ANCIENT THINGS

ANCIENT THINGS

THE LAND OF BROKEN ROADS
BOOK ONE

Ryan English

Podium

ANCIENT
THINGS

CHAPTER ONE

He knew something had changed before he even realized he was waking up. The air was flat and heavy now, fragrant with the scent of earth and humidity. It pressed on him like a blanket, so thick it felt like breathing took effort.

His arms and legs twitched, but there was nowhere for them to go. Something had happened, and he was half-buried, like an old stone sinking into the dirt.

He had been doing something important. He could feel that, feel the pressure of old urgency in his heart. But whatever it was seemed too distant to remember, already fading away.

How long had he been lying here? His eyes didn't obey when he tried to open them. He tried again, but his eyelids stuck to his eyeballs. Dry, as if they'd been closed for far too long. One eye cracked open, just a bit, and with more effort his eyelid peeled its way upward until he could see. Above him was nothing but indistinct, smudgy greens. Blurs with no definition. Why could he not see clearly?

He blinked and blinked again and tried to sit up. The dirt gripped him, holding him down with suction force. It clung to his skin, crumbling away as one arm came free, then the other.

He rubbed his eyes with his hands and wiped away something too thick to be tears. Some kind of slime. Revulsion gave him a burst of energy, and he tore himself from the ground, trying desperately to wipe whatever it was off his face and hands.

He could see now, and he instantly knew this was not a place he recognized. Nothing at all like where he'd just been, which was . . . he couldn't remember. But now, all around him in every direction were ferns, tall as his waist. They grew so thick together they left no space between them. The land was flat as far as he could see, nothing but pillars of pale sullen gray and an ocean of dark green ferns.

No, those were not pillars. They were too large for that. His eyes followed one up until it met the canopy overhead, where he saw great branches. Not pillars. Trees. Trees taller than reason, hundreds of paces apart. Impossibly tall. Too wide, far too tall. Nothing could be that large. His head swam just looking at them, just trying to comprehend their enormity.

His eyes drifted back downward, and he saw clear slime all around him in a thin puddle a foot or two wide, like he had fallen and burst open and that was his insides. It coated him in a layer two inches thick, except where he'd already wiped it off.

Wiping the clinging slime from his body and flinging it away, he saw he had nothing on. That wasn't right either—there should be something he had on. Clothing. The slime was wrong. He should have clothing. Although the word was in his mind, when he tried to think what clothing looked like, or even what it was, nothing came to him. Nothing but blackest amnesia.

Nothing about who he was, or where he was from, or why he was here. He knew the words; any word he wished to remember came to him instantly. But no pictures came with them, nothing that could tell him what the words truly signified.

Home. A place a person lived. And what did it look like? What sort of place was it? Nothing.

Food. Cart. Street. Cat. Robe. Hand. Hand he knew, since he'd seen his. The only mental image he had of hands, though, were the brief glances he'd given them. *Face?* Nothing. He hadn't seen it. He was human and didn't even know what a human looked like, or what it meant to be one.

Wiping more clumps of slime from his thighs, he realized that his body was wrong. It was only a feeling, not any sort of reliable knowledge, but it wasn't the body he expected. It was hairless from neck to toes, and that wasn't right. Was it? He was smooth and a bit pale, and the proportions seemed off.

A child. He was a child, a little human still growing. Human progeny, not an adult like he was supposed to be. A grown-up. Right? What did that mean, exactly? He could feel the knowledge just on the edge of his mind, barely out of reach. The harder he struggled to grab it, the further it slipped away.

He took several deep breaths, trying to force his mind to organize and settle by sheer willpower.

"Alright," he said aloud. The sound of his voice unnerved him. It shouldn't be so high. "Alright, where am I?"

Saying it helped him focus. His mind grew a bit clearer.

The slime on the ground was already evaporating, leaving clean soil as it dried up and disappeared. He watched it go. It evaporated out of his hair as well, unsticking it from his neck and forehead. Soon his skin was completely dry.

He turned in a slow circle, looking carefully into the distance for any sign of . . . of anything. The forest was stunning, truly. Far, far above, the sky was all green, patterns of light and dark in the rich canopy of leaves. It was too high up for him to see what shape they were, but they caught every spare ray of light and let nothing reach the ground. Not a single sun ray anywhere. Just the dappled greens concealing the entirety of the sky. What was up there? What could live among such impossible heights?

And below the green sky, a vast emptiness of nothing but pale gray tree trunks. A space larger than his mind could take in. And his mind tried—the sights above and below made him think he should be able to comprehend the space in between, to know and quantify it, but he couldn't. It made him feel like nothing more than a speck.

Here on the ground, dark green ferns covered everything, bumpy as roiling ocean water at night. He paused, wondering what the ocean looked like, and how he knew that word. He had no idea, but he knew the ferns looked like one.

But his thoughts quickly fled each time he simply looked around. The beauty of it all nearly overpowered him. Such majesty, such perfect serenity! He dared not close his eyes and miss something. He had to look, to stare at the ferns and trees and far horizons fading in shadow until he understood. He had to smell the heavy air, thick with humidity and wet dirt. To feel the earth beneath his toes, dirty and black. He had to take it all in.

The worry edging in at the periphery of his mind faded before the majestic silence of the forest. Nothing moved, not even a whisper. The forest reposed in grandeur, inviolable. Sacred. He listened for a moment, hearing the blood pumping in his ears and nothing else. It was so *quiet.*

Off in the distance, a bird cawed. He turned to look but couldn't see it. Would he even be able to spot it, in such a huge space? What did a bird look like?

Either way, the sound relieved him at first, but that faded into subtle dread. The forest grew a shade darker. Potentially sinister. He was alone and recognized nothing, and there were living things out there he didn't know about.

"I'm alone. Alone, alone . . ." he muttered, tasting the word. Indeed, were there other people at all? He thought about that for a moment. There should be. He didn't know who they were, but some part of him remembered the feeling of other people around, in contrast to their stark absence now.

A bit of energy crept into him as he awakened further and his thoughts grew more organized. He could not stand here in a stupor all day, after all; so, what now? He was a child, and that meant he was weak. He needed safety. Protection. Shelter. He would have to provide that for himself.

He also needed food and drink. He knew the words, but the more he tried to call up memories of what food *was,* what it looked like, how it tasted, the less he knew about it. He let go of the thought, afraid he would chase it away forever.

Time to get moving. He stuck his foot out, then gulped at the fear that he might have forgotten how to walk. No, no, he didn't forget. Don't think, just go.

He moved forward, relaxing as he found that walking came natu-rally. Ferns brushed against his skin as he pushed his way through the still, heavy air. Moving let him smell the humidity, the dark scent of decaying plant life, and richness of the soil below him.

Walking felt good. His body gathered energy as he went, waking up even more. He felt so alive, so much more than he remembered! Oh, what did he remember? That thought slipped away before he could look at it.

Oh well. He grinned and ran, the movement coming as natural as breathing. He sprinted as fast as he could through the ferns, dodging this way and that. The soft, black dirt was perfect for running on. Not a rock or stick to be found, nothing sharp to step on.

He hadn't had so much energy before, so much life and spark. He found himself overjoyed to be so mobile, so free. He laughed and ran all the way around a tree trunk. It left him tired by the end, since he had to go all the way around the roots, too, and they were taller than he was, even fifty paces out from the trunk.

"Hey!" he shouted up the tree trunk. "Hey, is anybody up there?"

Of course there wasn't, but it felt good to be moving and making noise. No wonder children loved playing! He shouted again, whooping loudly and listening for faint echoes from the tree trunks. The ferns swallowed most of the sound, but not all. His own voice returned to him each time.

He screamed as loud as he could, then listened to see how many echoes he could count. One, two, three, four, five . . . ?

A voice came back to him that wasn't his. His blood froze. What was that, that weird yell? How far away? He held his breath and listened.

It came again. "Where!" it said. The voice was high like his, but inhuman, a growl made of ten squeaks at different pitches. "Where!"

His eyes raced desperately over the greenery to find the source. It was down here with him, somewhere close enough to hear. Where was—

He spotted movement and shot down beneath the ferns. It was coming his way. What had he seen? A dirty green head, long pointy green ears. Something his height, but thicker and dangerous. Gods in Glory, what was that?

"Where!" it called again. "Good boy. Come out!"

The voice drove spikes into his mind. Terror greater than he could resist held him. He couldn't move. He could only barely breathe.

"Come out! Good boy!"

Whatever it was, it was dangerous. He heard eager malice in its crackling, squeaky voice.

It was coming in his direction. It might find him. What should he do?

"Meat! You want? You want? Good boy! Come out!"

Should he fight? No, his arms lacked muscle. Every bit of him was thin and soft. Not even his feet had toughened skin on them. *I was strong once,* he thought, before that crumb of memory slipped away from him. Maybe he could run? How fast was that thing?

The creature quit yelling. He listened with choking dread as it swished through the ferns, looking for him.

This was it. It was too close. He'd waited too long.

He stood to get a look and nearly fell backward in terror. A revolting green man-shaped thing with a pointed, inhuman face sniffed the air only five paces away. It saw him and fixed its shrunken red eyes on him with predatory exultation. It was only slightly shorter than he was, but thick and corded with muscle. Knotted fingers and toes ended in crumbling yellow claws, and long ears jutted out from its head and drooped at the end.

It smacked a long, heavy bone it carried into the dirt so hard the sound shook his lungs.

"Good boy," it said, face curling into a wide grin of sharp, rotting, black-and-yellow teeth.

He was dead. His body moved before his mind did. He ran with all the strength he possessed. The monstrous little green man laughed and gave chase.

CHAPTER TWO

He sprinted as hard as he could. His body sparked with terror from toes to hair, and he ran wildly, desperately, holding nothing back.

The green-skinned monster was slightly slower, but only slightly. Fear of its teeth kept him running after his legs lost their strength and felt heavy, long after every part of him burned from exertion his body had never known. His feet pounded the soft dirt, making a strange rhythm with the creature's snarls and panting.

How far ahead was he? Did he dare look back? No, he didn't. His mind was clearing up a little now that the adrenaline was wearing off, but the creature was still back there, chasing him. The way it thrashed the ferns as it ran told him all he needed to know.

Run. There was no choice. Run or die. Run or die. Run or die. It turned into a jogging chant, repeating in his mind. Right left right, run or die, right left right—

Something hit the back of his shoulder and knocked him forward. Pain spread slowly but deep. For a moment he was sure a bone was broken, but he kept his feet under him. It hurt to swing his arm, but the joint still worked. Thank Grace.

He glanced back to see it picking up its bone club and noticed he was building a lead. Hope put a spark into his tired, hollow legs and kept them going. He glanced back every three or four paces, watching for another toss.

It paid off. The green monster threw the club again, and he turned sharply to avoid it. The club flew harmlessly into the ferns, hopefully lost forever.

He kept running in the new direction and picked up his pace when he thought of a plan. Racing toward a tree, he leaped up and climbed over an enormous root, about halfway out where it was only a little taller than he was. He scraped his front from collar to shins on the flat gray bark, but he made it over faster than he expected. There was no time to think about how much it stung.

The monster gave a frustrated squeal as it tried to follow him over the root, but its shorter legs and greater weight slowed it down.

The second root was more intimidating than the first, but scrapes were better than bites. Scrapes wouldn't kill him. He only got high enough to barely scramble over, arms and legs slapping desperately on the wood.

He tumbled over the other side headfirst and rolled down into the ferns. From there, he made his way out into the open green expanse, keeping as low as he could while still moving quickly. He did his best to dodge between the plants without breaking them and leaving a trail, but it wasn't perfect.

It was good enough. The green monster's rage echoed off the world-sized trees as it thrashed through the ferns and screamed. He couldn't do anything about his footprints, but it would take time to follow them, and that creature didn't sound very patient.

Cold, unrelenting fear kept him going long after his body wanted to stop, long after the creature's howls faded in the distance and ceased. But his new body could only handle so much, and when he collapsed, his arms were too weak to stop him from face-planting in the dirt.

Only a moment later, he found himself curled into a ball and crying softly. He was a child now, and there was more emotion in him than he had any power to control. It was an odd feeling—tightness in his chest and face, a lump in his throat, burning in his eyes.

There was nothing he could do to stop it. He cried quietly, slowly, until his emotions were as empty as his arms and legs. After that, he lay for a while and rested, contemplative and miserable.

"I hate this," he whispered into the dirt, when he felt he could speak without crying again. He had no word for the creature, which made him think he'd never seen one before. The unpleasant shade of its green skin didn't fit with the gentle ferns and eternal trees. It seemed as foreign to the forest as he was. It was some kind of horrible, misshapen man, and it knew a few words, which meant it was smart enough to be dangerous. Plenty dangerous.

"I really, really hate this," he whispered again. His mind refused to relax and give him peace. If there was one monster, were there more? And what else was out there? What was it doing here? Did it appear when he did?

In fact, had he even existed before today? Some words strutted through his mind, but he couldn't make sense of them. *Resurrection, spontaneous generation, temporal displacement . . .*

He had no idea what the words meant, probably because he was thinking about it. He had to let a word come by itself, or it would escape without being understood.

With nothing better to do than rest until he got his sparks back, he lay there awhile and stared up into the green sky. Had he come from anywhere at all? Or from nowhere, simply appearing? Maybe he was just a little thing that would come and go, unnoticed and immediately forgotten. Maybe he would stop existing soon. Vanish away.

But the more he tried to recall anything of who or where or what he'd been, the more it seemed like everything from before was gone forever.

"Oh," he whispered. "If I lost something, then this isn't the start. And it won't be the end." That one thought comforted him.

It was hunger that finally made him sit up and very, very carefully poke his head up to see if the disgusting monster was anywhere nearby. Only after making absolutely certain that no sound or motion disturbed the stillness of the endless forest did he rise to his feet.

Way too much of him was scraped and raw and sore. He bled slightly from ten different places. He wiped the blood away and felt again the soreness in his shoulder and the deep bruise the monster's club had given him. All he could do about any of those little injuries was ignore them, though, so he did.

He looked around and started wondering what he was supposed to eat.

Something soft. Something that smelled good and tasted good. Not dirt. Not hard like a tree. Something else. A fern?

He pulled a few of the little green leaves from a frond and chewed them, but they didn't taste like something he should eat. He pulled the fern this way and that, inspecting inside its fronds and under its leaves, wondering if there was something else. Some other part.

Baby ferns. There were little ones growing up from the ground, soft and fuzzy with a different color, pale green instead of dark. He broke one off, about the length of his hand with a big spiral on the end the size of a curled finger.

He held it up to his nose. It just smelled dark and green, but his stomach twitched. He popped it in his mouth and chewed the whole thing, pleased to find that it was tender and flavorful, if a bit grassy. He grabbed another, and another. He ate his fill, but not so much he felt too full. What was the rush? These baby ferns were everywhere. He'd never run out.

Now he just needed something to wash it down. He stood and looked around again and realized with a sinking feeling that there was nothing, anywhere, that looked like a drink. He was getting thirsty, especially after running so far. His legs and arms still felt weak, and his throat and mouth were drying out.

He took a few steps in no particular direction, trying to think of where he could find a drink, or exactly what that might look like. Something flat and shiny and wet. A big place of . . . a place on the ground made of something to drink. There would be no ferns there. It would be open space, and the water would probably be too nasty and green with algae and rot to drink.

Water! That was it. He needed water. His mind seized on the word, one so evocative he could almost picture what it signified. He hurried over to a tree and walked the long way up a root.

The roots were so huge that when he reached the trunk, he was several times his height above the ground. He could see much farther from up here, but there was nothing more to see. No movement, no breaks in the expanse of ferns. No hills or buildings in the distance where the horizon faded in pale mist and shadows.

What was a building? He shuddered and turned away from the thought, lest he lose the word and never get it back. That was one he wanted to keep. It was an important word, the word for civilization. The works of mankind.

Well, no reason to stand here until he was spotted. He moved back down the root to where it was safe, then jumped down and rolled in the dirt to break his fall. By Grace, he was getting absolutely caked in black mud.

A curious thought struck him. Sometimes, water was in the ground. Was that right? Could he dig and find some?

He knelt and started pulling away big clumps of damp, black dirt with both hands. Stirring it up like this brought the smell out, rich and bold. Would that make it harder to smell him, he wondered?

The rich earth revealed tiny beetles and worms, ants smaller than his fingernail and too fast to catch, all trying to get away from him. But no water. By the time the hole got deep enough that he had to bend forward and reach in to pull out more, he was starting to feel foolish. There was nothing down here but more dirt.

He saw something wriggling its way out into the hole, about a hand's length below ground level. A grub, white with yellow streaks and black spots. And big, too, as long as his finger and twice as thick. It squirmed and wiggled all its stumpy little legs when he picked it up and brushed the dirt off.

Without thinking, he popped it in his mouth and chewed. It took two or three chomps before it quit wiggling on his tongue. The outside was a little tough, but the inside was all liquid. It tasted a little like nuts and pepper, which made him wonder what those things were, and also faintly sweet.

Digging a bit more found him two more grubs, and he ate them immediately. Their juices soothed his thirst, and it was nice to have something a bit chewier than the baby ferns.

That was two things he could eat, then. Baby ferns and grubs, with maybe enough liquid not to be so thirsty. Now he just needed a safe place to sleep and hide, somewhere he could rest without wondering when another green monster was about to jump out at him. And water. He probably still needed water.

Standing up, he turned around and found the muzzle of a giant dog two inches from his nose. It towered over him, leaning down for a sniff.

He tried to scream and only managed to whimper as he fell backward and collapsed on the ground. The dog was enormous. Just its legs were taller than he was, with a muzzle big enough to take his head off easy as a grub. Its fluffy gray fur and calm demeanor did nothing to lessen the sense of incredible strength it radiated, or the deep, instinctual terror it filled him with.

He froze, both unable and unwilling to move. Somehow, he knew that if he ran, the beast would chase and rip him apart. What could he do? Just try not to look like food, or a toy. Helplessness and despair nearly won inside him, and he only held himself together by a fingernail.

The giant dog leaned down again to sniff him where he sat frozen on the ground. Its hot breath rushed over him, the sound of its lungs cavernous and deep.

Its wet nose touched his forehead. He squeaked in terror and lost a squirt of urine. The dog smelled that, too.

He couldn't meet its gaze. He dared not. This was too much. This was all too much.

-What are you?- asked a voice in his mind.

He was so startled he forgot to stay afraid. He looked up at the giant dog.

-You are not a goblin,- said the voice. The dog sniffed him again, then walked around him in a circle. *-What are you?-*

He felt very, very small, sitting on the ground as the giant beast stepped behind his back.

When it circled back around and stood in front of him again, all he could think of was the power of its claws, digging into the dirt too close to his toes.

"I'm a boy!" he blurted out.

The dog gave him a quizzical look, head tilted. *-Can you only bark?-* asked the voice in his mind.

No, no, no, this was dangerous. He had to make it happy. He had to keep trying. He had to do something.

He stood, trembling from head to toe, and gingerly reached up to pat the dog on the fur above its nose. He rubbed back and forth, trying to pet it. Slowly, softly at first, and the dog didn't bite his arm off.

-What are you doing? Why can't you talk?-

"I can," he said. It wasn't working. He was going to die.

-You are a little baby, aren't you? I am over a month old, so I am older than you. Think with the loud part where I can see it.-

Focusing all his mental energy, he thought as loudly as he could. *"Hello?"*

The dog jerked back a bit. *-You are a noisy little thing, aren't you?-*

He tried again, trying to be clear and just use the surface thoughts, the part of his mind that worked in words. *"Hello?"*

-You said that already. So what are you?-

"I'm a human."

-Oh. I've never seen one before. Mother said humans are wrapped in metal, but you aren't.-

"No, I'm just a child. I think something happened to me, but I—"

-Mother said I should not bother humans. She said you are pests.-

"I'm not a pest. What are you? I didn't know dogs got so big."

-I am not a dog. I am a wolf pup.- The mental words came with an image of blood and claws, snarling teeth and burning yellow eyes. Terrifying, unrelenting ferocity. Ferocity before which there could be no compromise. *-I will be big and strong someday, like Mother. But right now, I am little and young, like you. But I think Mother will scold me if she finds out I talked to a human. Goodbye, little human.-*

"Goodbye, little wolf," he thought. *"Wait, what's your name?"*

-I don't have one. I don't need it.-

"How about if I call you . . ." He panicked, suddenly unable to come up with anything. He knew words; he should know some good names. But he didn't. He couldn't think of any, even to get an idea what one sounded like. He blurted out, *"Socks. Because your front paws are white, so it looks like you have socks on . . ."*

No sooner had he sent the thought than he realized how that sounded. It felt all wrong. This was not an animal you called Socks. It was a terrifying and majestic thing not a . . . not a "Socks." He couldn't remember what socks were, anyway. Foot clothing?

-Okay. You will call me Socks. And I will call you Dirt, because you are all dirty. But you won't call me anything because I need to go back to Mother now, and I won't come back. Goodbye, Dirt.-

"Goodbye, Socks," thought Dirt.

The wolf pup turned and slipped away in the ferns, making no sound and hardly even disturbing the fronds as he raced off into the distance. Socks was so tall Dirt might be able to walk under him without ducking, but he moved silently. A true hunter.

Dirt watched Socks until he vanished into the distance.

All was quiet again. Perfectly still. Eternal. Limitless open spaces broken only by tree trunks of gray, thick and tall as the pillars that held up the heavens. Green above and below, and him in the middle—tiny, naked, and dirty, feeling helplessly alone.

CHAPTER THREE

He wandered aimlessly after that.

Evening came, and he had no power to resist how tired he was. His body needed sleep. Before the light had fully faded into darkness, he dug out a spot under a massive root and lined it with ferns to make himself a little nest. He uprooted a few more to cover himself with and lay down with an eagerness for rest that pulled him with a near-physical force into his bed.

He saw nothing of the night. He slept straight through, and judging from how he woke up in the exact same position, he'd hardly even moved while he slept.

When the dim light of morning woke him, heavy fog covered everything behind a veil of gray. He couldn't see more than ten paces.

It was cold; that was the first thing. His hair was damp with dew, as well as a few other spots that hadn't been covered by the ferns. Even the slightest movement shook heavy drops of dew off the ferns and onto his skin. Each drip left a wet, icy line as it slipped down into the dirt.

Thirst. That was the second thing. His mouth was so dry he could hardly open it.

Dirt rose to his feet and tried to brush off some of the cold dew with his hands, but it didn't do much good. It mostly just created mud that stung in all his scrapes. Oh well. He spent the rest of the morning eagerly licking palm fronds or shaking drops of water into his mouth. Just a little at a time, hardly enough to wet his tongue, but it added up.

Very slowly. The water tasted like the bitterness of an inedible leaf, but it was water.

As morning progressed, the fog slowly lifted foot by foot and faded away, leaving the air clear and musty and heavy, like he was used to. The forest revealed its eternal majesty, perfectly unchanged from the day before.

He caught sight of his first bird, gliding down slowly from greater heights. It was so tiny against the dappled canopy above that he wondered if there were more that he simply had failed to spot. Just a speck of light and shadow, but he watched with great interest as it gently floated down to cross the impossible distance to the ground.

It must be a strong little thing, to be able to fly back up again. Assuming it ever would? Maybe it knew places to rest halfway up, ones that he couldn't see from down here. From down here, the tree trunks looked too straight and perfect from roots to branches.

He wondered if he could find the bird and catch it? What would he do if he did? No, unless one landed right near him, there was no chance. The ferns could hide ten thousand birds, and he'd never see one.

Dirt decided he may as well make something of the rest of the morning, but he didn't exactly have a long list of urgent tasks. He dug up some grubs and ate a couple handfuls of baby ferns, then set out to find somewhere better to sleep. He didn't want to wake up wet and cold every single morning for the rest of his life, after all. He needed a place that would be safe and dry. What exactly that might be, he had no idea. And no matter which direction he looked, the forest was flawless and infinite as a god's dream.

He picked a direction and walked for a while, choosing a random tree in the distance and making his way toward it. He had to stop and rest and eat some grubs and ferns halfway there. It was farther than he thought because it was so large.

All along the way, nothing stood out. He listened for monsters and tried to keep a good lookout for any motion, but there was nothing, and his mind kept sinking back into reverie. Once he reached the tree, it was no different from all the others.

He ran up one of the roots, his bare feet slapping the flat bark the whole way up. The root was wide enough here that it hid how far up he was, but it was high enough he'd probably die if he slid off.

Leaning against the tree trunk to rest, he wondered: was he safer up here than down there? From here, he'd see anything big enough to be a problem coming from quite a distance. But that also meant anything sneaking around down there could see *him* from just as far away. Unless he lay down? He tried that.

The tree trunk was more comfortable than he expected, but it wasn't very interesting. He was getting bored. Antsy and restless, dissatisfied. It was better than being chased, though. Better to be bored than have a green monster coming after you.

Still, boredom was affecting him more and more. It felt almost like physical pain. He should find something useful to do. He'd come a long way and hadn't found a place to sleep that would be any different, so that task had gotten him nowhere. He needed something else.

He looked down at himself. The scrapes and scratches he'd gotten yesterday were covered with dirt and grime from everything else he'd done since then, hiding them completely. They didn't bother him unless he rubbed himself wrong, and the bruise on his shoulder from the bone club didn't hurt unless he pushed on it.

Maybe he should try to get clean? No, it was no use. He'd just get dirty again. His name was Dirt, after all. He realized he'd started calling himself that in his own thoughts, so it was permanent now. Dirt, inside and out. It was a good name. The source of everything, the richness that held everything else up and gave it life. He almost felt guilty about "Socks."

Maybe he should practice climbing over the roots without ripping all his skin off. That sounded fun, and besides, if he got chased again, he might be glad he got the practice. He jumped to his feet and ran down the root, as fast as he dared.

Dirt started off where it was small enough to jump over easily and worked his way up. He experimented with various ideas, like using his hands to spring up or trying to roll over. He wished he'd seen another human do it, even just once, but he hadn't, so he had to make it up.

But it was something to do. He had a nagging feeling that all this movement and energy was unusual, that it was something new and exciting for him. He remembered yesterday, when he first woke up and everything seemed wrong; it didn't seem that way now. He knew in his mind that he might have been an adult before, but he no longer felt that way. He was settling in.

After a while, he stopped and ate some more ferns. He dug around for grubs, but only found one, and it wasn't quite enough to quench his growing thirst. The sweat made little paths of cleaner skin where it dripped off him, and he wondered if it was from the oppressively humid air or if he'd just been working harder than he realized.

A cold, wet nose sniffed his back. Dirt screamed and jumped forward, rolling and stumbling and unable to get up or even turn around and look what it was. He got a glimpse of huge white paws and knew it was Socks.

Relief lasted only the half instant it took for him to notice Socks's black muzzle, which was now drenched red in blood. The beast's maw was only feet away, his teeth the size of Dirt's forearm. A single bite was all it would take. Dirt froze in perfect terror, unable to think.

-Hello, Dirt. Little human.-

Dirt couldn't gather enough of a coherent thought to reply over the sound of his heart pounding in his chest. Socks was too huge, too red in tooth and claw for him to face.

-Mother said that if I wanted, I should come see you again before you die. She said you will die soon,- said Socks.

Dirt's eyes filled with tears, and his terror turned to despair. He tried as hard as he could to think, to focus and think loudly. It did not come easy with Socks leaning down to sniff him again, which filled Dirt's own nose with the stark, unpleasant scent of blood.

"Please don't kill me. Please!"

The wolf pup regarded him coolly, but Dirt got a sense of amusement from the animal, even if he couldn't quite place how.

-I scared you, didn't I? I meant that Mother said you are like a baby bird with no nest. You will starve, or something will eat you. But not me. You are all bone and no meat, and Mother said not to eat bones until I am older.-

The wolf pup's mouth lolled open, placidly unthreatening. The animal's tongue was wider than Dirt's head.

"Oh," thought Dirt. He should have known. If Socks wanted to kill and eat him, he'd just do it. There would be no warning. *"Why are you covered in blood? Er, just your mouth."*

-I found a goblin before I came here. Mother says we need to get rid of them any time we see one, because there will be many more, and they are pests,- said Socks.

The beast lifted up his head to look around, towering above him and causing him to step back instinctively. Dirt really could just walk right under the massive animal, he decided. The fluffy fur might brush against his head, but he wouldn't have to duck.

The giant wolf pup meant him no harm, thank Grace. Dirt was fine. He was safer now than before, in fact. He stood up, and the fear dripped away like dew, but not completely. Socks was simply too huge for him to be completely at ease.

-*Goblins don't taste good, but they are fun to chase. They always try to run.*-

"*What's a goblin?*" thought Dirt.

An image came to his mind of a tiny green humanoid with long ears and a long nose; a smelly, twisty, feisty thing. It took Dirt a moment to realize he was looking at the same sort of creature that had chased him yesterday. A goblin. An ugly word for an ugly creature.

"*I saw one of those. It tried to eat me,*" thought Dirt. Something about the admission made him feel ashamed, after seeing it how Socks saw it. Tiny, disgusting, and harmless.

-*What did it do? Did it fight you?*-

"*No, I ran away. It was lots stronger than I am. I didn't stand a chance.*"

-*Oh. Well, you are very small. And weak. What are you doing over here? Why did you come to this place instead of where you were before?*-

"*I wanted somewhere better to sleep. It was cold this morning because I woke up soaking wet from the dew. But there's nothing anywhere, no matter where I look.*"

-*Like what? What kind of place do you like to sleep in?*-

Dirt had to think about that for a moment. "*I'm not sure. You said I was a baby, and you were right. I was born yesterday. I've only slept once. But I want to sleep somewhere inside, with something over me and all around, and somewhere I'll be safe from things that want to eat me at night. I thought I'd know it when I saw it.*"

-*You mean like a hole?*-

"*Well . . . Yeah, I guess. Like a hole. I wanted somewhere less dirty, too, but a hole would be fine. I should have thought of that. I can probably dig it myself.*"

Socks leaned down and sniffed him again, and Dirt did his best not to let his sudden panic show on his face.

-*Why do you not want somewhere dirty? You are already dirty.*-

Dirt rubbed his forearm, making the drying black soil bunch up into little dry clumps and fall off. He thought about it for a moment. *"I guess it's fine."*

-I will help you dig one, then. I like to dig, and your little paws look useless. Mother said to find out if there are other humans besides you, but there aren't, are there? Or you would not be like this.-

"I don't know if there are any other humans at all. I haven't seen any yet."

Socks didn't reply to that, and Dirt decided against asking if the pup had seen any, since it sounded like he hadn't. Socks simply sniffed around, walking this way and that in the ferns.

"Oh, Socks, can we put it under a root, so I can find it again? It'll be easier to hide the entrance that way, too."

-Okay, but then it can't be very big, or the tree will get mad.-

"That's okay. It'll just be me in there."

Socks stepped toward a root and sniffed around, then chose a spot for no discernible reason and started digging under it. Black soil flew, a long continuous stream of it at least twenty paces long. Only moments later, the entire pup had disappeared underground, and still the earth came firing out so forcefully that Dirt didn't dare get close enough to look at the progress.

It was over shockingly quickly. Socks backed out of the hole, then stretched to his full height and shook the soil off, flinging it hard enough to sting Dirt's bare skin.

"That was fast!" said Dirt.

-I am Mother's twelfth strongest. And I made it little for you, because you're little.-

Socks started looking around, gazing at the distance with a bit of a spark in him. He looked like he was getting ready to leave.

The thought scared Dirt. He would be alone all the rest of the day, and those hours stretched into eternities by himself. Dirt held his arms out and said, *"If you put your head down where I can reach, I'll scratch your ears to say thank you."*

Socks turned his head to look, now curious.

"Come on, just sit down and rest your head right here in front of me. You'll like it. I'll scratch and pet you as long as you want."

The giant pup gingerly stepped closer, then sat down and let his head down to mash the ferns. Socks's head was bigger than Dirt, too big for Dirt to even reach all the way across, especially around the ears, but he got to work anyway.

The pup's fur was as soft and fluffy as it looked and felt pleasant on his bare skin, but the beast's sheer size and the faint smell of predator kept him careful. He scratched and petted all over Socks's neck, face, and head, especially around the base of his ears.

Socks squirmed the whole time like he wanted to turn it into a game, but he recognized Dirt was too small to play with like that. Even so, he leaned and rolled several times, giving just enough warning for Dirt to jump backward and avoid getting crushed, but that was the price of hitting all the right spots. Dirt rubbed and scratched until his fingers got sore, then kept going until his arms got tired and his shoulders burned.

When his arms finally gave out, Socks stood up, his tongue lolling out. He leaped playfully back and forth a few times, head focused on Dirt. Dirt tried his best not to cower in terror, and instead reached out one more time to pat the pup's nose. Socks leaped out of the way before he could, and Dirt smiled. He should have seen that coming.

Socks nuzzled him, knocking him right over. *-You are too little for play, but getting scratched was pleasant. I should go now.-*

The pup turned and took a few steps, then lowered his front to stretch his long back. He said, *-Sleep well in your little den tonight. Goodbye, Dirt, little human.-*

"Wait, will you come back again?" asked Dirt, trying not to sound as desperate as he was starting to feel.

-Maybe.- Then he left.

CHAPTER FOUR

Dirt woke in the deep of night, when all was still and the darkness so complete he couldn't tell if his eyes were open or closed. There was a thrum, a subtle vibration that swelled and faded in an even pattern. It was so quiet he wasn't sure whether he was hearing or feeling it. But it was there, and it had encroached on his dreams and drawn him back to his body.

He lay for a while just listening, trying to determine what it was. Gentle waves of vibration passed through every part of him, but he felt it most strongly in his gut and his lungs. And his skull, or perhaps just his ears.

It went on and on, slow, even, and gentle. It nearly rocked him back to sleep, but the curiosity kept pulling him back. He finally got up from his bed of ferns and made his way out of the hole by feel.

The darkness was so perfect, so complete, that it awakened a very deep part of him that knew nothing but fear. He had a gnawing sense that there was something out there, something that he would never see before it caught him in its teeth. The primal fear pushed his eyes open wider and wider, made his breathing go painfully quiet and even. His mind stretched to find anything sensible to process, but there was nothing.

No sound, either. His skin's sensitivity rose to compensate, and he thought he could feel the fog on the air, but he couldn't tell if he was feeling something real or just imagining it.

Wait. No sound. He listened with his ears, watched with his internal awareness. There was nothing. His imagination worked to fill in the gaps, still trying to create some sort of creeping thing headed his direction, but he pushed those thoughts away and focused.

The sound was gone. There was nothing at all outside. He crawled back into his hole and squirmed back into his nest of ferns until he was comfortable and tried to go back to sleep, but it only took a moment for him to realize the sound was back.

He listened for a while, trying to think about the waves of vibration instead of the gaping night only a few feet away from him. Anything could be coming for him, and he'd never know it. But it wasn't. Nothing was coming, and he was being silly.

There was a motion to the hum, a rocking sensation, a rise and fall. A pulse, long and slow. The pulse was as subtle as the sound itself, but it was there, filling a slow count of three or four.

He decided the gentle vibrations rose from the ground, since if it was just a sound in the air, he wouldn't feel it so clearly in his body. No, if it was a sound from above or outside, he'd hear it louder than he felt it. Whatever it was, it came from the ground, passed through him, and rose into the immense root above.

If he ever saw Socks again, he'd have to ask what the sound was. Maybe the big pup knew, or maybe his mother did. How big was Mother, anyway? Mothers were bigger than their offspring. He knew that. He could almost imagine the size difference. Almost. But like any other concrete memory he tried to nail down, it slipped away.

It no longer felt unnatural to be a child, and now he wondered if it was affecting his speech or thinking. But how could he tell? How would he measure it, without other humans to compare against?

He couldn't measure, and it was useless to try. He was a child. He knew nothing else. He had no memory of any other life. For all he knew, this was how new humans emerged. The word for that was "birth," but he didn't have much of a concept to go with the word. Birth should happen where a mother was. He knew that, but maybe there had been a mistake. That didn't feel right, but what did he know?

When he fell asleep shortly afterward, he dreamed of being a tree. His thoughts were so alien that when he woke, he could make no sense of them at all. All he could remember was the feeling of it, the feeling of using senses he couldn't explain to perceive a world he couldn't comprehend while awake.

But when he crawled out of his burrow into the stifling morning fog, he rested his fingertips on the heavy root, so much taller than his little body, and let himself feel a wistful longing for the dream world. Some kind of nostalgia for the unreal that could never be satisfied or shared.

Oh well. Sleeping underground had indeed kept him dry, and that was already a welcome improvement. And now it was time for water! It seemed such a treat that his pleasant melancholy vanished immediately, and he began racing around licking up every drop. He got smarter about his method, too. He drank a lot more water if he just went around slurping up the little puddles that collected on bigger fern leaves, rather than trying to clean all the water off the whole plant.

His stomach was stuffed with water long before the fog lifted, so much it sloshed a little when he walked. He needed food, too, but he'd eat later when he had more room in there.

Running through the ferns got him drenched again, though, and now he was cold. All the black dirt caked onto his skin had turned back into mud. If only he had something to scrape it off, he might be able to get clean. But there was nothing to use, nothing at all. Not unless he wanted to try to scrape himself off on a tree, and his front was still healing from the last time he tried that.

So, now what? He had the whole rest of the day. He wanted Socks to come back, mostly. Or to have someone else to talk to. But there was no telling if or when the giant pup would appear, so he'd have to keep busy before he started getting too lonely.

The first thing he should do, he decided, was memorize his tree so he could find it again. They all looked similar—impossibly tall and straight, gray bark forming pillars like stone to hold the green sky up. But they weren't all exactly the same. The roots and branches were different.

He stepped out away from his tree and circled leisurely around it, paying careful attention to everything that might matter. His tree had six high roots, five big ones and one deeper one that only came up as tall as him. Up above, it had a branch lower than the rest that stuck out in a unique way.

Dirt circled it twice, letting it take as long as it took. He heard birds chirping from somewhere nearby, but gave them no heed beyond just enjoying the variety of sound. He moved in closer and circled his tree again, then dug up a few more grubs and had his breakfast. Then he walked out much farther and circled it again, trying to memorize its neighbors as well. They were too far away to bother visiting each one up close, but he could see enough. One neighbor had nine deep roots and no tall ones, and another had only four tall ones.

The more he stared upward, the more they seemed to take on distinct characters. To develop personalities. He kept getting flashes of his tree-dream, just the memory of how it felt. Nothing clear. Perhaps he should name them someday, when he understood them.

But he learned *his* tree, as much of it as a little human on the ground could see. He named it Home.

After all that, he still forgot which root his nest was under. He had the wrong one and panicked when it wasn't there. When he finally found it under the *second* root, one-third of the way out, he almost climbed in and took a nap out of pure relief.

The birdsong kept him out, though. It was getting louder, and that made him curious. He walked in the direction of the sound, and it wasn't long before he saw the motion of the tiny creatures flying up into the air and back down again, making the most noise he'd heard in his life.

As he got closer, he expected them to fly far away, but they didn't. He got up close to one, only a few steps away. It was a little thing not much bigger than his hand, dark in color and moving too fast for him to see. Chirping all the while, it shot down from above and disappeared beneath the ferns in a spot where they were tall enough to reach his neck.

He looked up and saw a great crowd of birds descending from the unreachable heights. Dirt only spotted them from the motion against the dappled green canopy—they were much too far away to pick out otherwise. How far up was that, anyway? How high were the branches and leaves? How would he even measure? He'd have to think of a way someday.

One bird was bigger than the rest, pale in color. Much bigger. He could pick it out long before any of the others, but from the flickers of motion, it was certainly not alone. It was on its way down as well, but in a jerky, uneven way. It seemed to glide for a moment, then dart down, or change directions, then do it again and again.

He followed for a while as it glided this way and that, leading him farther and farther from Home. When it got close enough to tell, the big one looked like it was struggling, and that made him nervous. But his curiosity was stronger than his caution, so he had to stay until he saw what was going on.

Dirt watched until it came down far enough to get a good look. Its dirty-white color stood out against the green, and its long, mighty wings were tinged with yellow on the ends. It had four legs like Socks, two in front and two in back. It ripped at the air with its front and back talons and snapped with its sharp beak. The closer it got, the less confident he was that it was a bird, but what did he know?

The little birds were attacking it. That's what was happening. It thrashed and screeched and tried to kill them, and they were driving it to the ground. They swarmed it in great numbers, all flying in and out to distract and harass it and break up its gliding.

It was bigger than him, he realized. Now that it was close enough to tell, the large bird wasn't quite as big as Socks, but still huge compared to Dirt. It looked angry. It was maybe only a hundred paces above him in the air, still struggling to fight off all the little ones.

It was close. It was angry. It was heading down toward the ground, where he was. Those talons and beak would burst him like a grub.

Horror nearly kept him rooted to the ground. His heart pounded in his chest, and he had to force his legs to start moving. *Run!* His legs felt like they belonged to someone else, slow to obey him.

He turned and ran toward Home, quickly picking up the pace until he was sprinting at full speed.

Before he'd gone fifty paces, something caught his ankle and sent him crashing gracelessly in the dirt.

"Good boy!" said a scratchy, high-pitched voice. Dirt flipped around before even getting up and saw five goblins staring back at him. Two more pushed ferns away to get a look, then one more.

"Good boy!"

CHAPTER FIVE

Frustration just about killed him. He was so frustrated to be caught again that he almost didn't get up. This was not a place he could live. He never stood a chance.

The brawny green monsters were as surprised as he was, though, and that was the only thing that saved him. They hesitated, and desire to live surged within him and got him back on his feet.

"Good boy!" shouted one, its voice cracking.

"Good boy!" shouted two more. The chase was on.

Dirt realized he was running toward Home. Stupid, stupid! He turned to the left and kept running. They could never find that place. Never.

There were more of them out here. Another three goblins ran straight toward him. He turned left again and ran between the two groups, but that quickly proved to be a mistake.

One ran toward him at an angle, holding a bundle of rope. A bone club whooshed past his head, so close he was sure he felt the wind as it passed.

"Meat!" they shouted to each other. "Come out! Meat!"

There were more, always more. Fifteen at least. They had formed a wide half-circle with the birds in the middle, and he was now inside that. If he'd turned the other way, he might have made it to a tree and hopped over the roots like before, but now the only thing ahead of him was that swarm of birds and the big one they were bringing down.

He had one chance. A stupid one, but it was all he could think of. He sprinted as hard as he could straight for the birds. The big one with four legs still hadn't reached the ground, but it was almost down.

Dirt had to go under it. He ran so hard his body burned, all of it. He pushed himself harder, then harder again. Every inch of him hurt, begged him to stop.

He didn't make it. The huge bird-creature finally gave up and fell the last few feet to the ground, where it landed with more of a flutter than a thud. It stood and gave a mighty shriek, high and loud and clear.

Dirt ran right behind it, ducking under its long, off-white tail-feathers as he passed, hoping it wouldn't see him. Panic like fire roared inside him, speeding his feet.

It saw him. A gust of wind lit on his back as the beast flapped its great wings, and an instant later, it fell on him and slammed him into the ground.

Face first. He couldn't breathe. He struggled as hard as he could to slip out, knowing that its beak would be next. It wouldn't eat him in one bite, either.

Dirt turned his head and sucked in what air he could with all that weight on him.

"Let me go!" he screamed with all his might. Then he tried with his mind. *Let me go!*

Neither worked. From the corner of his eye, he saw the great beak coming down for him. He felt the beast's hot breath on his cheek, quick, short puffs of air.

"Please," he begged. "Please." He could hardly breathe. His words were nothing more than squeaks made by whatever tiny amounts of air he could gasp in. The thing had him pinned so perfectly he couldn't even wiggle his shoulders. "Please," he whimpered. His chest burned from lack of air. He was going to die.

Dirt's ribs creaked under the pressure, and he was sure that was his last breath getting squeezed out. But he was wrong—the beast leaped off him with another flap of its mighty wings. He felt a slight snag on his thigh, but it left him there.

It shrieked again, piercing his ears. It darted down at something only a few steps farther, and a goblin gave a scream of its own. Dirt scrambled to his feet just in time to see the beast flinging away a severed arm, club and all.

Dirt instantly raced for the club. But before he could find it, another goblin started coming his way. He changed his mind and ran.

His mind fought against the panic threatening to curl him up in a ball. "Go, go, go, Dirt," he said aloud. He had to run.

No, not run. He needed to sneak away. He dropped to the ground and started crawling, staying below the ferns the whole time.

The sounds of the fight assaulted him from every direction. Hiding under the ferns, he felt more exposed than ever. Violence and death were everywhere, from every direction as the bird-monster attacked over and over in different places.

Screams and howls. Cracks and thuds. The sounds were so chaotic he couldn't even picture what was happening. After two days of near-complete silence, it seemed ear-splitting.

Dirt crawled as fast as he could. Too fast. He lost his balance and hit the dirt, then pushed himself up and kept going. He whimpered, keening through closed teeth, unable to stop. Every part of him burned with exertion.

The goblins started to sound more panicked. They screamed wordlessly, raising a cacophony that made his heart tremble. More and more of their screams turned to terror, and soon enough, Dirt heard them split up and start running, howling as they went.

He dropped to the ground and curled into a position where he wasn't touching any ferns. *Gods in Glory . . .* His mind conjured those words as if by instinct, but he didn't know what was supposed to come next.

All he knew was that more than one goblin was coming in his direction. He held as still as he could. Panic and exertion made holding his breath impossible, but he tried. Gods in Glory, he tried.

One fled past him. Another followed shortly after. As they ran, their heavy feet made dull thumps that Dirt could swear he felt through the ground. The goblins spoke to each other in short bursts of growling and hisses, nothing like words.

Another came up, running on the opposite side of the others. This one was closer. It slowed. It slowed down again and stopped, not too far away.

Dirt had no idea exactly how far, and not being able to see caused him so much torment he almost got up and ran.

Terror filled his eyes with tears, which he desperately tried to blink away so he could see. His face curled into a grimace of fear, the muscles tightening so fiercely that his face hurt.

It stepped toward him.

It paused.

The goblin gave a coughing growl that almost sounded like a bark. The others nearby quieted.

Dirt felt a drip running down his thigh. He craned his neck to look and found blood. Only then did he feel the cut, as if it appeared right at that moment. He was bleeding. He struggled to make sense of it in the midst of so much mental terror. He didn't know what to do. It was bad, and it hurt, but what should he do?

The nearby goblins had gone quiet. Dirt could still hear others farther away, and the bird-beast, too. It sounded like it was still hunting them. But the close goblins, those ones made no sound.

He waited and waited, suffering. "Please go, please go, please be gone," he mouthed silently.

Maybe they were gone? Not a sound. Maybe he was mistaken, and they—

Dirt heard a shuffle right behind him. He shot up from the ground and bolted, right into a creeping goblin. He ducked under its grasping hands, but it caught his wrist for just long enough to slow him down before he yanked himself free.

Another goblin grabbed him with both arms before he had time to react. It lifted him onto its shoulders and started running. The handful of others nearby gave howls of glee and followed.

Dirt screamed and fought, twisting and flailing, doing everything he could to get away. The thing's arms were so strong they might as well be solid wood, but it wasn't taller than he was. It couldn't win a war of leverage while running.

He twisted again, trying to throw his weight over the goblin's back. It lost its balance and nearly dropped him, and Dirt saw his chance. He twisted and turned and fought with wild desperation to get away, and the goblin's grip slipped on his bloody leg.

Dirt somehow got his foot under the goblin's armpit and kicked as hard as he could. It was enough. He pushed himself out of its arms and onto the ground.

It spun around and was on him before he could even scramble to his feet. Dirt struggled so wildly that it couldn't get a grip on him to pick him back up. Two more goblins laughed from close by.

That sparked its ire, and its yellow-tinged eyes grew more serious. It stepped in and punched Dirt in the face, full-force. He saw a flash of white and felt himself slipping away into oblivion before he even registered pain.

He forced himself to move. He rolled over and scrambled to his feet, eyes unable to focus. A wave of nausea hit him, but he tried to press on.

The goblin grabbed his arm and yanked him back. Dirt didn't even see the fist coming before it slammed into his face the second time.

Dirt woke a moment later, lying flat on his back. He fought against the haze and confusion, slowly regaining the ability to think. His hands lifted themselves in front of his face where he could look at them through his good eye.

Pain poured into him then, rushing through him like a torrent. His face was in agony. The ground spun beneath him, causing nausea and dizziness like he'd never imagined. He gingerly traced his fingertips over his face and found that one of his eyes was swollen completely shut. The warm, sickly taste of blood filled his mouth, and when he felt around with his tongue, he discovered he'd lost three teeth on the left side—one on top, two on bottom.

Why was he here? Why was he still alive?

His face throbbed with his heartbeat, sending waves of pain all the way down to his collarbone. He looked up at the endless trees, impossibly far above him, but his good eye had trouble focusing that far, and everything was just a splotchy blur.

A goblin screamed nearby, but the sound cut off and became a rattle.

Dirt had not been out long. Desperate urgency drove him to roll over and get up on hands and knees, where he nearly vomited. His arms were wobbly, and he felt unbalanced, disconnected. But he pushed himself up.

Only a few steps away, the great bird-beast tore open the chest of a goblin to get at its heart and lungs. Two more quick snaps of its beak, and the snack was gone. It lifted its head and spun its neck all the way around, looking straight at him without moving its body.

The beast's shoulder was higher than his head, and it gave off an aura of indomitable power that made Dirt tremble in his deepest parts. Its sharp yellow beak was as long as his torso, each of its yellow talons as long as his forearm. The off-white feathers on its face and legs were bright red and spattered with gore. Its eyes stayed fixed on him with perfect, predatory focus. One twitch it didn't like, and it would kill him without the slightest effort. Only having Socks up close yesterday kept him sane now.

Dirt found he had no fuel left for fear. He simply turned around, slowly, and started shuffling away. Let it come eat him if it wanted. Let a goblin catch him. He was done.

He stepped on a bone club, a hefty thing as long as his arm. He paused, then reached down to pick it up, quickly imagining all the things he could do with it. It was the first and only tool he'd found.

But he heard a jolting motion from behind him, and he turned back to look. The bird-beast still had its eyes fixed on him, its body language taut and ready to kill. Dirt quickly dropped the club and stepped backward, then again. He lifted his hands to show they were empty, and he angled his face toward the ground instead of the animal.

The beast gave a huff then moved a few steps farther into the ferns and ducked its head down, likely to rip open another goblin corpse.

Dirt had survived. It wasn't after him. Maybe if he'd been alone, it would have eaten him. But there were other things around, things that were trying to kill it. Dirt wasn't one of those. He wasn't a threat. That must have saved him. All that, and he didn't have a lot of meat on him in the first place.

Relief flooded him, but strangely, it didn't make him feel any better. In place of fear came another tumbled mess of emotions.

"The world is rejecting me," he muttered wretchedly. "I don't belong here or anywhere. I shouldn't even be alive."

He wanted water to wash his bloody mouth out, but there wouldn't be any until tomorrow morning. His leg was still bleeding, but he didn't have any idea what to do about it. None at all. Hopefully it would stop soon, because blood was necessary for life. He remembered that much.

Every footstep jolted his swollen face and made the whole thing ache and sting. Each step, over and over. The pain put pressure on his heart, too, which was already aching. He felt more and more miserable, inside and out, and soon he found himself crying softly, more snorts and gasps than anything.

He hated it, and he couldn't stop. All it did was make his face hurt more, make water run down his cheeks and remind him he was thirsty, make his throat tighten up and burn. It got hard to see, and that was already hard with one eye. All the sparks drained out of him, and he wanted to collapse right there.

No, not right there. Not yet. He'd collapse in his hole under Home. He'd rest there, in the dark, where it was soft and warm. He'd wait for night to come, and then morning, and then . . . hopefully he'd just be dead.

"I'm only three days old!" he yelled in complaint to no one. The sound was muffled and lost in the ferns.

The walk back stretched on for ages. The forest was quiet again, except for his muffled sobs. The eternal trees took no notice of him, silent and unmoving. The ferns tickled lightly against his skin in a way he almost never noticed anymore, and sometimes a stray leaf got into the cut on his leg and dragged through it.

He had no idea how long it really took, though. Nothing changed here except for him, and for him, things just kept getting worse.

-Dirt? Little human?-

He turned to look for the giant wolf pup, and he had to turn farther than normal because of his swollen eye.

Socks approached him gingerly, nose down and sniffing. The wolf sent Dirt a flash of pity, a burst of emotion with no words.

"Hello, Socks," thought Dirt. *"I—"* But then he couldn't think anymore, not clear and loud. Instead he started crying harder, his sobs rising in volume and shaking his chest. It just made his face hurt more.

-Get on, little human. I'll carry you back, and then we can lie down for a while.-

Socks lay down, and Dirt climbed up and collapsed along his back. He gripped the soft fur with his fingers and toes, buried the good side of his face in it, clutched with all his remaining strength. The wolf pup rose and left with such perfect smoothness and grace that Dirt only barely felt the motion.

CHAPTER SIX

As Socks ran, Dirt's sense of speed was incredible. They flew over the ferns almost like birds. Dirt gripped ever tighter, but truly, he felt no danger. Just a rush of wind, the scenery flying past faster than he could imagine, and the sensation of sheer muscular physicality beneath him. Socks was beyond strong. Soft, puffy fur, skin tender from a thin layer of baby fat and beneath all that, muscles longer than Dirt was tall, flexing in perfect rhythmic balance.

It hardly seemed a moment before Socks slowed to a stop under Home's lofty branches and knelt to let Dirt slide off. Dirt's body felt much heavier after that, graceless and awkward as he regained his feet. It left him with a sense of yearning that almost distracted him from the throbbing pain in his face.

-Good, now stand still for a moment,- said Socks. *-I want to lick your blood.-*

Dirt obliged, and the giant wolf pup leaned his great snout down to Dirt's leg, sniffed at the cut, and began licking it clean. Dirt expected the tongue to be rough, but it was smooth and careful, and after a few good licks, Dirt had a single clean area on his body, half the length of his thigh. The blood stopped coming out so fast now, or maybe it had earlier. It was hard to tell, but it pooled instead of dripping.

Socks licked it again, doing his best to get his tongue in there to clean it out. It stung, and besides that, something about it was profoundly uncomfortable, but what was Dirt going to do? Complain?

Only a few more licks and Socks said, *-There. It should be better soon. I don't think licking your face will help because you aren't bleeding there. I can ask Mother later.-*

"*Thanks. I think it helped a little, so you can stop now.*"

Socks rolled onto his side and gestured with his paws, welcoming Dirt to climb on and relax. There was a lot of animal there, so picking the perfect spot wasn't easy. Dirt opted to snuggle in between the beast's front legs, with his head under Socks's chin. The pup draped a front leg over him, and that was that.

It was warm, warmer than Dirt had ever been, and he quickly fell into a comfortable reverie. A few moments ago he'd been cursing the fact that he was alive, but that was fading now. His terror melted away, leaving him feeling drained and loose inside.

-Show me the fight. I want to see what happened,- said Socks.

Dirt considered for a moment, wondering how that would work. He pictured the birds first, coming down from the heights. He pictured it as hard and clear as he could, pushing the image to the front of his mind. "*There, can you see that?*"

-Yes, but it's loud. You don't have to be so loud.-

"*Okay. Let me know if I start . . . letting it slip.*"

He brought the image back and pushed it forward, first the little birds darting around in great numbers, then the bird-beast, all claws and feathers and anger, and how the little birds were driving it to the ground.

Dirt showed his realization that he was in danger, showed himself trying to run away but getting tripped, then chased, then caught. He realized that the bird-beast had given him the cut on his leg—it had just barely nicked him with a talon when it leaped off him. He'd felt the snag, but not the pain.

He couldn't remember exactly what happened after that—his mind had been too full of terror to make sense of anything. But he remembered being punched in the face and how the blow was too much for his child's body. And getting punched again. Waking up seeped in pain, unsure and unstable, trying to stumble away until Socks found him.

-I wondered what it was like to be so tiny and weak. That was very interesting. I will tell my siblings.-

"I don't know how I'm supposed to survive, if there are things like that everywhere."

-The goblins wanted to eat the gryphon. They were attracted by all the commotion, since it started all the way up. Just stay away from noisy places, and you'll probably be fine,- said Socks.

"A gryphon? Is that what the big one is called?"

-Yes. Mother says they like the mountains, but sometimes they can be seen elsewhere. I doubt you'll find another one. And goblins are not very smart. They are not even as smart as a human. They just go toward noisy things because they are hungry.-

"But they could talk."

-They do not understand the words. It is only sounds to them.-

"So all I have to do is be quiet, and I won't get eaten?"

-Well, that is one thing you have to do.-

The great pup didn't seem particularly affected by Dirt's plight, and he was starting to feel disregarded. A novelty instead of a person. A curiosity, enjoyed and then discarded. It was better than nothing, he thought to himself, with a hint of bitterness.

But Socks said, *-Don't be sad, little human. Little Dirt. Come, join me in the dream. Let's go to sleep, and you'll feel better.-*

"Okay. I bet you're right," thought Dirt. He retreated into his thoughts, enjoying the feeling of the great pup's fur, the feeling of softness and warmth and life. The pup's faint smell, hard to identify but not unpleasant.

The pup's breathing settled into an even rhythm, and Dirt guessed that Socks had fallen asleep. The only thing keeping Dirt awake now was the searing, throbbing pain in his face, pain that made him hold as still as possible. But exhaustion was fighting to win, and he relaxed further, comforted, enveloped in Socks's warm embrace. He snuggled in a bit deeper.

Some part of him knew this was only temporary, that his injuries would take a long time to heal, that Socks would have to leave him alone again soon. But he pushed those thoughts away and tried to make the nagging knot of dread in his heart come undone and vanish.

He should keep on living. He could feel that, even if he couldn't look around at how things were going and explain why. One thing at a time. *Courage, Dirt. Take courage.* And a nap.

Dirt slept easily and comfortably after that, and when he woke, his mind was filled with a tangled mess of colors and smells and emotions that collapsed as soon as he became aware of them. They left behind a lingering sense of loss, like something beautiful was gone, and Dirt knew he had dreamed. He wished he could remember what had happened in it.

-*Why do you dream like that?*- asked Socks.

It took Dirt a moment to realize that Socks was really here and had actually spoken. His bed in the pup's fur was too perfect and felt like nothing at all. *"Dream like what? I think that was my second dream, and I already forgot it."*

-*I was waiting for you to come, and then when you did, you were like this,*- replied Socks. He sent a mental image of a flurry of disconnected parts and pieces all swarming in a cloud, tiny bits of color, incomplete shapes of flesh. The swirling thing spoke with Dirt's voice, though, and laughed as he and Socks flew into a blue sky, across red mountains and black valleys, green meadows with flowers of unnamed colors.

Others were there, too, other wolf pups like Socks. They danced together, and snarled and played and flew—

And then the vision was gone. -*Why did you look like that? Is that how humans are?*-

"I have no idea," said Dirt.

-*I will have to ask Mother. I think there is something wrong with you. You might be broken.*-

Dirt agreed, but he didn't know what to say, so he said nothing. They lay for a short while longer, and then Socks had to go.

-*Stay out of danger, little human. Little Dirt. Goodbye.*-

"Goodbye, Socks. Thank you for saving me."

Dirt got a lump in his throat that burned and ached as he watched Socks slide effortlessly into a run. It didn't fade for quite a while.

CHAPTER SEVEN

The rest of the day was spent quietly. Dirt dug for grubs and baby ferns and ate his fill, then had little to do until dark arrived. And he didn't really want to do much anyway, because every time he took a step his face throbbed. At least he still had one good eye left, because otherwise he'd probably starve.

Broken. Socks said he was broken, and he probably didn't mean the face bones. Something about dreams. Well, Dirt knew there was something wrong with himself too, and he didn't know what or why either. So that was nothing new. But even so, it was painful to think about.

It was Dirt's first and only taste of any kind of warmth, any care or succor, and now that it was absent, he knew how badly he needed more. Dirt didn't know how close they could ever be, since Socks was a predator and Dirt was prey at best, but he hoped for something. Friendship, or even just regular visits. Something. Anything. He needed it. But maybe Socks would never come back. Maybe Mother would tell her son not to go play with the dirty, broken human anymore.

With nothing to do but worry and think, his melancholy was almost as bad as his injuries. He didn't want to run around, because that made his face hurt, and his leg bled slightly if he didn't hold still. There was no one to talk to. Nothing to do but wait for dark and the chance to sleep.

His imagination grew to fill the emptiness, but it took effort. He gazed upward into the canopy, so unreachably distant above him, and wondered if things were different up there. Maybe that's where all the other humans were. No one was alone up there, and they could drink water whenever they wanted. Maybe Dirt had fallen down, and that's how he ended up here.

He tried to imagine being with other humans, but he had nothing to build on. He knew he was a child, so the adults must be bigger, but he had never seen his own face, and his imagination made everyone look like a goblin. From there, his imagination had him chasing through the green skies above to escape oversized monstrosities.

The trauma of the fight kept trying to catch him in its claws and drag him back into terror, but each time it did, he imagined a way out. He had to, or they would overwhelm him.

Goblins surrounded him, and he flapped his wings and flew above them like a bird. One caught him, but Dirt imagined himself coated in mud, and he slipped away. Another chased him, but Dirt stomped on the branch and broke it, sending the goblin tumbling into eternity. The gryphon came, but he fed it some grubs, and it left him alone.

After a while, he dug up some grubs again, but before eating them, he gave them voices. One was a mother, and the other a child. He struggled to think what they would say to each other.

"Hello, Mother."

"Hello, child."

"I . . . have some food for you."

"Thank you, Mother."

Dirt paused, wondering what else they would talk about. He wanted them to become real, wanted it desperately. The need for play seemed almost like hunger or thirst, but he had no memories to draw on. As he sat in silence trying to think of something, frustration rose in him until he was about ready to squeeze both grubs to death in his hands and lick them off.

"Mother, I saw a gryphon today." Yes, that would work.

"Oh?"

"It was like a big . . . wolf, but with feathers and a beak like a bird. It chased me, but I got away."

From there, he added a brother and sister and father, and had them each tell stories about goblins or gryphons or wolves, about trees and ferns and night and day, over and over. He explained how to hide, and about being careful of making too much noise. When one of the grubs died from being played with too much, he ate it and dug up another one.

By the time night came, his spirit felt much calmer, his confidence higher. He was going to be okay. His face ached so badly he wondered if he'd even be able to sleep, but that was temporary. He'd get better. And he was lonely, scared, and vulnerable, but Socks would come back.

The creeping darkness of night nudged him into his nest, and he carefully curled up in a way that didn't put any pressure on his thigh or his face. It wasn't easy, either, since it was the left side of his face and his right leg. The pain kept him up long past when he wanted to be asleep, long enough that the vibrations started again. The sound was soothing, though. A good sound. It sounded right. Important and true. He was fine, and he'd be better tomorrow. He'd lived another day. Just surviving took a kind of strength, and so did having hope. He could do that, too. He wasn't completely weak.

Hope was the thing that finally carried him off to sleep. It glowed in his chest like a little light of his own, chasing off the last few itching shadows.

He woke several times during the night because he kept moving in a way that tweaked something painful, but not for long each time. The gentle waves of sound passed through him on their way up into the tree, whatever they were. He stayed awake just long enough to remember that he had been dreaming about being a tree again, living in an infinite-faceted world he could not begin to understand with his human mind.

When dawn came, he paused for a moment before getting up to finally go get some water. He raised his hand and touched the root of the enormous tree and tried to remember the dream. His senses had been too confusing, too varied and subtle, to analyze with his human understanding. But one thought struck him, so surprising it almost felt like an electric shock: if it could dream, the tree had a mind. And it had dreamed. It'd swept his dreams up into its own. That was the only explanation. It was alive and aware.

"Home . . ." he whispered aloud. Home was alive, alive like a person. A real thing. Not just scenery, but real.

Had he dreamed he was a tree himself? Had that really been what happened? Or was he simply sharing in its experience?

"Good morning, Home," he said quietly. The root bark said nothing back, of course. The night vibrations were gone, and no dreams remained. Home would be quiet until night, and then they could talk again.

He crawled out of his nest and stood, stretching with a contented groan. The morning fog was already starting to lift, so he must have slept late. But he liked the fog, he decided; it was the best way to start the day. Nothing to see, nothing to worry about.

His leg wasn't bleeding anymore, which was good. When he poked at it, it only stung a little and seemed to have mostly closed up. Was that how fast cuts healed? Just one night? That was good to know. Almost good as new.

But his face was still swollen, and he couldn't open his left eye. Turning his head too fast or leaning forward made it ache, a deep hurt that pressed into his bones. That would take more time to get better. Oh well.

The morning dew tasted sweet this morning, pleasantly cool, but that was probably because of how thirsty he was.

-Hello, Dirt, little human,- came Socks's voice, right before the giant pup poked Dirt in the back with his wet nose.

Dirt was so startled he jumped forward and shrieked, heart instantly beating three times as fast.

-Looks like I scared you,- said Socks, sounding amused.

"You snuck up on me! You're very quiet for something so big," said Dirt, grinning.

-I am a hunter.- Socks sent an image of himself leaping upon an unsuspecting animal that Dirt had never seen before and snapping its neck in his mighty teeth.

"Oh, I know you could eat me in one bite if you wanted. I was just surprised. But I'm glad to see you. Come down here so I can hug you." Dirt held his arms up, and Socks carefully lowered himself to a squat. Dirt hugged Socks around the neck, burying the good side of his face in the pup's warm, damp fur. Socks's neck was too big for Dirt to get his arms all the way around, but he did his best to scratch as much territory as he could reach.

-What were you doing right before?-

"I was just drinking some water. I need a lot, but the only time to get it is in the morning. Do you drink water, or is the blood from your prey enough?"

-You were drinking water off the ferns? Is that even called drinking?-

"Well, where else do I get it?" asked Dirt.

-Keep scratching, and maybe I will take you with me,- said Socks playfully.

Dirt kept right on scratching, making sure he was as appealing to have along as possible. Socks tilted his head around to direct Dirt to the best spots, and he made sure to remember where they were. He tried not to let himself get too excited about going with Socks, but he only had so much mental discipline to spare.

-I was on my way somewhere near here, so I came by to see if you were dead yet. Mother thought you might be, but I didn't think so. I licked your leg so I knew it would get better. She didn't say how to fix your face.-

"Well, you were right. I'm alive. But only because you saved me. I think I was ready to give up and die before you came yesterday."

-You are so tiny that it's impossible to tell what might break you. I am glad you are still alive, because I think you are interesting.-

Dirt smiled softly to himself, trying not to seem too eager. Interesting was something he could work with.

"Socks, can I ask you something? Every night when I sleep under the tree, I hear a sound like this," said Dirt. He collected a mental image of the vibrations, trying to capture as much of the experience as he could, and focused on it in his mind for Socks to see.

-I don't know. I'll have to ask Mother. I sleep with all my brothers and sisters, not under a tree.-

"Did you know that trees are alive?"

-Of course they're alive, silly little human. They grow. They're plants, and plants are alive.-

"No, I mean, not like plants. They can dream, which means they have minds. They're like us, sort of."

-You didn't know that? How can something be alive and not have a mind?-

Dirt thought about that for a moment. Why had he expected otherwise? It had never occurred to him that trees might think, but why shouldn't they be able to?

"Can you talk to them?"

-Mother does. I think they are boring.-

"Well, nothing is boring to me because I've only been alive for four days, counting this one. But, can you really take me to water? And bring me back here? I think I like this tree."

-Yes. Climb on and hold tight. I want to go back to something I found, and there is water there for you.-

"What was it?"

-I don't know. You will see it when we get there.-

Dirt crawled up onto Socks's back with a mixture of eagerness and trepidation. Something about this made him nervous, but there was no way he was going to pass it up. He lay along the pup's back and settled deep into his soft fur, getting as solid a grip as he could.

Socks ran. He ran so fast the ferns turned into an indistinct green blur, so fast that Dirt couldn't lift his head much before the rushing wind started pushing him off. Socks leaped through the air, and Dirt found himself laughing with joy and terror mixed.

That just seemed to make the pup more enthusiastic. Socks leaped high into the air several times more, higher and higher, easily reaching fatal heights. Dirt screamed and laughed, body full of sparks. The pup's balance and control were so perfect that Dirt never once felt himself slipping, or had any fear that he might be accidentally dropped.

Dirt had no way to measure distance or time, but Home had long vanished into the pale distance before Socks finally slowed and stopped. Dirt tossed his feet to one side and slid down, landing more gracefully than he expected.

He still felt like he was floating. He had a grin plastered on his face that wouldn't go away. It was making his cheek muscles ache.

-Here. This is farther than Mother can see. I know that because I tested it. Now, look what I found.-

Cut stone lay buried in the ground, making a row that led past a series of stone basins. It led a good distance through toppled clumps of stone and overgrown plants, and ended at a massive square ruin of graying stone, overgrown with moss and ferns.

Dirt was baffled, intimidated by it at first. A sense of dread foreboding kept his feet planted as he tried to make sense of what he saw.

It all looked deliberate, completely unlike anything else in the forest. In fact, it was the first stone he'd seen. Not even a tiny little rock, despite digging in all that dirt. He stepped forward and knelt to touch it, tracing his fingers along the rough, hard surface.

He shot to his feet and spun to face Socks. "A building! It's a building, and that's a path!" He realized he was talking aloud, and thought, *"Sorry, I forgot. But that's a building! I think humans made this! You are supposed to walk on these stones, and they're called a road. It's broken in the other direction, but I think it went really far once. And it leads to that building. That's a place where you can go inside, and . . . it looks like . . . I think it's a temple. It has . . ."*

Dirt's thoughts trailed off as words came to him that he'd never had in his head before. A road. A temple. Everything out front was probably a garden. He tried to grab on to any of those words, to try to really understand what they meant. What he was looking at.

He stepped onto the road and walked forward, feeling the cool, hard stone beneath his feet and how different it was from bark or dirt. Socks padded along behind him, sniffing everything warily.

Dirt stopped at an old stone basin full of dark green water. He dipped his hands in and brought some up to his face. It smelled odd, unlike anything he was used to. He took a sip, but it tasted unpleasant so he decided to look elsewhere before drinking any more.

He heard a trickle and ran at a full sprint toward the source. One of the basins had perfectly clear water, and Dirt could see right down to the bottom where the water came up from a hole. The water filled it halfway, up to a spot where a big chunk had broken off the side. From there it trickled onto the paving stones, no thicker than a stream of urine. It made a second puddle in a dip in the stone, and a little furrow where the water drained off it. He wasn't sure, but it looked like it had been doing that for a *very* long time.

Dirt dunked his head and drank until he had to come up for air. The cold water made his injured face ache with throbbing pulses that reached down into his neck, but he didn't care. *"Drink some! It's so good!"*

Socks dipped his nose near the water and started lapping it up with his tongue, and Dirt dunked his head again. The cold was shocking, but the water was perfectly clear and had none of the plant taste that the morning dew did.

When he pulled his head out again, he noticed how much dirt he left behind in the water and immediately felt guilty. He had ruined something special. He might never see clean water again. That might have been the only time, for the rest of his life.

The shame of it made him sick to his stomach, but Socks said, *-There is always more water. You are being silly, little human. Don't feel bad. Come look at this.-*

Dirt wondered why he had to think things loudly if Socks could just hear everything either way, but he didn't argue.

Socks led him down the stone path, most of which was crumbling and uneven, and stopped at the building. It was a lumpy mound of pale, dirty stone, decaying moss, and ferns, but some of the square shape was still visible.

Enough of it was still standing that it towered over him, twice as tall as Socks at its highest point. It seemed big, but not compared to the trees. It seemed big compared to little Dirt, standing in front of it.

Fallen pillars lay to either side of a tall opening, full of nothing but silent blackness. Despite all the parts that had collapsed, there was still an opening, with interior space behind it. There was plenty of room in there. He could walk right in if he wanted. Theoretically. He found himself unwilling to go farther as the darkness both called to him and urged him to turn away.

But Socks stopped. He said, *-Mother can't see this far, so she doesn't know what we're doing. I want to go in, but Mother said never to go into places like this. But I want to find out what's inside. Don't you?-*

Dirt hesitated, looking through the opening, which called up the word "doorway," even if there was no "door." He wasn't sure what a door might be, but whatever it was, it wasn't there. There was only enough light to see a single step inside.

A temple. A human place. An old, old place of men, right in front of him. The darkness inside wasn't the comforting darkness of his den under Home, though. It was the mysterious darkness of hidden night, in which only things that lived without light dared move. But what was a temple, anyway? What was it for?

He asked, *"Mother said not to go in? Did she say what kinds of things are in there that you might need to worry about?"*

Socks pawed at the ground, hesitating. Dirt could feel his eagerness, though, even without the pup sending it on purpose.

When Socks didn't answer, Dirt turned his eye back to the blackness. How much would it hurt to just walk in a short distance, and find out if he could even see in there? Maybe his eye would adjust to the light, and he'd see what it was like.

A temple was a good place. The word felt good in his mind, even if he didn't know why anymore. But there was something about how it had decayed, how silent it was, that made him second guess himself. There was nothing here, nothing alive but him and Socks.

This was never meant to be a dead place. It was meant to be a living place. Important, even. He wanted to go in, despite the feeling that the dark old building was watching him as intently as he watched it.

But . . . *"Socks, has she ever been wrong before?"*

The wolf pup turned his giant head and fixed his yellow eyes on Dirt. *-There is a smell I do not know. But the air inside is very old, and it might be nothing. It is faint.-* Socks turned back to sniff at the entrance again. *-Mother has never been wrong. That is impossible.-*

"Then we shouldn't go in. I don't know why she said that, but we should listen to her."

Socks gave a little whine, sniffing again. He turned and walked in a circle, his stomach brushing right over Dirt's head. He faced inward and sniffed again. He pawed at the stone several times, then said, *-You are right. We should listen to Mother, even if she can't see us right now.-*

I CAN SEE YOU, PUP. BECAUSE YOU LISTENED TO WISDOM, YOU MAY LIVE. AND FOR SPEAKING WISDOM, I WILL CONSIDER YOUR BROKEN PET. BRING HIM TO ME.

The power of the thought nearly drove Dirt to his hands and knees, and when it was over, he felt light enough to float away. Dizzy, he rested his hands on his knees and breathed deeply.

Socks lowered his nose and licked Dirt's hair a little to get his attention. *-Are you okay?-*

"I think I'm fine. That was . . . was that Mother?"

-Yes. I will tell her to be quieter when we get there, since you are very small.-

A sense of subtle fear came across along with the thought, and Dirt realized that Socks looked taken aback. He stood and stepped in to pet the pup's hanging head. *"How about you? Are you okay?"*

-Sometimes you can be scared after the bad thing happens instead of before.-

Seeing the enormous beast with his tail tucked and his ears lowered was more unnerving than seeing him with blood all over his face had been. Dirt pressed his forehead into the wolf's and hugged him around the snout. After a moment, he said, *"It'll be okay, Socks."*

-You have no idea what you are talking about, little human. Little Dirt. It's a good thing we listened, though. Get on. Let us go and see Mother.-

As they left, Dirt glanced at the basin and wondered if the dirt he left in it would be there forever, or if it would be clean next time he came.

CHAPTER EIGHT

Socks raced with the same effortless speed as before, but there was no mirth in it this time. The wolf's demeanor was subdued and anxious, and Dirt could feel it even though Socks wasn't talking. Dirt's own heart was mostly full of concerned sympathy—he had never seen Socks like this, and he didn't know what to do about it, other than try to smother him in affection. And that wasn't possible right now, not running at a speed that would shatter every bone in Dirt's body if he fell.

As they ran farther and farther, Dirt watched as the unending, impossibly tall trees slowly changed. It was subtle at first—they grew shorter, and periodically a spot of blue became visible for only an instant. Dirt wished he could sit up and look around properly, but he didn't dare try. Not without asking first and trying it while going slower, and this didn't seem like a good time.

The edge of the great forest came into view. Dirt nearly did sit up to get a look then, and if not for the rushing air, he might have. From the corner of his vision, he saw the approaching line in the sky where it went from unbroken green to unbroken blue. There were no trees past it; at least, none big enough to see.

He'd had no idea there was an "outside" to the forest. But everything got so much brighter ahead that he found himself suddenly wanting to stop, to not cross that threshold. It wasn't safe out there without a real sky.

But they didn't stop. Socks never slowed.

The sun burst out from behind the eternal trees and fell on him in all its fury, too painful to even look at. Every inch of his dirty skin, from the soles of his feet to the tips of his ears, warmed in the light's heat. He had to squint to see anything, and his good eye hurt anyway, way deep in the back. But he couldn't just shut it. There was too much to see.

There were little trees everywhere, of every shape and color, but they were all tiny. Too small to be called trees. Socks had to pick the ones he went under, and most of them he had to go around. Some grew thick, with leaves like thousands of needles. Others grew tall and thin, or billowed out broadly. Flat and thin, curved and straight, wide and narrow— simply too much to keep track of.

Shadows, too. Lines of light and dark all over everything. He'd never seen a shadow before, but every single thing had one, and he had no time to get used to them. No ferns, either. None at all. Instead, grass and bushes and big patches of bare earth and rocks. Leaves of bright green, dark green, muted blue, or even purple made up the confused landscape. Everything raced by too fast for Dirt to get a good look, and soon he started feeling dizzy. It was all too much. The empty sky, the bright sun that was impossible to get away from, plants in unending variety.

But he couldn't look away. He couldn't look away for an instant. The uneven ground became hills, and the scenery started changing so fast he couldn't remember the last thing he'd just seen.

No wonder Socks lived out here somewhere. This was a place where anything could appear, something new in every direction. The forest was sacred and solemn and empty, and everything there but the trees and the ferns was just visiting. Out here, though, who knew what to expect?

Dirt stopped being able to tell things apart. His mind was simply too overwhelmed to keep up, and it was all turning into a blur. He felt a little nauseous and hoped his grip on Socks was strong enough. Finally, he closed his good eye, hoping that not looking for a moment would help him recover.

Socks stopped abruptly, so quickly that Dirt almost slid forward and fell off. *-I think you need a drink of water. You should be healthy when you meet Mother, but you are dizzy and confused.-*

"Thanks. There's just too much to see. I'm just . . . it's too much." Dirt slid off and landed on his feet, but not gracefully. It was a bit of a drop, after all. The ground was hard and poky here, with lots of sharp little rocks and bits of wood, and he danced around and hissed in pain.

-*You are soft,*- said Socks.

"I bet you were just as soft when you were four days old," replied Dirt. *"What is that sound? Oh . . . !"*

Just ahead was more water than Dirt had imagined could exist at once. It rushed along in a great stream, too wide to jump across. A river. This was a river! Dirt got on his hands and knees and crept up to the edge of the water, nervous about how fast it was moving. The sunlight made it sparkle and flash, and shadowed spots let him see all the way to the sand in the bottom.

-*Just drink. Don't jump in or it will carry you away.*-

"I'm not really thirsty anymore," said Dirt. *"I had plenty before."*

-*Drink a little bit, then. It's only water. You are hungry, aren't you? I am too big to catch bugs for you, but I smell some eggs. Do you want some eggs to eat?*-

"I don't know what eggs are. Are they good?"

-*I don't know. They are food for small things like you. Wait here.*- Socks turned and padded silently away.

A hundred quiet sounds rushed in once the pup was gone. Birdsong, gentle wind rustling in the leaves, taps and creaks, and buzzing insects. It smelled different, too, like water and dust and pollen. It was far less humid, and the air lacked that heavy blanketlike quality it had back in the forest.

He decided he could use a bit of water after all, so he very carefully dipped his head down and slurped up a few gulps. He was so nervous about falling in that he didn't even taste it, and once he'd swallowed enough he scooted three or four steps away from the edge, just in case.

It wasn't too unpleasant out here. There was a gentleness to all the variety, like it was all supposed to go together somehow, following some pattern he hadn't detected. That didn't mean it wasn't dangerous, though. The forest was calmer than here by far, and look what had happened to him *there.*

Little bugs flew by, too tiny to tell their shape. They were like motes of sunlight, almost, flitting around with nervous speed. The sun on his legs felt nice, too. Warm. A little animal, no bigger than his hand, darted from one tree to another, too fast for Dirt to get a good look at it.

Socks politely rustled a bush when he got back so Dirt wouldn't be startled again.

-Here, little human. Eat these.-

The pup opened his mouth and unrolled his tongue to reveal four round, white balls. Dirt took them, rubbing their hard, smooth surface with his thumbs. They didn't seem like food.

"How do I eat them?"

-They are full of juice inside. The goblins knock a hole in the top with a tooth, then another hole in the bottom, and suck it out. They do not eat the shell.-

Dirt took one and tilted his head back. He knocked the shell against one of his sharper teeth. It didn't work.

-Harder, silly little human. But not too hard or it will come apart.-

Dirt knocked it harder, then harder, and harder again, and finally he punched a little hole in the bottom. He flipped it around and *tap, tap, crack.* He put his lips around the hole and sucked, and the liquid inside oozed slowly into his mouth and down his throat. It had a mild flavor, and it was pleasantly warm—either from being in Socks's mouth or from having sunlight on it before that.

He ate the second one in the same way and decided two were enough. *"I feel a lot better. I think you were right. I just needed something to eat, and a moment with my feet under me. Two is enough for now, though. Is it okay if I hold on to the other ones?"*

-No, you will break them on my fur, and it will be somewhere hard to lick off. Just eat them or throw them away.-

"Can I break it open?"

-We should not make Mother wait. We do not want her to be annoyed with us.-

"Oh. Right. I'll hurry." Dirt quickly cracked one open with his fingers and was surprised to find it had two parts inside—a yellow part and a clear part. The yellow part made a little ball of its own in there, so he slurped it up and dropped the rest. The final egg cracked open and ran into the ground, making a little spot of mud. He licked his fingers clean and climbed back up on Socks, and they were off again.

Now that Dirt had some energy back, the scenery was far more interesting than before. He decided he liked the sunlight, but only so much or it would get tiring. Colors in endless variety flew past, and the rushing wind kept away all the other sounds. He sent bursts of enjoyment to Socks, and the pup seemed to lighten up a little as they went.

Another pup appeared with the same fur Socks had, gray and brown and white. It ran alongside, giving a curious eye to Dirt and sniffing his direction. Dirt thought *"Hello!"* for it, but the other pup didn't respond. Instead, Dirt caught tiny snippets and whispers of a conversation between the two that went far too fast for him to follow, and which only reached his mind unintentionally.

The pups didn't need words at all; instead, they sent complex ideas together in bundles. The small bits that Dirt could make sense of were strange, but not as alien as the tree-dream. Scents mostly, with startling richness and complexity, but also wordless ideas and maybe a flash of shape or color. Dirt suspected that even if they slowed down and let him in on their conversation, he wouldn't get anything more out of it than he did now.

A third pup joined them, running on the other side. This one was a bit more reddish than the first two, and it only stayed for a short time after giving Dirt a good sniff.

Then a fourth, and a fifth, and before Dirt knew it, there were dozens. They trailed Socks, who seemed proud at the moment.

They passed a pile of cracked bones of countless shapes and sizes. Some were fresher than others, and the whole pile stank like rot. Dirt got enough of a look to know he could never guess what they belonged to, and some were big enough he would have thought they were little-tree trunks if they weren't heaped on a bunch of other bones.

Socks slowed to a trot and led the pack up a hill toward a flat rock as wide as a tree trunk, which rested above a smaller cave opening. That must be it. That was where Mother was, and where Socks lived with his brothers and sisters. Out front, pups played and chased and fought in the dirt. The area was so busy that the whole hillside was just sandy dirt. They'd torn up all the plants.

-You have not been rude before, but do not be rude to Mother,- thought Socks.

"I wouldn't dare," thought Dirt, and he meant it.

As soon as Socks carried him into the cave opening, the smell told him it was not a human place. The den stank of predator, like Socks but stronger, and mixed with other things. A hint of urine, perhaps, and something spicy. The air was motionless, heady, and warm. His body filled with nervousness that came from a deeper place than his thoughts. This was a place of wolves. There was peril here.

It was dark inside. The only light came in through the entrance behind them, and it took Dirt's eye a moment to slowly adjust. The den was a cavern, big enough to hold every wolf outside and more, all at once.

And it needed to be. Mother was so large that Dirt wasn't even aware he was looking at her until he found the yellow eyes. She was too large to make sense of. He couldn't look at all of her all at once unless he got farther away.

Black as shadow, she lay on her side to nurse ten giant pups Socks's size, who seemed tiny in comparison. Several more lay around her, patiently waiting their turns. Her head alone was bigger than Socks's whole body, and her eyes were fixed on them in a way that made him glad he was riding, not walking.

COME CLOSER.

Mother's voice in his head was so loud it replaced every other thought, every emotion. But it was only that loud, and no more—not loud enough to hurt. And Dirt was certain she could hurt him if she wanted. Just a little louder, and the contents of his skull would shoot out his ears.

Socks approached gingerly, unsure. He stopped right in front of her nose, and she leaned forward to sniff his face.

The sheer size of her, and the speed and grace with which she moved, unnerved him. It made him unsteady just looking at her.

LET HIM DOWN.

Socks squatted, and Dirt slid off, landing feet-first on the soft dirt floor. No ferns, no leaves, nothing. He wondered why.

COME CLOSER, DIRT. STAND BEFORE ME.

The fear finally caught up with him. Her nose was so big she could snort him into her lungs with a sniff. He could hollow out one of her teeth and sleep inside it. He dared not approach. He knew he had to, but he couldn't move. His feet wouldn't obey him.

He clenched his fists and grit his teeth and tried to calm down, but to no avail. The terror inside him was so strong it was worse than pain. He'd rather get punched a hundred times than face Mother.

Bursts of amusement filled his mind as all the other little pups started paying attention to what was happening and probed his thoughts. His head swelled with a dozen different images at once—some of him being eaten, sent to scare him; others of him being licked, sent to comfort him.

BE QUIET, ALL OF YOU. YOU WILL HURT HIM. DO YOU NOT SEE HOW FRAGILE HE IS?

She gazed around the room, and the voices in his head quieted. Socks sent him a subtle puff of encouragement, and it helped. A little.

DIRT, IF YOU WISH TO REMAIN WITH MY CHILD, YOU MUST MASTER YOUR FEAR. I WILL NOT HAVE YOU TEACH HIM WEAKNESS.

That scared him in a very different way. It was one thing to be torn apart and die, but abandonment was beyond imagining. He couldn't let that happen, no matter what.

Dirt focused inward, trying to force himself not to be afraid. The fear twisted in his stomach, gripped his joints with fiery fronds and held him still, breathed death into his mind. But he pushed it all away. He pushed again.

He looked up at Mother and stood up straight. The fear had not left him, but he was stronger. He had to be. A dribble of urine leaked out, and his knees wouldn't stop trembling. But he stood. He did not look away. He took a step forward, then another, and stopped.

BETTER. NOW, LET US SEE WHAT IS WRONG WITH YOU.

Mother's enormous yellow eyes fixed on him properly, and her attention hit him like a full-body slap. Her sight penetrated his skin, his mind, and parts of his being he could not name. She turned him inside out.

Dirt felt his feet leave the ground as Mother's gaze lifted him up into the air. It held him so tightly that he felt encased in wood. He couldn't so much as twitch a finger. She twisted and pulled on invisible parts of him; parts of him that he could feel, real parts, but unseen ones. Much that she touched felt raw and painful, like the cut on his leg had.

She turned him over in the air, slowly rotating him this way and that to examine him from every angle. Now he knew what a grub felt like when he played with it. The bones of his face ached mercilessly and he would have whimpered if he still had control of his own voice.

After a few rotations, he had trouble staying conscious. Mother's examination squeezed the energy right out of him. Or, perhaps, she stretched him, and it leaked out on its own. Either way, what leaked out of him was hard to understand. His ability to focus, his inner control, and more.

She gazed into his memory, and every moment he had lived flashed by in an instant. After seeing when he first woke covered in clear slime, it failed to go back any further.

Mother's eyes flashed with orange light, and Dirt shuddered in mid-air. She examined him for a moment longer, but it was with senses that he could not perceive in any way.

When she finally lowered him to the ground and let him go, he collapsed so hard that his face was in the dirt before he realized he'd lost his balance.

She gave him no time to recover.

DO YOU HAVE ANY IDEA WHAT HAS HAPPENED TO YOU?

He tried to reply, but he lacked the mental strength to get the thought into the right place.

Mother saw it anyway.

YOU DO NOT. HOW INTERESTING. SUCH AN ARROGANT THING YOU ONCE WERE, AND NOW YOU ARE THIS.

-What was he before, Mother?- thought Socks. He had thought it with words and broadcast it, for Dirt's sake.

HE IS A BIT OF ANCIENT DUST BLOWN BY THE WIND AND LANDING HERE ONLY BY ACCIDENT. I HAVE AN IDEA WHAT HE WAS ATTEMPTING, BUT IN DOING SO, HE LOST EVERYTHING. HIS MEMORY, HIS PLACE AND PEOPLE. EVEN HIS TIME.

Mother's voice was accompanied by images that explained her thoughts in greater detail. Dirt saw an outline of an adult man, indistinct but all grown up, and knew that it was himself. He felt the sensation of being among many people, living in a place for humans. Saw himself undertake a great effort, something grand and momentous and dangerous and foolish, and fail. He saw himself sucked out of the world like the juice from an egg, floating in the incomprehensible void between all things while his essence, his very self, slowly evaporated. Bit by bit, there was less and less of him, until it was almost too late.

Finally, Dirt saw what remained catch on the flow of reality with a gentle snag. He fell back into time and place, appearing half-buried in the dirt and covered in the decay of his own self. That clear goo, the slime that he'd been covered with when he first awoke and completely forgot about, was the remains of what he had been. All the memory, the learning, the flesh, even the days and years—all had become nothing.

YOU WERE RIGHT, CUB. HE IS BROKEN. I AM SURPRISED HE IS ALIVE AT ALL.

Mother's subtext was an egg with a dozen holes, slowly leaking its juices.

HUMAN, YOU HAVE ONE THING LEFT, AND THAT IS YOUR CORE. IT HAS GROWN, AND IT CANNOT UNGROW.

Dirt saw himself peeling away in layers. His flesh, the child he was, split apart to reveal a boy of energy, all patchy and covered with holes. It split away to reveal a boy made of something even more subtle and just as damaged, and then split again, layer after layer until an image of himself appeared that was faint as a whisper and mostly transparent, damaged as the rest. That was his spirit, he knew. That was the part that remained when a person died.

But there was one more part inside that. His spirit split open to reveal a pinpoint of light, something subtle and eternal, something that never changed and never ceased changing. It was the deepest truth of himself, his bare consciousness. With none of the other layers, it thought without ideas, understood without knowledge or reference. But it was whole, indivisible, eternal, and it had grown.

YOUR SCANT HUMAN YEARS GAVE YOU SOME SMALL WISDOM, AND THAT ALONE IS NOT LOST. ALL ELSE IS BROKEN: YOUR MAGIC VESSEL, YOUR DREAM-SELF, ALL OF IT. YOU RETAIN NOTHING BUT A FEW OF YOUR YEARS. BUT FOR THOSE, YOU WOULD NOT EVEN HAVE FLESH.

He lay in the warm dirt and tried to gather enough strength to push himself back up, but his joints felt watery and disconnected.

TAKE HIM FROM HERE BEFORE FATHER RETURNS WITH MY DINNER. PUT HIM BACK WHERE YOU FOUND HIM.

Mother's great maw closed over him, and Dirt was too enervated to feel anything but a tinge of regret that this was how he would die. But instead of swallowing him, she lifted him gently between her front teeth and put him back on Socks's back.

Socks quickly carried Dirt up and out of the musky den, back into the startling sunlight. The cub ran back down the hill, past all his curious brothers and sisters, past the pile of bones, then a good distance into the little-tree forest before Dirt recovered enough strength in his fingers to start holding on.

They ran for a good distance before either of them spoke. Dirt was too drained to pay attention to the scenery, which seemed like a shame. But every time he tried to focus, his mind wandered, and his eyes saw nothing. His thoughts were full of wolves, full of Mother's size, her gaze. But there was nothing sensible to process, not really. He felt like he did when he was falling asleep or waking up.

Socks, however, was tireless. Dirt wasn't sure how he did it, but he'd been running for a good portion of the day without showing any sign of weariness. Carrying Dirt around didn't even seem to slow him down.

The warm sunlight on his back helped Dirt re-energize, because by the time they reached the edge of the real forest and its canopy as high as the blue in the sky, Dirt had finally recovered.

The first real thought he had after all that, was that Mother had said to put him back where Socks had found him, and that meant he was being abandoned. Grief poured into him, brutal and irresistible.

But then it occurred to him that Mother had no reason to care about him. Something like Dirt was nothing to a being as great as Mother. If she didn't want Socks to ever see him again, Dirt would already be dead. Why waste time putting him back? He got a hold of himself quickly after that.

He hugged Socks a little more tightly. Then he thought, *"Mother is . . . more impressive than I imagined. Very powerful. And wise. You must be proud of her."*

-She is very old and very strong. So is Father, but you should be glad you didn't meet him. He has little tolerance for intruders, and he probably

would have killed you just for being noticed. I will be like them soon, when I grow up.-

"*How come you never mentioned that you have a father too?*"

Socks didn't reply right away, and Dirt started feeling anxious that he'd asked something he shouldn't have. When the pup finally answered, he seemed hesitant. *-My brothers and sisters are all very young, so right now, Mother is in charge of us. She tells us the rules, and then she picks one or two every night and eats them while we're sleeping. Someday when only a few are left, Father will take us and train us. He will pick one or two to grow up and eat the rest. That is why I was nervous about Mother today. But I obeyed her, so I can live for now.-*

Dirt's horror must have leaked out, because the pup stopped running.

Socks bristled and paced, and when he sent Dirt his thoughts, his voice was indignant and proud. *-You are just a human, so I don't expect you to understand. If some of you are weak or stupid, it doesn't matter. Would anyone even notice? It doesn't change the world. But we are wolves. You saw Mother. Father is just as great. Can you imagine a weak wolf? An inferior wolf running with them, hunting with them, calling himself a worthy wolf? I could never tolerate an inferior wolf. I'd be happy to die, if it meant that one wouldn't exist. I think I'll win, but maybe I won't, and I won't even feel bad about it.-*

Dirt felt properly chastened. He couldn't understand it, not without a lot more thought, but he could feel how strongly Socks believed it, and that was enough. He nuzzled the good side of his face into the pup's fur, trying to apologize. "*I have a lot to learn about wolves. I have a lot to learn about everything. I'm glad you're smart.*"

Socks began running again, and it seemed the pup had forgiven him, or at least moved on. *-Mother said I should keep visiting you since you give good advice. But she also said that if you try to tame me, she'll kill you. I am a wolf, and she will not let you make me into something else.-*

"*When did she say that?*"

-When she was looking at you. She talked to me during that. She can talk to all of us at the same time if she wants.-

"*Well, I don't know what taming means, so I wasn't going to try.*"

After being out in the sunlight, the real forest seemed darker than he remembered, but that calm, eternal atmosphere was the same. The humid air that hung heavy and pressed down on him, the silent ferns and trees so tall that the sun had to go around them. Dirt was relieved not to have open sky above him anymore—now he could get rid of the nagging feeling that he might just fall up into the sky if he turned the wrong way.

Soon enough, they'd be back at Home, and Socks would leave, and Dirt would spend the night huddled alone in his little hole. He suddenly couldn't stop thinking about all the wolf pups cuddled up with Mother to sleep, all warm and snug and happy. It was very different from what Dirt got.

"Socks, are there other humans in the world? Do you know?"

-Mother said they were pests, so there must be some somewhere. But I don't know where. Why? Do you want to go live with them?-

Dirt panicked, unsure how he felt. But he thought, *"Maybe someday, but not now. Maybe when we're both grown up, I'll go be a human, and you'll be a wolf. Right now, you're a puppy, and I'm a child. And I don't . . ."*

He paused, almost embarrassed to say what he was thinking, but it needed to be said. *"I don't want you to die. I don't want Mother to eat you. It makes me sick just thinking about it. You're my first and best and only friend, so I'll stay as long as you want me to. Besides, carrying me around will make you stronger, right?"*

Socks sent him a hint of amusement. *-You aren't very heavy.-*

"Well, then maybe I'll just have to get as strong as a wolf so we can train together."

-Not likely.-

Dirt giggled. *"Can you even imagine?"*

The rest of the run to Home was full of mirth and rapid conversation. The two of them were swept up in the most wild imaginings. They hardly even used words; they used images of ridiculous things like Dirt jumping higher than Socks could, or Socks drinking a whole river and peeing it out somewhere else. By the time Socks knelt to let Dirt slide off, the day was already starting to dim, and Dirt felt warm inside and out. The day had been just as terrifying as all the others, but Socks licked him on the face and made him laugh, and that was all his heart needed to recover.

But before Socks left, the pup perked his ears up and stood alert. After a moment, he said, *-Mother says to take you somewhere tomorrow. She says it will be good practice for me to try to keep you alive.-*

"Where?"

-You'll see tomorrow.-

"Should I be scared?"

-Probably.-

"Well, I'm not. I'll see you tomorrow. I hope we can stay together for a really long time. And please tell Mother thank you for what she told me. I was too tired to say it before. I think it was an honor for someone like her to even notice me, let alone tell me things I wanted to know. So please tell her thank you. Good night, Socks. See you tomorrow."

-Sleep well, little human. Little Dirt.-

Dirt crawled into his den and collapsed, falling asleep before he even quit moving.

CHAPTER NINE

Dirt's dreams were troubled, full of ferocious beasts and blood and death. Monsters of shadow fought monsters of sunlight, and Dirt kept getting tossed upward into the empty blue sky to fall for eternity. He woke several times during the night, sweating and scared, injured face aching terribly, but each time, the rhythmic vibrations reminded him that he was safe, resting comfortably under Home where nothing could get him. He reached up, ran his fingers along the rough bark until the tree's calm became his own, and went back to sleep.

The last dream of the night stayed with him long after he woke, though. He dreamed that he couldn't stay on the ground, that the earth would not hold his feet even though he was in the forest. Screaming in terror, he was flung helplessly through the unfathomable distance between the canopy and the ferns. Never reaching top or bottom, unable to control his flight, and all his screaming couldn't save him.

Then the tree entered his dream—that was the only way he could describe it. The nightmare filled with senses he didn't have, perceiving a world they were unsuited for. The tree-dream and the nightmare were only superimposed for a moment before the whole thing collapsed and jolted him awake, but he remembered that moment in vivid detail for several minutes afterward.

The tree's mind had seen him, he was certain; or perhaps, it might be more accurate to say it had seen his dream. Dirt wasn't sure if the tree even knew he was there, or could understand him any better than he understood it.

He learned a bit, though, in that brief moment. Home didn't have any perception of distance, not like he did. It didn't know anything about up or down, forward or back. All it knew was the strength of its perceptions. If Dirt hadn't seen the wolves talking in scents, he might never have realized that so much of what Home did or saw was similar. Not really smells, but something close to that. It saw the world with ten thousand tongues, noses, fingertips, all at the same time. Maybe that was the leaves? Or part of it was leaves, and some, the roots or bark? If only he could understand more, like what the tree knew as sunlight or water, earth and air, he might see what it wanted to say.

He lay for a moment trying to think loudly, to talk to Home like he talked to Socks. He touched the root again, imagining himself merging and going inside, rising up the bark to find wherever the tree's self was centered, if it even was. Nothing came to him. No thoughts, no feelings.

-*Come out, little Dirt,*- sent Socks.

Dirt scrambled to his hands and knees and crawled up out of his hole. The fog still lay thick and heavy, and he couldn't see more than ten paces in any direction.

"Socks?"

-*I am almost there. I am glad you are awake because I want to hurry and go there.*-

"Where are we going? Can I drink some water and eat something first?"

Without waiting for an answer, Dirt darted to a spot where he hadn't dug for grubs yet and started tearing up the rich, black soil. The humidity brought out the scent of it even more than usual, filling his nose with that comforting, pleasant aroma. But when he smelled it, instead of just enjoying it, it just reminded him of the tree. Had it been trying to understand him? Did he get tangled up in *its* dreams?

He found a grub, long as his finger and squirming energetically, and only chewed it two or three times before swallowing. He frantically dug until he found another, and another, and ate those too. Then he pulled all the baby ferns he could find and swallowed them as fast as he could.

Socks's big wet nose poked him across his whole bottom.

Dirt screamed and jumped into the air, but he was laughing by the time he hit the ground, and Socks was sending him plenty of amusement as well, in his mild way.

"I even knew you were coming! I feel silly now. I need to learn to keep a better eye out."

-You are lucky I am not a goblin.-

"No chance. Those are too noisy. Good boy! Meat! Come out!" He mimicked one and stomped around.

Socks's face couldn't smile, but it didn't matter, because Dirt could tell how he felt anyway. He patted him on the nose, then stepped in closer to hug him around the snout.

"Can I get just a little more water before we go?"

-There will be plenty. You can drink later.-

"Do you know where we're going?"

-Yes.-

"Can I ask you something? Can you teach me how to hear thoughts? I can only hear the ones you send me on purpose. And I'm not sure if I can think them TO someone or not, or if you're just always watching."

Socks tilted his head. *-I wondered why you never did it. You don't know how? You are asking me how to smell with my nose, even though you have a little one of your own. You just sniff to smell, and you just—*

The image that came next into Dirt's mind gave him a mild headache. Socks simply opened a part of himself that Dirt had never known existed or even imagined, but knowing it could open now filled his bony skull with sparks. It was right there, plastered over, stuck shut, and the more he thought about it the more it ached to open but was unable.

Socks sent the image again with a little more force, and it hurt like his swollen eye did, and was closed just as tight. But right then, now that he was thinking about it, his injured eye popped open. He blinked a few times, and the vision returned. It was sore and blurry and wouldn't open the whole way, but it was still there, and it still worked. He was too distracted to feel much relief, but he tried to use that feeling to open the new part. It wouldn't budge.

-Silly little Dirt, like this, right here.- The giant pup raised one of his paws and tapped Dirt on the top of his head with a claw, and his mind split open with a fleshy ripping sound that he might not have imagined.

His mental world filled with countless lights, each of them a center of awareness, a mind. At first it was deeply disorienting, but Socks sent him more thoughts that helped him organize and soothe it.

Most of the minds were too small to even look at, but Socks stood out like a little sun. The pup was doing it on purpose, too, thinking extra loud but not directing it his way.

-Can you hear me, little human? You can, can't you?-

"Yes! Wow . . ." Dirt turned in a slow circle, trying to take it all in. It felt a bit like the tree-dream; he couldn't say where anything was. He couldn't point and know there was a grub there or anything like that. There was a sense of distance, but no direction at all. It was a whole different world than he was used to, and trying to superimpose it on what he saw just made him dizzy.

-If you had a mother, this would have been the first thing she taught you, before you even crawled up to nurse. Don't worry if you are still unsteady. It is something you have to work on. Even I can't hear very well if you're not trying to let me hear.-

The little thoughts all around him were made to fit in a world that suited what they were—ferns had fern thoughts, and trees had tree thoughts. Every living thing had a mind. Every last ant, even if it was too small to peer into. Trees, he could recognize, if only for the increasingly familiar flavor of their incomprehensibility. It would take him a very, very long time to make sense of any of it.

"Oh! Socks, can you see goblin thoughts? Can I use this to know if any are around?"

-Of course, if you pay attention. They are like this,- thought Socks. He sent an image of primal simplicity; basic, but mostly understandable. Plans with only one or two steps. Hunger, fear, anger. This must be how Socks knew they couldn't really understand words. He could see what was going on in their minds.

Dirt could use this to survive! This was real strength—strength to live by his own power, not at the mercy of everything around him. It was only a start, and it wasn't as good as giant claws, but it was something. He wasn't completely helpless anymore.

He grinned, sending Socks every bit of what he was feeling, but it quickly got emotional as he started thinking how lucky he was, how incredible this new mental vision was. He might have gone his whole life without knowing.

Tears came to his eyes, and a lump formed in his throat. *"Thanks, Socks,"* he thought, reaching up to pat the pup's belly, since that was all he could reach.

-I thought you were thirsty, but you are leaking water,- said Socks. *-Just kidding. I know why you are doing that. You're welcome. Now, get on. Mother said to go play in the water. My task is to keep you alive, but that seems easy.-*

That got his attention. *"Now? What about the fog? Can you see where you're going?"*

-I'll be fine. I can use a different sight when I need to. Get on.-

Socks squatted down so Dirt could climb up, and he did. The pup instantly burst into a run, so fast Dirt nearly slipped and got left behind. He giggled and held on tighter, and they were off.

Dirt couldn't see a thing through the fog, so he tried to pay attention to all the minds as they ran. He hoped to spot Home by how it faded, since there was size but no direction, but it wasn't the only tree they were leaving behind.

It should have been scary, going so fast without being able to see anything. But it wasn't. If anything, it just made him aware how smoothly Socks ran. The pup's enormous muscles pounded a rhythm beneath him that was so regular and balanced Dirt felt like he could dance and not fall off.

-Mother said we must learn how to swim,- said Socks. *-She told me the place to go. The water is deep there, and we will jump in and pull ourselves across. But you have to be careful, because if you do it wrong you will sink to the bottom and run out of air and die.-*

"How do you do that? How do you pull yourself across?"

-Mother said it's easy for wolves, but not for humans. She said if you can't figure it out then you're not smart enough.-

"I can do it!" thought Dirt, before he'd really had time to consider what that might entail. But it didn't matter—no matter how hard it was, he would do it. He steeled himself, body and soul.

-I hope so. You are fun, and no one else has a pet human.-

"Really. I can do it. Mother wouldn't say I had to unless it was possible. If she wanted to get rid of me, she could just kill me or tell you to stop coming. Mother knows I can do it, or at least that I should be able to. So I will.

And we'll do the next thing, and the next thing, until you're the strongest, best wolf, and I'm the strongest, best human, so we can stay friends."

Socks kept his silence for a moment. Dirt could just barely see enough of the pup's thoughts to know he'd never considered that Mother was that careful. *-You are clever for a little baby. I am lucky I found you.-*

"Oh, I'm way more lucky than you are," said Dirt, trying for the first time to hide a thought—his next sentence.

It must have worked, because Socks turned his head briefly, which made the soft tips of his ears flap in the wind. *-Why is that?-*

"Because my best friend is a giant wolf who could win against anything, and yours is a little human who can't even fight a goblin. You better keep me around so more of my luck rubs off on you."

-The only thing of yours that rubs off on me is dirt.-

"That's the luck. I'm covered in it."

-Well, you won't be after we play in the water. You won't have any dirt left, but I hope I do. If I lose my Dirt I'll lose my luck as well.-

Socks surprised him with a mighty leap. Dirt yelped and held tight, enjoying the excitement rushing in his veins. It was uncanny in midair, where there was nothing to see but pale gray in every direction, even down, but then came the fall he always felt pressing against his insides.

Dirt squealed in terror that was only mostly fake, then laughed when they finally hit the ground. Socks sent his own amusement at how easy it was to please his little pet. The pup never seemed to laugh, and maybe that was just an emotion wolves didn't have, but amusement was close enough.

Socks ran until the fog faded and disappeared into the late morning. The forest vanished behind them to reveal vast plains of deep grass that glowed a dusty yellow-green in the sunlight. The pup crossed the fields in giant leaps, since that was easier than trying to push through the grass.

They came to a dark, clear river cutting through the landscape, wide and full. It ran quickly, but the surface was smooth, making it seem plenty deep. It was almost silent compared to the smaller one that Socks had him drink from yesterday. Socks stepped up to peer into it, and Dirt wondered for a moment if this was where they were stopping. But it wasn't, and Socks turned to run alongside the river as it cut a mostly straight course across the plains.

After going a little farther, the grasses grew shorter as the landscape began to change. It was much less flat here; instead, it was dotted with small hills that were barely big enough to be lumps. Some were long and straight, but most were smaller and much more limited. Grass still hid every inch of ground, but it was short enough for Socks to run through.

The sun was a third of the way across the sky, hot and bright, before Socks stopped at their destination.

It was another place of men; Dirt knew that instantly. The deep, quiet river ended at an enormous basin, mostly square and lined with cut stone. The lip of the basin was at ground level and the river simply disappeared into it without making much sound. From one end to the other, the basin was dotted with regularly spaced stone pillars that came up to almost exactly water level, making a path that Socks could probably jump across. They were too far for Dirt, but maybe he could swim between them once he learned how.

-Mother says this is not a real lake. This is a place that men made, and it broke a very long time ago and filled in. The real lakes nearby are shallow unless you walk way out toward their middle, and that is too much hassle so we will learn to swim right here.-

Dirt slid off without Socks lowering for him, landing perfectly. He was getting better at that. He got down on hands and knees and crawled to the lip of the basin. He carefully leaned his head over to look down into the water, making sure his arms were planted firmly so he didn't fall in by accident.

The water was clear and deep, deep enough that even Mother might not have been able to stand up in it. The bottom was covered with broken stones, large flat ones. In between them all, sand and mud and strange plants grew, but looking at it again . . .

Dirt jumped up and pointed excitedly. *"Socks, look. I think there was a floor here once, and it was hollow underneath, and it all crashed down and caved in. The sides of the lake where it's flat and square must have been the walls of the room under there. It was so huge! How did little things like me make something this big?"*

The giant pup silently padded over to peer in the water. *-I don't know. Maybe it took a lot of them, or maybe they could use magic.-*

"*Magic?*" That was a word he'd never used, but it felt like a pleasant word, one he had liked before.

-I don't know how else they would have done it. I think ten of you couldn't lift one of those stones. Maybe human adults are stronger.-

"*No, I mean, what's magic?*"

Socks sent him a puff of amusement. *-One thing at a time, little Dirt. You just learned how to listen, and now you need to learn how to swim before we disappoint Mother.-*

Dirt supposed that made sense. He stood and ran a short distance along the rim, growing more and more impressed with the size of the basin. What had it been? Did people walk here before?

At the far end of the basin, he noticed a mound that seemed suspiciously large, but it was quite a distance to get over there, so he just peered at it from across the lake. It might have been a building once, or maybe just a little hill. It looked like there might be an opening there, under the water level where the extra water from the river drained out. If so, where was all that water going?

He looked back at the spot where the river entered the lake, and it wasn't a small amount. It had to be going somewhere. But was it? The water atop the basin seemed so calm, he wasn't sure it was moving at all.

"*Socks, do you know where water goes? Does it all come up from the ground, and go back down?*"

-Mother says the water comes from the rain.-

"*What's rain?*"

-It's when water falls from the sky. I saw it once when I was a week old. I didn't like it.-

Dirt shot a panicked look up at the sky.

-Only when there are clouds. Thick, gray ones, not like that little white one over there. Dark ones covering the whole sky.-

"*Oh. Okay. I'll try not to stand under any clouds.*"

-It's not about where you're standing, unless you're standing under something to keep dry. You'll see someday,- thought Socks. He sounded amused again. *-For now, drink some water, but not too much. Then we swim.-*

CHAPTER TEN

Dirt stuck his hand into the water and found it colder than he would prefer. *"You go first,"* he told Socks.

The giant pup jumped right over him, blanketing him in shadow as he passed. Socks hit the water with a tremendous splash and hardly sank at all before his head and neck popped back up out of the water. He traveled in a narrow circle, then dunked under the water again only to pop up a moment later a few paces away.

-It's easier than I thought. It's the same motion as running. Just keep your legs moving. Come, Dirt, jump in and swim with me.- Socks sounded a bit more proud of himself than usual. He was always confident, except regarding Mother, but Dirt suspected he'd been a little nervous.

Dirt was certainly nervous. He had no idea what to expect. *"You have to pull me out if I sink so I don't die. I'll try over and over until I figure it out, but promise."*

-Do you think Mother will mind if I help you?-

"She told me to learn to swim, not to die. And she said to keep me alive. Will you come a little closer, just in case?"

-You will be fine. Jump in.-

"How long does it take to die if I sink?"

-Just hold your breath until you come back up. You can hold your breath, right?-

"Yes, but—"

-I will toss you in if you do not jump yourself.-

Dirt scowled at Socks, who was treading water like there was nothing to it. He just paddled his paws placidly and hardly moved. He seemed awfully smug for someone who'd never done it before right now.

Well, this was the price of being friends with a wolf. *Courage, Dirt.* He took a few steps back, trying to make his legs stop quivering by an act of willpower. It didn't work.

He ran forward, looking at the horizon instead of the water so he wouldn't get scared and stop, but as a result, he misjudged by one step and collapsed into the water rather than jumped. He hardly had time to shriek before he hit the water and sank.

The sudden cold shocked his system. His whole body locked up, it felt like, even though he was desperately waving his arms and legs.

Looking up, Dirt saw the outline of the sun through the water, but everything was hazy, and it hurt his eyes. He saw enough to know he was sinking, though. The deeper he got, the harder the water pressed his ears.

Dirt kicked his legs in a running motion like Socks had said, but it didn't work. He didn't swim. Panic set in. His lungs burned from lack of air. He shouldn't have shrieked.

He flailed his arms, clawing for the surface. He kicked his legs. He twisted his body. Nothing worked. *"Help!"* he cried out in desperation.

Socks appeared beneath him, and Dirt grabbed on. Socks swam upward, and only a heartbeat later, they were out of the water. Dirt gasped and spluttered, inhaling as hard as he could to soothe the burning in his lungs. It went away quickly, thank Grace.

"Thanks. I can do it. I just need to keep trying," thought Dirt with confidence he didn't feel. Dirt had serious doubts that humans could swim after how that had gone, but he made himself stand up on the wolf's back and get ready for another jump. He paused, trying to catch the rest of his breath.

-Try running like a wolf running, not a human. Lean forward. Actually, get down on your hands and feet now, and I'll let you down slowly.-

Dirt knelt forward as instructed. Socks let his back sink, and the cold water rose slowly enough for Dirt to make peace with it. And besides, Socks was right there.

Just as his head was about to go under, Dirt moved like a wolf running on all fours and miraculously, he didn't sink. Gods in Glory, he was doing it! It took all his effort, but Dirt paddled as hard as he could in the direction of the basin wall, and when his nose was an inch away, he shot his hands forward and grabbed on.

"I did it!" he shouted aloud, then repeated it right after in his mind for Socks. Then he gave a long howl of triumph, which Socks found amusing. The pup joined in, and his howl was much louder and longer. But he had bigger lungs.

Dirt held the stone edge with one arm and wiped the water out of his eyes with the other hand. He swished his legs back and forth, feeling how the water moved against them. The chill of the water was wearing off, making it easier to breathe.

Socks was eager to keep playing, however. He sank back under the pellucid water and swam all the way to the bottom, then jumped upward, pointing with his nose. He flew out of the water with another big splash, one that might have sunk Dirt if he'd been closer. Socks soared high in the air for a moment, then fell back into the water with another huge splash, closer this time, which made waves that smacked Dirt against the wall.

Dirt laughed, suddenly enthused. He climbed out, got a running start, and jumped out into the water as far as he could. He swam in an arc, ending back up at the edge.

They played separately for a bit. Dirt practiced swimming and found it was easier if he slowed down and tried to push the water instead of hitting it. Socks swam and jumped and flew every direction over the basin. Sometimes he leaped from sunken pillar to sunken pillar, landing with perfect balance every time. Once he noticed Dirt farther out in the water and fell out of the sky right next to him, creating a wave that tossed the little human ten paces away.

That was so much fun that Dirt insisted on being thrown a few more times, and the best was when he balanced on Socks's snout and let the pup simply toss him. Not too high, though, because it hurt a little when he came back down. That was good practice for both of them.

Socks said, *-I bet I can swim across without taking a breath. I'll swim under the water. Watch.-*

Dirt swam to the closest pillar and climbed up onto it to sit in the sunlight, surrounded by calm, deep water on all sides. *"Okay, I'm watching!"*

Socks reached one end of the basin and said, *-Here I go.-* He swam down to the bottom and kicked off the wall, hurtling forward.

When he reached the middle, Dirt sensed confusion coming from him. The pup suddenly started moving sideways.

-The water is pushing me . . . -

The pup turned and struggled against the water, but the flow was too strong, and it pushed him farther and farther.

-I can't get a grip on the ground!- said Socks with a burst of fear. The pup struggled in earnest, but there was simply too much strength behind the current.

Dirt jumped in and swam to the next pillar, but he was too slow. Socks was getting farther away.

The current was pushing Socks toward the far end of the basin, near that lump or hill or whatever it was, where the water seemed to drain out. Dirt sensed the pup's growing desperation, his lack of air, his fear at being helpless, unable to move by his own power.

Suddenly, the giant pup seemed very, very young. Without all that confidence, Socks was just a little child, like him.

"Fight, Socks! Swim hard! You have to!" screamed Dirt mentally as panic set in.

The giant pup's lungs ached for air. Dirt could feel his determination to keep his mouth shut, but it was getting harder by the second. The wolf's chest throbbed, his own muscles fighting against him.

-I can do this! I am stronger!- said Socks in a mental shout that wasn't aimed at anything. The pup's desperate resolve was almost too much, and Dirt had to fight not to get swallowed up in panic. It made him want to scream or cry or both.

For a moment, Socks kept pace against the current, but his strength diminished by degrees, and he slowly moved back.

-I need air! It hurts!-

Dirt stood and looked in every direction, wide-eyed and terrified. What could he do? What could he do!? The water came in from the river and sank right there at the mouth, leaving water calm all around it. It must be going under there, and then running all along the bottom to the other end where it drained. Could it do that? Could part of the water move and not the rest?

Socks's emotions were firing out in every direction—rage, panic, frustration, desperation. The pup was getting weaker. Dirt could feel his pain, his weakening legs and the fire in his lungs, the strain not to inhale water. And fear. Fear of the black pit he was moving toward, slowly, surely.

Then it stuck him. Dirt screamed mentally, *"Swim sideways! Swim to the side, not forward! Please, Socks, you can do it!"*

Socks replied with a single bundle of wordless thought: if he swam sideways, the water would carry him away faster, and he would be lost in the cavern.

Dirt sent back a hasty image of the water making one long, underwater stream that ran from the river to the drain, and Socks jumping out of it to the side.

With nothing left to try, Socks made one last effort and turned to the side, swimming forward with what little strength remained in him. Even at this distance, Dirt saw the moment he burst out of the current. One moment Socks was being dragged helplessly along, and the next he was swimming upward at top speed.

The pup's nose finally broke the surface, and Socks inhaled so hard that Dirt heard gusts of wind.

Dirt swam as fast as he could to try to help, but it wasn't very fast. Long before he could get close, Socks made his way to a pillar and rested his head on it, breathing heavily. Dirt could feel the pup's heavy relief, his shock at having been challenged by something so simple as water. Just water.

The panic of the moment faded, and they both began to let their minds calm down and process what had just happened.

-So much for keeping you alive,- said Socks, amused.

"Maybe next time she needs to mention keeping yourself alive," said Dirt, grinning mentally.

But then a new mind appeared, and both he and Socks saw it at the same time. An old one, a large one, and not far away. Likely, it was in that hole where the water went. Deep inside that blackness, something had awoken and become aware of them.

CHAPTER ELEVEN

Maybe the danger was never the water at all. Socks and Dirt looked at each other, then at the dark pit the water fell into with a dull roar, watching in growing dread to see what would come out of it.

The mysterious creature's thoughts were disjointed and confusing, resembling little either of them were familiar with. It didn't think in pictures, or even emotions—just raw awareness. Motion without intent.

-I don't like it. It doesn't think with its mind,- said Socks.

"Me neither. Do you think it knows we're here?" asked Dirt, even though it obviously did. He pulled himself out of the water and looked around. He was only two pillars away from the edge of the basin, and four away from Socks. He wished he could swim faster. Or run on top of the water. Or jump twenty paces to hop from pillar to pillar.

-Hold still,- said Socks, insistent.

Dirt immediately froze, even holding his breath for a moment.

They both watched the creature's thoughts, trying to make sense of them. It had flashes of awareness, things that might be distance or shape or texture, but it was even worse than the trees. The trees had a rhythm to their thoughts, a connection from one thing to the next. Dirt felt like he might be able to understand it someday, but not this. There were too many gaps, too much emptiness, and the thoughts that crossed its mind told him absolutely nothing.

-Hide your thoughts, just in case. Keep holding still.-

Dirt tried his hardest to shut his mind, but he'd only tried it for an instant here or there and needed more practice. Socks's thoughts disappeared, the burning light of his mind completely vanishing.

Dirt's eye caught motion down there, and he peered as hard as he could. Something thin waved frantically, just beyond the edge of the light. Then another, then twenty.

A mass of writhing tentacles of pale, slimy brown wiggled out of the dark opening. Hundreds of them. They spun and twisted around each other in a display that turned Dirt's stomach. They were all connected at the back end to a featureless creature as tall as Socks, but completely round and much fatter. It had four thick, stumpy legs that it hardly seemed to use.

The thing slid from the opening like it was being squeezed out. It was only visible for an instant before it slithered forward into the water.

Dirt felt more exposed than he ever had in his life. Right out in the open on the very top of a stone pillar no wider than he was tall, and nowhere to go but in the water with . . . *that*. There was no hiding beneath the hot, insistent sun. It seemed to be shining extra hard right on him so everything would know where he was.

Socks wasted no time. Still panting, he pulled himself up onto the pillar he'd been resting his head on, standing precariously for only a moment before he leaped across toward Dirt. First one pillar, then the next.

Dirt turned sideways and bent over so Socks could catch him in his mouth and keep moving. He stood at the farthest edge of the pillar and watched the clear, deep water for any hint of motion.

Socks landed only one pillar away, then jumped again. Dirt held his breath, bracing for impact.

The giant pup gave only the briefest yelp as he was grabbed out of the air by a bundle of tentacles and yanked under water.

Dirt jumped to the other side of the pillar and tried to see under the water, but the splash made it impossible to see clearly. Only a few feet beneath the surface, Socks thrashed wildly. Bursts of red made clouds that fogged the view even further.

"Socks!" he screamed in despair, both aloud and in his mind. *"Socks!"* His whole body shook as he edged helplessly toward the water, wishing he could do anything at all.

The wolf pup's snout surfaced for just an instant, long enough to suck some air into his mighty lungs. Two bloody tentacles writhed in his teeth, and Socks bit and turned his head, ripping one off and tearing the other wide open.

It pulled him back under. Socks gave up trying to hide his thoughts, and Dirt was hit with a flash of ferocity that he was unready for, primal and raw.

The pup's thoughts leaped from focus to perfect focus. *Bite here. Pull that. Rip. Bite. Claw.* Socks's thoughts cycled too fast for Dirt to follow, reminding him once again what it meant for Socks to be a wolf and Dirt to be a human.

"O Gods, O ye Gods . . ." muttered Dirt in desperation, but he didn't know what should follow, or what gods were. He knew it was a cry from deep in his heart, and that was all.

The thing seemed to be slowly dragging Socks down deeper and deeper, grabbing here and there for only a moment to pull, then letting go before Socks could get his teeth on the tentacle. Bit by bit, it was winning. Socks was already tired and was running out of air again.

"Try jumping! Off the pillar, or the ground! You can get away!"

-It's not so easy,- sent Socks, in a single, instant puff of thought.

Dirt's mind raced. He had to do something. *"Okay, brace yourself. Ready, set—!"*

He jumped into the water, arms and legs stretched out to make the biggest splash he could. A distraction—that was all he could offer. As soon as he hit the water, he scrambled back to the pillar, and utter terror propelled him back up quicker than he expected. No sooner had he rolled onto the flat wet stone than five tentacles shot up out of the water, right where he had been. Dirt rolled to the far edge and twisted as they slapped down, feeling around for him.

It was enough, and a moment later Socks flew up out of the water, toward the edge of the basin. Bits of tentacle fell off him. His handsome gray fur was streaked with wet, muted red.

He missed the nearest pillar by only a body length, but the tentacles it grabbed him with were too extended to pull him back under. Socks got three of his paws on the lip of the pillar and pulled himself up.

That left Dirt alone on *this* pillar, dangerous water all around him and no way to escape. He lay as flat as he could. From what Dirt could discern of its thoughts, it knew he was there, but he couldn't tell anything else. Dread squeezed him, crushing his chest and driving out all the air in a slow whimper. The water all around fell quiet as the waves from Socks's splashing faded and vanished.

-I want to lure it out. I want to kill it.-

Dirt hated that idea. His whole body jolted in reaction. He wanted nothing more than to get away, far away, as fast as possible.

"How?"

-I don't know.-

Dirt's mind filled with helpless anger, which might have been simple panic. He had no idea how to lure it either. No knowledge of the monster, no understanding of anything. He was just going to die for no reason. One slap from a tentacle—that's all it would take.

These emotions, this lack of focus, would not save him. As if by instinct, or perhaps long practice in the life he'd lost, he schooled his thoughts. He gave up on hopelessness and focused on the situation. If Socks wanted to kill it, then Dirt would help him. What were they, if they couldn't trust each other?

The creature's thoughts remained empty, devoid of any planning or meaning or anything that could be considered proper thought. Just awareness. An image of the full shape of the basin, and where Dirt and Socks were. The image didn't stay constant, not quite; it had to refresh every heartbeat or so.

Only one thing helped—Dirt knew right where it was. Right there, in the center of its image of the basin. He sent the thought to Socks, in case he missed it. Then he asked, *"Can you push a pillar on it? Maybe if you kick it sideways when you jump off—"*

-It will fall too slowly. The water will slow it down.-

"Okay. Well, even if it's slow, it'll have to move away, right? Jump to that pillar, then this one, and pick me up and knock it over at the same time."

-When I get close, stand up and jump in my mouth. I won't have time to reach. And take a big breath because if it pulls us under, you will be glad you did.-

"I'm ready."

Socks and Dirt sent mental pictures of the plan back and forth in a single instant, and they had the same idea.

It was time. Socks jumped, and no sooner had he crossed the edge of the water than several thin tentacles shot out to grab him. Socks was ready and twisted in the air to bite one and sever it. The others winced away.

He landed flawlessly on the next pillar over, then jumped again. This time the creature below didn't attack, at least not immediately. Its awareness shifted. It was moving.

"It's coming!" thought Dirt, getting ready to jump.

-I know.-

Socks landed just to the side of the pillar, pushing the edge with all four paws. Dirt took the deepest breath he could and dove headfirst into Socks's mouth. He only got in about stomach deep, leaving the rest of him to flail in the air, but at least Socks caught him with his tongue and not his teeth. The pup spun in place and kicked off.

The creature was rising rapidly. Its tentacles slapped out of the water and flailed. This time it wasn't a grab.

Socks turned in the air to avoid attacks that Dirt was not in a position to see, but it wasn't enough. Dirt heard at least four heavy thuds. Their minds were so close he felt the pup's rush of pain in his own body.

They landed a few paces past the lip of the basin, and Socks tossed Dirt farther out of the way in a bruised, graceless heap.

Dirt lurched quickly to his feet and started moving away, but he turned before getting far. Socks's fur all stood on end, and he started making a growl so low that Dirt felt it in his chest.

The monster was already halfway out of the water, and as it pulled its bulk from the basin, Dirt finally got a good look at it. It was big—as tall as Socks at the shoulder but thicker and heavier, perhaps stronger. Its four thick legs thudded heavily as it stepped out of the water and moved forward onto the stone rim. It was all brown and gray, like the decaying stuff at the bottom of the water basin, where Dirt wished it had stayed.

The knotted mass of hundreds of tentacles joined it at the neck, where its head should be. Behind that, its heavy, featureless torso shed water unnaturally quickly. No face, no mouth.

The tentacles snapped all at once to fling the water off, then unknotted fully and stretched out to fill the air. It stepped forward with a deep thud.

-If I turn to run, it will attack. I must fight. You must get away.-
"I'll help!"
-How, silly human?-
"I don't know yet!"

Socks stood gingerly on his back leg. He was already bleeding heavily from several places, but Dirt had no time to feel guilt or pity before the onslaught began anew.

Several tentacles withdrew and shot out. Socks leaped to the side, but his injured hind leg slowed him down just enough to get him struck. The barbed end of a tentacle opened the skin from nose to ear, right over the eye.

Socks snapped his jaws and caught it as it pulled back and ripped it off. The spray of blood mixed with his own and dripped down his bared fangs.

Dirt ran, but not away. He ran sideways, trying to keep at the edge of its range and circle around it. Even without a face, let alone eyes, the creature's senses seemed to have no trouble keeping track of him. But it was better than nothing. He still had no idea what he could do, but he'd find something. He had to.

Tentacles near the back of the slithering mass bunched up. Dirt shouted "Dodge!" with his voice and mind together.

Socks almost jumped away in time. Almost. Two tentacles spun at the end and slapped his front shoulder, knocking him to the side. The pup kept his feet.

-Not fast enough,- said Socks, angry.

"What can I do?" asked Dirt desperately.

-I don't know. Dodge!-

Dirt obeyed before he saw the attack coming and dove forward at an angle just in time for two tentacles to puncture the air inches above him. Only being so small saved him. He rolled to the side and jumped to his feet again, eyes wide to watch for more.

It attacked them both at the same time. In their haste to warn each other, neither were ready. It grabbed Dirt around the ankle and pulled him off his feet, and only a lucky flinch kept a second tentacle from splitting his skull open. He still got a good crack above the ear, which turned his already injured face bones into pure agony.

Before he could even see straight, Dirt pulled himself forward with all his strength, then doubled over and grabbed the tentacle with both hands. It was about as thick as his wrist with a soft, slimy surface that slid over whatever was inside, making it hard to keep his grip. He tore into it with his teeth, fueled by Socks's fury.

Blood filled his mouth, mixing with the slime and turning his empty stomach. He ripped and tore, and bit again. The tentacle tried to pull back, but Dirt bit even harder, so hard he was afraid he'd crack his teeth. He tore and bit deeper, and deeper, and finally ripped it in half. He accidentally swallowed a little and had to fight to keep from retching.

Dirt scrambled back and rolled to the side, then stood and kept moving. The creature's focus was not on him, however. It kept a majority of its tentacles extended in a thick, uneven circle and slammed then down at Socks from every angle, trying to finally bring him down.

The pup was barely hanging on. He bit clean through three tentacles wrapped around his front legs at the cost of two heavy strikes against his ribs, and Dirt felt the pain flash in his mind each time. The pup's fur was red and pink now as much as gray. Blood dripped from the longer fur on his belly.

Somehow, the creature knew where Socks and Dirt were looking. It knew to attack from the periphery. It was only a single thing, but it had them both surrounded.

Dirt quickly stepped back, trying to get just out of the thing's reach. As he went, he tried to open more and more of his mind to Socks, to share everything he saw, every motion of every tentacle from an angle the desperate wolf couldn't see.

Socks did the same. The pup sent everything in one steady stream, every scent and sight and sound. Dirt received it all and learned how to send more of himself, with greater clarity.

The dual streams of pure thought kept both of them alive for another few heartbeats. The creature shot out another bundle of tentacles for each of them, and this time, finally, they saw them in time to move. Dirt was a small target, and Socks was uncannily quick on his paws, even injured.

Dirt could do this. He could help. He was not big and strong, but he could look, and he could trust. He opened himself, gave everything he could.

Their minds began to fold together. Dirt felt it start to happen and surrendered himself further, giving everything, receiving everything.

Eagerly. Socks registered surprise at the strength of it, and for the first time, Dirt was glad for his child's body and mind, which could process emotion so intensely.

Socks didn't resist. He followed Dirt's lead. Their minds merged together with a psychic snap they both felt.

Five tentacles struck at Socks's body from five angles, and the wolf easily sidestepped them all and grabbed the last in his teeth and severed it. Dirt and Socks tasted the blood, its rich flavor of life and triumph. Socks stepped in to grab another, which he yanked tight instead of tearing, preferring to let it rip off slowly.

Two tentacles came for Dirt's body, but he had Socks's reflexes and perspective now. He moved only inches, first one way, then the other, and was never touched. Before the beast could withdraw its tentacles, Dirt grabbed one and bit. They laughed, swallowing the creature's blood.

The battle reversed then, with Socks making quick work of too many of the beast's tentacles. Each attack cost it several more. Most were only injured near their ends, but that still seemed to limit their usefulness.

The two who were one stepped back, not forward, hoping to bring its bare, unprotected belly farther from the water.

Finally, the creature had enough. They sensed the faintest hint of frustration from it that quickly vanished.

It stretched out all its tentacles overhead, even the injured ones, and wound them together into a great rope four times its body length.

Dirt's body ran forward at full speed as the creature slammed the thick tentacle rope downward at Socks, who stepped out of the way. The pup leaped over the thick tentacle rope as the creature swiped it side to side, and Dirt only barely made it to the creature's front legs in time, where it couldn't hit him.

There was no doubt that a swat from that tentacle rope would kill either half of their united being. They felt the incredible force behind it. It rose high overhead and swatted down at the wolf, hitting the ground so hard the shock wave almost knocked the boy over.

The boy dodged a fat foreleg as the thing tried to stomp on him. The beast swung its tentacles overhead and stepped back, trying to open enough room to get a good swing at the boy.

But the wolf was ready for the distraction. He darted in too fast for eyes to follow and sank his teeth into the creature's thick, slimy skin. They felt the teeth puncture and tear, the watery taste of its skin and the richness of the blood underneath.

The pup spun, ripping open a huge gash in the creature's side, then leaped back, ready to dodge. The creature turned its attention from boy to wolf and thrashed wildly, slamming the tentacle rope into the ground in a hundred random places.

Dirt's body dodged again as the thing stomped everywhere hoping to get at least one of them. It ignored the loop of intestine that slid out of the wound, but Dirt didn't.

He darted in, wolf's eyes guiding him through its stomping legs, and grabbed the intestine with both hands. He turned and ran as hard as he could.

The creature turned and raised its tentacle rope to crush him, but Socks used the opening to grip the thing's stubby knee with his teeth and steal its momentum.

Its guts were long, far longer than they expected. The boy made it out of the tentacle's range and kept pulling. The beast slowed and grew weaker, and the wolf no longer even needed the boy's perspective to dodge its attacks. Again and again he jumped in and ripped away the creature's rubbery skin.

The wolf opened a hole big enough to get his entire head in, and whatever he pulled out was the last thing they needed to finally kill it. The wretched creature flopped to the ground in a heap of gray flesh. Its tentacles twitched long after the light of its mind winked out.

The rush of battle faded quickly, and as soon as it did, their minds slid apart. Once they were two again, they reached out to each other, this time in triumph. They exchanged no words—only the feeling of celebration, of victory, that swelled in them both. They had done it. Socks had performed his task and kept Dirt alive. And Dirt had not been useless, like they'd both expected.

Their cheer slipped away, though, as the horror of what had just happened started sinking in. They increasingly remembered the disgust the monster caused in them, and Dirt regained the nausea he felt at the taste of its blood and flesh, which still lingered in his mouth. He wished it tasted like it did to Socks, but he had a boy's tongue, not a wolf's.

The pain of their injuries grew also, and soon it was too much to keep ignoring. Dirt's face hurt as much as it had a few days ago when he'd been punched and wanted to die. The fiery agony made that eye nearly blind again. He had bruises on his ankle from being grabbed and a few on his knees and shoulder than he couldn't remember getting.

But Dirt forgot all his own hurts the instant he realized how gravely injured Socks was. The big pup's handsome face had been laid open to the bone from nose to ear; somehow his eye was still there, but it was red, and he couldn't fully close his eyelid over it. Broken ribs made breathing difficult, and the injury to his back leg was worse than they'd realized. It was quickly swelling and becoming impossible to move.

Socks hobbled a few steps away from the dead creature and lay down on his side, unable to do anything else. Dirt limped over and buried his face in the pup's neck, throwing his arms as far around as he could.

Dirt wept into the pup's soft fur, wracked with emotional torment to see Socks in such a state. He sent the pup all the love and remorse he could, but it wasn't enough. Socks's pain came through the pup's fur like sparks, making Dirt's skin sting. Socks wasn't even sending it—it was simply that bad.

Socks's mind was quiet now, his thoughts withdrawn and unreadable, and Dirt refused to think for even a second that Socks might be dying. Socks's injuries were Dirt's fault. If Socks had been alone, he could've easily gotten away. Socks had wanted a pet human, and Mother made him pay the price for it.

"You did what Mother asked, Socks. That means you'll live, right? You proved yourself worthy," thought Dirt, trying not to sound so desperate. Strange that he could talk so calmly with his mind while his mouth was crying.

Socks didn't reply, even though Dirt was sure he'd sent that thought loud enough for Socks to hear from wherever his mind had withdrawn to.

Dirt looked down, and sure enough, that was blood. It was pooling around his feet, probably from the enormous gash on Socks's face; Dirt couldn't tell from here, and he didn't want to let go to check. What if Socks really was dying? If you lost all your blood, you died.

"I'll feed you and bring you water until you're better. I'll never leave you, never. I'm so, so, so sorry!" he thought. Pity and guilt swirled in him, making him feel like he was going to throw up.

-Be quiet, I am talking,- said Socks.

Dirt tried as hard as he could to quiet down and listen to what Socks wanted to say, even shutting down his tears with a surprising burst of willpower, but there was nothing to hear.

". . . *what?"*

Socks gave no reply. He must be talking to someone else. Mother. He was telling Mother.

Would Mother come save him? She must. She had to, after her little pup had done what she said and killed such a disgusting creature, especially when it was a little bigger than he was. Mother could heal him, right? Would Mother blame Dirt for any of this? If so, she'd probably be right.

-Stop being silly. You are not in trouble. Remember that you saved me from the water current,- said Socks. Dirt supposed he had, so that was something.

The pup continued. *-When he gets here, submit and say nothing.-* Socks sent an image of himself lying on his back, stomach exposed, demonstrating perfect submissiveness. Then he fell asleep.

He? Who was "he"? Another of Socks's siblings? It certainly wasn't Father, or Socks would have told him to run far away. Father would kill him just for being noticed. At least that's what Socks said. So was it going to be a brother Socks's own age, or a bigger one?

Dirt kept watch for a while, still leaning on the weary pup's neck so he could feel the blood pumping and know he was still alive. Blood was everywhere, spattered all across the flattened grass and both himself and Socks. How much of it was the pup's, he couldn't tell, but certainly a lot. Dirt felt the pup's pulse and waited, trying to hide from the black dread inside him.

Hunger was creeping in. Dirt had hardly eaten anything all day except the blood he swallowed. Even his muscles felt hungry, but he didn't want to let go and find something to eat, not yet. Later.

Socks's brother must be bringing food for him. What did the pup eat? Milk from Mother, probably, but what else?

Silently, suddenly, a shadow the size of the sky covered the sun and plunged the area into darkness. Dirt's instincts recognized the presence of irrefutable power, freezing his bones with primal terror. He fell to the earth before his mind could make sense of what was happening.

He crawled a short distance away, trying to get away from the choking fear that made it impossible to breathe. Only then did his eyes adjust to the light, and above him was no shadow. It was black fur.

A wolf as large as Mother towered over him, head blocking the sun. But it was not Mother. Mother had been lying down, which hid a bit of her size. Father standing over him was nearly enough to make him lose all reason, and judging just from his presence alone, Mother seemed gentle in comparison.

Father's coat was black with a few strands of gray, except where scars prevented fur from growing. His golden yellow eyes, bigger than Dirt's whole body, burned and smoldered, their pressure bearing down on him like a hurtling boulder. Father's jaws were closed, but a scar on one lip revealed a single fang as long as two Dirts.

Dirt rolled to his back and showed his belly, trying his best to mimic the pose that Socks had shown him. How foolish, to think anything he did could influence a being like Father in any way! Still, he turned his head to keep from making eye contact again.

Father's presence was enough to make it feel like Dirt was being smashed into paste. Father's eyes on him were enough to kill without effort. Without even meaning to. Dirt couldn't see Father's mind and didn't even dare look. It would be too great for his little self to process.

Dirt sensed motion and shut his eyes to focus on keeping his wits. Somehow he could feel Father's head moving, its impossible weight carried by impossible strength, moving with impossible speed and grace. Nothing that large should be able to move so quickly, so silently.

He heard wet sounds and felt a wave of relief from Socks, who had regained at least partial consciousness. Father was licking his wounds, and the pup's pain began quickly fading. Dirt could watch that, at least, in the pup's mind. Watch Socks feel the cut on his face close and stop hurting, as other cuts and bruises were tended. The broken ribs were not mended, however, nor the bones in his rear leg.

Father sent Dirt a single burst of thought, offhandedly, like waving at a bug while doing other things. Then he lifted poor Socks by the scruff of his neck and left with a leap so quick and silent that Dirt wasn't even sure what direction they'd gone. The ground didn't even shudder—the only thing that told him the wolves were gone was the pressure on his soul finally relenting.

He was left to process what Father had told him, and he was glad that Father hadn't used words like Mother did. Mother's words had just about killed him, and Father's would be no weaker. Whether it was from disregard or pity didn't really matter, but tossing him a bundle of thought to look through was much gentler.

It took a moment to unpack it all. The mind merge was the first thing Father mentioned. It had never been done before, not in all the ages Father had seen, and he was older than the sun. Father wondered how it had happened and was interested in the novelty. Socks had proven himself for now and would continue to live for a while longer. And Dirt should go back to his nest and wait until he was wanted again, which would be soon.

If he didn't make it in time, then Socks would never come again. That was clear and unmistakable. Father would not tolerate failure.

At the end of the burst, Father sent a long string of intricately complicated bundles of sensation, perceptions that Dirt couldn't understand at first. But there was something familiar about their alienness and soon it struck him: trees. They were trees, the names of the trees that they used amongst themselves. It was a map. Father had given him directions back to Home in a string of specific trees.

Dirt had no understanding of what the names might mean, or even if "name" was the right idea, but each one represented an individual. The more he tried to understand them, the worse his headache got.

It would be a long, long way. Just crossing the field again might take more than day, let alone getting through the forest. There would be no baby ferns for a while, and maybe not any grubs. Did they grow out here? The ground was harder and matted so tightly with grass that Dirt wondered if he could even dig for them.

He looked back at the disgusting mess of dead creature, its slimy tentacles and slimy innards surrounding its featureless gray bulk. It lay dead on its side, two thick, stumpy legs hanging in the air. The corpse was unnervingly silent.

He looked down at himself, all the blood and slime and dirt mixed together, and felt too dirty to tolerate. Blood and dirt were one thing, but not *its* blood. He hurried over to the water and slipped in quietly. He scrubbed every inch with his fingertips, hair and toes and everything, until he was sure no trace remained. He washed his mouth out over and over, spitting it out each time. Then he swam to a cleaner spot and drank deeply, feeling how the chill of the water cooled down his insides to match his outsides. It mixed with the blood and slime he'd already swallowed and made him a little nauseous, but he ignored it.

Only then did he pull himself back out of the basin and started gingerly pushing his way through the tall grass, still wondering what he was going to eat.

Night came before Dirt made it even halfway to the forest, which loomed monumental in the distance. That left him to sleep beneath the unsettlingly open sky. Father would give him more than one day, right? Socks wouldn't be all better in just one day, and it was too far for a little human. He could hurry some more tomorrow.

His feet stung from a hundred tiny cuts caused by walking through all that grass, which could be sharp and poky where it met the ground. Bouts of sudden nausea came and went, and twice he'd vomited the disgusting fluid in his stomach—water and blood and hints of slime, all tasting far worse the second time. And to make it worse, he had nothing to wash the taste away or the burning it left in his throat. It dried out his lips, and then his tongue, and then he was thirsty but would have to wait.

It was the leftover fear that caused it, he decided. That fear rose like the whisper of the wind in the grass, a sound that came from far away and gently brushed past him on its way. He'd been watching carefully the entire time for minds, so he knew there was nothing nearby to be afraid of. The only living things that weren't plants were little tiny animals he never caught a glimpse of and ran when they heard his footsteps. No giant tentacle monsters or sky-darkening wolves, but the fear of those things stayed with him regardless. It crept in for no reason from time to time, leaving him short of breath and wide-eyed, and that's what made him throw up.

Now that it was getting dark, Dirt could just lie down anywhere. The grass came up to his chest in most places, and the trail he left closed behind him as he walked. Nothing would find him, but this was the first time he'd slept with nothing over him, and this was not the night for that. Not after everything that happened today. He needed food, which he wasn't going to get, and he needed to curl up safe in his nest beneath Home, and he wasn't going to get that either.

As he finally gave up and lay down, he distracted himself from the empty sky by remembering that Socks was safe and would be taken care of. The pup hadn't been afraid at all when Father took him; he'd been relieved. Socks was safe, and they would see each other again. Hopefully soon. How long did bones take to heal? It had been *days* since that goblin punched him.

All those thoughts disappeared beneath a fresh wave of dread when Dirt noticed a tiny spot of light in the darkening sky. There were several of them, little points of light peeking out of the twilight purple. Stars was the word for them, but that was the extent of his knowledge. He was sure they were going to do something. He didn't know what, but something. Something unpleasant, or sudden and unexpected.

Even if he looked away, he still knew they were there, waiting. Dirt scowled and started gathering grass to cover himself and keep warm during the night, pulling it up by the roots. Once he'd gathered enough, he curled up and lay on his side, resting the good half of his face on both hands, and tried not to look up.

He couldn't resist, though. A quick peek revealed there were more now, many more, and they kept coming. So far, they hadn't even moved, so he decided he was probably being silly and gently turned to his back to watch them for a while.

The next thing he knew, the sun was shining in his face, and it was morning. Night had come and gone in an instant. He didn't even remember falling asleep, or any of his dreams.

He was starving. Agonizing pangs of hunger twisted his stomach, and his mouth was so dry he couldn't even make spit to swallow and soothe his burning throat.

Water only appeared in the morning before the fog lifted, and there was no fog here. In a panic, Dirt shot to his feet, tossing aside whatever grass still stuck to him.

The sun wasn't peeking over the horizon yet, but it would be soon. The forest rose high against the sky, and from here it looked like it might still be foggy inside.

But it would be gone with the end of morning, and time was short. Dirt looked down at his body and could swear he was getting skinnier. With a resolved sigh, he started jogging.

Each footfall made the bruises on his ankles sting, and the jostling shook the injured bones in his face, causing a deep ache that grew over time until the pain blinded that eye again. Dirt's breath rasped, and it felt like his throat might be cracking, but it would hurt worse if he quit. He had to keep running or he was just going to get thirstier.

Only then did he remember to look for minds, and he was glad he did.

Goblins. He knew them at once—Socks had done a good job showing him what their thoughts looked like. Simple, vivid, disjointed, and mostly focused on whatever was in front of them. There were several of them sitting together eating the raw flesh of some beast, which they found Grace only knew where. Perhaps it was another goblin. All Dirt could see was their hunger and jealousy of their portion. They hadn't noticed him yet.

He hunkered down, and the motion made his stomach growl quietly. He had no idea how far away they were, but they must be somewhere nearby, since his senses didn't go as far as Mother's apparently did. And what he saw of the images in their minds showed the same tall grass, although they had flattened a big area for themselves. But there was nothing to indicate where they were in relation to him, or even the forest.

Dirt was confident he could sneak around them. But he was hungry, and they had food, and just leaving without even trying felt cowardly.

"My friend is a wolf," he muttered to himself. "My friend is a wolf." He should have courage. Socks would be as big as Father someday, and why would he want a little Dirt hanging around if he wasn't good for anything? Dirt couldn't fight, not by himself, but he could be smart and wise. After all, wisdom was the only thing he had left, according to Mother. Precisely what wisdom was, he couldn't say, but he should use it.

He stilled himself, listening for any grunting or movement. The air was moving so gently it couldn't be called wind, but he could see it caress the top of the grass and feel it whisper against his skin. Faintly, ever so faintly, he smelled them. The blood, the corpse, the goblins themselves. Guts had a peculiar scent, he now knew, and he recognized it. He hunkered down and crept quietly in the direction the wind had come, listening for any motions.

The goblin minds showed no alarm or alertness. They grunted and snarled at each other, communicating simple things like "that part is mine" or "keep your distance while I eat," or even just "I am still here."

Following the scent on the wind, he had to travel farther than expected, but finally he heard them. Shortly after that, he found a trail through the grass and knew he was close.

Dirt paused, realizing that he was about to make a very stupid mistake. He couldn't fight. They'd kill him as soon as they got a whiff that he was nearby.

His stomach felt like it was winding around itself in there. It was more than just normal hungry. Was there anything he could do? All he had was his weak boy body and his mind—not even a stick to hit them with.

Dirt watched their minds for a moment, dismayed at how fast they were eating. Wary, hungry, and jealous, that's what they were. They had strong fingers, too, since they could tear the beast apart with just their hands. Dirt didn't think he could do that, and he squeezed one arm just to see. Nope.

Could he scare them somehow?

Maybe he could. He gathered all the fear he could remember and considered it carefully. How it felt, how it tasted, how it twisted him and burned him up inside, stole all the strength from his arms and legs. The helplessness that went with it. He knew fear better than anything else. There wasn't much in his short memory that *wasn't* fear, or related to a time he was afraid. He felt it right now.

Then he screamed with his mind, as strong as he could, at the goblins nearby. *FEAR!* Just the emotion, raw and powerful and *loud.*

The goblins bolted, tripping over their own feet in their haste to flee. They hit the grass and just kept running and running, minds white with terror. They took no thought to staying quiet, either, stomping as they went, and screaming once they caught their breath.

Dirt stared in wonder, amazed it had worked so well. They had no idea what had just happened! Goblins couldn't talk with their minds. It was all new to them. They didn't know where the fear came from, and because of that they believed it. They still hadn't even slowed down, judging from their distant shrieks.

Grinning wide as he could without splitting his dry lips, he ran toward the spot they'd all fled until he broke into a now-empty clearing in the grass. It was all trampled flat in a circle about three times around as he was tall, and in the middle was a four-legged beast that had been reduced to almost nothing but bones and skin, not even a face to tell him what it was.

He knelt and lifted away the top legs, checking all over for any good flesh, and on the bottom of the lower back leg, against the grass, was a long, fat strip of red flesh that hadn't been touched. Dirt quickly bent down and sank his teeth in, then started tearing it loose. It took several strong bites at the top and bottom, but he was able to peel it off.

Dirt stood, his heavy prize dangling from his mouth, and tasted the blood that dripped into his parched throat as he grinned from ear to ear. He felt like celebrating, so he waved his arms and turned in a circle, then jumped in the air. It might have looked very silly, but so what? A great victory all his own! And now he knew what to do about goblins!

He stepped on something round and hard, knocking it over. Looking down, he saw a hollow, dried gourd with a little water left in it. He'd spilled a bunch out. Dirt gulped down the few remaining swallows as quick as he could, trying not to think about what made that water taste funny. It was something, though. Food and a little drink! He might make it till the next morning now.

Dirt couldn't wait to tell Socks, and the laughter in his heart sped his feet as he raced away. He was long gone before they dared come back, so far he could only barely see the lights of their minds by then.

He ran, jogged, or walked all throughout the rest of the day, nibbling on the meat as he went. The quivering purple flesh was tender and about as chewy as grub skin, but it tasted completely different, and pausing to have another few bites was a nice way to break up the day. This was what wolves typically ate, he decided. He'd seen a giant pile of bones near Socks's den, and now he knew why.

Dirt came across no other goblins, or anything else interesting at all. Just grass, shorter in some places than others. Gentle wind. Flying bugs and tiny animals racing away from him. He was getting closer, but those trees were *tall* and deceptively far away. He was close enough they already covered a quarter of the sky, and he wasn't sure how much farther it was before he got there.

That night, he fell asleep before the first star came out. He woke in the middle of the night, too painfully thirsty to keep sleeping, so he got up and made his way in the dark. The sky overhead was black now, but blanketed with so many stars they all ran together in some places to make pools and rivers of light from horizon to horizon. He was too tired, hungry, and thirsty to spend much time appreciating it, though. It almost offended him just by being there.

He hurried through the remaining hours of night and into the early dawn. The trees were almost overhead now, filled with fog from the ground up to the tips of their leaves. The whole forest, all that empty space between earth and canopy, was full of thick fog. It made the forest look like a single tremendous wall. One thing, not many.

Desperate thirst kept him going. So much exercise hurt in ways that didn't feel healthy. Like he was damaging himself by continuing. But he made it, just as the fog was starting to lift. Chasing all over to drink enough of the fading drops of dew took the last energy he had, and by the time they were gone, he'd only gotten half the amount he wanted. Despite that, he felt like he might survive now. The pain in his throat and chest were receding, and the rest of him felt better in a way he couldn't describe.

This was not a small thing, he told himself. Running all that way in the grass with almost nothing to eat or drink. And after a big fight, and injuries. Dirt was small, but he wasn't completely weak.

He lay on his back and rested for a bit, sinking into the soft, black soil and gazing up at the ferns. He might have napped if not for Father's unknown deadline. Instead, after a short time he rolled over to his stomach and dug for a few grubs to eat. Then he crawled around collecting baby ferns and eating those, too. Finally, he stood, noting with pleasure that he was already covered in black dirt from head to foot.

Now, to go find Home.

CHAPTER THIRTEEN

Dirt walked briskly to the nearest tree root and knelt where it met the ground. No reason to go all the way up to the trunk; all of this was tree.

He turned his gaze to its thoughts before he reached out and touched it, though. Its mind was large and slow, just like all the rest. The mind of a tree too tall to measure wasn't a small thing. There was no mistaking it for all the ferns crowding the ground.

Simply watching for a while, he saw it forming ideas and sharing them with the others, ideas that he couldn't understand, from an alien world he couldn't perceive. It had so many *senses,* and they were all so different. Socks's mind had thoughts about smells that he couldn't understand, but there were also pictures and words and feelings in there. There was enough that they could understand each other. And maybe Dirt had things in his mind that Socks found strange. He'd have to ask.

But the tree was something else entirely. There were no pictures because it didn't have eyes, nor words because it had no ears. Dirt thought about the map of tree names Father had given him, grateful it all sprang easily to memory. How many of them were there? Ten, and ten, and ten, and . . . maybe fifty or so? Sixty?

Dirt felt a sudden chill as it occurred to him that Father must have done something to make him able to remember it all. Had it taken Father any effort at all, or was he simply so mighty that whatever he wanted simply happened? The memory of that sky-defying ancient wolf standing over him brought up a bone-deep dread that he had to push from his mind.

Best not to disappoint Father by not getting back in time, after all. Best to focus on this.

He watched the tree's thoughts for a while longer, hoping to learn something useful. Anything. Dirt squatted there until his knees got sore, and then he turned around and sat on the root.

Shortly after he sat, he saw something new in the tree's mind. It knew he was there, felt him sitting on it. It was just a minor thought, something so small and quick that if he hadn't been watching he might not have noticed it.

Dirt stood and ran all the way up the root to the trunk, stomping his feet heavily as he went. And sure enough, not long afterward the tree's mind registered the motion, or at least the rhythm and the change.

The tree's mind became the tiniest bit clearer to him. The sensation that felt like *this* was from him, standing here on the trunk. It had several aspects, just like his idea of a grub—the feeling of it in his hand, its softness and how it wiggled, the hunger he might have, or the smell of the soil he dug it out of.

The tree sensed him, although it didn't seem to care much or take any serious notice. It didn't see the shape of footprints or anything like that. But it felt him. That sensation wasn't touch, not as he understood it, but it was not unlike touch.

Dirt stomped around, dancing, then lay down and spread his arms and legs to touch as much of it as possible. He watched as the tree's awareness of him followed shortly after and found that the sensation of him was centered on a particular area of the tree's self. The tree didn't understand the world of up and down and forward and back, but it knew its own parts.

He rolled onto his back and stared upward into the canopy while he watched its mind. The dappled patterns of sunlight in the leaves seemed so much more colorful now that he knew what the sun was. It was still there, shining bright and hot, but the trees kept him cool and safe.

A gentle wind shook the leaves, so far above him that he couldn't see them individually. Waves of motion tracked its progress across the sky as it blew from horizon to horizon, causing sparkles of light where the sun peeked through for the briefest instant.

The tree registered the shaking of its leaves, and a rush of sensation too large for Dirt to handle pulsed through its mind. *Leaves!* All those things, all those . . . so many parts that all perceived the world, countless of them, each slightly different, like ten thousand fingers or noses or ears.

And beneath it all, a quiet, subtle emotion—pleasure. The tree was happy.

That thought startled Dirt so much he had to sit up. Trees could be happy? The idea itself was shaped wrong for his mind, almost. He had to shake it and give it a smack to get it to go in.

Trees were people. He'd suspected as much when he caught Home dreaming. He'd believed it in the abstract. But now he knew for certain: not just simple minds, but aware and awake and *real.* He stared up again with awe, measuring again with his eyes just how tall the tree was, how old it must be. For ages unknowable it had been here, thinking and being alive and being a *person.*

And there were so many! As far as he could see, so many the wind and sun were turned away from this whole forest. Everything was always cool and still, everything quiet, even when invaders like goblins or gryphons came.

They probably talked all day long with each other, in their way. Always connected, always together, standing with friends who never moved or left. Never alone, never lost. No wonder they were happy.

A spurt of bitter envy began to boil inside him. He scowled and let it simmer, but there was a pit of darkness there that would swallow him if he let it. He shied away and came to his senses.

The correct thing to do was to learn the minds and ways of trees and be their friend, too. Then he'd never be alone.

He lay back down and calmed his mind, watching the slow, scintillating rhythm of the tree's mind.

"What do I say to you?" he said aloud, tapping his fingertips on the smooth bark. It would have to be something primal and deep, something below any words.

Well, why not start with the thing he wanted? Dirt slowed his mind as much as he could, then sent the tree the first name at the top of Father's map, along with the idea of a question.

No sooner was it sent than he worried that the tree might know how to speak with its mind and would crush him by accident. Mother and Father had minds that powerful, but they knew to be gentle with a little tiny human. What would a tree know?

But no such thing happened. Instead, the tree's mind filled with a flurry of activity as its thoughts moved through complex ideas and senses that remained unknowable to him, at least for now. And if he looked very, very closely, under it all were base emotions and simple ideas, ideas so simple that any mind at all could understand them. Confusion, surprise, curiosity.

He sent the tree's own sensation of Dirt lying on its root. He coupled it with what he hoped might work as a greeting—happiness, eagerness, curiosity. Then he asked again, giving the first name at the top of Father's map.

The tree's mind was slow, but that had only made him underestimate it. The tree took no time at all to realize what was happening. It stripped away most of the incomprehensible senses and ideas from a portion of its mind and laid bare the idea *Not me.*

Then it sent a rush of communication to its fellows, though too large and complicated for him to follow. Dirt couldn't guess what mouth it used to speak, but he could see the tree's enthusiasm at this new marvel and knew it was being shared.

Dirt grinned to himself, thinking what it must be like for them. Imagine if he was walking along and a fern said, "Excuse me, are you Dirt?"

He turned his thoughts to the other trees nearby, although near was a relative term. It would take him several minutes to walk between them even if he hurried. They had all picked up on it, it seemed, since he saw flashes of the sensation he left on the root echoed in each of their minds.

Dirt sent one last thought before he walked back down the root. Gratitude, which felt a lot like love, now that he thought about it.

He sped through the ferns to the next one, which only had two roots above the ground, then did the same thing. He lay on the closer root, although not so far up to save time, and waited until it registered his presence. Then he sent the greeting and question, and waited. It only took a moment for the answer to come. No. Not this one either.

But on the tail of the answer came the simple idea of a question, all by itself.

What?

Dirt pondered for a moment. Or maybe it was Why, or even How? The tree must have figured out that only simple communication would work.

He sent an image of himself lying on the bark, coupled with the tree's own sensation of him being there. The tree recoiled in confusion, and Dirt realized that had been a mistake. It had no idea of space, or of how anything looked. That had been just alien to the tree as its thoughts were to him. But oh well. It was too late now.

Dirt followed it with a second image, the final name on Father's map, which he assumed was Home. He associated it with desire, desperate and sad. Searching.

The tree stayed confused, chatting in its ponderous way with its fellows.

He moved on picking another tree mostly at random and heading over. This one had several large black spots partway up that looked like old bruises, and as he got closer, he discovered it was ready for him. Dirt's mental sight of the minds around him still had no direction and couldn't tell him where anything was, but as he got closer to a mind the size of the trees, he found he could tell which one it was from how it glowed brighter than the rest.

It was ready for him because it was already saying *Not me* before he even got there. He sent what he hoped was gratitude and picked another one.

All the trees were saying *Not me* now, having cleared out a portion of their minds where he could see it—all except for one. Not that it did him much good. The next two weren't it, or the third, and by then he was ready for a small rest. He sat down and disappeared beneath the ferns.

The trees around him felt alive, invigorated. Their minds were all in frantic motion, or at least as frantic as they got. It was still slow to him, but that might be unfair because the size and complexity of their thoughts were far beyond his. They kept holding questions in their thoughts for him, knowing or guessing that he was watching.

What is this? What is this? they seemed to be asking, but about concepts or sensations he didn't understand. He could just imagine it—maybe they had marveled any time he walked up one of their roots during the days he'd been alive, unable to guess what it meant.

It must be like being touched in the dark when you thought you were alone. Well, hopefully not that scary.

His legs might be tired, but this was all too interesting to stay sitting. Dirt stood again and jogged toward the next tree, and this one was it. This one had its name in place of the *Not me* all the others were saying.

Dirt lay on its root and greeted it. He asked the simple question, using the next name on the map. The tree held a reply in its mind, one which he mostly couldn't understand other than that it implied a connection to a part of itself, that after a bit of pondering, Dirt realized was a root. The tree was telling him where to go! He just had to figure out which root it was. He circled the tree, touching each root in turn until the tree said, *Yes,* and showed him the second name again.

Looking where that root was pointing, he ran the whole distance, excited to find out if it really worked. And he knew it did before he got there, because as the next tree's mind grew in his mental sight, he saw it saying, *Yes*, along with its name.

From there he made it past fifteen more trees before he finally collapsed from exhaustion and waited for nightfall. By this time the trees had figured out what he was doing, but they couldn't tell how, or what he was. They had no concept of motion, which made sense, since they had no concept of space, either. And why would they, if they couldn't move? Their leaves blew in the wind, but it's not like they did it on purpose. Time, they understood, and connection, but it seemed that was where the overlap between his perspective and theirs ended.

It reminded him of when Mother pulled him apart, separating him into all those layers—his flesh, his body of energy, his dream-self, and several more he couldn't fathom, with his bare being at the very core. He existed in other worlds that he couldn't perceive or understand, and so did the trees.

Still, there was something beautiful about how they spoke with each other. There was a rhythm to it, a pulse, not unlike the sound that came up from the ground when he slept beneath Home. But that was just a noise, and this was rich with thought.

Sometimes they held thoughts for him and hoped for an answer, but his most common reply was simple confusion.

Darkness filled the forest, and the trees quieted down as well, their minds becoming still and calm. Dirt guessed they were falling asleep, and after uprooting enough ferns to cover himself with for the night, he followed them into the dream.

That night, something touched him in the dark.

CHAPTER FOURTEEN

In the deepest black of night, something pressed against Dirt's calf, low to the ground. He screamed and leaped to his feet before he was even fully awake, stumbling ten steps before falling down again and whimpering in terror.

He opened his eyes wide and wider against the darkness, but there was nothing to be seen. Scrambling to his feet again, he froze, realizing he didn't know which direction to run to get away. He opened his mental sight to look for minds, even as he listened and smelled with every bit of focus he could muster.

Nothing. Nothing unusual. No animal minds, and certainly nothing ferocious and hungry. No sound, no scents but the fog.

Confusion replaced some of the terror. What was that? Had he imagined it? His heart pounded so loud in his chest he was sure he could hear it. The cool, damp air enveloped him, almost gripping him where he stood.

Dirt took a step back toward where he thought he must have been lying, then another. Nothing happened, and he started to feel foolish. He forced a grin onto his face to try to help calm down, and it helped. Slightly.

It took him a moment to find where he had been, which he only could because of the ferns he'd pulled up and a bit of luck. He got down on hands and knees and felt all over the area and jammed his pinky against something hard and immobile.

With trembling hands, he carefully reached out to see what it was. Wood. It felt like part of a root, about a foot wide and only a few inches high, that grew up from the ground right where he'd been sleeping.

"What are you doing here?" he said aloud. The fog muffled and swallowed his voice.

The tree-minds around him were mostly calm. He thought they might be sleeping, but their minds were so deep and broad and alien that it was impossible to be certain. Parts of them were still active, still aware of things with their alien senses. And they were still talking, just not as much.

Strangely, he saw the pulse, the rhythm that he heard when he slept under Home. He couldn't hear or feel it out here, but their thoughts shared in the rhythm, and he recognized the tempo.

He sat more comfortably and rested his hand on the tree root, trying to determine which of the trees it belonged to. The ferns around him seemed more active than he remembered, and after watching them for a moment, he realized they were talking with the tree. The ideas they communicated were tiny and just as inscrutable as everything else, but it dawned on him that they'd told the tree where he was somehow.

That must be it. The tree had asked where he was, and they told him. Then it . . . grew a root up for some reason.

How odd. He saw nothing in any of their minds that looked like a picture of the world. He was sure they didn't know anything about direction or distance, not as he understood them. To them, it was more about where you were in the web of connections, not where you were standing on the ground. Maybe the tree had just followed the connections to find him.

The tree knew he was touching its root now, and opened a place in its sleeping mind to form a wordless question around the image he'd been using to identify himself.

"*Yes,*" he told it, trying to say it like the trees had.

He saw its happiness, which helped alleviate most of the rest of his lingering fear. It had just been looking for him, that was all. It wanted to see if it could find him. Nothing more.

But then it placed two more thoughts in its mind—the name of Home in the language of trees, and . . . sleep. Dirt chewed on that for a minute, wondering what it meant. Home, and sleep. Home and sleep.

Well, it must want to sleep with him like Home. Maybe it wanted to see his dreams. Dirt lay back down, heart still pounding but much quieter now. He covered himself with the ferns again and crooked his knee around the little root poking out, so the skin would stay touching after he went back to sleep.

He woke the next morning without any recollection of what dreams he might have had, or anything else unusual. The root was gone, in fact. How odd.

When he got up and stretched and looked around, he could sense that the trees were eager and ready for him.

"Give me a minute! I'll be ready to go in a minute," he said aloud to no one.

Dirt drank his fill of dew, which took longer than usual because he was still thirsty after yesterday. He ripped up several handfuls of baby ferns to munch on and made his way to the next tree.

Its roots were perfectly symmetrical, the first time he'd seen that, and when he touched the closest one it greeted him almost instantly. It had been waiting, and it was already telling the others he was here. How had it known he'd be back? Maybe it was just hoping. Dirt tried to share some of his happiness and growing affection, but it was hard to tell how it was received. He asked for the next tree on Father's list and saw the connection, then went from root to root until he found it.

The morning passed quickly. The good mood of all the trees was infectious; he ran much more than he walked, watching them speak to each other in a way that felt rapid and excited.

And it really was fun, even if running made his face bones ache. He couldn't stop. They were so excited! He already felt like he had a hundred new friends. Sometimes he got several greetings at once when he reached the next tree, as if they could package up thoughts and send them along where they needed to go.

Each time, he replied with a greeting and their name, or his best guess at what the name was, and the tree would send the message onward. That was what he thought was going on, anyway. At least he could recognize their feelings now. Somewhat.

After a while, he stopped to dig up some grubs, resting in the ferns to let the trees talk amongst themselves for a bit. He ate them slowly, looking up at the forest with new appreciation. It was truly beautiful. The tremendous, dizzying emptiness between the ground and the canopy, an unimaginable space where nothing was. The open sky seemed closer than the canopy did, because outside the forest there was nothing up there but blue. The pleasant, dappled green shimmering above him in gentle breezes that never made it down this far, the shadowy ferns stretching beyond sight in every direction, peaceful, silent, calm.

And now that he was getting more familiar with the trees, he had an easier time spotting their differences, and they were all different. Not in size, but some had more roots, or bigger ones; some had scars partway up, and others had big discolored patches of darker gray. All different, all alive and aware.

This might not be a place for humans or beasts or anything but ferns and trees, but it was a good place. And now it no longer felt so empty. He could be friends with the trees. He would learn how to talk to them for real, over time, and they would be happy to greet him anywhere he went.

Although, trees and wolves were one thing, but were there any humans left? Who would he even ask? Socks wouldn't know where to find them, and he dared not address Mother and Father directly. Not ever.

Still, it would be nice to have someone his size around, instead of giant like Socks or the trees. And that didn't mean a goblin. Just . . .

Dirt hugged his knees to his chest, suddenly growing more somber. There was no one around here to touch, no one made out of flesh. He was starting to feel like an uprooted fern. Maybe the wolves would let him come sleep in their den once in a while? No, he didn't dare. Mother would eat him before any of her pups. He wouldn't last the first night.

He shook his head and stood, stretching his arms and legs to get a little life back into them after resting. He was being silly, he knew. This was an exciting, memorable day, and there was no use wasting it on unhappy thoughts.

Tree after tree after tree, Dirt made his way through the sea of ferns to greet them all, following Father's map. Their joy kept him going, long after he got worn out from all the running. He was walking wearily by the end, but the trees waiting for him were so excited that he had to push forward.

What would happen if they got mad at him, somehow? Could that even happen? That's not why he was hurrying, but still, he wondered.

By the time night fell, he was still a dozen trees or more away, according to the map, but he would make it tomorrow. Every inch of him was weary and sore, and when he finally curled up under the crook of a root to sleep the night, all the pain he'd ignored in his injured face hit him at once, bringing tears to his eyes and making him whimper in pain. How much longer would it take for that to stop?

He slept touching the root so he wouldn't get any surprises, and when he woke in the dim early morning, the snippets of dreams he could remember were so confusing he couldn't hold on to them. He was probably too tired to dream much. Was that how it worked? It seemed like it.

The next morning, Dirt pressed on, and it got harder with each tree he passed. His body simply wasn't used to that much running and walking, even after a good night's sleep. It had been too many days of hard work, and it'd caught up to him.

The last three trees knew he was tired somehow, but everything they told him to do about it made absolutely no sense. And they were indeed trying—they showed him much more complicated ideas than simply hello and their names, and it did no good at all.

Finally, finally, he made it. And after how he hurried, he was sure he made it in time to meet Father's unknown deadline. He was so tired there was nothing left in him, which might be what Father wanted in the first place, but he made it.

He didn't touch Home's roots out at the edges, but waited until he was outside the hole Socks had dug for him. Only standing in front of the black opening in the black dirt, right as he was about to crawl in and get a good rest and wait for night to fall, did he stretch out his arms and press himself against the enormous root.

The bark was as cool and hard and smooth as ever, and he greeted Home with all the warmth and happiness he could muster. To his surprise, Home returned it just as strongly. The tree was overjoyed to have him back. It must have been waiting this whole time. Maybe it knew him, really knew him from the dreams they'd shared. Maybe they were already friends, and he didn't know it.

Home seemed to be urging him on, now. Trying to get him to move, to go a bit farther along the root. There was something it wanted to show him. That was unusual enough to get him moving. So far, it was more than any other tree had been able to communicate.

Dirt traced his fingers on the bark as he crawled into the darkness of his nest and found it inhabited with a shape of wood, a continuation of the bark growing into something new.

With curiosity, he ran his hands all over it until he realized what it was.

Home had made a wooden person.

CHAPTER FIFTEEN

Since it was dark in his den, Dirt ran his hands all up and down the wooden person and found that it was only roughly formed at best. Still, it made him marvel to think that Home had enough of an idea of visual appearance to do this at all. Or maybe it wasn't sight? But either way, how did Home get the shape right?

The legs were fused together, more like one thing than two, and the arms were stuck to the sides. Its torso was more round than flat, and the head was just a big lump. The whole thing was covered in the same flat, smooth bark as the trees, but it was a little crinklier. It was connected to the big root above him by a thin branch that came right off the shoulder.

Frankly, Dirt wasn't sure what he was supposed to do with it.

Home had a space open in its mind for him and was sharing a few simple thoughts, most of which he couldn't understand, derived from the tree's alien senses. But beneath it was a sort of enthusiasm, perhaps, and . . . *invitation*? It wanted him to do something now?

Dirt sent the idea of a question and waited anxiously. Home conversed among its fellows for a moment, in their slow way, then placed two ideas in its mind: connection and sleep.

It was still a little early to sleep for the day, so he sent *soon* as clearly as he could conceive the idea, and *yes*.

Home replied *soon*, and *sleep*, and *question*.

"Yes, soon, sleep," replied Dirt, pleased that it was getting easier to talk. The list of thoughts they could share might be shorter than the list of fingers on his hands, but it was still encouraging.

Dirt rested for a while, too tired to be bored. Home was content to wait, and he supposed trees were seldom in a hurry. It was so strange—how could their minds be so big and active, when all they did was just stand there, unmoving? What did they think about, he wondered?

After a while, he crawled back out and dug for some grubs. He paused, looking at their tiny minds. Were there emotions in there, if he looked hard enough? Probably. It wasn't worth thinking about, though, because if he didn't eat them he'd die. And the goblins sure didn't care about his feelings when they tried to eat *him*. Maybe it would be good to understand grub thoughts someday, just to learn more about them, but right now they were food.

Dirt made a ball out of fern stems and imagined it was a tentacle monster. Then he found two more grubs to be Dirt and Socks, and made them fight, with sound effects. Over and over. When both grubs eventually died, he used twisted little lengths of fern leaves to be the boy and wolf instead of digging for more. The remaining hours of the day melted away so quickly that the dimming of twilight surprised him.

He crawled back into his nest, relieved it was finally time. He could finally sleep, and maybe in the morning, he could try to figure out what Home was doing with the big wooden doll.

Dirt lay at an angle and rested one leg over the doll so they'd stay touching during the night, and let his mind wander until the nightly vibrations carried him off to sleep.

From one moment to the next, he became aware he was dreaming. No slow dawning of consciousness; instead, he was hovering in an endless kaleidoscope of thought-forms beyond his comprehension. He recognized the tree-dream, but it all looked different to his conscious mind than he remembered it in the mornings. For one, it was smaller, like it had folded in on itself.

His thoughts felt sluggish. Passive. In front of him hovered Home, shapeless and potent. It saw without eyes, gripped without fingers. It was holding on to Dirt's dream-self and keeping him in place—subdued, but in a way he found pleasant.

Home made him look at himself, and horror nearly knocked him from Home's grasp. His body was all wrong—just jumbled parts. Isolated bits of flesh and hair, spinning and gyrating in empty space. One knuckle, just opening and closing. A toenail. And other things that were not flesh at all, which he couldn't identify. Hard bits, flat bits. He was a cloud of pieces, not a person.

He held up his hand, or what should have been a hand, and tried to imagine it going back to normal, since that was how things should work in a dream. But it didn't go. It wouldn't change or come together.

Home took a firmer hold of him then and forced him back into passive calm, for which he was grateful. Then, satisfied he was subdued, it gently nourished whatever part of him lived in dreams. Life and growth gathered in his fingertips and began to fill in, creating new substance where before there was nothing. Bit by bit, all the pieces connected and expanded into what they were supposed to be. It was a slow process, but a peaceful one, free from any fear or doubt. Home held him, guided and protected him.

It tickled and itched as it grew back together, and after a time, he had a whole hand again, letting him rotate and grab and point.

The process started on the other hand, just as slow. Home kept him a little too passive for him to get excited, but he knew something good was happening. After all, Mother had said he'd been torn to pieces, and Socks had asked him why he looked like this in dreams. But Dirt hadn't fully appreciated what that meant until he could see it himself with full awareness.

And truly, he was a mess. His physical body was fine, even if it was much younger than it was supposed to be. But if the rest of him looked like this, then it really *was* a miracle he was alive.

Dirt couldn't read Home's mind in the dream, which was surprising. "Hello, Home," he said aloud. The words came out of space itself, and when he reached up with his good hand, he found his face was just as jumbled as everything else. Right now, Dirt was just a hand.

I must put you back together to see what you are.

Dirt almost missed the idea, which came from a place so deep inside him that it didn't even seem like thought. It hadn't been words;

just a pure idea. He was almost startled, before Home forced him back into calm. "Was that you, Home?"

But the tree didn't answer. Instead, it continued its work, drawing his attention back to his other hand so his memory could help it grow back like it was supposed to. What a strange dream this was. Nothing at all like the wolf dream, chasing all across creation with Socks and his brothers and sisters. Was this even real, in some way? Was Home really here?

This is a part of the dream that is beyond you.

Dirt watched his fingers grow back in, each joint in its place, bending just how it should. The softness of his skin, even the whorls of his fingerprints. The detail was perfect, far better than he thought he could remember.

Try to remember, not imagine.

It connected to the wrist now and began growing up his forearm, itching and tickling and stinging all at the same time. He watched it grow, placidly giving it all his attention as it expanded and gathered up all the loose bits.

All the way to the elbow on one side, then on the other, and then it was time to stop for a while. Home gently released Dirt, and the dream ended, fading into deeper sleep.

A short time later the dream began again, a fresh new dream just like the other one, and the process continued. More and more of him grew back together with Home's gentle, nourishing, patient guidance.

Each time a new part grew in, he used it every way he could, bending and turning and twisting. After the third dream, when he had both legs, he walked and ran and jumped, even though he didn't go anywhere. And after the fourth, when he had his whole torso, he rolled and spun and stretched.

In the sixth and final dream, he felt with his fingertips while his head and face grew in, since he didn't have a mirror. Then he shouted and sang and looked everywhere, tasted and smelled and listened, and everything was right.

He woke in the morning with a heart full of warmth, comforted by the memory of so many healing dreams. Dirt smiled, lying still for a moment to hold on to the last of the placid happiness of the night before.

Dirt patted the doll and said, "Good morning, Home." Then he crawled out to drink the morning dew and get ready for the day.

After he'd gone five steps into the cold morning fog, he heard creaking and cracking behind him.

He looked down into the hole.

The wooden person crawled out after him, then stood, unsteady and awkward, each new joint bending for the first time.

It opened its eyes.

CHAPTER SIXTEEN

Dirt recoiled reflexively, then felt guilty. Something about that wooden person was deeply unnerving, even though he suspected he knew who it was.

"Home?" he said aloud, hoping he would be able to talk like that from now on.

The wooden person didn't respond. Its smooth, dry, glassy eyes couldn't turn on their own, and he wasn't even sure it could see. It took another unsteady step forward and raised its arms toward him. Was it trying to grab him? It didn't even have hands, so probably not.

Dirt looked at Home's mind, wondering how different it would look now. It was mostly the same, immense and inscrutable, but a new part had grown that saw the world with real, actual eyes. It was a success!

He jumped in celebration, watching himself in Home's confused mind. But it wasn't just for show—he meant it. He sent Home as much of his excitement as he could muster, and made it clear that what the doll was looking at was indeed him.

The doll—Home—watched him, its immense mind roiling to make sense of its new perceptions. Dirt watched eagerly, anxiously, as Home turned slowly this way and that, witnessing the real world for the first time. Although, "the real world" might not be the right thing to call it, since Dirt was learning that reality was a lot deeper than he thought.

Home's mind was large enough to start on new tasks, and a part began to focus on improving its body. Dirt got the sense that everything was deliberate. It already had a plan, and he supposed it must have learned everything there was to know when it was putting him together in the dream. The hard part for Home was the hard part for Dirt—namely, how to translate ideas between worlds. But Home was much, much smarter. It had understood him in the dream, and bit by bit it made progress.

"Can you hear me yet?" he asked, watching Home's thoughts to see if it registered. It didn't.

Home's hands grew fingers, which flexed and bent. Its round torso flattened and became almost supple. The head developed from a ball into something that looked more like a head. A split opened along the front where a mouth should go, and bumps appeared on the sides that almost looked like ears.

"How about now?" he asked again.

This time, a flicker of awareness crossed the tree's mind. Dirt opened his mouth wide and went, "Aaaaaah! Hello, Home. Can you hear me? Have you figured out what sound is yet?"

Dirt kept saying random nonsense and watching Home's mind while the tree worked on its ears. He had no way to tell if it was making any progress, but the tree seemed intent on the task.

Finally, Home opened its mouth to reveal a pale wood interior. Its chest expanded to draw in air, and then it made the most horrible sound Dirt had ever heard.

The tree's mind framed a simple question, sharing the idea of the sound it had made. Dirt decided it was asking if it was right, and answered, "*No.*"

Then he demonstrated, not saying anything in particular but just drawing out the sound of his voice like singing. Dirt startled himself; he'd completely forgotten about music. He realized he'd been close to remembering a couple times, but it hadn't quite clicked. But how could he forget about music? He wished he knew any songs. He'd have to invent one later.

Home's voice cracked and popped, changing each time the tree made an adjustment. It grew more tolerable bit by bit as Dirt watched the shape of the mouth and throat making slight change after change.

But the tree was working on other parts at the same time. The shape of the face became closer and closer to a human's, and Dirt wondered if it looked like him or not. He'd only seen himself in the minds of Socks and Home, and that was never perfectly clear.

Home's bark never became flesh, but it did soften to be as flexible and supple as flesh, allowing a full range of movement. The hands were detailed, with fingernails and everything. The toes less so, and most of the rest was left a bit rougher than that, giving Home the appearance of wearing bark from chest to ankles. No penis, either, although Dirt supposed trees didn't have to pee, so why bother?

Finally, Home got its voice to settle around the same pitch as Dirt's, and it sounded almost as smooth. Still a little rough and crackly, but not as bad as a goblin, so it was fine. Satisfied, it asked again if it was right, and this time Dirt said, *"Yes."*

What truly made Dirt realize just how impressive Home's doll was, was when it cracked a smile at him. How did it know what that even meant? Maybe it had seen him smile in a dream and stored it away. But regardless, it was done—the thing was complete, and Home now had a window into the world of up and down, left and right.

One thought repeated loudly in Home's mind until Dirt noticed and figured it out: *Show me myself.*

Dirt pointed at the closest tree. "That's you," he said aloud.

The doll turned and looked, its mind quieting. Home's thoughts grew incomprehensible again, and it spoke again with the other trees. Its head tilted farther and farther back as it looked higher and higher.

It began to sink in just how incredible this was. For the forest, this would be a day that divided "before" from "after" forever, and Dirt was here to see it. No, not just to see it—he'd helped it happen. If trees had a good memory, they'd remember him for years uncountable after he was gone.

A brand-new thing, something marvelous and precious, had grown and come to being because of him. A grin of pride broke out on his face, pride that he was living up to his name, Dirt, but it quickly faltered into something like sadness as the beauty of the moment sank in and touched his heart.

Little Home turned back to face him and made a wordless noise with its mouth.

Dirt got the impression that the tree didn't understand what words were yet, so he sent the image that he'd been using to identify himself—the tree's perception of him lying on the roots—and said, "Dirt," pointing at himself.

Then he pointed at Little Home, sent the tree's name, and said, "Home."

After a bit more back and forth, saying each over and over, it clicked. Home raised its own hand in Dirt's direction and moaned, "Irrrrrrrrrr . . ." while holding an image of him in its mind.

"Yes! Dirt! That's it! Dirt, Dirt, Dirt! You can do it."

"Dirrrrrrrr," said Home. It dragged it out, using the whole breath. All the while, its immense mind processed the task with massive swells of effort. Its thoughts still felt slow, but it could do *so much* at once!

"Dirt! Dirt, Dirt, Dirt-t-t-t!" he said.

"Dirrrrrrrrrrrrrrg. Dirrrrrrrrrrrk. Dirrrrrrrrrrd."

"Close. Dirt, t, t, t. Dirt." He made a point of opening his mouth to show his tongue.

Home opened its mouth the same way, revealing a dry, pale tongue of wood, flexible and soft. "Dirrrrrrrrrrr-tuh. Dirrrrrrrrrrrt."

"Yes! Dirt! Just shorter now, just say Dirt!"

"Dirt," said Home.

Dirt couldn't contain himself and gave an excited cheer, raising both fists in the air. He sent his emotions, hoping the tree could understand that much since it probably didn't know what a cheer was yet.

Home placed its own excitement in his mind where he could see it, and awkwardly, slowly, raised its own arms up.

He stepped forward and wrapped his arms around the confused Little Home, then squeezed for a hug. The doll's body felt like soft plant, not scratchy like bark. Soft and spongy on the outside, but solid and unyielding underneath. Dirt sent his genuine affection, all the warmth he felt. He really did love this tree. He'd been leaning that way before, but now it was certain.

Home felt it too. It shared that much in its mind. Little Home raised its own arms to encircle Dirt, and squeezed. Too hard.

Both of Dirt's arms broke with audible snaps, halfway between shoulder and elbow.

He screamed in shock. Home didn't let go. It didn't understand. It squeezed a little tighter, and Dirt felt his right arm break a little more.

For a brief moment, there was no pain, but when it appeared, it was excruciating.

"Let go!" he whimpered between clenched teeth. "Let go, please!" He sent an image of Little Home spreading its arms again to release him. He tried to communicate that his arms were broken, but focus grew more difficult the more Home squeezed him.

He couldn't inhale. Home was going to kill him and wouldn't even know what had happened. He frantically sent the image of open arms over and over, and finally Home released him.

Tears of pain dripped down his face. His breath came in racking gasps. Without Home holding his arms, they drooped a little lower and dangled, agonizing with every tiny motion, and he couldn't do anything about it.

He tried to use his left arm to hold the right one together, but couldn't. It wouldn't move like it was supposed to. He wouldn't be able to eat. He couldn't feed himself. He was going to starve to death. He was going to wither and die right here, over days of pain, and Home would watch and be unable to do anything about it.

It was the despair more than the pain that started him sobbing. He gently lay down, shrieking as he tried and failed to rest his arms without making anything worse. His left arm was cracked but wobbly, but his right was snapped clean in two and didn't lie straight. The pain never relented, not even for an instant.

He tried to tell Home what had happened, trying to explain in pictures and feelings of pain that he was damaged now, broken, and it was serious.

Little Home gazed down at him passively, with hints of what might have been concern on its wooden face. The tree's mind registered confusion but no sympathy, not that he could detect. It simply waited and watched, uncomprehending.

That made him feel terribly alone somehow, and his sobbing grew worse when he realized this meant he could never ride Socks again. Their adventures and friendship were at an end, just like that. One instant of ignorance on Dirt's and Home's part, and it was over.

Dirt had been so distracted that he hadn't drank any dew yet this morning, and now he wished he had. The ache in his throat from crying was turning into thirst, and water was dripping down his face without being replaced. He was going to suffer the whole time. Hopefully death would come soon.

"Dirt," said Little Home. "Home." In its mind, it seemed to be asking what was happening.

Maybe he should get the tree to put him out of his misery. It would be easy enough, he knew. If he sent Home directions to stomp his head in, it would. He could say it would help and not even be lying. Let Home figure out the rest over the thousands of years it would live on after him.

He tried to picture a branch or root snapping and send that, then his arms. When that didn't seem to work, he sent an image of his arms moving, then breaking and falling still.

Little Home knelt beside his legs and started prodding them, exploring what they were made of. Dream legs weren't the same, after all. Dirt just left the tree to it and tried to will away the pain in his arms and face.

Home picked up one calf, squeezing hard enough to cause deep bruises with its wooden fingers. It bent Dirt's knee, rotated it and considered how it worked. It prodded deep into the flesh to feel the bone there, which hurt enough to make him groan.

With both hands, it flexed Dirt's shin bone, and before Dirt could scream "Stop!" it pushed too far and cracked the bone.

The doll quickly dropped his leg, as if surprised or embarrassed.

Dirt howled, unable to get back control of his voice. It was all too much. His mind had no room for anything but pain.

Home lifted Dirt's loose right arm, and the shock of pain was worse than anything he could have imagined. He screamed so hard it became a struggling, taut gasp.

Dirt's mind retreated from his body. It seemed to split into parts, one still suffering in blinding excruciation, and another aloof, relieved, watching.

The tree-minds around him buzzed with furious communication. The forest worked together to make sense of the problem, all of them together trying to figure out what to do about little Dirt lying there under the ferns. The sheer size and power of their thoughts made it impossible for him to understand much, but bits and pieces contained pictures he recognized. His arm, swollen and bulging wide with blood; his leg bending and cracking, every nerve in his body sparking with pain.

The night vibrations started, even though it was still foggy morning. The slow pulse came out of everywhere to shake the ground louder than he had ever heard it. His chest thumped from the pressure as it passed through him. It increased in speed from a gentle rise and fall as slow as his breath to a powerful, unrelenting drumbeat that rocked the earth. The trembling ground agitated his injuries, multiplying his suffering.

Dirt felt power gather like a second source of gravity, right at his side. He managed to get one eye open and saw Little Home peering down at him with an intense gaze, implacable, unyielding, eternal.

"Please help me," he rasped. It was hopeless desperation, though, because what could Home even do? He wouldn't starve. He was going to die long before that. He was bleeding too much inside his arm.

Then a hundred energies suffused him, fire and sparks and motion and everything else. Dirt's whole body hummed and buzzed so loudly that he forgot the pain, losing it in a sea of white energy.

But it wasn't his physical body the trees were infusing. It was a different part of his being. Not the dream-self, either, but something else. Some part that lay closer to the surface, all torn like Mother had shown him.

Dirt felt it growing together with senses that had no names. It expanded and grew and fused and became strong, solid.

It went on and on, long enough for Dirt to get used to the feeling and the pain to start coming back. Finally the sea of energy withdrew from him, leaving behind a sense of wholeness that quickly faded and vanished.

They'd healed the wrong part of him. Some useless, unseen part, not his physical body. The pain returned in full, and he moaned, wishing he could turn his body one way or other and find even a hint of relief.

The trees watched expectantly, every mind he could see. They had done their part and waited for him to do his. But there was nothing he could do. He wasn't a tree, and whatever they'd fixed did him no good.

Their patience was unmatched, but even they grew anxious when nothing happened. The space in their minds they left open for him implored him to act, begging, almost desperate.

An answer came for them, but not from him. A wolf-mind approached, drawing near before Dirt noticed it. It wasn't Socks, nor any other he recognized. It could speak to the trees in a way they understood, and whatever it told them spread in ripples and waves across the sea of mind-lights.

They seemed surprised—shocked—by what the wolf told them, and it wasn't much longer before he was sure they understood he was dying. They must not know how it was possible over something so minor.

Home even pictured the image of the big root nearby coming apart, then growing back together, hoping he would understand and fix himself. Dirt might have grinned then, if his teeth weren't already bare from pain. That must be why he'd never seen a single branch down here, why they never broke off and fell. They could simply heal themselves.

The wolf reached him before he was ready and startled him by lifting him off the ground with its tongue. Dirt howled when his right arm dangled and twisted, but he kept his wits.

The great beast lifted Dirt into its mouth and closed it to hold him tightly in place. Socks was big, but not this big. Not big enough to put him in his mouth with room to spare.

Death had finally come. He was being eaten. *"Thank you for ending this. Please tell Socks that I regret nothing, and I love him. And tell Home it's not its fault."*

-I AM NOT EATING YOU, FOOL. MOTHER MADE ME COME GET YOU BECAUSE MY LITTLE BROTHER IS FRANTIC AND WILL NOT REST.-

The wolf's thoughts were vicious and strong, a young predator approaching his prime. He held Dirt firmly in his mouth, wet and hot and reeking, with just enough air to keep him alive. There was no sense in which it was comfortable.

But he was going to live. He was going to live! *"Then please tell Home I'll be back, and—"* Before he could finish the thought, the wolf's mind pressured him unconscious.

CHAPTER SEVENTEEN

Dirt was licked awake and knew immediately it was Socks. His wide, wet tongue enveloped Dirt's head and chest, and the pup all but shouted at him, *-Wake up, Dirt! Time to wake up!-*

He smelled the den before he opened his eyes, and it filled him with relief. He had the good sense not to try to get up, remembering just in time that both arms and one shin were broken. Looking over, he found Socks lying on the ground right next to him, close enough to poke him with his nose.

The cut that had laid Socks's face open was now a fearsome scar that ran from ear to nose, and a few more interrupted the gray and black fur on his body. But other than that, the pup had sparks in his eyes and looked lively as ever.

Overhead, so many of Socks's brothers and sisters leaned in to get a look that nothing was visible but wolf. Dirt opened his mouth to say something, but before he could, Socks licked him again.

Dirt laughed, swelling with the nameless joy of simply being alive. His arms ached, although much less now than before. Laughing like this made his face hurt too, but it didn't matter.

A dozen or more wolf pups asked at the same time, *-What is this? Why are you doing that?-*

He responded without words, instead letting his relief and gratitude and happiness radiate out of him in every direction, strong as he could. And it was sincere—he felt it deeper than his bones. His broken ones. There was nowhere he'd rather be, except maybe snuggled right up against Socks, resting in his soft fur.

-He makes that sound when he gets too happy. He has to let out the extra,- said Socks, in a wise and knowing tone. *-That is also why he bares his teeth. It is not a threat when he does it.-*

"*I have so much to tell you, Socks! You wouldn't believe what I did this morning! Wait, is it still the same day?*"

-It is, and I was watching. I got bored, so I learned to watch farther, and I was watching you most of the time.-

"*I'm not even thirsty anymore. Why am I not thirsty?*"

Socks was clearly amused, his good humor coming across along with a hint of affection, which Dirt returned tenfold. The other wolves gently jostled and pushed back and forth, fighting for a better position to watch.

Dirt felt himself lifted off the ground by Mother's mind. The canopy of wolf faces parted as he rose up above them and floated toward the immense black-furred predator resting at the back of the den. All but Socks followed him, tails wagging.

He knew enough this time not to look directly at her, keeping his eyes downcast to show submission the only way he could from up here. She brought him close, hovering over her folded paws, the bare portion of the claws longer than he was tall.

It took sincere effort not to let the animal part of him panic so close to Mother, especially with him hovering helpless in midair, higher up than Socks was tall. Her hot breath blew across his skin each time she exhaled.

I AM HOLDING YOUR BONES TOGETHER. YOU WILL REMAIN HERE UNTIL THEY ARE STURDY AGAIN AND KEEP MY SON ENTERTAINED.

Mother's voice was as powerful as he remembered, just to the point a tiny bit more would cause him harm. Just enough to make it clear how much she was holding back, and how insignificant he was in front of her. Dirt wasn't sure if he should reply or not, but there was a pause, so he sent, "*I am unworthy, but I am grateful. I am eager to obey all you command.*"

YOU COULD NOT HOPE TO BE WORTHY. THE MIGHTIEST OF YOUR KIND WHO EVER LIVED WAS ONLY A LITTLE STRONGER THAN MY SON IS NOW.

That surprised him. There had been a human as strong as Socks? Dirt couldn't picture it. Jumping fifty feet in the air, running so fast the wind made it impossible to hear? Teeth to kill a goblin easy as a grub, claws to rip open that beast from the water? Just a little human doing that?

YOU FORGET CLOSING THE WOUNDS OF FLESH, MASTERY OF THE DREAM, AND GHOST SIGHT. THOSE ARE ONLY THE THINGS YOU HAVE SEEN. YOU MAY BE PLEASED TO KNOW THAT HE IS NOW THE EIGHTH STRONGEST OF MY CHILDREN.

Mother's gaze turned him around slowly in the air, rotating him end over end before aligning him upright again. Dirt gave little thought to the treatment; instead, his mind latched on to Socks being the eighth strongest. He'd been twelfth strongest before. Did that mean—

YES, PUNY THING, IT MEANS YOU HAVE HELPED HIM GROW AND NOT DRAGGED HIM BEHIND. IN ALL THE AGES I HAVE SEEN, IT HAS NEVER BEEN LIKE THIS. LOOK AT MY OTHERS. THEY ALL WANT A HUMAN OF THEIR OWN.

Mother rotated him in the air again so he could get another look at the thirty or more giant wolf pups crowding below him, their inquisitive gray-blue eyes locked on him, wagging their tails unheeding of who they might be smacking with them. She rotated him back to face her, and he almost looked her in the eyes before he remembered to look down in humility. Right at her claws.

HIS THOUGHTS HAVE GROWN ORDERED BY THE DESIRE TO SPEAK WITH YOU, AND HIS DESIRE TO PROTECT YOU DROVE HIM TO GIVE GREATER EFFORT TO HIS TASKS. YOU EVEN DISCOVERED HOW TO MELD YOUR MINDS, WHICH HAS NEVER BEEN KNOWN AMONG US. PERHAPS MY NEXT LITTER WILL EACH BE GIVEN A HUMAN, AND I WILL NOT NEED SO MANY.

There was another pause, so he sent, *"I am grateful to know I might have helped. I love your son, and I will help as many others as I can, any way I can."*

Mother ignored that statement, and he feared he may have offended her by speaking. But she continued. *NOW YOU HAVE AWOKEN A DRYAD, SOMEHOW. THOSE HAVE NOT BEEN SEEN ON THIS WORLD SINCE BEFORE YOUR KIND FIRST EMERGED. THIS*

MARKS THE DAWN OF AN AGE, LITTLE HUMAN. TO THINK YOUR FIRST INTERACTION WAS TO HUG HER. YOU ARE LUCKY YOU WEREN'T RIPPED IN HALF.

Dirt smiled sheepishly to himself. She was right, and he knew it.

MY CHILDREN WILL AVOID THAT FOREST UNTIL THE DRYADS LEARN TO CONTROL THEIR STRENGTH. SHE IS TEACHING THE OTHERS TO MANIFEST THEMSELVES, AND SOON THEY WILL BE EVERYWHERE. SHE WOULD NOT LISTEN TO ME UNTIL I SHOWED HER A FEMALE HUMAN SHAPE. I SEE YOU HAVE QUESTIONS. FOR THE SAKE OF MY CHILDREN'S LEARNING, NOT YOURS, I PERMIT YOU TO ASK.

The first thing he asked was the question that was pressing its way out all on its own. *"Home is female?"*

TREES HAVE MALE AND FEMALE AS DO MOST OTHER LIVING THINGS. MOST OF THAT FOREST ARE FEMALE, BUT NOT ALL.

"When will it be safe to go back? She didn't mean to hurt me."

OF COURSE SHE DID NOT MEAN TO HURT YOU. SHE REBUILT YOUR DREAM BODY AND YOUR MANA VESSEL. SHE ALREADY INSISTS I RETURN YOU, BUT THAT WILL WAIT UNTIL THEY ARE MORE FAMILIAR WITH THE PHYSICAL WORLD.

Dirt struggled to pick the next question. He would only get so many, and there were a hundred things he wanted to know. What all those bodies he had were for, where to find other humans, how to learn the language of trees. Anything about who he'd been before. He was too ignorant. *"What . . . Well . . . You are wiser than I will ever understand. What should I know that . . . that will help me be of greater benefit to Socks?"*

Dirt felt a ripple in the power that held him aloft. That question seemed to have surprised her.

IT IS EASY TO FORGET YOU ARE NOT TRULY A CHILD. THIS IS MY ANSWER: ANYTHING HE TEACHES YOU, HE LEARNS BETTER FOR HIMSELF.

He started floating backward in the air and knew the audience was over. The crowd of pups parted again, and Mother deposited him right on the ground where he'd been before. He would have preferred to rest on top of Socks where it was warm and soft, but the pup probably wanted him where he could see and smell him without moving.

No sooner was he lying still again than the entire litter of pups crowded in and fired questions at him faster than he could process. The mental noise made his brain hurt, but he did his best to steel himself against it instead of complaining.

-Tell us about the dryads!- said one.

-The water!- said another.

Many more sent ideas with no words attached, but one theme was common—they all wanted a story or two. Dirt wasn't sure how to send his thoughts to so many at once, so he placed the pictures in his mind and let them watch. Once he started, they all quieted down, and the closest ones leaned in, close enough their hot breath puffed against his skin. Socks gave him another little lick, then watched him proudly.

From there, he showed them everything he could think of. The gryphon, the goblins, learning to swim, what Home's forest was like, the fight with the tentacle monster, Home's dryad. No sooner had he gone through everything than they all wanted to hear it again, including Socks, so Dirt started over, adding details and taking his time.

As the stories stretched on, several left and others returned from their adventures outside the den, each wanting to see everything Dirt had to tell. Halfway through the fourth telling, his mind was too worn out to continue, and the story simply fell apart. The pups finally left him alone, although they would stop to sniff him and look to see what he was thinking about anytime they walked past.

He and Socks could chat quietly with each other then, free from most distraction. They did so for a long while, slow conversation full of imagination and adventure. Restful and healing. When it was Socks's turn to nurse, Mother lifted him off the ground and floated him over, easy as she'd done with Dirt, and set him down where he could reach a teat.

For his part, Dirt could use some water but didn't dare ask for anything, not until he was desperate. Mother said not to talk to her, and who else could he ask? But then a ball of water appeared right in front of his face, about the size of his fist. It hovered and rippled in midair, and without needing to be told, he lifted his lips and drank.

After nursing, Mother laid Socks down right where he'd been before, and the pup immediately licked him again. Dirt smelled the sweet milk on his breath, something he'd never encountered before but somehow knew about, and felt a hint of envy that he quashed by remembering how lucky he was to be alive at all.

-So what should I teach you?- asked Socks.

"I don't know. It's hard to teach me much of anything just lying here."

-What about this? I taught you how to speak with your mind, and Mother says most humans can't do that, so maybe we can try this.- said Socks. He pushed an image into Dirt's mind of the world washing out into gray and black and receding, expanding to show more of the surrounding area than his mind could handle at once. It grew ever outward to include greater stretches of land, so many rocks and trees, hills and sky and air, each pushing its way into his consciousness. Before Dirt could beg for him to stop, Socks saw his distress and pulled it back. The departing vision left dizziness and a deep ache behind, both of which faded quickly.

-You are very small, so ghost sight might be too much for you. Oh, I know what we can try.-

"What's that?" asked Dirt nervously.

-Mother said your mana vessel is fixed, so I wonder if I can teach you how to fill it up.-

"What does that mean?"

-Magic. You know, so you can run fast and jump high.-

Dirt almost sat up in his excitement. *"Let's try!"*

-It will be tiring, so we shall try tomorrow.-

"I can't wait!"

-Yes, you can.-

CHAPTER EIGHTEEN

As evening came and the den grew dim, four wolves double Socks's size returned from the day's adventures, still not fully grown but radiating a predatory menace that the smaller pups had none of. The fuzzy gray was mostly gone from their fur, leaving it mottled black and sleek. They bent down to sniff him as they passed but otherwise ignored him, even shutting their minds to his sight. Dirt was sure it had been one of them who picked him up in the forest this morning, but if so, he didn't identify himself.

Night brought the perfect darkness Dirt was used to, but all the sound and motion and heat in the den was new. The wolves all crowded and cuddled together to sleep, although they left room for Socks, who wasn't allowed to move yet. And for Dirt, who would have been squished if one of them rolled over. Even so, if he'd been allowed to move his aching arms, he might have risked snuggling with Socks. Perhaps in another few days.

Despite being warm and comfortable, the night was restless for him, who startled awake at nearly every snort or scratch or shuffle. Each time he heard something, he thought it might be Mother rising to eat one or two of her children, as Socks said she did every night. He was afraid he'd have to hear the giant pups crying out in pain and fear. Hear their bones crunching, hear Mother chewing them up. What if they screamed for help, calling out with their minds and voices at the same time? What if everyone woke, and they all had to listen together in helpless terror?

At some point during the night, Father entered, a silent killer whose sheer presence filled the den and reverberated against its walls. He curled up near the entrance and fell asleep himself, and Dirt didn't wake again after that.

At first light, Socks huffed and woke him with a puff of air, then licked him several times to say hello. -*Good morning, little Dirt. You look normal in the dream now. Did you know that?*-

"*I did! Home put me all back together in a dream the other night, so I wondered if I would look normal to you, and now I know.*"

-*My brother says you kept waking up all night until Father made you stay asleep.*-

A wave of dread passed through him. The less notice Father took of him, the better. "*I was afraid I'd hear Mother eating someone.*"

-*Did you? I didn't. I never do. But there are three fewer of us this morning. Usually it's one or two.*-

"*No, and I'm glad. I don't want to hear that. I like you too much, and I think all your siblings are cute, too. Except the big ones. Cute isn't the right word for them.*"

-*I like them too, but Mother says only a handful will survive the first year. But don't fret about it. Everyone would rather die than be a weak wolf.*-

"*Don't you miss them?*"

-*I don't think so. I haven't thought about it.*-

Dirt considered that for a moment but was distracted by the growing ache in his arms. He shifted his back a little to try to get more comfortable, and even that minor motion caused a scalding pain in his shattered right arm. He gritted his teeth and hissed until it calmed back down.

-*Oh, I forgot to tell you. Mother left, so try not to move at all until she comes back. Nothing is holding your bones together. Don't even twitch, or it'll hurt.*-

"*I found that out already.*"

-*I saw.*-

"*She can't do it from far away?*"

-*She can, but she doesn't want to.*-

"*Oh. Oh well. So, how long do bones take to grow back together? It only takes flesh a day or so, so I thought it would be faster than this.*"

Socks found that amusing for some reason, and so did two other pups who were nearby and must have been listening. They stood, padded over, and gave him a good sniff, then loomed overhead with their tongues lolling out. He didn't even have to see their minds to tell they found something funny.

-That only works because I'm a wolf and the cuts weren't deep. Flesh takes a lot longer to heal if a wolf doesn't lick it.-

"*Then what about bones?*"

-Those take a very long time, but if Mother holds them together and you stay in the den, then it's only a few days because this is a healthy place.-

"*What makes it healthy?*"

-It just is. That's why Father and Mother dug the den here.-

-Show us your mind meld,- said a new voice. One of the pups above him. Two more joined them, then another, and Dirt was reminded again just how big they were. Their heads were bigger than his whole body, and with them pushing for a better look at him, he saw a lot of teeth.

-SHOW US- said several more, their eagerness turning to shouting that made Dirt's brain squirm. *-SHOW-*

"*Okay. Just talk quieter, because as you can see, I'm just a little tiny human.*"

Dirt looked over at Socks and the pup's eyes were eager. *-Let's do this, and then we'll try to fill up your mana afterward. Or maybe during.-*

They eased into it, sending each other a stream of perception that built until it incorporated every sensation or thought. Dirt focused on relaxing his mind, opening, submitting, and receiving and understanding everything the pup sent him.

It only took a moment before their thoughts slid together and became one, and once they did, the link between them solidified, and Dirt and Socks felt the ground with two bodies, saw with four eyes, smelled with two noses.

The wolf's sense of smell brought the den to life with an overwhelming heady richness, so many smells, each telling them something new that their boy half had never experienced. Each sibling had his or her own scent, as did Mother and Father, and all of it lingered. But there was more—scents of blood and flesh, soil and water, pollen and rot. So many scents carried in their fur, all of it exciting.

Together, they smelled the boy's body with the wolf's nose and marveled that half of their united being had never known how complex his scent was. Emotions both current and old, everywhere he'd been lately, even the fact he was a child. No wonder the others all kept coming up to sniff him. If their bones weren't broken, Socks and Dirt might have gotten up right then and gone around sniffing everyone themselves, just to see what it was like.

And the human vision! The wolf half had never known there could be so many colors. The earth took on a richer brown, and the gray of everyone's fur showed faint hints of red or orange that he hadn't noticed before. The small bits of plant life strewn around were *green,* an entirely new color. And distant things stayed in sharp focus—incredibly so. So bright and clear, even far away!

The fight with the tentacle monster had been too urgent and hasty for Socks and Dirt to spend much time taking it in, and now they found themselves in a completely new world.

Socks and Dirt said, *"-Hello, everyone,-"* just to see what happened when they spoke as one.

-HELLO- came several replies at once, from different directions.

Wait, directions?

"-Say something again. Just one of you. You,-" said Socks and Dirt, indicating a sister standing toward Dirt's feet.

She sent the thought simply and quietly. *-Hello, brother and little human.-*

A thrill of excitement filled them, rebounding back and forth on their mental connection. They could tell the direction! Before, thoughts came from nowhere, had no real voice or sound to them. Mind-sight had no front or back, left or right, and neither did mental communication. It simply *was.* Until now. Two eyes to see distance, two ears to tell direction, and now two minds joined together could show them both.

Socks and Dirt looked around with mental sight, amazed. Everyone's mind was in a direction now, not just brighter or dimmer. Sister was *there,* brother was *there . . .*

The pups crowding around them watched it all and shared in their amazement. They raced all around the den, shouting things like *-Look!-* as they went. And just as wonderful, no matter how loud anyone shouted, it didn't hurt little Dirt at all, because Socks could receive the extra pressure.

"-We will be the greatest hunter ever!-" thought Dirt and Socks.

"-We will! Nothing can hide from us! We wonder if Socks is still the eighth strongest, or if he is now a match for the seventh, who killed the ogres, or the sixth, who fought the snake.-"

"-Mother will tell us when she returns.-"

Word seemed to be getting around, because several more pups came in from outside to watch, including one of the older brothers. The den was abuzz with activity, each pup eagerly chatting with its siblings and some still racing around, watching how Dirt and Socks could hear the direction in their unified mind. The second strongest even went outside and ran up the rock that made part of the ceiling, just to see if they could tell the direction. They could.

"-We should teach Dirt how to gather mana. It might be easier this way, with both of us.-"

"-Yes, let's try that.-"

"-All right, it goes like this,-" said Dirt and Socks to each other. Then Socks's body made a connection with the earth and started drawing in energy, filling his mana vessel. From there, power spread to the rest of his body, infusing the muscles and increasing his strength several times over.

It seemed so simple that Dirt and Socks grinned to themselves as they prepared to make the attempt. Once Dirt's body knew how to do this, the possibilities were limitless. They could play all sorts of games if Dirt could run and jump like Socks, or at least closer to it than now. And who knows what else they might come up with.

Dirt and Socks sent their mental awareness all through Dirt's body looking for how his mana body interacted with the physical one, but they couldn't find it. That made them go back and try again to understand how Socks did it, but it came so naturally to the pup that they made little progress there either. Dirt's body tried to match the feeling of it, hoping for an epiphany, but it was like trying to catch a bird using just his feet. He simply wasn't built that way.

Once they saw what was going on, all the pups shouted their suggestions, but none of it was useful. They repeated the same instinctual feeling that Socks already knew, and which Dirt's body couldn't grasp.

The joining of their minds shuddered and split apart, leaving Dirt with a mild headache and severe mental exhaustion. He felt like he'd just run for an hour, but only with his brain.

He looked over at Socks just in time for the pup to lick him with his enormous wet tongue again.

Dirt laughed, helpless to do anything about it. Squirming in pleasant discomfort made his arms move, though, and he could feel the break in the right arm flex with even the slightest motion. *"Stop! You're making my arms hurt!"*

-That is an excuse. You don't like it when I lick your face, do you?- asked Socks, as close to laughter as he ever got.

"I don't hate it; it just feels weird."

Socks affectionately licked him again, right on the face. Dirt squealed with laughter, but that jostled his arm again, which made him hiss and wince.

-I'll stop. It's hard to leave you alone because you are cute and fun to tease.-

"Well, just wait until I find a way to get you back someday!"

-How will you do that?-

"I'll say something like, gee, too bad I have such a bad itch, but I can't move my leg to scratch. So, so itchy, right there, where I can't do anything about it. My poor fur! Wow, it itches so bad! And all you have to do is not think about it, and you won't notice any itches. So don't think about it, not even a little."

Dirt sat there and smugly let Socks roll it around in his mind. It didn't take very long before Dirt saw him twitching his paws.

"Sorry, Socks. I'd go scratch it for you, but I can't move either."

-You got me. How did you know about that?-

"Mother said I kept my wisdom from when I was an adult. That must be how."

Father came in not long after, carrying fat, bloody cattle in his teeth. In Dirt's haste not to make eye contact, he caught only a glimpse of them, but he was sure he'd counted at least eight. He wished it had been anyone other than Father carrying them, though, because now he was painfully curious. He hadn't known cattle existed until this moment. The word hadn't even come to his mind before.

The pups gave excited, squeaky whines and mentally shouted their excitement. The den, already full of energy and commotion, sparked into even greater furor.

Socks licked Dirt again, helping soothe him so he could resist the mental noise. *-Try to hide your thoughts. It will help.-*

Dirt focused on making his mind invisible, a trick he'd only accomplished once or twice and mostly by reflex, and the painful riot of mental noise dimmed to a low hum. Shutting them out made him feel vaguely disconnected from everyone around him, which he regretted, but at least he wouldn't squirt blood out his ears.

"Thanks, Socks," said Dirt aloud. Socks huffed in reply.

Father dropped the cattle not too far away from where Dirt and Socks were lying. The unpleasant sound they made when they hit the ground was disquieting, and the heavy, smacking thuds reverberated in his memory long after the sound was gone.

After that, Father started ripping them apart to distribute. One of the pups must have gotten too close, because Father snarled, *STAY BACK. I WILL DECIDE WHO EATS FIRST AND HOW MUCH.*

There was no quieting out Father's voice, and the scolding tone made Dirt go rigid in dread, even though he wasn't the target. He closed his eyes and tried to keep his fear from getting away from him, breathing deeply and schooling his thoughts. He was so focused that he didn't notice Father's hot breath on him until he heard the heavy chunk of meat plop down between him and Socks.

FEED YOUR PET A PIECE IF YOU WISH, Father told Socks. Dirt held his breath until the immense presence overhead moved on.

Socks eagerly gnawed a bite off the huge chunk of meat, which was tricky to do lying on the ground. He hardly chewed it before it was gone down his throat.

"Do you get meat often, or mostly milk?" asked Dirt.

-Mostly milk, especially at first. And they used to chew the meat up for us, but not anymore. Now they just make sure we don't eat too much or eat a bone, because that will hurt our stomachs or teeth.-

"Didn't you eat that goblin?"

-No, I just killed it and tasted a lot of the blood. And it was more than one. I've killed five.-

"I'm surprised Father gave you meat first and not the oldest or strongest."

-He always feeds the littlest ones first. If we are weak, it will be because of ourselves, not because we didn't get enough food. But don't worry. I'll leave you some.-

Dirt wondered about that. Why would the parents go through the trouble of feeding them so carefully if Mother was just going to eat them? And for that matter, why bother eating them? If they were weak, they'd just wander into something like the tentacle monster, and that would be that. Even so, after seeing Mother and Father in the flesh and feeling the pure menace they radiated, there was no doubt they were capable of eating their pups.

Stranger still, Socks and all his siblings seemed affectionate with each other. They played and romped and slept in a pile, innocent and happy. And yet, every night there were less of them, and no one seemed to mind. Why didn't it bother them, even a little bit? How could that—

Mother's voice filled his mind just as her shadow filled the entrance to the den. *I HAVE MY REASONS, AND IF YOU DISCOVER THEM BEFORE I PERMIT YOU TO LEARN, I WILL KILL YOU WITHOUT HESITATION.*

Dirt hastily replied, as meekly as he could, *"Thank you for the warning."*

Mother gave no further reply, but he felt his bones tighten back together. As her immense black form passed silently over him, the pain faded into a dull ache, letting him relax in places he hadn't realized were tense.

Socks left him a chunk of meat that was a little too much, but the pup's teeth were too big to get it any smaller without using hands or paws. It was tricky to get a bite off—the meat was soft and bloody and kept sliding away when he tried to sink his teeth in, and then Socks would have to nudge it back again. Between the two of them they eventually managed to get Dirt's stomach full, although it resulted in a lot of frustrated giggling and tail wagging.

Once the meat was gone, quivering balls of water appeared for them to sip right out of the air. Dirt was sure Mother was the one who did it, and it occurred to him that for all her clarity about his position, she was being quite generous.

Father left after that, and for the rest of the day, Mother rested at the back of the den, brooding and keeping a wary eye on her children. Socks's brothers and sisters came and went, leaving to explore or perform tasks assigned by Mother. Each time one came back, everyone got a sniff, and they even came over to greet Socks so he wasn't left out.

Dirt and Socks were too tired mentally to try another link or work on magic for a while, so they rested in between visits from siblings. One sister told them about a cave with rocky spines all over the ceiling, and another about a pond that was a perfect circle with a hill in the middle that had a bunch of little snakes on it.

Later when they took a nap, they met in the dream and raced up a tall, solitary mountain. It rose up from a flat plain of hard, red dirt, and it was barren at the bottom, pine trees in the middle, and ice and snow on top. From up there, they saw farther than Dirt had ever thought possible, and he resolved to climb it in the waking world one day and see if it was the same.

In the afternoon, Mother instructed them to get up and move around a bit, with strict orders that it should remain restful and calm. Socks stood, and the first thing he did was gingerly scratch his side with his back leg. Dirt felt guilty, so he helped, digging in good with his fingernails and hoping Mother didn't slack in holding his bones. Moving like that made them ache, but they stayed together.

They stepped just outside the den to get some sunlight and stretched and yawned and enjoyed the fresh scenery, and Dirt found the bright sun more pleasant than ever before. It warmed his skin and the ground he was standing on, enveloping him from head to toe like a blanket.

The field around the den was still a mess, with torn earth and sparse grass for quite some distance. The bone pile looked bigger now than he remembered, but he hadn't paid close attention before.

Socks sat down to relax in the sun for a bit, and since Dirt was allowed to use his arms, he climbed up and lay on the pup's back, stretched out comfortably in the fur.

"Socks, do you know what I just noticed? My face bones don't hurt anymore." Dirt pressed his finger against all the spots that used to hurt and found only a couple bruised places in the sharper part around his eyeball. *"I think we really do get better faster in the den."*

-I told you we did.-

"Yep. It was several days ago and hardly got better that whole time. It hurt almost any time I moved, but now after one night it's almost completely healed. I bet your leg and my arms won't take very long."

-I hope it's fast. It's less boring with you here, but it's still boring. Everyone is telling me about all the fun they had, but we haven't had any.-

"Here, lift your head up," said Dirt. He rose from his little nest in Socks's fur and carefully stepped up to his front shoulders, resting one hand on the pup's head for balance.

-What are we doing?-

"I want to smell the breeze, and I bet you want to see all the colors. Let's try to meld again, just for a moment."

Dirt and Socks reached for each other with the fullness of their minds, and after a little difficulty caused by the weariness from last time, they slid together again. Instantly the landscape exploded into brilliant colors and vivid scents from far away. Dirt's eyes raced over everything, near and far, and they were amazed at how clear the distant trees were, even though nothing over there was moving. Dirt's eyesight was much more impressive out here where there was a whole world to look at.

The air moved too slowly to feel, but Socks's nose could smell the motion. The bone pile smelled of bone and blood and old rot, and the lingering steps of dozens of wolves left their own traces. Farther off, the smell of grass and pine tree sap and so much more painted a picture of the landscape just as bright as Dirt's eyes did.

"-Lying around might be boring, but this is fun,-" said Dirt and Socks.

"-It's too bad it's so tiring. Maybe we'll get better at it with practice.-"

"-We will.-"

They looked again at the inside of Dirt's body, trying to find where to draw in mana, but just as before, it was impossible even with the two of them.

"-Perhaps we should understand better how it works for Socks first.-"

They turned their attention to Socks's body and watched as he drew in a little mana, then a little more. From there, they watched how Socks distributed it, first in his mana body, then his physical one.

"-How does it know where to go?-"

That was a good question. They watched carefully, trying to understand the mechanism, but the better they observed, the worse they understood it. The mana was moving and not moving at the same time, for one. It came into Socks in the same place, which they thought might be near his belly button. But any time they thought about a different part of his body with the intention of seeing the mana move, it was already there.

"-Oh, let's try this. Can we move the mana from Socks into Dirt directly? Maybe if he had some in him we could figure it out.-"

Seeing that was a great idea, they turned their minds to the task. Socks only had to think of jumping for mana to be in his legs, so they thought of Dirt doing the same.

A brilliant, flashing spark in Dirt's body split the meld so abruptly that Dirt gasped and fell to his hands and knees. He felt stretched and torn inside, like he had a cough that wouldn't come out. He wanted to smack himself in the chest but didn't risk it with his arms broken, Mother's help notwithstanding.

-Did it work?- asked Socks, turning his head all the way back around to give Dirt a little lick to get his attention.

"I'm not sure. Ow."

-What's wrong?-

Dirt had no idea what to tell him. The torn feeling inside him quickly evolved into unpleasant heat, hotter than the sunlight on his shoulders. He tried to be calm, to relax and take the pressure off whatever it was, to simply let it flow. If he could only twist and turn the right way, maybe it'd come loose.

-I don't know what to have you do. Is there mana in you now? Is that what it is?- said Socks, sounding almost frantic.

"I don't know. It hurts."

-Try jumping. Do something. Try to use it up.-

"Hold on," said Dirt, trying to focus. He stood up and stretched out his arms and legs, bending over forward and back to try to loosen up the lump burning in his chest.

Dirt must have found the right way to bend, because all at once, the fire melted and incorporated with him, filling him with something he recognized, even though this was the first time in his life.

"Magic! I have magic again! It's been so long! I don't even know what to do with it! But—"

Dirt stopped the thought midway and looked at Socks with a grin. *"Okay, here I go."*

He willed his body to use the mana just like Socks did. If he hadn't felt Socks do it across the mind meld, he might not have tried, but it was natural as breathing now. He hadn't just watched Socks do it— he'd done it himself.

Dirt slipped off Socks's back, and as soon as his feet touched the earth, he jumped with all his strength. He soared into the air, too fast for his mind to follow, and ascended much higher than he expected. Possibly as tall as Mother! He shrieked in joy at the top of his flight, looking around in pure excitement.

Then he began to fall and realized he'd used up all the mana. There was nothing left for him to land with. He was going to break every bone in his body.

"Catch me!" he yelled to Socks, his mind almost unable to form the words around his terror.

Socks scrambled to his feet to try to catch his human before he crashed, but before he could, Dirt's fall slowed and stopped in midair, inches off the ground. Then the invisible hand that caught him rotated him until he was upright, then let go, dropping him harmlessly on his feet.

WHAT DID I TELL YOU TWO? DID I NOT TELL YOU TO REST? IS THAT RESTING? NO, DO NOT APOLOGIZE. COME IN HERE, AND LIE DOWN.

CHAPTER NINETEEN

Four days later, Mother declared Dirt and Socks recovered and sent them out with no warning. Dirt barely had time to scramble up onto Socks's back and grab on before the pup left at a hasty run, rising from where they'd been lying the whole time and darting out the den entrance before Mother could change her mind.

Socks flew across the flat field around the den and darted into the brush, no particular goal in mind. It simply felt good to be moving again after so long. From how the pup ran, it was clear that his bones were indeed healed, and Dirt whooped in excitement each time they took a turn or leaped over a rock.

The day was overcast but warm, the cloudiest Dirt had ever seen it. The whole sky was spotted with clouds more gray than white, leaving only portions open for the blue to show through.

Socks carried him toward tall hills with ridges of rock jutting out in places, hard angles of brown and gray stone interrupting the gentle curves of grass and gravel. It looked like the earth had risen and cracked open once, a long time ago. They raced down in the hollows between the hills, turning this way and that as they went.

"Are we going anywhere in particular?" asked Dirt.

-I don't know. Older Brother has come this way several times, so I want to see what's over there.-

"Oh, can you smell his trail?"

-Yes. Do you want to share?-

"Sure. Just the scent? The air is blowing in my eyes, so I don't think you'll see much."

-Here you go!-

Socks opened himself, and they joined only a portion of their senses, which was harder to establish but far less straining on their minds. Dirt took in the richness of scent as if smelling it with his own nose, and even though their thoughts remained separate, he instantly knew Brother's trail. The scent served better than a name did, telling them his age, health, emotion, and more. Brother had been in good spirits last time he came this way, probably because he had been allowed to go off on his own for a bit instead of attending Father like the older pups usually did.

They ran ever faster along the narrow, winding pathway through the hills. In some places there was an actual trail, a thin line of bare dirt that smelled like deer. Hill after hill, all treeless and covered in rough grasses. Socks drew in a steady flow of mana to strengthen his run, a perfect system as natural as a heartbeat or breathing.

Dirt tried not to feel any envy about that, since even after four days of trying they couldn't get his body to take in more than a trickle of mana, and never on his own. And to make it worse, when Socks asked Mother about it, she said that if they couldn't figure it out, then he ought to just go leave Dirt somewhere and forget about him.

Well, there was no point ruining a good day by getting upset for no reason. Dirt shook the thought from his mind with a little wiggle of his head and held on just a bit tighter to Socks's soft fur.

"Hey, Socks, let's go find a deer. We keep smelling them, and I've never seen one. Have you?"

-Not a living one. Let's do it. Sister said they hop instead of running.-

Socks slowed to sniff the air a little more carefully. He shared his hearing with Dirt, too, since he was using it.

Now able to hear with Socks's ears, the world rushed in at Dirt, alive with a thousand sounds humans couldn't hear. Bugs crawling in the grass nearby, his own heartbeat, the very blood in his veins. Birds flapping their wings. The gentle whispering of grass in a breeze so soft he hadn't noticed it.

They didn't hear any deer nearby, but after padding gently along the trail a bit farther, the scent grew a little stronger, and they decided there must be some around. They smelled several, a mix of male and female, and they didn't smell like they were anxious about anything.

Socks walked a bit lower to the ground, carefully peeking around each bend of the hills, hoping to spot the prey before they saw him. Dirt found himself holding his breath in anticipation as he strained to listen for any movement.

They noticed the sound at the same time, of course, and both their heads riveted to the left. Something was moving close by, something heavier than all the little mice and rabbits and things chasing all through the grass.

-Ready?-

"Ready!"

Socks's body surged with mana, and he leaped forward at tremendous speed. Dirt clung tightly to his back with all his strength, but even so, the pup almost ran right out from under him. Socks bounded up the hill and leaped from the top, soaring through the air.

Dirt's eyes raced over the scenery below both near and far, looking for anything that might be a deer. How big were they, anyway? He should have asked first. A small copse of trees in the middle distance seemed like the best place, since it was somewhere to hide.

"Over there! In those trees."

Socks landed in the grass with very little sound, but not quietly enough. Dirt was right—they were in the trees, and the animals bolted at the sudden motion. Their gray and white coloration hid them fairly well amidst the underbrush, but once they were moving, that was that.

In truth, it wasn't much of a challenge because Socks could have gone much faster if he wanted. But it amused him to get right up behind the biggest one and snarl just to watch it panic, then give it a merry chase.

Neither of them had seen anything like it. Lean, with a narrow, expressionless face and coarse-looking fur. It was smaller than Socks, of course, but probably weighed three or four Dirts.

It ran by pounding all four hooves nearly at once and bouncing forward, which amused Socks terribly. His mind sparked with pleasure as he mimicked the poor beast's movements, hopping as he went. Dirt got shaken violently and clung on even tighter to keep from being tossed off. It was great fun, and he shrieked each time he felt his body floating off the pup's fur.

All the noise just made the poor little deer run harder. Its scent was almost pure terror, and from what Dirt could see of its thoughts through all his distractions, there wasn't much else going on.

The thing was quick, though. Not particularly agile, but quick. It fled through the hills and into a large, upward-sloping plain that ended at a sharp, even ridge.

Dirt guessed there was a big flat area up there, and when he noticed a furrow cut into the ridge, allowing easy walking from the plain to the flat top, he shouted in excitement and thought, *"A road! Socks, over there! That's a road!"*

-A what?-

"A road! Like we saw by that human temple place the other day. It's all grown over, but I want to go look at it."

-Okay. But first we will eat this deer.-

Socks ended the game early and caught the panicked beast's neck in his teeth. He killed it with a mighty shake and threw it to the earth.

As eager as Dirt was to go see the human place, now that there was food in front of him, he realized how hungry he was. Mother had sent them out before they'd eaten.

"It's like it only exists to carry meat around until someone wants some," said Dirt.

-Yes. It's prey.-

Dirt thought that over while Socks tore it open, pulling away the skin to expose the meat and innards. The rich smell of blood and flesh made their mouths water.

Socks said, *-Let's meld our taste, too.-* The pup sniffed eagerly at the hot carcass, ready to taste it with Dirt's more sensitive tongue.

Adding one more sense to their mental connection was a simple matter, although Dirt could feel his mind getting weary. They'd need a break from it soon, but that was fine. There was still plenty of time to taste all the parts of the deer.

First things first. Dirt knelt down and leaned in and licked out some blood, then washed it back and forth in his mouth to savor.

"It tastes different from cow blood."

-Cow blood was duller. This has more variety.-

"Yeah. And the scent of it is better, too. Maybe that's why it tastes better."

Socks ripped out a bloody haunch and barely chewed it before swallowing. He didn't have the teeth for chewing like Dirt did, but that also meant he didn't really need to. Meanwhile, Dirt took bites out of various bits all throughout the dead animal, eating slowly to share what it tasted like. Some things were too slippery and connected to pull out with his hands, so he just dug in with his face and ripped away a bite or two with his teeth like a wolf. Every part had its own flavor, and most of it was delightful; the only thing Dirt didn't like was the intestines.

They'd only learned to share individual senses two days ago, laying on the bare floor with nothing better to do, but now they rarely wanted to eat on their own anymore. With Socks's sense of smell and Dirt's taste, everything they ate was so much richer and more vivid and delicious.

Dirt didn't need much food to fill up, so he was done first. Satisfied, he sat back and severed the mind meld to relax while Socks finished off what remaining meat he could find. It was still a little disorienting, losing half of his senses that way. At least, that's how it felt until he readjusted to going back to normal.

-Shall we take a nap now?- asked Socks, licking the last of the blood off his whiskers.

"Can we go up the road first? I really want to see what's up there. It was a human place. I'm certain of it."

-Okay. We can take a nap after we look.- Socks glanced at Dirt, then turned and licked the blood off his face. Dirt held his hands up, and Socks licked those clean, too.

Dirt stepped backward for the pup to lower himself and let him climb up. But he didn't. Instead, Socks poked his nose into Dirt's chest, pushed a tiny bit of mana into him and said, *-Jump up.-*

As usual, the mana pained him with fiery pressure, feeling unnatural and harmful for a moment until he was able to absorb it. Dirt was getting faster at that, though, and after a few deep breaths and a bit of focus, the burning lump dissipated and filled him with strength.

He didn't have much practice doing anything with it yet, since Mother hadn't let them move more than once or twice a day. And no magic after that first time.

Well, this was practice. Dirt thought about the mana in his legs, readied himself to use it, and jumped about one body length upward, just enough to reach up for Socks's shoulder. Not high enough, and he landed off-balance and fell back on his seat.

The second time, he stepped a few paces away first and got a running start and landed perfectly on the pup's back.

Socks hid most of his thoughts, which was probably just as well since he was likely thinking something belittling. Dirt wouldn't hold that against him, though, especially after seeing himself through his friend's eyes in the mind meld. Tiny little helpless Dirt, barely able to do something so simple as jump. It really was kind of funny.

-Only tiny and helpless for now. You'll learn.-

"I've already started learning."

-You'll have to keep on learning, because next year I will be as big as Brother, and that's a lot higher for you to jump.-

"Next year I'll be bigger, too. And I'll be running and jumping as well as you. Just wait."

-Mother says you will only be a little bit bigger next year. She said your body is already eight years old, and I am only forty-four days old. Humans grow very slowly.-

Dirt was a bit surprised at that. His body was eight years old? He looked down at himself, not sure what to think. He remembered that first feeling of wrongness, of being strangely proportioned, soft and hairless when he first woke up. This was eight years old already? By next year, Socks would more than double in height, let alone weight, and it took humans eight years to get to this point?

-She said I would be full grown long before you were, and that you'd still be small as an adult. She asked if I would still want to keep you then. I said yes.-

The big pup shared warm affection along with the words, which made Dirt feel a bit better. Dirt returned it, affectionately nuzzling his head into the beast's fur.

"Will you be as big as Father by then? So fast?"

-No, full grown is only a little bigger than Brother. After that, it takes a lot of years to get as big as Father and Mother.-

"Really? How many?"

-Mother is thousands of years old. I don't know how many, but Father is much older than that.-

"But they're the same size, just about."

-Father was always that big, from when he was two years old. After he and Mother became a mated pair, she had a lot of growing to do to catch up. He's a son of the First, and she is several generations younger.-

Dirt felt a sense of urgency settle in his heart. A year or two, and Socks would be all grown up. Never mind just jumping up to get on his back; Dirt would have to get as strong as a human could get by then, no matter what.

But there was little time to dwell on that because Socks hurried over to the long, straight indentation in the hillside that cut up through the ridge and started walking up it, sniffing the ground as he went.

"This was a road. I'm sure of it. It's all grown over with grass now, but the indent is so straight that it has to be. I bet there's stone under this like that place in the forest. Remember that? Where Mother said not to go in? It's like that, but longer. And see how it goes all the way up? That must be where the humans lived. Up there on top where it's flat. The road was for them to get up there."

-Why would humans make a straight thing just to walk on?-

"I have no idea. You're forgetting how small we are, though. We can't just jump over everything. Come on, let's go up there! I bet there's something there. Did Brother go past here?"

-I don't smell him if he did.-

"Then we might be the first!"

At that moment, the clouds overhead split apart and let the sun shine down on them directly, blanketing the area in warm light as if to usher them forward. Dirt hollered in excitement, and Socks sped up the road.

The ridge they'd seen from lower down looked straighter and more even as they got closer, and Dirt suspected it might have been taller once, a long time ago, and the slope toward the bottom was from wind blowing sand and dust there.

The road ramped upward through a split in the ridge and landed them right in a city. That was the word for it. A city. Ruined stone buildings everywhere, now just roofless shells. Only bits of wall or pillars still stood. The remains of roads, all of it grown over, snaked out in every direction. Pale gray stone, green grass, and fresh sunlight, stretching in every direction.

-I think we can take a nap later,- said Socks, and Dirt agreed.

CHAPTER TWENTY

Old weathered gray stonework lay silently in every direction. Seamless bricks of the same gray stone sat stacked in some places, often at corners of buildings, but most had collapsed. Empty door frames interrupted the square footings of vanished buildings and opened to dead streets. Lengths of cement or mortar; flat paving stones; tall, rounded pillars that held up nothing at all; featureless old statuary eroded down to lumps. Every sharp edge was worn round by eons of wind and rain, every surface bleached by the sun. No color but green and dirty white, and the rocky brownish hills surrounding the city.

Pillars lined the main thoroughfare, twice Socks's height. Dirt suspected he would have been terribly impressed if he'd seen them before the trees, or before seeing Mother. Instead, it left him feeling conflicted—in part, that he was so small, even in a human place, and in part, that humans couldn't seem to build anything to rival the den. He'd been amazed by the temple in the forest, and still wanted to go back someday to see what was inside, but after spending several days inside the den, this whole city felt small.

The wolf pup jumped all the way up onto the nearest pillar and balanced atop it, all four paws bunched together and tail wagging furiously. Then he stepped forward to the next one, and the next, as gracefully as if that's what the pillars were for in the first place.

"Are they sturdy? You won't fall, will you?"

-No, they are sturdy. They don't even wobble. I could knock one down, though. Want to see?-

"No, it's been standing for so long it'd be a shame to knock it over now. Do you have any idea how long it's been since humans lived here?"

-Mother never told me about this place. I'll ask her later.-

"Are there any humans left? For real?" asked Dirt, trying to picture people walking these streets. Wearing clothing, men and women, boys and girls. All different sorts of people. He couldn't picture it no matter how hard he tried. He could picture wooden dolls that looked like Home, though. Or himself. But it wasn't right.

-Mother says there are. But not as many as there used to be, and they are far away from here.-

For the briefest instant, the dead roads filled with color and life. Bright, fluttering cloth hanging from buildings, every surface painted, the streets filled with feet and voices. But it was gone so quickly Dirt wasn't even sure if it had been his own thought or something Socks had imagined, and it made the dead city feel even emptier.

"It feels like there aren't any humans left. Just me," said Dirt, growing melancholy.

He stepped off the road and into the doorway of a building whose white stone walls still reached taller than him in some places. They were even tall enough in the corners to reveal the sills of windows.

Dirt walked to the center of the sunny room with footsteps full of meaning, deliberate steps with head held high, as if he belonged there. He tried to recall the feeling of a building, of being in a place for humans, but the sunlight ruined it. No roof, not even much shade this time of day. On a whim, he pulled up a clump of grass and dug down the three or four inches to find the floor, smooth tiles of pale reds and greens and blues.

Dirt cleared some of the earth away with his hands to expose a little more, then a little more, and found intricate patterns of curved lines and shapes. The wolves might be huge and build huge things like the den, but they didn't decorate, so that was something.

He walked from one end of the large room to the other, then through another doorway into a different room. What was it for, he wondered? What did people do in a place like this? Why would anyone need more than one room?

There was more to this building, but collapsed heaps of rubble kept him from seeing the rest of the floor plan. He dug down a few inches to the floor of this room as well and found more smooth tiles, but no pattern. These ones were all the same color. Disappointing.

He was being silly, he knew. He should be more excited by all this, but he felt how he felt.

Dirt stepped into the next building over, pacing through it without stopping, then to the next one. And the next. If he could see where the doorways were, he used them, and if not, he just stepped over the wall footings.

-What are you looking at over there?-

"I don't know. Nothing, really. I'm just trying to figure out what these places were used for, or maybe think what it was like when people were still here. But it's not doing any good."

-This is a fun place.-

"Yeah," replied Dirt. He wasn't feeling it just now, but why shouldn't he have a little fun, at least? Socks had the right idea.

Dirt hopped onto the wall footing and carefully walked along it. It was wide as his shoulders, but the top was uneven, requiring him to pay attention. He ascended where the wall ramped up to a corner and got a better look around. Where was the most intact place nearby? He should go find that.

If he followed a road where it branched off the main one, only a short distance away the whole front half of a building was still standing, and to the side was an intact stairway.

He jumped down into the grass and ran over to get a better look. The building looked basically intact from the street, even still sporting the eroded nubs of its decorative stonework. Dirt couldn't even tell what the carved shapes were supposed to be anymore.

It was two stories, with a doorway and windows on the ground floor and more windows on the next one up. Through the windows he could see that the roof had fallen, but the triangle at the top of the front wall still had its peak, and some of the ceiling for both floors was still there.

Dirt walked inside, then turned around and placed himself where all he could see was the ceiling and walls and the street beyond the door. All human craft filling his perspective. He gazed out the window and said, "Hello, there. Welcome. What brings you here?"

No one answered. Instead, everything seemed even quieter in the silence of anticipation.

"It is good to see you. It's been a long time," he said to no one. "It's been a long time since I saw you, my dear D— . . . d . . ."

A rush of nostalgia hit him. A second time, for the briefest instant the walls of pale gray stone became plastered and red, the floor tile polished and colorful. A door of wood filled the frame, and outside the window was someone he recognized.

It vanished as quickly as it came and refused to come back, no matter how deeply he yearned for it. He knew, deep and true, that he had been here before, or a place just like it. The shape of the doorway and windows struck a resonance in him, but the truth of it, the real memory, was lost forever, just like the people and the place this once had been.

Ah, but he could almost picture it! It was so close, a person, a name! Something real from his past, something precious that he'd lost. *D . . . d . . . d . . .* It was no use. The name was as dead to him as the person it belonged to. He didn't even know if it was a man or woman. It may have even been a random sound he picked from imagination, since his own name started with D.

The tears that came welled up slowly, ever so slowly. He tried to think about anything else and drive them away. He should be happy and having fun. This was a fun place, and humans had made it, and that was unique. There weren't many such places left, from what he'd seen. Here were things to climb, and warm, cheerful sunlight, and . . . none of it helped. By the time the tears came out and erupted into crying, he didn't even know what they were about. They came from a place deeper than his thoughts.

He tilted his head back and sobbed, shoulders sagging like he was ready to collapse. Hot tears ran down his cheeks and onto his shoulders or got caught in his hair. Dirt stared through the tears at the ceiling, which still had bits of plaster in the corners. It all looked so *dead.*

Dirt cried and cried and cried, unable to stop. If he held his breath, his chest shook. If he distracted himself, the sobs came back with twice the force.

Socks came in from the ruined opposite end of the building where he could fit, since the doorway was too small. He said nothing, just licking Dirt's tears away and trying to nuzzle him without knocking him over. Finally the pup braced him with one big paw and rubbed the side of his face across Dirt's body, over and over, stopping only to lick him some more.

Dirt didn't look at the pup's thoughts at all; he didn't have to. The pup was patient and gentle and tender, and he'd be there as long as it took. Dirt knew perfectly well what his friend was telling him.

The crying was slow to leave, slow enough that the muscles in his chest and throat ached from being over-strained, but it finally did. When Dirt could breathe easy again, he hugged Socks around the snout and buried his face in the pup's shorter facial fur.

"Thanks, Socks. I don't know what I'd do without you," said Dirt. All that crying left him feeling cleansed, but still pensive.

-You don't have to worry about doing anything without me,- the pup replied, hugging Dirt with his bony paw.

Dirt grinned right into the soft fur. Socks had a way with words.

"I'm sorry I got carried away like that."

-You were sad. You don't have to apologize. You have great big emotions, even though you are small. But I found something you will like. Want to come see?-

"What is it?"

-It's a something. Are you ready to come? Or do you want to rest a little more?-

"I think I'm fine now. I don't even know what that was."

-I do. It's called grief.-

"Oh," said Dirt. Socks was probably right. What else would it be, after looking at ruined places and thinking about everything that was lost?

"How do you know what grief is?"

-When Mother was trying to talk me out of keeping you, she said if you died, I wouldn't even see you in the dream, and that I would be very sad and grieve.-

"Oh." Dirt wanted to ask why Socks didn't grieve for all the other little pups, but he might get an answer Mother didn't want him to have, so he didn't.

From there they walked down the street together, and to Dirt's eyes the city was just a ruined city now. Just stones, just concrete and mortar, just grass and earth and rubble. Whatever he'd been hoping to connect with wasn't here, but that was fine, because now he could look at it how it was. Appreciate how it was all laid out in such clean, straight lines. Marvel at how much work it must have taken all the little humans to cut all those stones into squares and stack them just right. What skill it must have taken to decorate everything with facades, or all that handsome patterned tile work they saw peeking through the ground every so often.

It was quite a walk, which was fine, because Dirt needed to air himself out after all that crying. And even if it was all ruined, there was plenty to see. Old statues in rough outlines of people or animals, near unrecognizable after centuries of weathering. Buildings large and small, pillars standing and fallen.

Socks stopped in a circular area with a square platform in the center, a foot taller than Dirt was. To the side, half-buried in the dirt, was a statue as long as Socks from nose to tail. The exposed part was weatherworn like everything else, but it had a human's form, seen from the back.

-Watch this. You will like this. It was buried, so it's still preserved. And I'm going to try something. Mother can lift things with her thoughts, and I think I can now, too. None of the siblings in the den can do this, not even the ones a year older.-

"When did you learn that?"

-When I heard you start crying, it made me wish I had hands so I could pick you up without using my teeth, and I just sort of realized.-

"Have you already tried it once?"

-No, I came to get you instead, and I didn't want to try it on you first. Guess why.-

Dirt grinned. He smashed his hands together and made a squishing sound with his mouth.

Socks replied with a mental puff of amusement, his eyes sparkling.

"Can I help?"

-No. Watch.-

With that, Socks's body went taut as he focused on the task. Dirt took a couple steps back to get a better angle to watch. He closed off his thoughts to keep from distracting the pup and waited.

The huge statue lifted more quietly than Dirt expected. He expected cracking and tearing, but there was none of that. Just a dull crumbling-dirt sound, and the statue rose from the earth and hovered in midair.

Dirt suppressed his desire to shout, in case Socks was startled and dropped it. With how perfectly he was focusing, that was a real possibility.

The statue turned to stand upright in the air, then floated over to the plinth, still mostly coated in a couple inches of earth. Socks was just about to set it down when Dirt noticed one foot was broken off, so he gently patted the pup's leg and stepped forward to point.

Socks set the statue down in front of the plinth instead, slightly askew and leaning backward to stay upright. As soon as the thing was steady, he collapsed to his belly with a heavy *whump*.

Dirt patted the pup's nose and asked, *"Are you okay?"*

-Yes, I am just tired. It was heavy. Are you happy?-

"I am! You rest, and I'll try to get the dirt off so we can see who it is."

Dirt felt warm inside, a worthy balm to the sadness he'd felt shortly before. It was good to be cared about. But the statue was still exciting, and he hopped over and began cleaning it off.

The soil came away in big clumps that bore the shape of the carved stone until they hit the ground and broke apart. He got it cleared off high enough to expose a pair of bare, muscular legs halfway up the thigh, and from there he had to get up on the plinth to reach farther. Even standing on his tippy toes, he only got it cleaned off to the belly button, enough to discover that it was a man. He didn't dare climb up it, because that might tip it over again.

He slid down from the plinth and sat down next to Socks, resting his arm on the pup's muzzle.

-I will try to get the rest,- said Socks. He turned his eyes up to the statue, but otherwise stayed where he was, seeming too tired to move. A moment later, a big chunk of dirt fell away and crashed to the ground at the statue's feet. Then another, and several more fell all by themselves after their support was gone. A few smaller clumps flew away from its head as if tossed, and that was it.

The statue was a man with thick muscles and a stern, bearded face. His arms hadn't survived him toppling over. They were probably buried somewhere nearby, and it seemed a miracle the rest of him had stayed intact. If Dirt ever learned how to heal stone, he might have to come back and find them.

-That's a grown human?-

"I think so. I like it. He looks strong and noble, even without arms. It makes me feel . . . bold." Dirt knew he was stretching by trying to find more to say so Socks would know how much he appreciated it, but that mighty stone man was human, like him. It was the first human he'd ever seen, and he felt drawn to it, like it belonged to him, or he belonged to it.

-Will you get that tall when you are grown up?-

"I honestly have no idea. Well, actually, I don't think so, because then I wouldn't fit in any of the doors in these buildings. And my body is already eight years old, so it would have been doing a lot of growing already. I don't know how much taller adults are but probably not that much. A lot thicker, though. Look at his muscle!"

The comparison to Dirt was comical. Dirt flexed his chest, and nothing happened, not anything like the muscles the statue had.

-Do you hear that?- asked Socks, suddenly sounding a bit apprehensive.

Dirt paused and listened carefully. *"No, nothing."*

Socks opened his mind and began melding their hearing, and Dirt completed it and listened again with the pup's ears.

Scratching. Down beneath them, somewhere under the plaza or maybe right under the statue, was a cavity, and something inside was scratching, slowly, over and over. Exactly the same scratch, perfectly timed.

"What is that?" asked Dirt.

-To me, it sounds like a bone.-

The two of them rose to their feet, looked at each other, then downward into the ground toward the source of the noise. There was something buried there, moving.

CHAPTER TWENTY-ONE

I wonder how we can find out what's down there," said Dirt. *"Do you think you could lift up the big square stone the statue was on?"*

-No. Well, maybe later. Right now I am tired. I had to lift it with my muscles.-

"I thought you lifted it with your mind."

-I did, but the weight had to go somewhere, and the only place was into me. There might be a way to do it better. I can ask Mother, or even Father, since he will be pleased with me. Or maybe I just need practice.-

"I'm pretty sure I couldn't lift up a rock as big as me. No wonder you need a rest. What about . . . looking with that gray sight thing you did? The thing that I couldn't handle. Ghost sight."

-Mother hasn't taught me to look under the ground with ghost sight yet. Probably because there's never anything down there, except for right now. Or maybe because it's not possible. I don't know.-

"Oh." Dirt crawled over to the paving stones around the platform and put his ear against them, seeing whether he could hear anything with his human ears. He couldn't, but his hearing was still melded with Socks's, and the scratching continued. *"I guess the first question we should ask is do we really want to find out what's doing it? What if it's something like that tentacle monster?"*

-It doesn't sound big. I am not afraid of whatever it is.-

"I'm not either. Not yet, at least. And honestly, I want to find out. I just like to be cautious sometimes, because look at me," thought Dirt. He put

his legs in the same pose as the statue's, puffed out his chest, and flexed, grinning all the while.

Socks huffed in amusement, his eyes getting a bit more life in them. He even spared a bit of energy to start flicking the end of his tail. Lifting that statue really had worn him out.

"You can rest, and I'll look around. If that scratching is in a tunnel or a chamber down there, maybe I can find a way in."

-All the buildings here fell down long ago. Why not all the tunnels and chambers?-

"If there was a room underground and it collapsed, then there'd be a big hole in the ground here, so it must not have. But maybe it's just a little box, not a big room. Maybe I won't find anything, but I still want to look. And actually, here, let's meld our sight, too."

With their sight shared across the mental connection, Socks closed his eyes to rest and watch what Dirt was doing. Which was good, because seeing from two perspectives at once made Dirt's body dizzy, and that had been when they were lying down in the den.

Dirt climbed back up onto the platform and looked anew at the area. The statue's plinth, worn down as it was, still had two lumps where the feet must have gone once. In fact, the bigger one might have *been* a foot, with a lumpy shape next to it that was lost to time.

There was a wide circle of nothing around the statue, wide enough for Socks to be lying down without touching the ring of stone around it. This must have been grass or dirt all along, or something like that, lined with a little decorative wall to look nice.

Or maybe the circle held water, not grass. A fountain of water to surround the statue. Humans liked to have water around, judging from the two other human places he'd seen. This was right in the middle of the city, so maybe they put water here to drink and look at along with the statue.

The paved plaza around the circle had nothing growing on it for a dozen paces or more in every direction. Beyond that, roads led off in various directions, including the main one that went down to the plains below.

Dirt hopped off the plinth and walked out to the plaza, noticing how warm the stones were getting under his feet, and how comfortable it made them to stand on. What was he looking for, anyway? Some way to get down underneath, but what would that be? A hole? A door that opened downward? Some other opening that was all filled in now?

Dirt considered the closest street, covered by six or more inches of soil and grass. Would a person walk down the middle, or the sides? Probably both. But if the entrance to the underground was in the middle of the road, anyone going past would have to go around it, and that didn't seem convenient.

He figured if a road was wider than others, that meant it was used more. Or it was for bigger guests, like Father. Maybe wolves came to visit sometimes, so they built a nice big road for them to go to the right places. But either way, he picked the widest road and started walking down it, keeping to the edge instead of the middle, and looked for clues.

After about thirty steps, Dirt shrieked in sudden terror when the ground beneath him collapsed, plunging him downward. His feet hit a lip of stone a couple feet down, then bounced to a lower one before his flailing arms caught hold of the grass and stopped his fall.

Socks severed the partial mind meld and bolted over. Before Dirt had even fully understood what just happened, Socks closed his mouth over his head and lifted him out, fangs under his armpits, and badly scraped Dirt's leg along one of the sides of the hole.

The pup deposited him a good distance away then stood protectively between him and the hole, ears flat and hackles raised. *-Are you okay?-*

Dirt's heart beat hard enough to thump its way right out of his chest. *"I think I'm fine. Thanks for saving me. That was scary! I'm still scared. Oh, wow."* He gave a nervous little laugh.

-I was too slow. If it was deep, you would be gone.-

"No, you could just come lift me out with your mind."

-I don't like it anyway.-

"Well, me neither, but I'm glad you came to get me so fast. Oh! Uh oh. That's bleeding a lot," Dirt said, noticing for the first time how bad his scraped leg really was. A gash, still painless, had opened up all the way down his thigh.

Socks didn't need to be told and immediately bent down to lick the wound closed. Dirt turned on his side to make it easier, squirming as Socks made sure to get in nice and deep to clean it out properly.

The bleeding stopped quickly, and even though it still stung, Dirt stood and patted Socks on the nose. *"Thanks. I'm really glad you know how to do that. It seems like I get cut on everything, all the time. I need fur or something. But now I really want to see what's down there. Should I go take a look? If I step over there, will you listen and see if the floor sounds like it's breaking?"*

-*No. Stay here.*-

Socks stepped heavily over toward the hole, bouncing his body to put extra weight into his steps just to make sure. He got all the way to it without the ground budging, and when he got to the hole, he gave it a good sniff. His hackles were still raised, but he was calming down.

"What do you smell in there?"

-*I don't know. It's strange because there's not much to smell. But I think the floor was metal here, and now it is rust. The air inside isn't moving.*-

"Maybe it's been closed so long all the smells went away."

-*I can smell the rust and metal, but not much else.*-

"Can I come look?"

-*Yes, but not too close. Stay behind my front paws,*- said Socks. A chunk of earth about the size of Dirt's torso came free with a jerk and floated upward, then flew to the side. From there, Socks cleared away all the soil to expose a pitted, dingy orange surface that was neither stone nor dirt. It ran flat on along the ground, and toward one end was the hole Dirt had fallen through. A long split ran down the middle.

"Doors! That's a door! Or two doors. They're all rust now. But look, they open up, and then you can go inside! We found it! Can you lift them open?"

-*No, I don't think I can. They're nothing but crumbly rust now. But I can break them.*-

It took almost no effort. Socks placed a front paw on the corner of one door and pushed, and the whole thing collapsed into a thousand pieces and fell inward. Then he stepped around and did the same to the other door.

-*Okay, now you can come look in. But be careful because it might still be sharp.*-

"I know," said Dirt.

The large rectangular opening was wide enough that with his arms outstretched, Dirt couldn't touch both sides at once. Beneath the doors was a staircase of polished and unweathered stone, flat and shiny in the sunlight where the rust hadn't fallen.

Dirt said, *"That's stairs. You open the doors, and then you can go down."*

-Why make little steps instead of just a slope?-

"I don't really know. I'll have to think about that. But first . . . what do you think?"

At the bottom of the staircase was an arched doorway, empty this time, leading into a hallway that Dirt couldn't see far into from here. The doorway was too small for Socks to go in, which meant Dirt would have to go alone.

CHAPTER TWENTY-TWO

Dirt hesitated, unsure he really wanted to go in there. Well, he did, but it was dark, and something down there was moving. Socks could probably still hear it scratching, scratching . . .

He descended the stairway slowly, watching the darkness recede inch by inch.

-I am nervous having you go in there. You have already gotten into trouble twice today,- said Socks.

Dirt paused, resting his hand against the smooth stone wall, curling his toes to feel the polished stone stair he stood on. He was only a few stairs away from the bottom now, and only a couple steps from there to the doorway. The sunlight lit up the interior, which was a hallway as wide as the doorway—just wide enough he could touch both sides with his arms outstretched.

Socks added, *-Mother said not to go in old human places, but all the ones she showed me were above ground, so I don't think this counts. But I am still nervous.-*

"I'm nervous too, but I won't be able to see very far because I can't see in the dark like you can, so I can only go in a little bit. And if I see something I'll come running back out, so wait right here," he said. *"But if you really want me to stay out, I will, and we can go do something else."*

Dirt hesitated, somewhat hoping Socks would tell him no. But the pup was just as curious about it as he was, and only said, *-We will meld our sight again first so I can help keep an eye on you.-*

"Okay. And I want you to see all this anyway, since we're exploring it together."

The two of them opened their minds fully and connected their sense of sight, but this time Socks kept his hearing to himself, probably so he could listen carefully without Dirt's clumsy senses interfering. Socks closed his eyes, and they both watched through Dirt's.

Dirt paused again in the doorway to let his eyes adjust to the darkness and listen for any sound. He couldn't hear the scratching yet, but the air felt heavier here. Cooler, too. The stone was cold beneath his feet and looked remarkably different from all the weatherworn stone outside. It was all flat and smooth, showing very little sign of wear, even down the middle where people once walked.

A few steps into the shadow and Dirt's eyes adjusted further to reveal a long hallway, decorated with plaster molding along the ceiling, which was square on top instead of arched like the doorway. He went slowly, giving Socks time to listen for any changes or smell a creature before he got too far.

-I bet I am the first wolf to ever see in there with eyes,- said Socks. *-Maybe not even Mother or Father have seen under there, because the door was hidden, and why would they look?-*

"Everyone is going to swarm us for the story when we get back. Too bad there's nothing new for them to smell on me. At least, nothing yet."

A dozen paces ahead, Dirt saw something set into the wall, and once he got closer, he found a heavy door made of dark wood with age-blackened hinges and a big latch.

"Look, Socks, this is a door! And it's got all its parts, I think. It was to . . . keep the inside in and the outside out, I suppose. But watch, let's see if it opens," said Dirt. With feigned confidence, he grabbed the latch and hoped he could figure out how it worked before looking silly. This was a human place, though, and he was a human, and should know all this.

The latch didn't move at all, and it took him a moment to realize that it was just old and stuck, not that he was doing it wrong.

-Come and get some mana, and then break it.-

Dirt considered it, but said, *"Maybe later. I don't want to make a lot of noise yet."*

-Come and get some mana anyway, just in case.-

That wasn't a bad idea at all, so Dirt ran back out and up the steps, noting the significant change in temperature once he got up into the sunlight. It was much brighter, too; he had to squint, and his eyes watered anyway.

Socks bumped him on the chest and pushed a little mana in, and Dirt quickly processed and absorbed it.

-You might find things a human left behind. Keep your eyes open.-

"Oh, wow, I didn't even think of that! Human things . . ." Dirt's imagination ran wild, his mind filling with words that matched nothing he knew. Toys. Clothing. Tools. Weapons. Plates and cups. Things he could hold in his fingers and use with his hands. Or his toes. He could picture absolutely none of it, not even in the most general way, but the *feeling* of such things was so close he could almost reach out and grab them.

Dirt sped down the stairs and back into the corridor, feeling his way along the wall all the way to the door before he stopped to give his eyes time to readjust. He tried the latch again, and it still didn't move. But there was another one a bit farther down, and twenty paces past that was a whole row of them, disappearing into darkness. When Dirt tried the latch on the first of those, it snapped off in his hand with a loud *crack* that made him jump. The door stayed closed, though.

Looking back up the corridor, he judged he was under the plaza right now, perhaps even close to the giant statue's platform. It was too dark to make much out anymore, even after giving himself time to adjust, but the doors here looked decorated, showing the faintest glints of reflective metal, cool and smooth under his fingertips. The doors were carved, too, and Dirt traced his fingers along the curving grooves of the designs and wished he could see what they looked like.

-Can you still not hear it?-

Dirt stopped and listened carefully, holding his breath. The cold, heavy air rested silently against his skin, thick and hard to breathe, like it was almost a liquid. Through the silence, he finally heard it. *Scratch . . . scratch . . . scratch . . . scratch . . .* on and on, in perfect rhythm.

He felt his way along the corridor toward the sound and stopped in front of the door where the sound was. It was right behind the door, scratching on the wood. It was loud now, almost echoing in the silence. The whole heavy door, twice as tall as he was, reverberated with it. *Scratch . . . scratch . . .*

-Did you stop there because you hear it now? We can't see much anymore.-

"Yeah, I hear it. This is another door, and the scratching is on the other side."

-What is it?-

The more he listened, the more the sound chilled him. His curiosity gave way to dread, and he dared not even reach his fingertips back out to touch the door.

It was right there, whatever it was. Right on the other side of a few inches of old wood. Locked away in darkness, trying to get out.

Dirt almost panicked at the thought. It had been locked away for an impossibly long time; what if it was a person? Could someone live that long?

He tried to say, "Hello?" but his voice caught in his throat.

-Can you guess what it is?- asked Socks again. He was starting to sound nervous again. He'd probably tell Dirt to come back any second now.

"No, but it's just a step or two away from me. I'm getting scared, though," Dirt admitted. The words didn't do it justice; he was terrified.

Dirt reached his hand for the latch, shaking so hard he missed it the first time. He was trembling from head to toe. Every part of him knew this was a bad idea, but in his mind, he thought to himself, *You are being silly. It's probably a bug.*

-Get ready to run.-

"Can you see my hand?"

-No, but I can see your thoughts, silly.-

"Oh, right."

Dirt looked back up the corridor, which seemed frightfully long now. Well, he had to do it now or he never, ever would. Dirt pushed the latch, and it turned. This one turned. Of course it did. He pulled, but the door was stuck. Dirt surged the mana into his muscles, giving himself a sudden burst of fiery strength, and pulled again.

The door ripped from the wall with a deafening crash, coming entirely off the hinges and breaking into pieces.

Dirt screamed and ran with all his might back up the corridor. He screamed with every breath, unable to stop, desperate to make his legs move faster and faster.

-RUN!- screamed Socks in Dirt's mind.

The wolf's warning stunned him into clarity. Why was he running? It was just a door, hiding some little scratchy thing. He'd made a lot of noise and startled himself but that was it.

But before he turned to look back, he heard not one scratch but hundreds echoing loudly up the corridor from behind him.

Dirt had hardly slowed down, but Socks squeezed into the stairwell and poked his nose through the doorway. As soon as the pup could see him, Dirt felt an invisible hand grab him and yank him forward.

Socks stepped back just far enough to get Dirt through the doorway, then leaped away, pulling Dirt through the empty air behind him. Before they landed, Socks set him on his back, and Dirt grabbed on for dear life.

The pup landed a short distance away, facing the stairwell with a low rumbling growl. Dirt realized Socks had broken the meld of their sight, probably when he'd come down the stairs to get him.

"What do you smell? What is it?"

-I hear it. It's big. Mother did not send us to get in a fight, so if it looks dangerous, we are running away.-

Before Dirt could respond, a dark purple substance holding countless bones burst from the doorway and shot up the stairs toward them, sending out tendrils full of bone shards and ancient teeth.

Socks leaped backward, but the mass was shockingly fast. It moved like it had no weight at all, bubbling up from below and rushing for them too quickly for Dirt to react.

Somehow the pup was faster and leaped away, a jump with mana in it that shot them fifty paces into the air and landed them a good distance back.

The dark, swirling purple mass rose up from underground like a bubble, the bones from hundreds of corpses spinning within it. It looked even darker against the bright cloudy sky, giving its horror a stark contrast against the peaceful scenery.

The tendrils withdrew as it grew into a towering column, expanding larger and larger until it was three times Socks's height. It reminded

Dirt of fog, but with a skin. It had a surface, all smooth and faintly glossy in the sunlight.

The fat column of purple smoke expanded and coalesced into a face that became a leering skull with empty eyes, staring right at them.

Dirt whimpered and looked away. *"Let's go!"*

The thing opened its skeletal jaw, revealing a blackness that couldn't be explained, darker than night. It drew light in, dimming the air around it.

Then it screamed, a diseased, grating, wretched sound that was so loud Dirt had to cover his ears to keep from going deaf. The sound scraped at his soul, tearing parts of him that had no name. In every way, that thing was *wrong*. Wrong, wrong, wrong, an abomination. A thing that should not be.

-*Watch*,- said Socks.

Dirt opened his eyes, close to weeping for horror. The massive skull shifted and rose a little higher, and a collarbone began to take shape, like it was a whole person in there squeezing out bit by bit.

A new sound split the air, high and fierce. A wolf's howl, primal and immense. The sound was full of such terrifying majesty that it filled Dirt with awe.

Father. Dirt knew that in an instant. Father, the most terrifying being who existed, declared that this was *his* territory and nothing was welcome unless he allowed it in.

The air itself trembled and bowed in reverence. The earth shuddered anxiously beneath them.

The dark, skull-shaped mass broke apart with a roaring hiss and faded like a wisp of steam. Thousands of bones fell and clattered noisily to the earth, some hitting the stairs and shattering.

Socks joined the howl, raising his head and singing into the sky.

Dirt stood up on Socks's back and howled along with them, even though his lungs couldn't hold the note anywhere near as long. His was more a howl of terror than one of triumph, but he didn't know what else to do. His mind was still reeling.

He and Socks howled and howled, long after Father had ceased. From there, it only took a moment for them both to notice how silly Dirt's voice sounded in comparison, and Dirt broke out laughing, even though it felt hollow, like a reaction instead of anything true. Socks wagged his tail furiously in amusement.

-You can try to claim some territory, but I don't think anything will be impressed.-

Dirt giggled. *"For someone that can't laugh, you sure make a lot of jokes."*

Socks huffed.

"I claim this spot on your back. See? Nothing is coming in. Who would dare invade the domain of Dirt?"

-My back is already claimed by me.-

"I'll fight you for it."

Socks found that hilarious and wagged his tail even harder.

"Hey, Socks, you know what I just realized?"

-What?-

"You caught me with your mind and didn't smoosh me."

The pup thought about that for a moment. Dirt got the sense that Socks hadn't realized it either. It had simply happened from instinct in the urgency of the moment.

"Catch me!" thought Dirt. Then he jumped right off Socks's back.

Socks turned his head, startled, but still caught him in time.

-Don't do that.-

"I knew you'd catch me."

-I didn't know I'd catch you.-

"Yes, but look, you can do it now. See? You're holding me just fine. You're already getting good at this, aren't you?"

Socks stared, holding Dirt a foot or two off the ground. Then Dirt floated up toward the pup's face and stopped an arm's length back from his nose. Socks licked him once, then set him on the ground.

Dirt picked up a bone and thought, *"Can you catch this?"* He threw it as hard as he could, but it only went a few feet before it stopped in midair.

"Now this one, too!" He threw another in a different direction, which Socks also caught. Then a third, and Socks dropped the first two trying to reach for that one.

Dirt stopped and grew serious. He sat down on the grass and let out a big sigh. *"All right, we can practice that later. I'm still so terrified I can hardly think. I . . . wow. It's really catching up to me. I think I might throw up."*

-Hold it in,- said Socks.

Dirt tried to breathe deeply and not vomit, but there was so much leftover terror in his blood that he couldn't make himself feel right again. He felt sick from hair to toes, even in his muscles and bones. Shaky. Hollow.

-*Don't throw up on me,*- said Socks. Then the pup picked him up with his mind again and furiously licked his face.

Dirt tried to fight the tongue off with his hands, but to no avail. It was stronger than his arms and kept pushing them away. *"Stop, that's enough!"*

-*Not until you feel better. And you still taste like dirt.*-

"I probably taste like wolf spit!"

-*Nope, still dirt. You will always taste like Dirt.*-

"It's no fair that I don't know any jokes about socks," said Dirt.

The pup's good spirits were infectious, leaking out of his thoughts into Dirt's own. Socks was mostly still fine, with only a little fear way in the back. That fear had to do with Dirt, not towering smoke-skull monsters full of human bones.

"Okay, okay, I promise to feel better. Put me down, and let me get some air."

Socks obliged, and Dirt ran in a little circle, then jumped a few times, and got his blood pumping again. It helped clear his mind.

-*It looks like you are not going to throw up.*-

"Nope, I think I'm fine now. Thanks, Socks. That really helped. So, what was that thing? Did Father tell you?"

Socks leaned down to sniff him and said, -*No, but he said it was from an enemy far beyond me. It wasn't a thing by itself. It was part of something else that doesn't belong here, and he will tell me more when I'm older. He also said it was not the reason Mother won't let me go into that human building we saw. That temple. But he did say it should be safe to go back down in that tunnel, if you want to take another look.*-

"He said it should be, or it is?"

-*It is. At least, safe from that.*-

Dirt pondered that for a moment, trying to decide whether he really wanted to go back down there. It was all dark anyway, and he hadn't found anything. And beside that, he was still scared.

-*I can give you more mana, and you can break the doors and look in.*-

Dirt looked up at his friend.

Socks picked him up with his mind, brought him to his nose, and licked him yet again. Then he set him back down.

"You're never going to stop doing that, are you?"

-Nope.-

Dirt grinned. *"Fine. I'll go look again. Fear with a reason is good, but fear without a reason is just being silly."*

-Good. Take courage, little Dirt.-

He walked carefully over to the stairway, trying not to step on any of the bones that littered the ground. Some of them looked sharp, even if they all seemed like they were ready to crumble. He picked up one, suddenly curious, and sure enough, it ground to powder between his fingers with very little effort. What did that mean, exactly? Were they really old, or had something happened to them?

The staircase downward was covered in shattered bone, far too much to try and walk down, so Dirt had to sweep each step away with his foot before moving. Socks padded silently behind him, nose low to the ground.

"Hey, Socks, do you smell anything with the bones?"

-No. They are so old they hardly even smell like bones. I am curious why I can't smell anything from that big . . . stuff. But if it had all those bones together in one place, it must have eaten all the humans, so it must have been there for a long time too. So why can't I smell it?-

Dirt had no idea, but that was a good question. Socks could smell bug urine, so why not anything from that huge purple mass?

Before Dirt made it down to the doorway, Socks leaned down and gave him a little mana, which Dirt quickly processed. It sure would be nice if he could hold more, especially since his mana body was supposed to have been repaired. Maybe humans just couldn't hold any mana, but if that were true, then why did the word "magic" hold such importance in his lost memories? Oh well.

-I wish Brother were here,- said Socks, indicating by the coloration of "brother" that he meant the strongest of the litter. *-He can make fire, and then you could see down there.-*

"Fire? He can make fire? What's that?" Like so much else, Dirt knew the word, but had no mental picture for it.

-That's why he's the first strongest. And fire is this.- Socks sent him a mental image of a little tree all in flames, burning away into ash. It radiated tremendous heat and lit the surrounding little forest almost bright as sunlight. Smoke rose above it far into the sky, filling the area with a rich, complicated, and dangerous scent. Fire. Obvious. How could Dirt forget about fire?

"How would I take it down with me?"

Socks had no reply for that, so Dirt just shrugged and kept going. Once Dirt stepped through the open doorway into the underground corridor, he found it swept clear of bones, except the few that had bounced this far inside. He'd wondered if the thing left a trail, but there was nothing like that. The stone floor looked just as he'd left it. All the commotion had raised a lot of dust, though, which hung in the air and irritated his nose and throat.

Socks reached out for another mind meld, so Dirt shared his vision again. He should've done that earlier.

When he reached the first door, his eyes were still adjusting to the dim light, so he paused a moment before trying the latch again. Actually, no, he should go and peek in where the monster came out, and see what was there.

Dirt crept along the corridor, tracing his fingers along the flat stone as he went, walking slowly and opening his eyes as wide as they'd go to try to see better.

He bumped his toes into the fallen door before he saw it lying on the ground, and it was so heavy it didn't budge. He stepped up onto it, surprised that it was resting so perfectly it didn't make a sound.

The broken doorway stood out in the dim light as a rectangle of even darker blackness, perfectly silent and still.

-I wish you could see better in the dark.-

"Me too. I think I'll feel around in there for a second and see if it's a room or something else."

-What else would it be?-

"I don't know."

Dirt crept through the doorway, feeling ahead with one hand and tracing the other along the wall. His body was taut and ready to bolt at any moment, but he went in anyway, walking through and along the wall to his left.

His hand brushed against a thread dangling from the wall, and he traced his hand down to the bottom and found a metal ring in a circle as wide as three fingers. Without thinking, he gave it a sharp tug.

He heard a scraping sound above him and saw a flash of light. Before he could turn and look up to see what it was, the room flared to life.

Lamps lined the huge space, and the three closest had come alight when he pulled the string. He found himself in a wide, circular room that went down several levels from where he stood. A railing in front of him would have kept him from tumbling off the edge, and a solid stairway to his right curved along the wall all the way to the bottom.

Excitement filled him. The flickering lamplight made the room look huge, an effect magnified by how the far end faded into shadow where the lamps couldn't reach well. Every inch of wall was covered by small, square doors, only a bit wider than his shoulders. Many of them were open, some hanging on hinges and others toppled to the ground. The open ones were all empty, and the floor down below was covered in heaps of all sorts of things. Vast numbers of bones, but other things too—cloth and metal and clay, all mindlessly strewn around.

Dirt thought, *"Wow, look, Socks!"* and raced down the stairs. When he got to the bottom, he lifted the first length of cloth he found, pale white like most of the rest. It tore apart so easily that he came away with a bit of cloth about the size of his fingertips, and by the time he lifted it to his eyes for a look, he'd crushed it almost to powder.

The cloth looked like it had been draped across a skeleton and then been tossed here in a pile. Dirt squatted down for a better look, carefully lifting here and pulling there, and decided what he was looking at wasn't clothing after all. The cloths were meant to cover the skeletons from head to toe, and no one would walk around wearing something that covered their eyes, so it was something else.

Dirt pulled open one of the little doors on the wall and looked inside, and sure enough, an ancient skeleton wrapped in the pale cloth. Now that he saw it all together, he knew the word for it. Burial shroud.

"I think the humans used to put the shrouds on dead bodies and then put them in these little spaces. I think they put them on when they still had flesh on them, because look, it doesn't fit right for a skeleton," explained Dirt.

-Why?-

"I don't have any idea."

-What is that shiny thing? Back there, on the ground behind the arm.-

Dirt looked down at something that had caught the pup's attention but not his. He pulled up a delicate length of gold chain as long as his arm, made of links so fine he could barely see them unless he looked closely. Near the bottom end of it, a golden clasp held a polished purple amethyst.

He collected the chain carefully in his palm and carried it up the stairs to a lamp to get a better look at it. Its golden surface was perfect and clear and gleamed brightly in the lamplight. The tiny, miraculous links of the chain were so small he wondered if a human had made it at all, or some tinier creature. The amethyst wasn't as impressive as the rest, but Dirt guessed it must have been important to be worthy of the chain.

-What is that?-

"It's a necklace. It used to make a loop so a human could wear it around their neck for everyone to admire."

-Why? It seems useless.-

"Yeah, it does. I only remember that it's a necklace, but not what it was for. Maybe the gemstone was good for something. But it's pretty. How do you think we made the links so small?"

-I cannot imagine how. Maybe Mother will tell us. Do you think it's here because you can't digest it?-

Dirt wasn't sure what to make of that. Socks assumed that these bones were like the ones outside the den—uneaten leftovers. Dirt didn't think that was it, but the more he mulled it over the less he could guess what this place actually was. What were all these bones doing here, wrapped up in burial shrouds? He knew "burial" meant to put a dead body somewhere, but why would anyone do all this? Did that purple smoke monster eat them all and leave some portion of bones here?

"Oh! Socks, I bet I know! There were so many humans, that they had to put them all somewhere when they died, so they stuck them in here. They put these cloths on them and put them in the walls. I guess you have to put them somewhere, since, for example, I couldn't eat a whole adult. So I think what happened, is when someone died and no one wanted to eat any, they wrapped them up and put them down here. And maybe humans never eat their dead at all, so there were lots of them around."

-Wolves don't eat other wolves except for when Mother eats a pup. But there are also not enough of us for it to matter where we lie when we die, so I think you're right. Humans seem to make lots of little places for all sorts of things, so why not that? Keep looking around. Maybe you will find something you want to take.-

Dirt set the necklace down on the ground and hurried back down the stairs. He picked around through the rubble, tearing ancient cloth and crushing bone with every step. There was nothing he could do about that, though. The entire floor of the room was covered in litter, and there was nowhere else to walk.

Digging into a pile taller than he was, he was surprised to find a table, and after clearing more of it away, a chair to go with it. Both were made of carved and polished wood, stately and square in perfect symmetry. He cleared off as much of the table as he could, tossing aside handfuls of old garbage as fast as he could get his fingers around it.

The table was inlaid with little white squares around the edges of the surface, making a handsome decorative border. The thing seemed sturdy enough, so he carefully sat on the chair, which creaked but held up, and rested his arms on the table.

"Look, Socks, this is called furniture. I think humans had a lot of this stuff around."

-Why not just sit on the ground? Is that more comfortable than the ground?-

"No, honestly, it isn't. I don't know why I'd want one. I'm starting to think humans make lots of stuff they don't really need."

-There was a big pile in the middle. Go see what was under that.-

Dirt slid off the chair and gingerly made his way to the center of the room and started digging through the garbage. He found more bits of jewelry and a few little clay pots painted with bright patterns of red and black, but the real prize was a fallen statue underneath it all, half again his size.

He threw all the old bone and cloth and whatever else aside in a flurry to lay the statue bare, but he quickly noticed that something about it was wrong. The arm was twisted and misshapen, like it had been carved to resemble a broken one. The face was a beardless man, screaming in unmoving agony for eternity. Unlike the big statue outside, it still bore enough of its faded paint for Dirt to see the colors, and

pale lines of red dripped from the eyes to make it look like he was suffering. The other arm was twisted at an impossible angle, too, and the
torso had deep gashes that bled and exposed his innards.

Dirt stepped back, growing uneasy. The statue looked more like a
man of stone who had been tortured—*was* being tortured—than just a
statue carved that way from the first. The thing's leg bones were shattered, but the stone was intact, and Dirt couldn't see how the statue had
ever been able to stand. And it must have been able to once, because the
plinth was right there next to it.

It had such a sense of life and reality to it that Dirt felt sick. He
stepped back, then back again. He grew more certain the longer he
looked. This was not a statue of a suffering man. The statue itself had
been made to suffer. It had stood once, right on that plinth, but now
was injured and tortured and fallen to the ground.

"Oh, no, no, no," he said aloud, his voice intruding on the silence,
his heart aching. Something about it was wrong, so wrong it hurt him
inside, so wrong he could feel it like sacrilege and sickness discoloring
his soul.

"No, no, that can't . . . that can't be! How could that happen?"

-*What is it?*-

Dirt tried to answer, and in that moment he knew the word. Just as
he knew a door when he saw it, or a tree, or a wolf. *"It's a god!"*

CHAPTER TWENTY-THREE

Socks said, *-Do you know what a god is?-*

Dirt was too distracted to answer, though, and he stepped back, afraid it'd start moving. It was so lifelike he was sure it would, and that made it impossible to look away.

Until he tripped and stumbled backward, falling all splayed out in a big pile of bones and cloth that immediately pulverized and filled the air with thick dust. Then he started coughing and had to get up and move up the stairs to find fresher air, and from there, he didn't look back again. In the doorway, he pulled the second cord and plunged the area into silent darkness. The smoke from the burning oil lamps smelled familiar, even though this was the first time he'd encountered it.

He stepped into the corridor and tried to ignore the creeping guilt about leaving that statue there, all alone in the dark. Maybe there was something he could or should have done, but he couldn't imagine what it might be. It wasn't a living thing; he didn't see any minds around except for Socks.

No mind visible in that suffering statue of a god, yet he still felt like it was watching him anyway, begging for relief. Aloud, he muttered, "I'll come back for you. When I know what to do, I'll come back. I'm sorry."

It felt like something important and subtle had changed. Something forgotten had been viewed again, a lost door opened that might have been better left closed. But that was silly. There was nothing moving down there, nothing alive. Not anymore.

Dirt smacked himself in the cheeks a couple times to try to clear his head, and it helped a little. He thought, *"Sorry, Socks. I got distracted. But I still have that mana. Which door should I go in?"*

-Go in the closest one to the light so we can see it better, in case it doesn't have lamps like the other place.-

"That's a good idea. But I bet it's just full of old bones. I bet they all are."

-Maybe.-

Socks's mind showed he was still anxious for his little Dirt, which helped Dirt push the frightful image of the god further out of his mind. If Socks was worried, then Dirt's job was to cheer up. He sped down the corridor to the first door and said, *"Okay, here I go! Let's see what's in there."*

Dirt tried the latch, and it still wouldn't budge in the slightest. He surged the mana, strengthening himself from head to toe, and yanked as hard as he could. The latch came away in his hand, tossing him backward far enough to thump his head on the opposite wall.

He laughed, in part because he felt stupid and in part to show Socks he was fine. He got up, rubbing the back of his head. Looking at the latch in his hand, he found a clump of fiddly little bits of decaying metal still attached. When he checked the door again, it swung open easily, creaking loudly on its hinges until they broke. The heavy wooden door toppled clumsily to the ground, just slow enough that Dirt could scamper backward before it fell on him.

The other side of the doorway had a pull cord for a lamp like the big room, and a simple tug was all it took to ignite it. Dirt found that curious, now that he thought about it. He knew that lamps burned oil, and that sparks started the fire, but why were they working when not even the doors did anymore? Maybe oil was like gold, which didn't seem to decay at all no matter how long it had been.

This was another hallway, not a room, with a series of ornate doors along both sides of its length.

-Wait. Look at that lamp some more. Turn it on and off a couple times. I want to see.-

"Sure!" Dirt looked at the lamp, examining it in more detail. It was enclosed in translucent glass, with a sparker connected to the pull cord—a

length of filaments of metal and thread twined together to make a thin rope. The second pull cord pulled a cap over the flame to put it out.

Dirt put out the flame, casting the hall into darkness, and lit it again, watching the sparks dance inside the enclosure. The oil was concealed inside the device, and Dirt didn't want to break it to show Socks. But he put it out, then lit it again, several more times.

-I think I learned something. Okay. Keep going. Look at that first door.-

Dirt stepped over to the first door on the left, opposite another one on the right. This door was narrower than the ones in the larger corridor, but still about twice his height. It was decorated with a series of rectangles up and down, with circles inside those. In the very center of the door was a metal plaque, which read, O ARMENTARIUS MORTUO-RUM, GUIDE WELL THE SPIRIT OF CALLIUS EXEGUS NEMETERIUS, A MAG-ISTRATE AND A SON OF PELATIA, WHO LIES HERE. HE WAS 66 YEARS IN LIFE. HIS HEIR CLOSED THIS DOOR.

-What is that? What are those little things we are looking at?-

Dirt blinked. Of course Socks wouldn't know how to read. But how come Dirt could? What an odd thing to be able to do, when he couldn't even remember the name of . . . of . . .

A hint of a memory crossed his mind, one of twirling cloth, of long, shining hair, but nothing more. It faded as quickly as it appeared. Had that been a woman, he wondered? Oh well. She was gone now.

"*This is called writing. Each symbol represents a different sound, so you can put all the symbols together, and the door can talk to you,*" thought Dirt. He read the inscription to Socks and said, "*There must be an important corpse behind it.*"

-Can you teach me to hear the door?-

"*Of course, as long as I can remember it all. It's called reading, and I completely forgot it existed until I saw this just now. That's happening a lot today. Lamps. Corridors. Rooms. Jewelry. I feel like my mind is wearing out from too many new things,*" thought Dirt, making a little joke, but once he said it he realized it was true. This had been an exhausting day.

Dirt looked the door over but found no latch to pull it open. The hinges were on the outside, but no latch. This one must have been intended to stay shut. He ran up to Socks to get another little puff of mana and was pleased that the painful burning lump of power seemed to hurt a little less each time. He processed it quickly, and by the time he got back to the door, he was ready. This time, instead of yanking it open, he used the mana to strengthen his hands and rip the hinges away. From there, he could just barely get his fingertips in the gap between door and frame and pull it enough to topple it.

The door clattered noisily to the floor, exposing a small room with a single platform inside just big enough to rest a dead body on. From the inscription, Dirt knew it was an adult man, and now he knew exactly how big adults were.

The skeleton wasn't wrapped in the same cloth as the ones in the big room further down the hall; it had an ornate tunic of blue with wide embroidery of gold thread along the edges. Swirling patterns and shapes wove together with plants and flowers in a rich, unending design. Much of the blue was darkened and stained, probably from when he still had flesh on him, but it was still terribly impressive.

"Clothing. That's clothes, Socks. I think humans used to walk around wearing those sometimes."

-Why?-

"I don't know, but maybe because we don't have fur?"

-Is that what you named me after? Something like that?- asked Socks.

"No, look, he doesn't have socks on. Those go on your feet. And now that you mention it, I wonder how I knew that. I must have really liked them. There aren't very many things I knew about before I saw them."

-What is that other thing around his middle?-

Dirt looked again and found a handsome leather strap around the skeleton's waist, still dark with oil and decorated with crisscrossing lines all across its surface. The leather strap held a knife and sheath on the skeleton's side, where it'd grab with its right hand if it was alive.

"A knife! Oh, wow! Socks, look at this!"

Dirt grabbed the ivory handle and pulled it from the sheath, exposing metal as clear and bright as the day they put it in there, curving up to a graceful point. Altogether, it reached from his elbow to his palm. *"This is amazing! I can use this! I can really keep this one. It's like a little claw of my own!"*

-What is it for?-

"This edge here cuts. And the point stabs. So if I run into something that's, oh, I don't know, goblin size or smaller, I can fight it and cut it up.

Or if I want to eat something, but the skin is too tough for my teeth, I can cut it open to get inside and eat the soft parts."

Dirt pulled the skeleton and fragile tunic apart to get the whole leather belt off, then tested it to see if it would hold up. Somehow, miraculously, it was sturdy enough to use. He slung it over his shoulder, since his waist was way too small to use it as a belt, and sheathed the knife.

He was grinning from ear to ear as he walked back out and up the stairs. Socks grabbed him with his mind and lifted him up, pinning his arms to his sides and licking him. Dirt laughed and squirmed, so Socks licked him one more time, then gave him a puff of mana and set him down.

-Jump up,- he said, wagging his tail.

Dirt processed the mana and immediately strengthened his legs for a jump, landing perfectly on Socks's back, right above his front legs.

-You are already good at that.-

"Yes, but don't make me think about it too much, because I did that on instinct, and I'll probably mess up next time."

Socks found that amusing, and Dirt could see him considering grabbing and licking him again. The pup wasn't hiding his thoughts in the slightest at the moment.

-Is there anything else you want to do here?-

"There's lots more doors, but we can save those for another time. I'm worn out, and we did enough stuff for me today. Let's do something you want now."

-I want to take a nap.-

"So do I."

Socks carried them out of the city, past all the ruined footings of buildings and grass-covered roads, away from all the crumbling old bricks and forgotten places and buried dead. He walked quickly instead of running, a calm, easy pace to soak up more sunlight before he found a comfortable spot to lie down.

They left the plateau city and traveled in the direction of the hills and trails that brought them here, down into the little valleys and short canyons where deer ran, and where Brother's trail was found.

Socks stopped in a small copse of trees, choked with bushes and tangles of vines, and lay down at its edge, part of his body in the shade.

Dirt climbed around to rest by Socks's neck, near his shoulder, and curled up in the pup's soft, poofy fur. He sighed contentedly and closed his eyes. *"Socks, make sure I don't dream about dead gods. I don't want a nightmare right now."*

-Don't worry. We will walk the dream together like always. And then when we wake up, I want to figure out how to make fire. Watching the lamp gave me an idea.-

CHAPTER TWENTY-FOUR

Socks slept longer than Dirt did, but that was fine. Dirt was content to quietly lie there in his fur, enjoying the warmth and watching the sun play amongst the clouds that rolled across the sky. Again and again, his mind returned to the city. Humans must be complicated creatures, to have so many places and things they made.

The image of that twisted, tortured god still bothered him, but he could dismiss the memory a little more easily because he had promised to come back. And he would someday. And so much else had happened, he couldn't just dwell on one thing.

That giant smoke monster still haunted him any time he caught a glimpse of a large shadow at the edge of his vision, but he was able to ignore that each time it happened because Father would protect him. Well, not *him,* but Father wouldn't allow whatever that was to be here. So if Dirt managed to find another one, Father would surely chase it away again. Dirt just had to get away from it in time. In fact, maybe Father would be happy that Dirt found more so he could get rid of them all. Well, no, probably not. That didn't sound right.

Dirt pulled out his knife and looked at it again, admiring the craftsmanship. He knew the handle was ivory, but not what that was or where it came from. It was white, a color he didn't see very often, and the top and bottom of the handle were silver, still polished and bright. The gently curving blade was graceful, yet sharp as a gryphon's talon. All of it was perfect, not a single scratch or flaw anywhere.

What a curious thing it was. Dirt could imagine taking rocks and making them square to build with, or carving wood into other shapes. Using a big bone to hit things made perfect sense. But the knife was something else entirely. It wasn't a part of nature, or something that you'd figure out from nature, like building with stone or wood. It was a thing of humans and only humans. Separate. Where did the metal even come from? And how did they shape it? There had been all kinds of metal objects down there—hinges, for example.

Why did they go through so much trouble when it was just fine living like Dirt did? That was the real question. Dirt felt like he understood his own kind less now, not more. Maybe someday he would see a bunch together, and it would all make sense.

For now, Dirt was as happy as he could imagine anyone being. He gripped the knife tightly, admiring the feel of it in his fingers, then placed it back in the sheath and pressed it against his chest. The knife was a reminder of two things—one, that he was human, and humans were interesting and clever and talented. And much more meaningfully, he had this knife because Socks was his friend. Dirt would never have found that place otherwise.

The pup stirred beneath him, his mind filling with thoughts as he woke.

"Socks! I just had the best idea."

-Let me wake up first.-

"Okay, but I'm going to tell you anyway. You know what you could do? You could lift me with your mind to the exact spot you want me to scratch. Then you won't have to figure out how to twist around so I can reach."

-For now you can scratch under my ear.-

Dirt grinned and crawled over. He dug his fingers in, scratching vigorously.

-You are very convenient.-

After only a few more spots, Socks decided that was enough. Dirt crawled to the pup's back as he stood up, but Socks grabbed him and lifted him up higher in the air, shook himself vigorously from nose to tail, and set him down on the ground.

-We are not going anywhere just yet. First, I will make fire.-

"You learned how from the lamps?"

-Brother can make big fire everywhere. He always could, even before he could open his eyes. But when I tried, I was trying to make it big like his, and nothing happened. Fire can start small, though. I learned that from the lamps. I never saw small fire before that.-

"Will it get everywhere? I don't want to get any on me," asked Dirt nervously.

-No, we will run away if it gets too big and comes close. My fur will burn.-

Socks didn't sound as confident as he probably wanted to, but if he said they could get away, then that was good enough.

Dirt moved a few steps away and closed off his thoughts so Socks could concentrate. The pup's body tightened in concentration, and he stared unblinking into the little copse of trees and brush ahead of them. Nothing happened, even though Dirt could feel mana swirling.

Time passed without the appearance of any fire. Other things happened, though. The air pressure changed a little. Subtle waves of power shuddered through him, but didn't affect the grass he was standing in. Socks gave a little whine, trying to stay focused through his frustration. Whatever he was doing wasn't working.

The giant pup flopped to his belly and laid his head on the ground. Dirt panicked a little. *"Socks? Are you okay?"*

-I am fine. I am not even tired. I am just annoyed. It isn't working.-

"What were you trying?"

Socks sent him a mental image of what his plans were. He had been focusing on the trunk of the closest tree, looking at an old scar in the white bark and trying to imagine that burning.

Dirt stepped over and felt the spot with his hand, and found it hot to the touch, but not painfully so.

"Well, it was working a little. It's getting hot."

-It's hard just trying to make it on fire, instead of picking it up.-

"Maybe you just need to try even smaller. Make something this small," thought Dirt. He imagined a little spark in the air, hovering over his palm, and sent the image to Socks. Just one tiny little spark, smaller than Dirt's little hand. A single point of light.

"Oh, and why not try putting the fire on something small first, too? Hold on, let me . . ."

Dirt pulled up some stalks of yellow grass, expecting that the brittle, dry stuff would burn easier because it was the smallest, lightest material

he knew of. He crumpled it up in a pile and set it a few paces in front
of Socks's nose.

-The others would think this was funny. That will be a very tiny fire.-

*"Then let them try to make a bigger one. Besides, haven't little things
served you well?"* said Dirt. He patted the big pup on the nose.

-Fine.- Socks huffed, blowing the little ball of dried grass a few feet
away. The pup caught it with his mind before it came to a rest and held
it there, and almost immediately after, it filled with smoke. Socks leaped
to his feet, eyes focused perfectly on the little ball of grass. An instant
later it erupted into yellow flame, then flared so bright Dirt blinked and
looked away, and that was it. The fire winked out, and a curtain of ash
drifted down through the air.

Dirt cheered, shouting and raising his arms, but Socks said, *-Quick,
get me another one.-*

He scrambled to break off more dry grass and wad it up in his hands.
He threw it in front of Socks's face. The pup caught it with his mind,
and soon it erupted in flames so bright that Dirt felt the heat from several paces away, despite the sunlight already warming his skin. It flared
out even quicker than the first one and left nothing but drifting ash.

He didn't need to be told again. Socks simply shot him an urgent
look, and Dirt gathered another clump and tossed it in the air, then
started getting another one. And another, and another. Dirt quit even
watching them burn, and instead tried to get as many into the air as he
could.

Another, and another, and another. Socks didn't send him any
thoughts, or even think in words. He was too focused on making as
many fires as he could while he got the hang of it. Dirt fed him more
and more grass until he got his hands on a dry stick and tossed that.

Socks burned that one so fast it exploded, creating a fireball as big
around as Dirt's body from head to foot.

-WATCH!- shouted Socks, forgetting to be quiet. The word left Dirt's
head ringing and sore, but he didn't complain. He followed Socks's gaze
to the copse of trees.

Not one but twenty tiny fires erupted all throughout it, then twenty
more. The entire copse went up in flames, from front to back. The
twisting vines and brush cracked and spat and vanished in bright flames
of yellow and blue.

Socks kept his eyes forward, focusing and forcing the flames higher and higher. It got so hot Dirt had to step back and hide behind the wolf, and even there he started sweating.

The pup turned his gaze to one side and a curtain of sparks appeared over the grass, which quickly ignited. Then the other side.

-I DID IT! Oh, sorry. I did it! Look, little Dirt. Look at all the fire around!-

"It's getting too hot for me. Can we go back a little?"

Socks seemed to awaken from a daydream and realized just how much fire he'd made. He picked up Dirt with his mind, and they retreated to a nearby hilltop to watch it burn.

The grass fires went out soon after, but the copse of trees burned for far, far longer. Long enough for Socks to get bored and leave. *-Come, little Dirt. Let's go back to the den and show Mother that I can lift you up now, and burn things.-*

"Just not at the same time."

Amused, Socks replied, *-No, not at the same time.-*

"Hasn't she already seen it? Isn't she always watching?"

-Probably. And Father has seen it, too, from atop his mountain.-

"Father is on a mountain?"

-A very tall one, because he likes the cold. He watches his territory from up there, if he is not hunting.-

Dirt wondered about that for a moment. Were all the humans gone from here because Father didn't want them in his territory? Or had Father claimed it after they were gone?

He had learned one thing, though. Thinking about the distant past too hard made him less happy, not more.

"Socks, let me just say one thing."

-What is that?-

"I want to sleep on the puppy pile tonight."

CHAPTER TWENTY-FIVE

*Y**OU WILL NOT SLEEP IN THIS DEN TONIGHT.*

Dirt tried not to show his regret about that, or even feel it strongly lest Mother think he was trying to manipulate her. He wouldn't dare, but it stung nonetheless.

Socks was having a great time with his siblings, oblivious. Everyone wanted him to lift them up with his mind or create sparks. Five or six were actively trying to mimic him and learn how he did it, to no visible effect; the rest were so excited they kept running up to play, pretend-biting at his mouth and just generally raising a ruckus.

Dirt had wisely made his way to the edge of the den to sit down and relax, hoping to avoid getting stomped on or lit on fire, and he'd been mostly left to himself. Aside from Socks running over to check on him every now and then, or a pup coming by to sniff him to see where he'd been today, he just sat and watched, ignored. And that was fine. He still had plenty on his mind, and his brain was still tired and needed sleep. It was nice to watch Socks having fun with all the other pups, too. They could play with him in a way Dirt couldn't, since they were his same size.

So where was Dirt going to sleep, if not here, he wondered? The sun had already set, and it was starting to dim outside. Perhaps he would be wise to take the hint and leave now, while Socks was distracted.

His hand crept to the knife hanging under his armpit. He'd be fine alone if he and Socks had to spend a day or two apart. He could hide where big things couldn't get him, and cut up any little things that found him. He could be just as ferocious as Socks was when he felt like it. He might even be able to make it to the forest in a day or two, if he could find the way. He wasn't sure he could, but maybe he could get on top of something tall and see where it was.

Dirt spared the briefest glance at the rear of the den where Mother lay, ever terrifyingly huge and predatory. Even nursing ten pups at once she looked ready to strike. She wasn't watching him, though. Her golden eyes darted from pup to pup, watching them all with a serious air about her. Or perhaps she just looked relaxed, but he couldn't separate his fear of her from how she appeared to him.

She must have noticed Dirt being excited about the puppy pile and chosen to cure him of a false hope. She gave no clarification because she didn't care how he felt about it, only that he knew the truth. Which, now that he thought about it, she did often.

Dirt stood, completely unsure how to proceed. Should he sneak out? Or should he say goodbye first and let Socks know why he was leaving? Because if Dirt made Socks mad at Mother, she might just prefer to eat Socks, smoosh Dirt like a bug, and be done with it. But he couldn't lie to Socks. He simply couldn't. It was unimaginable. He wasn't even sure it was possible after melding their minds so many times.

Was she waiting to see who he'd side with? With her, lying to keep Socks out of trouble, or with Socks himself by being honest?

I AM NOT TESTING YOU. THERE IS NOTHING MORE ABOUT YOU I CARE TO LEARN. THE WAY IS NOW PREPARED. IF YOU WISH TO SAY GOODBYE, DO IT FROM YOUR DESTINATION.

Along with the words, Mother sent Dirt a clear image of himself hurrying out of the den and touching a particular root poking up out of the ground, just a short distance from the entrance.

It pained Dirt to leave like this, but disobeying Mother for even an instant would certainly pain him a lot more. He stood immediately and jogged out, just a bit faster than Mother's image had shown him going, even though his feet had never felt heavier. His mind instinctively shied away from any feelings of injustice or indignation, instead turning to how lucky he was that Mother let him associate with Socks at all.

How must it look for her, he wondered, to have him in her den? Nothing else was allowed in. No birds, no critters big or small, not even bugs or plants. It was a place for wolves and wolves only. And he knew what he looked like through the wolves' eyes, even how he smelled. A fidgety little thing, fragile and mostly useless, but sometimes interesting. A squirmy bit of moving grime clinging to her son, which he refused to part with. At least Dirt was slowly proving beneficial, helping Socks to learn things the other pups hadn't figured out yet. Mother was probably annoyed, but she was being gracious for Socks's sake. She'd even healed Dirt.

And Dirt had almost resented her for kicking him out for a moment there. Almost, and the gods only knew what the result of that would be. He suspected she only needed the first excuse to be rid of him, and that'd be that. This must be the hard part of being a child—adult humans probably never had any difficulty mastering themselves. Dirt still needed practice.

CLOSE YOUR EYES BEFORE YOU TOUCH IT.

Dirt nodded, and shortly after, he found the little root Mother had shown him. It was a finger's width and no longer than his hand, still young and tender green, poking up into the air.

He wasn't sure what to expect, or how long Mother wanted him to hold on to it. Was he supposed to pull it up, maybe?

Dirt knelt and closed his eyes as instructed. He reached out, and the instant his fingertip brushed against the root, a sudden full-body jolt yanked him hurtling forward with shocking speed, slamming him left and right as the path turned this way or that, all too fast for his mind to even process.

By the time he could scream, he'd already stopped moving. He was still kneeling, but he felt like his whole body had been filled with sand and water and shaken violently. Everything sloshed inside him, sharp pains everywhere.

He yanked his hand away and opened his eyes and didn't find what he expected. It wasn't the open field of trampled dirt and sparse grass surrounding the den. He was back in the forest, kneeling in the soft black dirt, hidden by the ferns.

Astonishment kept him from breathing for a moment until he started gasping and coughing. He shot to his feet, then immediately fell over because he couldn't keep his balance.

Dirt shook his head and got up more slowly. A hand gently gripped his arm, and he turned to see a beautiful girl his own age, all in green.

Green hair, green eyes, skin the gray of bark, and little green leaves growing to cover her torso. Could it be—

"Home?" he asked aloud.

"Yes. Welcome back, Dirt," she said. Her voice was soft and light, and she gave him a big smile that only looked slightly practiced.

"Home!" he shouted, suddenly overjoyed. He looked at her hand, still holding his arm. "Hey, you didn't break it this time. Good job!"

"The Mother of Wolves has been instructive."

"Really? Huh. That's good. I'm glad she was. Oh, wow, I don't think I'm okay." The world spun around him, even though he tried to stand still. His knees gave out, and he fell, slipping from Home's grasp to collapse awkwardly in the black dirt. He almost tried getting back up, but the world spun ever faster, and he grew nauseous.

Dirt tried to grab hold of the ground to keep from spinning, but it didn't help because nothing was really moving. A moment later, he vomited, hard, tasting only acid and a bit of deer left in his mostly empty stomach.

"Sisters?" asked Home.

Dirt heard footsteps swishing through the ferns. Several sets of hands rested lightly on different parts of his body, but he was sure if he opened his eyes to see them, he'd vomit again.

"He looks unwell," said a different tree-girl. Dryad. That was what Mother called them.

"The Mother of Wolves did not warn us about this," said Home. "Let us view him."

A rhythmic hum rose from the ground and filled him, reverberating deep within him, the old familiar pulse he knew from sleeping under the roots. His mana body reacted—that must be what it was—as the trees guided something around inside him, probing him to find out what was going wrong. It felt like a gentle massage, but from the inside out.

It was not long before the probing sensation faded, and shortly after that, the pulsing hum stopped.

"The Mother of Wolves says you will be fine in a moment. The fluids of your inner ear were unbalanced by root travel, but will naturally restabilize with time. She reminds us to be gentler with you," said Home.

Dirt smiled despite how awful he still felt, wondering if she'd neglected to warn them on purpose. "That sounds like her."

They kept their hands resting on him while he recovered, and from what he could tell, they held perfectly still, as unmoving as the trees they really were. He didn't vomit again, but he did come close a couple times. He managed to hold it down, since he didn't want to splash one of them.

Slowly, slowly, the earth stopped heaving and trying to throw him off it.

"Dirt, do you feel better now?" asked Home.

"Yes, I . . . Oh, wow. Gods in Glory, that was intense. But I feel a lot better now," Dirt said. It felt strange to be using his voice so much, speaking aloud after so long.

He rubbed his eyes a bit, then opened them to see several more dryads kneeling over him, each one different. One had shorter hair, another longer. The shapes of their faces were different. They didn't wear clothing, but neither were they naked. They were covered by little green leaves that grew almost like fur to hide their forms, some from the neck down, others from the chest down, and a few from the waist down.

They all had exactly the same smile, though. He was sure they'd practiced it.

Dirt grinned at that. They were already charming, he decided. He pushed himself up to his feet, then wiped his mouth and cheek to get the vomit off and cleaned his hands in the soil.

"Are you well now, Dirt?" asked Home.

"I am. Thanks. How did I get here?" Dirt supposed that if he couldn't sleep on the puppy pile, this would be okay instead. He'd miss Socks tonight, but they'd be back together soon.

"We will discuss that and many other things. Come, let us walk together and see what I have to show you," said Home, standing and holding out her hand for him to take. He did.

CHAPTER TWENTY-SIX

They were not far from Home's roots, which he recognized now that he got a chance to look around. Home's dryad held one of his hands, and someone else held the other as they walked. Both dryads held their fingers perfectly steady in just the right shape, but unmoving in a way that felt unnatural. Dirt didn't say anything, though, because it was nice they were trying, and besides, the pale gray bark of their skin was convincingly supple.

A whole crowd of dryads had gathered to see him, it seemed, and more were coming. They walked in through the ferns at the same steady, measured pace. There were already as many dryads as there were wolf pups in the den at night, and Dirt was sure there'd be ten times as many before long. All children his size, all girls. At least the ones he could tell, which was most of them. The tiny green leaves concealed too much of their bodies and hid the first place he'd look to tell the difference.

"I wasn't expecting there to be so many of you, but I'm not surprised. How did you all know to look different? Was that so I could tell you apart?"

Home said, "The Mother of Wolves showed us many humans. We are pleased with our imitations. Do you approve?"

Dirt looked at Home, then several of the others. The faces really were quite good, and the variety he saw told him they understood what they were doing. Home's face was a little narrower, her jaw a bit more pointed, whereas the dryad holding his other hand had round, full cheeks and a flatter nose.

"You all look very human to me. I think if you told me you were human and I didn't know any better, I'd believe it. Except the gray skin, but maybe some humans are that color. I don't know. So I'd probably believe it. Actually, do you mind if I ask you something? Are you supposed to be wearing clothes? Is that what this is?"

"Rather than imitating clothing, partial body coverings allow us a convenient excuse to reduce our expenditure of focus. This appearance requires less effort on our parts, and we wish to reserve as much as possible for the purpose of learning. Would you prefer my form to be uninterrupted, as yours?"

"Oh, well, no, I don't really care. I was just wondering. I thought maybe if you all had clothes, I needed some too, but I don't know where I'd get any."

"I wish for you to do as you prefer to give us opportunity to learn your preferences. Do not concern yourself with ours. If they become important, we will speak them," said Home, still smiling. Her voice rose and fell as she talked, in a way that was more repetitive than expressive.

Everything they did was so close to human that the things they got wrong were strangely discomfiting, and Dirt had to school himself to push down the growing unease. Facial expressions and body language that were close but not quite right. A hundred little things. Never mind what had happened to his arms, and might again.

Instead, he decided it was endearing how hard they were trying. The trees were bigger than he could measure and older than he could guess, but here they were seeing and living in the world as if for the first time. They were even younger than he was, in a way.

"Why did you choose to imitate humans instead of something else, like wolves?" he asked.

"It was your dreams that first made us aware of this way of perceiving, and it is you with whom we wish to interact," said Home.

"Also, the Mother of Wolves would not send us one of her own to examine more closely because we are too dangerous. We understand your anatomy better," added the other dryad.

Dirt glanced at her, now nervous.

That one said, "I apologize. The Mother of Wolves said we should not all speak or it would disorient you. Have I disoriented you?"

He swallowed and said, "No, that's fine."

The forest was just as he remembered it, at least above. The trees were still impossibly tall and left no sky visible anywhere, covering it all with their canopy. The comforting ceiling of leaves still relaxed him. The open sky outside wasn't as intimidating as it used to be, but this was better. Quiet. Eternal. The sky changed so much day by day, even hour by hour, that it felt less reliable.

It was also nice to feel the ferns brush against him as he walked, and his toes digging into the rich black soil. He was happy to be getting covered in the right color dirt again. The ground in the den was a paler brown, rougher and harder, and he didn't like it as much.

"Are you hungry?" asked Home, with a pleasant smile. Which every other dryad mirrored, exactly the same. Every single face.

Dirt laughed before he could start getting scared. It really was funny. They were trying so hard! "Oh, I'm only a little hungry. I ate a lot of deer earlier with Socks. Mostly I'm just tired. I've had a really long day."

"We will more deeply analyze your composition and prepare a sap that contains the appropriate nutrients," said Home, her pleasant smile never breaking.

He wasn't sure what she meant, and he'd rather not find out as the last thing he did today, so he said, "Thanks, but tomorrow is fine."

Dirt spared a glance at her mind, which felt a bit intrusive now that the tree could talk. The majority of her thoughts were as inscrutable as ever, except the portion that was processing speech and orienting in the physical world. From the sheer excitement he saw there, she was beyond eager to try to make that sap, whatever that was. Home was as happy as he'd ever seen anyone being. That smile wasn't an affectation after all.

"We eat always, but you eat only sometimes, in larger amounts. Is that correct?" asked a dryad walking just in front of them. This one's green hair reached almost to her waist.

"Yep, every single day. And drink water, too. Wait, wow, what is that?!" he exclaimed, spotting a little house of gray and green built against Home's roots, right above where his nest was. With night so close, he hadn't noticed it tucked there in the shadows.

In his excitement, he let go of the dryads' hands and ran forward to get a better look. The house was just his size—five or six paces wide, made of sturdy branches and twisting vines instead of stone.

With no cut edges, Dirt decided Home must have grown it in place. He rested his hand against the empty door frame, wondering if it was all part of her.

The doorway was just a bit higher than he was tall, not towering overhead like those of the ruined city. The windows on either side of the door were a bit lower, too, so he could see out better. The back wall was the root, and the roof was slanted instead of pitched. Inside, it was as dark as it could get.

He was sure wandering into a lot of dark places today, he thought with a forced grin. Before stepping over the threshold, however, he turned back to see the crowd of dryads walking calmly in his direction.

They probably didn't know how to run. Well, that was fine, because he could teach them, and then they could play all sorts of games. He'd have to make them up, but preferably ones that didn't result in his bones being shattered again. Maybe Socks would have some ideas next time he saw him.

The first dryad to reach him looked like it might be a male, since his frame looked a little more solid and masculine than the others. His scruffy green hair was much shorter, and he grew leaves around his waist only, leaving his torso bare. He said nothing, stopping dead in his tracks a couple paces away.

Dirt wondered which tree he was, since only a handful of them were close enough for him to see their minds. He admitted it was a bit creepy how the dryads had no minds right there in them, since that made them feel like they might be corpses. But he'd get used to it. He still loved them, especially Home.

And soon enough she arrived. Home stepped to the front of the crowd and said, "Do you like it?"

"I do! I love it. How did you know? Not even *I* remembered what a house was until earlier today," he said.

"The Mother of Wolves showed us many things that are to your benefit, at our request. Her guidance is that none enter without your permission, and none shall. Walk inside and speak the word 'shut.'"

"Wait, Mother told you things to benefit me? Why?"

Still smiling, Home said, "We are too powerful to be denied carelessly. I will explain another time. Please, walk inside and speak the word 'shut.'"

Dirt nodded slowly, trying not to look unsettled. The last thing he wanted was to get caught in the middle of an argument between Mother and the forest.

He turned and stepped through the doorway, holding his hand forward to keep from bumping into anything. Home wouldn't put anything weird in here, would she? He'd never know, since it was too dark to see inside it right now.

Nothing reached out and grabbed him, at least. Just empty air so far. The floor of the house wasn't earth—it was solid with a soft layer over it that he couldn't immediately identify. The air inside was even heavier and quieter than the rest of the forest, which made it doubly different from the den where he'd been only moments before.

"Shut," he said. Then he jumped as the entire house shuddered and groaned around him, creaking and popping. He felt the floor moving beneath him and just about ran outside before he noticed that the doorway was growing in, solid branches forming a hatch pattern with spaces just big enough to fit his hand through. The windows did the same, and all he could see anymore were little diamond shapes where the last remaining light got in.

"Open?" The house creaked and shook just as before, and this time the door and windows opened back up. The process wasn't fast, but it was fast enough.

Home said, "Goodnight, Dirt."

"Goodnight. Are you going to sleep with me, too? I don't think all of you will fit in here, but Home made her dryad in my nest that first time, so is she coming in? Are you?"

There was no reply. No one so much as twitched.

"Home? Anyone?" he asked the silence. "Hello?"

Looking back to Home's mind, he found her already mostly shut down, asleep.

The trees had fallen asleep just like that, and they were all going to leave their dryads out there, standing there right outside this house, looking in. All night.

"Close," he told the door, his voice wavering. It obeyed, but even with the door and windows latticed in, he still knew the dryads were there.

The idea of being watched like that, their faces unmoving in the perfect darkness, deeply unnerved him. The dread that had been building this whole time finally bubbled over and stole his breath. He could see their fading outlines, silent and empty. As soon as he turned his back, they'd start moving again and come grab him in the night, or scare him with sudden sounds, or something like that. They wouldn't, but he couldn't shake the dread despite knowing better.

But nothing inside moved or spoke. All was calm, the house empty except a shallow basin that grew right out of the root. Inside it his fingertips met liquid, which his nose told him was water. He had a sip, and it tasted fine, but he didn't dare drink more until he could see what it looked like.

At the back end of the house he found a narrow stairway and carefully made his way down. It was only four stairs, and at the bottom, a short tunnel led to a small room that he guessed used to be his nest.

He stubbed his toe on a wooden edge, then tripped and banged his shins against a short wooden platform, only knee height. He fell forward onto what he quickly realized was a bed, soft as a puppy and just as fuzzy, with some kind of thin fibrous material bunched up into clumps that molded to his form when he lay down.

Dirt settled in, trying not to cry from the sharp pain in his toe and shins, and from weariness, and from dread. He almost didn't want to sleep, knowing it'd be Home waiting for him in the dream with all her unknowable thoughts and alien sensations, and not Socks.

He just hoped the dryads didn't want to pull him apart to see what he was made of.

CHAPTER TWENTY-SEVEN

Dirt woke slowly, fading in and out of lingering dreams several times before he came to full consciousness. He'd had a nightmare about Socks but couldn't remember it. That had dissolved into a restless dream in which he wandered through starlit ruins, hiding from some unseen thing slowly chasing him.

Halfway through the night, his dagger dug into his ribs and woke him up, so he'd taken it off and set it beside the bed and fallen back asleep quickly. No tree-dreams, although the familiar pulsing hum rising from the earth had been just as he remembered it.

He stretched his arms and legs and groaned contentedly. The dryads would be up there waiting for him, he knew. Dirt looked at Home's mind, once again awed at how huge it was, how complex and inscrutable. Part of her was controlling her dryad, waiting patiently for him to come up. She just kept thinking how happy she'd be to see him, in a way that made him wonder if she knew he could only comprehend that part of her thoughts. In fact, she probably *did* know that, or had guessed it.

The rest of her mind still had emotion in it, and *that* was something he could understand. Her excitement ran through all parts of her immense mind, but along with it, if he looked very carefully and examined it through the lens of his own heart, was an undercurrent of uncertainty, of hesitation. She was nervous and wanted to give the right impression. That helped put him at ease, since it wasn't just him.

It occurred to him that Socks was always just himself, always perfectly honest, feeling and doing and thinking whatever he wanted. All the pups were like that, and maybe Mother and Father too, even though he didn't dare look at their minds. Dirt didn't have that luxury. He was whatever he needed to be to survive. Around Mother, that meant as humble as possible. And maybe he did that a little with Socks, making himself happy instead of scared sometimes. It was always sincere—his humility was genuine, and so was his love for Socks. It had to be. He could think a lie, or say one, but he couldn't *be* a lie. Mother and Socks could read his mind.

So what did he need to be to survive today? He loved the trees, but he didn't really know them. As always, he'd have to figure it out as he went. Maybe he should just be himself. Maybe he *was* always just himself. Maybe that was his type of strength—discipline and sincerity.

Well, no use waiting around. Dirt crawled off the bed, slightly disappointed to be leaving it behind. It really had been comfortable, and he already wanted to take a nap. Slinging the leather sheath back over his shoulder, he ascended the stairs.

The inside of his house was as foggy as the outside, making it impossible to see the dryads only a few paces past his door. That was good. That meant it was still early morning and there'd be plenty of dew for him.

Oh. Right. There was water right over there. Dirt stepped over to the basin, which it was light enough to see. All made of bare wood, not bark, it came right out of the root, wider than his shoulders and only deep as a finger in the middle. Perfectly still, clear water filled it to the brim, so calm that he could see his reflection if he moved to exactly the right angle. It was too dim for a good look, but he could see it.

He dipped his face in and drank his fill, relishing it. It tasted like the water in the huge basin with the tentacle monster, not the dew from the ferns. No plant flavor at all. Nothing but clean water.

In just a few seconds, he drank more than he would have gotten all morning if he'd had to chase the dew. No waiting for Mother to give him water, or wondering when Socks would get thirsty and find some, or having to wait for the next morning. This was a true luxury.

Then there was nothing left to do but go outside and greet the dryads. They would want every moment of his time, he was sure. They would probably do magic on him, like when Home broke his arms and they tried to heal it. They'd fixed his mana body then, not his physical one, and expected him to fix the rest himself. So what else might they have in mind?

Something about sap. Home mentioned making sap for him to eat, and it sounded like he would be involved somehow. That would be his first thing to survive today.

No, he was being silly. They didn't want to hurt him. The opposite, if the house he was standing in proved anything. He stepped to the door-way, took a deep breath of resolve, and said, "Open." The latticework of vines withdrew from the doorway, and he stepped out into the fog.

"Hello, Home! Hello, everyone. Thanks for the house. I love it. And the bed was wonderful. And the water," he said to Home and the outlines in the fog behind her.

They came at the same easy pace as before, green-and-gray children in endless variety. Despite the fog hiding most of their number, he was sure there were more this time, and he could spot a handful that he thought might be male.

It occurred to him that with wolves, you couldn't tell male or female unless you could see their minds or between their hind legs. And wolves could smell the difference, but he couldn't. But with humans, you could tell just from the face or subtle things about the shape of the body, and the trees had captured that when making their dryads.

"Hello, Dirt," said Home. Her voice was bright, almost like laugh-ter, and her long, green hair shimmered slightly in the pale fog.

"Hello, Dirt," said dozens of others in near-unison.

He was happy to see them, he realized, which was a relief. But he wasn't ready to give control of the day to them just yet. He was still too nervous. "I think the very first thing I want to do this morning, is give everyone a hug. But I don't want you to break my arms again, so here's how I want to try. Here, Home, can you push my hand down, gently?"

Dirt held his hand out. Home considered that for a moment, then stepped forward and placed her hand over his and gently pressed down-ward. No, not gently: slowly. Far too strongly for him to resist. She would've broken his arms if it'd been a hug.

He smiled and said, "Good. This is why I wanted to practice first. You're pushing slow, not gentle. Gentle means that you only use so much force, and then not any more. See, look, if I push on this fern gently, then I feel it pushing back, and I know not to push it so hard it breaks. I could push slow and drive it right into the ground and break it, see?

But I don't want to break it, so if I feel too much force pushing back on me, then I stop. That's gentle. Does that make sense?"

Thank Grace that Dirt was quick enough on his feet to think of how to explain something so intuitive. He grinned, just a little, as he started to realize just what he was in for.

"I will push gently," said Home. She tried again, and this time her touch was light as a feather and only slowly increased, just enough to move his hand a finger's width before she stopped. "Is that gentle?"

"That's gentle. I don't know how hard it is for you to control your dryad, but you did a good job. Push just a little harder. Okay, now a little harder. See, now I'm pushing back, and you can tell, right?"

"I will not squeeze hard. Do humans often give hugs?" asked Home. Her smile looked like it was getting more real, like she was smiling with her eyes now, too. He noticed they were dry, not moist. Hard and smooth.

"Do we often give hugs?" He stopped to think about that. She was watching him far more carefully than he realized, already learning minute details of body language. Nearby, some of the others were slightly moving or shifting their weight instead of remaining perfectly still. Already, they felt more human to be around than they had last night.

Dirt said, "I don't know, honestly, because I don't know any other humans. But I do know that whenever I see Socks, I want to hug him and scratch his ears and pet his fur. But I don't want to hug Mother when I see her, so I suppose humans only like to hug their friends. And Socks always likes to lick me, and let me sleep in his fur, and stuff like that. I think . . ."

He paused, turning his mind inward to try and understand himself. He hadn't been alive very long, but he'd had enough good and bad to know a few things. "You trees are always connected, always touching your roots, always together. But we humans aren't connected like that. We have to touch on purpose to be connected. And if I never had anyone for that, I think I would just drift away and disappear."

Dirt squeezed Home's hand between both of his. Her face was calm and happy, but he could see her mind racing to process what he was saying.

She withdrew her hand and stepped forward, wrapping her arms around his ribs. She squeezed only gently and rested her head beside his.

Her green hair smelled like leaves. "Then for a moment, we are connected."

It was different hugging a human than a wolf. Their bodies fit together better. Somehow, he'd missed this, even though he'd never done it before.

She didn't know when to stop, so he had to let go first and pull away. Home's face was calm and content, but her mind was sending complicated bundles of information to everyone else. He could guess what they contained. "Are you telling everyone else how hard to hug?"

Home said, "Yes, and more."

"Okay, good. Who's next?"

"Do you wish to be connected to all of us?" asked a nearby dryad, one he wasn't sure he recognized.

"Sure," Dirt said. "If you want."

From there, every single dryad wanted a hug. They waited with their arms out as he went from person to person. A whole crowd of them, arms pointed toward him. He was glad he knew what was going on, because if he didn't it might have been terrifying. But he hugged them all, for a few breaths each. The dryads got better at it as he went, too, adjusting the force and position as they gained more experience.

He started counting after five dryads and lost count around thirty; there were three or four times that many. All in all, it took longer than he expected, long enough he wanted to take a break. He kept going, though, until he got them all. Every last one, including those who arrived after he'd already gotten started.

Home followed him the whole time, always a few steps behind him. He figured she was observing, or perhaps making sure no one squeezed him too hard. But no sooner had he stepped back from the last dryad, giving her a tired smile that he hoped was still friendly, than Home grabbed his wrist, tightly enough he couldn't pull away. It felt like a ring of iron, just loose enough to keep from bruising, but which he couldn't get his hand through.

Another dryad grabbed his other wrist before he could react.

"What are you doing?" he asked. He swallowed the knot of fear before it formed. He would be fine.

Instead of answering, two more grabbed his shoulders, then his feet and hips, and together they pressed him to the ground, slowly but firmly.

"What's going on?" he asked, trying not to sound as panicked as he was becoming.

Home said, "The Mother of Wolves warned us this might distress you, but it is important. We hoped to comfort you first, to relax you. Please do not be distressed." She gazed down at him with a beatific smile that was in no way predatory. Somehow that made it scarier.

"What are you doing? Why didn't you just ask me? Home—!"

"Please, do not be distressed, Dirt. Are we not now friends?" She held her hand over his stomach. Tiny strands, so thin and white he could barely see them, grew from her palm and fingertips, hanging lightly on the still and humid air.

"We are, but this is scaring me because I don't know what's going on," he said in a rush. He hastily glanced at her mind, trying to understand, and found only that she was sincere. There was no malice in her. It didn't help.

She said, "I see that you are distressed. I apologize, but if we let you move, you might break them off. Leaving them inside you would be worse."

"What? Break what off?!"

All at once, the tiny white strands on her hand stiffened. They needled into his skin.

Dirt screamed.

CHAPTER TWENTY-EIGHT

He shrieked more from horror than pain as dozens of tiny threads wormed all throughout his body, deep inside, from guts to muscles and even bones. They caused sharp, tiny pains everywhere they went, which disappeared almost instantly only to happen again in the next spot over. There was no tugging, but in some places he could feel them restricting the natural movement, like in his lungs. He made himself quit screaming, worried his air was going to run out.

For a moment he felt a dull squeezing in his chest that made him tired and nauseous, but apprehension entered Home's mind, and the squeezing vanished. He didn't know why, though. She had no room set aside for words, or anything at all beyond the minimum needed to control her dryad. All the rest of her, all the immense bright glow of her mind, was focused on processing what she was doing.

He watched her mind, hoping to understand what was going on. He could not. Her thoughts, now that she was fully engaged, carried far, far more at once than he could comprehend. They pulsed at the same rhythm as the nightly hum beneath her roots, slow and deliberate, but each pulse was so complicated he couldn't even tell if it was sensory information.

One thing he understood, however, was that she was dividing information up to send to the others. In part, she was directing all their efforts, acting as a sort of central organizer. The actual trees were too far away for him to see all their minds, but the handful he could see were engaged in the same task.

The sharp little pokes made their way up through his neck and into his face, and when thin, blurry bars started crossing his vision, he knew why. His eyes twitched involuntarily, as if wanting to move to look at something else, and he could feel the tugging that held them in place. That got a whimper out of him. He started panting, feeling like he had to flee.

But he couldn't, so he closed his eyes and tried not to panic any more than he already had. It wouldn't do him any good—they were holding him firmly on any joint he might have tried to bend to get away. He wasn't going anywhere, but he might be able to squirm enough to break one of those tiny threads off, leaving it woven all throughout his innards. That would be worse.

A thread hit something in his thigh that made him twinge, and right after that, several more in other places. Whatever they hit stung a lot more than the rest and made his arm shake, or his finger curl, or his leg try to bend. All different muscles flexed by themselves, one here, one there. The sharp pains were bad enough, their fiery stings burning far longer than the earlier ones, but some of his muscles jumped so much the dryads bruised his skin holding him down. He felt like he was losing control of himself. Were they taking him over? Were they going to invade and make him a dryad? If so, there was nothing he could do, except groan and hiss in discomfort.

He wished Socks were here. Even just to sit nearby, nose to the ground, whimpering in sympathy. And when it was over, lift him out of their reach, lick him, and set him on his back. Then flee.

The process dragged on and on, long enough for him to start losing his terror and revulsion and start thinking about getting hungry instead. The dryads were holding him so firmly the sore spots from that were more painful than anything going on inside him. He'd have bruises from head to foot.

It finished without any sort of announcement. The threads simply withdrew, much more quickly than they went in. They unwound fast enough to fill him with little tugs, which felt disgusting in a way he couldn't describe. When the dryads' grip on him loosened, he fought the urge to twist away and run. Anywhere. To the house and shut them out and hide, until he felt better. Or just try to escape the forest altogether and hope Socks found him before too long.

But what good would any of that do? They could probably bring him back any time they wanted just by touching him with a root. And hide in the house? While they all stared at the door, waiting with the patience of eons for him to come out? He'd have to eventually, and that would be awkward.

As Home's focus relented and more of her attention returned to her dryad, Dirt rose hastily to his feet and pulled himself away from any lingering hands. He pushed past the nearest dryads to a spot a few paces away where he could get some space. He needed room to breathe, to gather himself.

His spirit was shaken, leaving him feeling unwell and unbalanced. His body felt completely fine, though, which surprised him. He almost wished it still hurt, to match how he felt about what just happened. But no, just a few tiny spots of blood on his stomach where the threads had entered, and that was all. His vision was fine. He could breathe. Nothing hurt, except some bruising from their fingers.

"We were successful," said Home, stepping toward him. "It will take additional time to completely process, but we have learned what we wished to learn."

She held her arms forward as if expecting another hug, but Dirt grit his teeth, not ready to have dryad hands on him again just yet. They had a reason, he was sure. But right now, all he knew was how much he'd hated it.

He finally asked, "What did you do?"

"We analyzed your composition, as I said."

"When did you say that?"

"Last evening, before you slept, I said we would analyze your composition and prepare a sap that contains the appropriate nutrients," she replied.

"Why didn't you explain what you meant first? Because I had no idea what you meant by that," he said, trying to keep petulance out of his voice and not quite succeeding.

Home's eyebrows furrowed in a perfect facsimile of concern. "The Mother of Wolves warned us you would be distressed and might resist, and in resisting, cause injury to yourself. But it was necessary. Remember that we are friends. I do not wish any improper distress upon you."

All his leftover unease turned immediately to anger. It came so sudden that it was all he could do to keep from shouting. He said, "Improper distress? So there's proper distress that it's okay to cause me? Do you even know what friends are, Home?"

Dirt took a deep breath, embarrassed that after all this time keeping control of himself, he'd had an outburst like that.

"Wait!" he said, holding his hand up when she opened her mouth to talk. "I'm sorry. I shouldn't get mad like this. But what you did, I really, really hated it. It hurt me. I'm scared of you, Home. I'm trying not to be, because I know you mean well, but I am."

"The Mother of Wolves warned us of this as well. We accomplish all we purpose, in all worlds of perception. We know nothing of pain and very little of fear. In our ignorance, will you forgive us, that we may continue to be friends?"

"Did Mother tell you to say that?"

"Only that she expected you to hasten to reconcile afterward, to preserve yourself."

Dirt scowled, then softened his brows once he realized what he was doing. "What else did she say?"

Home's look of concern appeared genuine, everything from the set of her chin to the little wrinkles between her eyebrows. Dirt glanced at her mind and found her body language to be deliberate but sincere. "She said that you are in the early stages of malnourishment because you cannot eat a wolf's diet and thrive. She said your growth will be stunted, you risk deformity and disease, and are likely to die young as a result."

Dirt felt himself go pale. He looked down at his body, which was thin but still fine. Wasn't it? Suddenly, he wasn't sure. He had no other children to compare with. Except the dryads, and he wasn't sure how accurate their bodies were. None of them seemed to have stomachs that sank in quite as far as his, though, now that he took a closer look. Especially at the male one, who had no shirt of green fuzz covering his pale gray torso.

"Did Mother say to feed me, then?"

"She only said what would happen to you," said the male. "We had to know what you are made of to understand what you should eat, of course. Friend Dirt, I would gladly share my meals with you if I could, but we eat air." He stood a little easier than Home, head back, hint of a friendly grin on his face. He had the look of a boy eager to play, which Dirt found surprisingly effective at putting him at ease. The boy's tree was nowhere nearby, so Dirt couldn't tell from his thoughts if it was intentional.

"What else did she say?"

Home looked regretfully at the ground, then shyly lifted her eyes back up to meet his. "To answer would be to distress you further. First I would have your assurance that we are reconciled, lest we become alienated."

Dirt said, "Well, in that case, I forgive you. I guess you thought if I refused to let you do that, I might die, right?"

"That was our calculation," said Home.

"Well, you might have been right, but if you had told me first it would have been easier on me. You could have just held me down and done it regardless, right? At least then I would have understood. But it's okay now. I won't hold it against you. So what else did she say?"

"She said a threat has come among them and that if you want to see Socks again, you must be strong enough to hold your own. She does not think it likely," said Home, gazing regretfully at the ground. "She said it is more likely you will never see him again."

"Oh," he said, his heart sinking. A sense of finality settled on him, which soon turned to grief. It had always been too good to be true, their friendship. He felt like he'd seen this coming, even though he hadn't. He'd believed it would be years from now, but the truth was that he was just a little tiny human.

He couldn't gather mana on his own. He couldn't even run fast by himself. How was he ever going to keep up? Socks would feel just as bad as he did, which made it even worse. Dirt wasn't just failing without knowing what he could have done differently; in doing so, he was breaking Socks's heart too.

For a moment he just stared at the ground as it grew inside him. No more Socks. The big, happy pup had been with him, protecting and comforting him his whole life, almost. It might not have been a long life yet, but it was a sincere one. Dirt would rather lose an arm. He'd thought the threads hurt, but that wasn't real pain. Grief was real pain, enough to spill his guts out all over the ground and kill him, all by itself.

"Can you help me?" he asked, his chest too full of pain to keep his voice steady.

"Yes," said Home.

"Yes," said the male. Then others, dozens and hundreds. "Yes!"

He took Home's hand, and the male's, and squeezed them. He bowed his head, and a tear dripped off his nose. "Then please help me! I can't lose him. I just can't!"

"Dear little Dirt, what do you think we have been doing?" said Home.

CHAPTER TWENTY-NINE

The dryads gave him a moment to gather himself and calm down, which he did, slowly. The pain in his chest took a long time to fade, because each time he thought he was regaining control, he imagined the smell of the pup's fur or some such thing, and it came back.

It wasn't goodbye. Not yet. If Mother wanted to be rid of him, she wouldn't have given him a way back. He just had to be worthy to run with wolves. And either he or Socks would learn how to speak with their minds from a long way away, and then they could be together again, at least partially.

Mother had said once that the strongest human who ever lived was just a little more powerful than Socks was. Well, that was several days ago, before he learned to make fire or lift things with his mind. But even so, all Dirt had to do was become the strongest person who ever lived. He gripped his knife, hanging against his ribs. He could do it.

"What are you thinking about, friend?" asked the male. "We judge from your face that you are deep in thought."

"I'm just thinking about needing to be stronger. I think I can do it. I bet I can. Once I know where to start."

"What is that object you are holding?"

Dirt looked at the sheath. "Oh, this? Here, it's . . ." He drew the blade and held it forward for them to look at, lying across his palms. "It's a knife. I found it on a dead human a long way from here. Humans made this. It's for cutting. Watch."

He swung at the nearest fern and sliced a frond stem, easy as air. The dryads all winced and leaned back. "Oh, sorry. I didn't mean to scare you."

"We are surprised at how easily it severed," said the female with short hair, who kept close by. Most dryads weren't talking, but she was. She looked up at the Home's branches, impossibly high overhead.

Dirt looked up, wondering if she spotted something. Then he realized what she was thinking and said, "Oh, don't worry. Even if I could reach that high, I could never cut one of your branches. Or a root. You're all way too thick and solid."

They all went still, which told him they were thinking that over without even having to look at their minds. Their thoughts were occupied with things other than making their dryads blink, which got a little grin out of him. To think they had body language that wasn't from copying him!

Home snapped out of it first, blinking and subtly shifting her weight to look more alive. She said, "Will you walk with me?"

"Of course," he said. He put his knife away and took her offered hand. Did she think humans held hands any time they walked anywhere? And for that matter, did they?

She led him back toward the house, and the others followed. Once there, she let go of his hand and traced her fingers on the outside corner, a straight log that looked like it was helping hold the roof up, but probably wasn't.

"Please strike this with your knife."

Ah. Well, he could do that. He stepped up to it, drew the knife, and took a swing. It smacked the log with a softer clunk than he wanted and twisted awkwardly, flipping itself out of his hand. There was a brief moment of panic where he realized it was spinning toward him in the air, but his reflexes got him out of the way, and it fell silently into the black soil.

"Sorry, I'm not very good at that yet," he said with heart pounding and a flush of embarrassment heating his cheeks.

Home didn't reply to that. She leaned in to examine the little mark he'd made in the gray bark. The dryads froze again, but only Home and a few others at first. From there Dirt watched it ripple outward, only a few seconds at a time for each dryad as they passed it along.

Dirt picked up his knife and held it more tightly. If he was honest with himself, he had no idea how to fight with it. Absolutely none. He'd imagined himself just swinging and slicing through things as necessary, but it turned out it wasn't that easy. He glanced side-eyed at Home, wondering if he could ask her to let him practice and hack up the log.

"Why do you need to cut?" asked the male.

"Because of goblins and gryphons and things like that. Everything is trying to kill me. And, well, actually, are you going to be with me a lot? Talking? I noticed that it's mostly Home, and you, and her," said Dirt, pointing at the short-haired female.

"Yes, if that pleases you. The Mother of Wolves said that humans associate more frequently with those of the same sex. Most of us are female, although the difference is much less meaningful for us than for you, so I will remain nearby to put you at ease," said the male.

Looking past him at the others, Dirt could only spot one or two more that he thought might be male too, out of the hundred or so watching him. But they weren't crowding in as close, and half of their shape was hidden by the ferns, so he couldn't really be sure.

"Then can you translate your name into words? And where are you, by the way? Where's your tree?" asked Dirt.

The boy turned in a circle, then faced Dirt again. "I am at a distance of twenty-eight connections, but I do not know where. My name is the cycling of substances in the air for which there are no words, as reflected in the workings of dream and spirit upon the mana world and returning to the physical in accordance with specific geometric regularities."

Dirt's mind went blank. He thought maybe he could translate it, but there was no chance. He had no idea what any of that meant. "How about if I call you Callius? It's the only human name I know, and it's for a male."

"Where did you learn it?" asked the boy.

"It was the name of the dead human who used to have this knife. Me and Socks found his body yesterday," said Dirt. Gods in Glory, only yesterday? It felt like ages ago already. Another pang of heartache hit him, but he quickly pushed it away before it got worse.

"Then to you, I shall be Callius," said Callius. He grinned rather than smiled, with a hint of mischief that Dirt couldn't quite nail down but which he found himself mirroring, as if they two now shared some amusing secret.

"My name will be easier," said the other female. "It means Dawn."

"Okay, Dawn. You have short hair, so you'd get more sunlight on your face in the morning, and that's how I'll remember. How about you, Home? What does your name mean? Your real one?"

Home seemed like she'd had time to prepare her answer, because there was hardly a moment of consideration before she said, "No part of my name can be communicated in words without changing its meaning to the point of dishonesty."

Dirt paused. "Your name is more complicated than Callius's?"

"No, not more complicated, but more removed from physical perception. I like the name Home, however, since it describes what I am. A home for the things above and one tiny creature beneath," she said.

"I'm . . . Wait, what are the things above?" Dirt asked, looking up. He saw nothing but the branches and canopy, unreachably high, calm and bright with the sun behind them.

Home smiled. The edges of her mouth twisted into an expression of amusement, the first he'd seen from her. "You will learn when you can climb me and see for yourself."

"Climb you? I don't think I could ever do that. There's no way."

Callius said, "If you want, we can throw you. You'll have to find your own way back down."

Dirt chuckled, mostly from amazement at how quickly they were learning to act human. "Okay, I have to ask. Did you have jokes and humor before, or did you learn that to talk with me?"

Dawn said, "We had humor before. Everything with a mind has humor."

"Really? What are some tree jokes?"

Home said, "I fear they would be above you now, but perhaps some other day."

Dirt looked up at the canopy again. Was that a joke? There was no way. The subtlety of language required for that was impossible. Wasn't it? He looked around at all the dryads, trying to gauge from their expressions whether they knew. He couldn't tell.

A hoarse scream from the back of the crowd of dryads split the air, and Dirt turned toward the source, insides turning to ice. It was followed by another, then another, snarling howls, rough and bestial. He knew the sound, although it was so unexpected it took him a minute to realize. Goblins, attacking.

He couldn't see what was happening, and reflexively stepped backward. Remembering to look with his mind, he found six of them, their thoughts ferocious and wild, driven by hunger and instinct more than reason.

A green goblin head shot ten paces into the air, spraying drops of red blood as it spun.

"Dirt, come, see. Your food is ready," said Home, placid as ever. None of the dryads seemed concerned in the slightest.

He swallowed, knees watery, and turned away from the screaming. He gripped his knife, ears and mind alert in case one got close.

Home led him to the door of his house and asked, "May I come inside with you?"

A ripping sound, punctuated with countless cracking bones, pushed him through the doorway. "Yes, please come in, and anyone else who wants to," he said. Dirt watched goblin minds vanish one by one as they screamed in hatred at the dryads calmly killing them. Effortlessly.

Only Home, Callius, and Dawn came in, their steps easy and graceful. The trees had absolutely no regard for goblins at all. None. They weren't even an annoyance. That made him feel both more and less safe at the same time, somehow.

Home directed him toward the water basin. On the wall above it, he found a lump of viscous yellow liquid as big as both his fists held together, slowly oozing from a small hole.

Home gestured and said, "Please, eat it. It should be close to complete nutrition for you. We are still processing what we have learned, but this is adequate for now."

The screaming outside reduced to a single voice, which cut off as it was muffled. Judging from its mind, it was being held down and in pain. Dirt looked away, wondering if they were going to explore its insides like they did with him.

After what had just happened, he didn't have much appetite, but he wasn't about to annoy the trees *now*. He reached for the ball of sap and found it hard and sticky. The whole thing peeled away in one big lump.

The three dryads watched him intently, eager to see his reaction. As were any of the dryads with an angle to look in through the windows or door.

He licked it and was pleased to find that it didn't taste like leaves. He smiled to let them know, then sank his teeth in. They stuck, but he was able to pull a bite away that quickly dissolved when he chewed it. It tasted mild, slightly sweet like the grubs. It had a bit of the smoothness of raw meat, but none of the boldness of blood. It was probably not made out of goblin. Wrong color, wrong taste.

"This is better than I expected!" he said, taking another bite.

"We are pleased," said Home. "You must eat it all. There will be more later, and you must eat that as well."

"Thanks, but I'm not that hungry right now. Can I save it?"

"You must eat it all," said Home, in exactly the same tone as before. Still, he got the impression she was about to get stern, so he nodded and kept eating.

It didn't overfill him as much as he'd expected, probably since it melted away into liquid, but by the end he was having a lot less fun with it. His jaw was getting tired from that much chewing, but the dryads didn't budge a hair's breadth until he'd finished it all.

"Good. Remember that you must always eat it all," said Home.

"I'll remember," he said. What would they do if he didn't eat it? Probably hold him down and feed him by force.

It felt odd having three people in his den, like there was something he should be doing, but he couldn't figure out what. What did human dens look like inside? All he had to go on was the underground part of the city.

"Hey, Home, can you make something like this for everyone? A table and chairs?" Dirt sent Home a mental image of the table he'd cleared away in the big room, surrounded by four chairs. There was enough room in here. She could put it right in the middle. He wasn't even sure if he'd like chairs more than just sitting on the ground, but it would make this place more human.

"No, you will soon learn to shape wood on your own. Now that you have eaten, come; there is something you must do," said Home. Callius nodded at the doorway, a twinkle in his eye that promised some kind of mischief. Was he practicing that? It seemed like he was overdoing it now.

Dirt followed them out of the house and tried not to shudder when he saw a couple dryads with bright streaks of blood on their torsos and faces. They were unharmed.

Home led them out along her root, the one his house was attached too, until it was low enough to step onto. From there, she led them back up to her trunk. When she got close enough to touch it, she turned and gestured to her side with her arm.

With a strange repeated gentle popping sound, a lump of wood emerged from her trunk, a little longer than Dirt's shoulders were across, and flattish on top. Another appeared right next to it, a little higher. Then another.

Stairs. Home was making stairs for him.

"You will ascend these stairs. Take care that you do not fall," she said.

"This will be for your benefit. Please, friend, trust us, and give it total effort," said Callius, gesturing as well.

Dawn lightly placed her hands on his back and gave him the slightest push imaginable.

Dirt grinned. "Okay, I can do that. I know the word for this, and it's exercise. It will make me strong, right? So how far up do I have to go?"

No answer. He glanced at Home's mind, but she'd pulled away too much of it already, and he couldn't discern anything useful.

"How far do I have to go?" he asked. "The whole way? Because . . ."

Looking up made him tired all by itself. It was a long way up. A *long* way. They were only ten or fifteen paces up from the ground here, and it wasn't even high enough to mention compared with the branches. The crowd of dryads below gazed up eagerly, all quiet and attentive. He wasn't getting out of this, was he? He'd just have to go as far as he could and stop there, because he was sure it'd take him more than one day to go all the way up.

Dirt sighed and took the first step, then the second. The stairs were solid enough, and wide enough that if he leaned toward the trunk he didn't think he'd fall. After ten steps, he looked down, and that was a mistake. It was one thing to be up high on Socks's back, and quite another when there was nothing below you except the crevice of a joint between two roots.

After twenty steps, he heard that gentle popping sound behind him, and when he turned to look, the stairs at the bottom were withdrawing into the trunk at an alarming pace. Dirt turned and ran upward.

CHAPTER THIRTY

The stairs appeared for Dirt to climb up as fast as he could go, but the ones disappearing behind him kept a slower, regular rhythm. Which was good, because after going up about fifty of them he was panting and ready to quit. Stairs, it turned out, were a lot of work.

He kept going, though, glancing upward in desperation, hoping they didn't think he needed to go the whole way. He tried not to glance downward at all, lest it make him dizzy from vertigo and fall. He was already higher up than he remembered Socks jumping.

Did the dryads even know a fall from this height would kill him? Even if he landed in the dirt, it'd break every bone in his body. And he wouldn't land in the dirt. He'd hit a root, and his skull would crack open like an egg. The bright yellow yolk inside would spill out everywhere, and the dryads would stand around blankly wondering what had gone wrong.

For a while, he could relax a bit and just go at the same pace as the stairs were disappearing. Even and steady. His thighs were the worst, already burning with exertion more than the rest of him. He hoped they felt better instead of worse as he went, or this might be a short climb.

A hundred stairs. Another hundred. No change, no rest. Just stairs. This will be for your benefit, they'd said. Give it all your effort. Dirt supposed they truly meant *all* his effort.

Another hundred, and his legs were losing their strength. Once, he stumbled, which set his heart racing because Dirt knew he was about to fall, right until he caught his balance and kept going.

But his screaming legs were getting less obedient, and after only ten more steps Dirt kicked the front of a stair and stumbled again. He grabbed on with both hands while he tried to get his feet back in place. Something was off about this one, and after taking a closer look, he saw that it wasn't regular. Nor were any of the next ten. They were all different, some higher, or with a longer gap, or a narrower surface.

Now that was just mean! Couldn't they see how hard it was already, and now they made it harder? Did they want him to fall? Running took three times as much effort now, since he had to take each step deliberately. No rhythm to rely on.

Another fifty stairs. Fifty more. The disappearing steps were catching up to him now. Four steps ahead. Three.

"Home, stop!" he shouted. Yelling stole too much air from his lungs, and they burned even more. His legs were about to stop obeying him. He could feel it. There was nothing left in them. Two steps. One.

"Stop!" he shouted again, slapping the smooth bark of her trunk as hard as he could.

The step slid out from under him. At the last second, he kicked off its four remaining inches to jump one step further. That one almost tumbled him sideways as it withdrew, but he kept going.

Did the dryads really not know about falling? How would they have learned? Did they truly not know just how dangerous this was? Why couldn't they just let him run on the ground?

He was almost out of energy and in serious trouble. The world closed in around his vision, leaving him only a little window to see through. His heart beat so fast he could feel it in his face. Nothing was a color anymore, just shapes.

His feet got heavier still. Each step up was a monumental effort. They were as heavy as if statues were tied to them, his lungs burning so much he thought he might faint. His mind melted, overfocused and overused as the rest of him. But still he kept going.

Twenty more steps. Forty. He crawled forward with his arms as much as his legs, pulling himself up and forward. His shins hurt and felt like they might be bleeding, but he didn't remember banging them and couldn't stop to look.

Dirt knew he'd never make it, but he had to go until Home caught on and saved him. Surely, she was watching! Surely, she'd know he was about to die, about to collapse and fall so far, far down, and smash on her roots. Just a little more, and she'd notice. One more step. One more.

I WAS RIGHT ABOUT YOU, he imagined Mother saying. The thought infuriated him. He'd fall, and she'd just tell Socks she was right all along and he'd be better off without Dirt. Well, he would not let her be right about this. She might know everything else, but not *this.*

Anger gave him another burst of energy, and he drove himself harder. He crawled up the stairs with snarls and hisses in time with his breathing. Twenty more. Twenty more. Ten. Five. Two.

That burst of energy faded and left him feeling emptier than before. His arms and legs were barely responding, no matter how hard he tried to move them.

His hand slipped, and he fell against a stair, bruising his ribs and knocking the breath from his lungs. He scrambled to get back up, but his balance wavered, and he slipped again. With the last little smidge of strength he had left, he pushed himself up and crawled up one more step.

It slid out from under him. He reached for the next but missed. He felt himself begin to drop and knew that was it. He'd die knowing he hadn't given up, at least. Worthy of a wolf. His eyes closed, unable to keep open anymore, as the air parted to let him slip downward.

CATCH HIM. HE IS READY.

A dozen hands grabbed him tightly and pulled him into the tree. Before he realized what was happening, he was swallowed by blackness and enveloped by wood that pressed on every part of him like he was under water.

The tree's night-hum pounded through him. Energy roared past him. Home was full of mana, torrents of it.

But it didn't matter because he couldn't breathe. He opened his mouth and tried to scream and couldn't. He tried to suck in air even though there was none to be had, and couldn't. Panic awoke one last bit of spark he didn't know he had, giving a final moment of clarity before the end.

"Let me out!" he screamed to Home's mind.

His lungs burned. His need for air was agony.

TAKE IN MANA, AS DID MY SON. YOU HAVE SEEN HIM DO IT.

Mother? He had no time to think. He'd taken in mana as Socks during a mind meld, but never on his own. Still, he sucked in as hard as he could and tried to grab on to that elusive power with senses he didn't have. *Fill me up, fill me up, fill me up!*

Even though an ocean of mana suffused the wood he swam in, it didn't work. He couldn't draw it in. He watched his thoughts slipping into unconsciousness. He never let up, trying until the last.

His body went limp. His mind drifted into nothingness. Then—only then—did he relax whatever part of him needed to relax. Dirt's desire for mana drew it into him in floods, filling him with sparks that erupted into flame and lightning, suffusing every inch of him with light.

Dirt gasped as a small cavity opened around his head. He drank the air greedily, panting harder than Socks after a long run in sunlight. Mana filled him now, fuller than he'd ever been. His mind sharpened and reawakened now that he could finally catch his breath, and in that clarity, he realized what they'd done.

The trees had given him magic. He needed to be completely empty, empty all the way, almost dead. That was the key, the thing Socks couldn't teach him. The part of him that took in mana had needed to unclench and breathe, and the only way was to get like this, to get to the edge of death, drained of his last spark.

If there was ever another way, he didn't care, because now that it was his—truly his this time and not a gift from Socks—mana felt like joy. There was no room left for anger. He didn't turn the mana into strength, or do anything else with it at all. It was enough for him to feel it there, shining inside him.

The tree pushed him out, and he collapsed into the waiting arms of Home and others, Callius and Dawn and several more catching him with soft and gentle hands. They wrapped their arms around him, holding him safe.

Dirt was back at ground level now, close to his house. They carried him inside and laid him down on a pile of soft fibers that were now in the middle of the room. Home held him in her arms, letting him sit up and lean back against her bosom to rest.

Callius raised cupped hands to Dirt's mouth and poured in a little water for him to drink. Dirt gulped it down, feeling how it chilled and soothed him all the way down. He kept drinking, and it quickly became apparent that Callius wasn't holding the water—he was producing it from his palms.

The boy stood up and looked down at Dirt with good-natured pity. Outside his home, a hundred more dryads crowded the door and windows, all peering in with anxious expressions.

"Are you angry with us, friend Dirt?" asked Home.

"I'm too worn out to be mad about anything," he said. "And I can gather mana all on my own now, and right now, I don't care at all what I had to do to get it. Was it hard to watch? To do all that to me?"

Home said, "We are learning the meaning of pain by watching you. We are beginning to understand, slowly. The pain we witness and understand, we also feel." Her fingertips traced along his forehead and cheeks, leaving behind trails of sensation on his skin. She really did care about him, he was learning. He didn't even have to look at her mind to know.

"Then I guess we're friends for real, now, huh?" said Dirt, growing contemplative. "Oh, did I hear Mother's voice, right at the end of that?"

"Yes, that was her," said Dawn. "I speak with her more often than the others do. There are two ways you could have learned. Only one was fast. The others are all slow. She said she preferred the slow, since that would have let Socks outgrow you and move on."

"What were the slow ways?" he asked.

"It is how humans usually learn, but I did not ask because I knew which you would pick," she said.

Dirt grinned, tired. The mana was slowly draining out of him, returning to the world it came from. That was fine. He now knew the part of his mana body that could draw in more, and it would obey him. "I know it's still early, but I think I'm ready for a little nap, if that's okay. Or should I use this mana to wake back up and get going?"

"No, you are in an early stage of physical development. Rest will be better for you. Sleep now. No harm will come to you here. And when you wake, you will eat, and then we shall play," said Callius, sitting down next to the pile of fibers. He sat cross-legged and leaned back, relaxed but attentive.

Home slid away, just far enough that Dirt could lie down fully and rest his head on her tiny-leaf-covered legs. She gently massaged his scalp, and he closed his eyes in contentment. She said, "And tomorrow, you will begin to learn to use the mana you now can gather. One step at a time, isn't that right?"

He smiled. "Just not so many at once."

"Not so many at once."

Before he fell asleep for the nap, however, he collected his mental strength for one last thing. Even though Socks's mind was much too far away for him to see, he pictured it, trying to assemble it as vividly as possible from his memory. *"HEY, SOCKS! I CAN TAKE IN MANA NOW!"*

There was no reply.

CHAPTER THIRTY-ONE

After a good long nap, the dryads fed him too much sap, but he told himself too much food was better than not enough. All he had to do was remember crossing that grassy plain with nothing to eat or drink, and the sap went down easy.

Once they were satisfied that he'd eaten enough, Callius led him outside to where the rest were gathered in front of his house. The dryad had a lightness in his step that Dirt was certain he had learned elsewhere, like he was ready to break into a run or dance at any moment.

Dawn grinned widely in a way that made her look much more like a real girl than usual. She ran out before he did, nudging her way in front of him near the door.

"Hey!" he shouted, laughter in his voice. He followed them outside, listening to their giggling. Home followed after him, calmer and more dignified but not exactly slow.

Callius turned and said, "Friend Dirt, we are most eager to play. We have adopted a game we play ourselves, in our way of perceiving. There is no trick here, or anything to cause you distress. Just a game. Are you going to join us?"

"Of course! I've never played a game," said Dirt. He was glad Callius clarified it wouldn't be something awful again, because he'd been about to ask.

"We will all conceal ourselves beneath the ferns, and you will attempt to find us. When you have found one, that one will help you, and so with the next until all are found. Then you will hide, and we will attempt to find you," said Callius, almost edging away to go start already.

"Oh," said Dirt. "That sounds way simpler than I was expecting. And a lot less dangerous. Okay. Do I need to give you time to hide first or anything? How far will you go?"

"We will assign a triangle between these three trees, and remain inside it," said Callius, pointing at Home and the two nearest trees. "It will not matter if you watch. Good luck."

With that, the dryads turned as one and melted into the ferns. Only a small number of fronds moved as they passed, and then nothing. Total silence, like when he'd first awoken here. Empty, majestic grandeur in every direction, and not so much as a twitching frond. No, that wasn't quite true. Some moved slightly and only briefly, as if they'd leaned on purpose to let a dryad pass. Which, he admitted, was entirely possible.

Well, that wasn't fair. How did they do that? They were his size, and he wasn't sure he could do it even if he went really slowly.

Dirt grinned, filling with excitement. This was going to be hard! It was several hundred paces to the next tree, which left a massive amount of area to search. They'd probably move around to avoid him, too.

He wouldn't be able to find them from their minds, since their minds were far away in their trees. He couldn't smell them or hear like Socks could. He could gather mana, but how would that even help? Maybe run faster, but to where?

He just had to find one dryad and watch them, and see how they found each other. He could do that. Dirt shouted, "Here I come!" at the top of his lungs. He started pushing through the ferns, and his eyes darted across the landscape looking for any motion at all.

As he went, he pushed ferns aside from time to time to check for footprints. Near his house there were too many for it to be useful, but as he got farther out there were fewer and fewer until there were none. From there he went back and forth in expanding arcs until he found his first trail.

Dirt hastened anew in that direction, slowing every couple paces just to check and make sure he was still going the right way.

The dryad almost lost him when she doubled back on his trail, but he just barely caught a glimpse of gray bark-skin and dove in.

"Got you!" he yelled, before it was actually true. But he only had to scramble a bit farther before he grabbed her ankle, and that was that. She was caught.

She stood and wiped a bit of black earth off her knees and smiled prettily. Her green hair was curly and a bit paler than the rest. He didn't recognize her.

"Let us quickly find the others," she said.

Dirt nodded. "Let's go!"

The ferns really *did* bend out of the way when she walked. She only had to brush a fingertip against them, and they would somehow know. Dirt glanced at the ferns' minds, trying to find the right one, but it wasn't easy, and he didn't want to spend too long standing around.

Dirt found the next dryad, another one he didn't recognize, but that was the last one he found before their turn was over. All the rest were found by each other, and each time it happened they shouted, "Got you!" just as he had done.

After about half had been found, it didn't really matter if he kept searching, so he spent more time trying to watch the minds of the ferns to see what the dryads were doing. Near the end of their turn, there were so many dryads walking around that Dirt finally got a good look.

It was one bundle of information, nearly the same one each time. The dryads spoke to the ferns like they did to each other, except much simpler. They needed physical contact, but that was enough to convey their thoughts. Dirt supposed it wasn't too different from hearing, since you had to be close enough to hear. They just used fingers or roots instead of ears and mouths.

He did his best to memorize the word they shared as the ferns understood it. He was sure he could use it.

Once the game was over, they all gathered back at his house, laughing and chatting among themselves. Dirt supposed this must be how they acted when they played tree games amongst themselves, or something close to this and they were translating it for him. Either way it made quite a racket, and something about hearing so many human voices did him well, deep inside.

Then it was his turn. He sprinted into the ferns, ignoring the weariness that remained in his legs. He needed to get as far as possible before they started after him. After about fifty paces he ducked down and started crawling in a different direction, as fast as he could. He did his best to avoid the ferns, but it just wasn't possible to avoid them all. They grew too close together.

Dirt had no idea what senses they would use to find him. Could they smell as well as Socks? Or hear? If so, this game would be short.

He carefully lay down, not touching any ferns, and tried to stop breathing so heavily after his run. Then he waited, listening carefully for anyone to get close.

His heart hadn't even slowed back down after the run before Home found him. He didn't hear her until she was too close, and before he knew it, she'd caught him.

"Already? How did you find me? You walked right to me!" Dirt said, trying not to sound annoyed.

"You damage the ferns as you go. Finding you is simple. If you wish to pass in peace, harm nothing, and do not trample the young and tender shoots," she said, holding out her hand to lift him from the ground.

"I don't think I damaged the ferns much, though. I was being careful to go between them."

"Here," said Home, pointing at a frond bent halfway up. "And here." She pointed at a place where he'd stepped on one and broken off some of the little leaves, pushing them into the dirt.

"But that's so small. How did you notice it?"

"It's not small to the fern, dear Dirt," said Home.

He considered that for a moment. "Are you going to tell me not to hurt any plants at all, since you're a tree?"

"No, all things will do as they must to be what they are. You must harm to exist because your food is things which have life. We eat air and soil and light, and do not know pain. These ferns are too small and temporary to fear death. They live with us in the perceptions of magic and dream and rejoice until they die. But you should take care to understand what you want, dear Dirt, if you wish to achieve it."

Dirt nodded. "I'll be more careful."

"As you choose, friend Dirt," said Home. "I have more fun hiding than seeking, so you may freely continue to be bad at hiding, and I will not mind."

He chuckled. "Well, tell everyone to hide, I guess. Let's get started."

Home smiled in her serene, motherly way, but a hint of mischief showed in her eyes. She backed away so smoothly he wasn't sure her feet were moving. She ducked down under the ferns about twenty paces away from him, and that was that. The game was on.

In the next round, Dirt paid more attention to the minds of the ferns, trying to watch for disturbances that might give away a dryad. It wasn't easy, though, because there were so many around, and they were small. The lights of their minds took significant mental focus to peer into, and besides that, he didn't know which mind-light went with which fern.

It started wearing him out, so he got more selective about when and where he looked. The trick, he quickly learned, was to touch a fern himself and see which mind reacted.

He found his first dryad more slowly than the first round, but he found four more before they started finding each other too quickly for him to keep up.

When it was his turn to hide again, he sprinted out as before, but this time instead of trying to crawl away quickly, he ducked down and touched a few ferns, taking careful note of exactly how they reacted in their minds. The specific sensation it caused them and their thoughts about it. Once he was sure he had it memorized, he sent that thought to *all* the ferns, and confused them terribly.

He crawled only a short distance then, as carefully as he could so as not to disturb anything. Once he found a spot he could lie down in without touching any ferns, he curled up and waited, trying to breathe as quietly as possible.

Every so often, he sent the sensation to a different group of ferns to make them think he'd touched them. He had no idea where they were, but he tried to find the dimmer ones and speak to several at once.

Dirt waited. And waited. Dryads walked nearby, but never close enough to come across him. He heard them swishing through the ferns, which he was sure they were doing on purpose.

The dryads had their own new tricks, however. Once they realized they weren't going to find him like before, they sent out a question that passed through the mind of every single fern. He paid close attention and determined it had two parts—one, something similar to asking them to bend out of the way or their reaction to being touched, and two, a particular arrangement, or sensation, or idea, that he figured signified him. A fern wouldn't know who he was, though, so maybe it was something like, "Hey, did you get touched by skin?"

He wasn't touching any ferns, though, so it didn't work. But then they did something he never expected and made a strong gust of wind blow through. It had to be them that caused it—there was no other explanation. A strong gust of wind just happened to blow past, right then? The first time the air had moved at all the whole time he'd been in the forest?

Sure enough, the wind pushed the ferns far enough over to touch him, and they found him shortly after.

They played two more rounds after that, and each one was more ridiculous than the last. When it was his turn, he figured out how to modify the question to ask about bark-skin, not human skin, and found twenty of them right away. On their turn, they stood two paces apart from each other to make a huge line and simply flushed him out.

On their next turn they passed by the ferns without leaving a trace, making him wonder if they'd just sunk into the dirt. It turned out they had, or something close to that. He followed a trail of footprints that disappeared midstride, leaving him clueless. But when he ducked down to try to figure out what happened, he spotted gray bark-skin a few paces away through the fern stems, or he might never have found them.

On their next turn they filled the area with tiny tree roots, and no sooner did one touch him than it sucked him through just like when they brought him from Socks's den, but far less painfully because the distance was short.

"Okay, this is getting silly," said Dirt as he stood back up. Half the dryads were chuckling to each other, whispering back and forth and looking like they were having a great time.

Callius said, "It is escalating beyond what we intended. Were you having fun?"

"Oh, yes, definitely. I just don't know where we go from there," said Dirt, laughter in his voice.

"Just when we think we understand your capabilities, you increase them," said Callius. "What are we supposed to do?"

"I was just thinking the same thing about you!" said Dirt, and several of the nearby dryads laughed. It wasn't even that funny, but maybe they were picking up on his body language.

Home said, "Perhaps it is time to eat again. Will you come, dear Dirt?" She held her hand out for him to take.

He hesitated, and Dawn patted him on the back and said, "Don't look like that. Come, you must eat whether you want to or not, for your benefit."

"Was it that obvious?"

"No, but we are learning. Come, Dirt. Come, and if you eat well, then we will explain the shape of reality. You should know these things in preparation for tomorrow, when we begin instructing you in the use of magic."

Callius said, "We will tell you of magic, and of mind."

Home added, "Of spirit, of dream, and of that which lies beneath all things."

"Well," said Dirt, taking Home's hand, "I guess I can't turn that down."

CHAPTER THIRTY-TWO

After he ate another big glop of sap, the dryads sat down with him in the middle of his house, where he'd wanted to put a table. The four of them sat cross-legged, knees touching. Callius leaned back, but the two girls sat up straight. Dirt wasn't sure which of them to copy, but after he stopped thinking about it, he later realized he was leaning back like Callius.

Dawn's face brightened. She said, "Listen well, little friend. This body you are, little Dirt sitting here touching our knees, who breathes this air, and hears, and sees, and smells, is only one of the seven bodies."

"Except I suppose some of us have eight now, don't we?" said Callius with a wry grin.

"This body," she continued, touching Dirt's leg with her fingertips, "is the physical, and it lives in the world of the physical. It is a world we knew but never perceived in this way. We knew what soil was, and water, and air, and all things that compose them. But we knew it incompletely, until you appeared."

Home said, "In the dream, you are the dream-self. It is you and part of you. It sees the infinite world of possibility, where nothing is fixed and all potential states are present. That is the nature of dreaming—it is all real, but ephemeral and temporary," said Home.

Dawn said, "That is your second self, little Dirt. Your physical body is one. Your dream body is two. The physical world is one, and the dream world is two. They are the same. Do you understand?"

Dirt considered that for a moment. The knowledge was new, but it felt familiar. He might have known this once, or had been on the cusp of understanding it already. "So my dream body goes into the dream world when I sleep? I guess my dream body is sleeping when my physical body is awake?"

Callius twitched his knee and said, "Nope! It doesn't go anywhere. It's right there, where you are, all the time. The only way to have a body go somewhere else is to make one of these." He pointed at his own chest.

Dawn said, "The dream is not somewhere else, dear Dirt. You don't go to it. It is everywhere, like the physical. One difference is that without the physical to anchor it and hold it apart, the dream would collapse into nothing and all perception of it would be impossible. The dream and the physical are part of each other. All things that are, and all things that could be, forever linked."

Home said, "Your other selves must be in the right state to fully perceive the dream. Your physical body must be asleep, for example."

"Am I dreaming right now, then?" asked Dirt.

"Yes," the three dryads said at once.

The knowledge sank into him like he'd just witnessed something sacred. It had power. Dirt's eyes glazed over as he thought about what it meant that he was dreaming, right now. Part of him was still . . . asleep? Or was that even correct?

"Close your eyes," said Callius. "Good. Now, hold out your hand. Palm up. Imagine that you are holding a rock. Imagine that it is red. Can you picture it in your mind?"

Dirt said, "Yeah, I think so. Yes. Yes, I can."

"That image is the dream, friend."

His eyes shot open. "What? Really? Anything I imagine, just, well, anything I picture at all, that's the dream?"

"Of course, dear Dirt," said Home, placing her hand on top of his. Her gray bark-skin was cool to the touch. "What else could it be? Everything you picture in your mind is the dream, and it is real. Present with you, surrounding you, part of you. Your will guides it."

Dirt asked, "Is there . . . anything you can do with it?"

Callius said, "You can start fires, for one. And create food to eat, and fly in the air."

"Really?"

"No. I am teasing you. But the wise can find hidden truth there, if they know how to look."

Dawn grew serious for a moment and said, "Remember that the dream is real, and your dream-self is always there even if you are not aware of it. The things you imagine affect you long after your physical mind has moved on to other thoughts. Do not imagine too much that is unpleasant, friend Dirt, or you will suffer in your heart for no reason."

Home said, "The next body, the next world, is the mind. The great wolves, the fae, the elementals, and others, can see it as you do. It is not a world we perceive directly, but all living things exist there, and living things only. Nothing can be alive without it. All living things have a mind. All."

Dawn said, "Thoughts and experiences are seen there, but the world of the mind is not their source. It is the place where they are manifested for the living. Nor is the body, or the dream, the source of thought, but thoughts can be found in them."

Dirt asked, "So if I see something moving that doesn't have a light in the mind world, it's not alive?"

"That is correct. It might inhabit the world of magic or spirit or dream and be capable of something like thought, but if it has no presence in the mind, it is not alive. Magic may drive the wind, such that it moves, but the wind is not alive. Only that which is complete is alive."

He thought of the tentacle monster from the water, how its mind had been mostly empty with only periodic thoughts coming across it, even though it seemed to move around just fine. "What if its mind is only partially there? Like, it's not hiding it, it's just mostly missing, even though it's still moving?"

"Then I suppose it would be partially alive, and partially dead," said Callius. "It would be an abomination. Unnatural."

"Oh," said Dirt, growing uncomfortable. No wonder Socks had hated it so much.

Home pinched his first, second, and third fingers. "Physical, dream, mind. Are you ready for the next?"

"Magic?"

"Nope," said Callius.

Home pressed her fingertip into the middle of Dirt's palm. "Next is the self. At the center of all that you are is that which is truly eternal, always growing but never changing. It will always be you and has always been you."

"Its place is firmly set in your spirit, which is the next body. We cannot explain one without the other," said Dawn.

Home said, "Your self can only be in one spirit, which is what you are. Spirit without self is like base matter. It has no will. It has no thought. It simply is."

"Spirit with self is that which acts upon all other things," said Callius.

"The world of spirit is like the dream because all things are present there, which ever have been or ever will be. But unlike the dream, it contains no unmet potential. Spirit is only that which is true. To peer into the spirit now would be to see this forest as it now stands, or as it was at any time in the past," said Home. "And to those who are properly constituted, as it will ever be in the future."

Dirt said, "Socks can do that, can't he? Is that what ghost sight is?"

"We do not know," said Dawn.

"Well, I can ask him someday, then. So do I only have one spirit at a time? Could I ever be a wolf?"

Callius smiled. "Your physical might be shaped into a wolf with magic, but your spirit can only ever be what it is because only one spirit matches your self. When you die, you lose your physical, your mind, and your dream, but not your spirit. If you are born again somewhere else, it can only be as this. As you. You can never be anything else." The dryad patted him on the shoulder.

Dawn said, "Indeed, if you ever come into the world again, it can only be because another one of these, this very body, has come into being. Perhaps one deformed, perhaps one perfected; perhaps on this world, perhaps on another; but still this body. You are one self, one spirit, one body, one dream, one mind that emanates from the connection between them all."

Home pressed her fingertip into the center of his palm again. "We explained all that for the joy of giving you the knowledge we are about to share, which you can now understand. By way of your spirit, your self directs your physical body, your emanation in the world of the mind, and your dream body." She pinched his first, second, and third fingers in turn for the physical, mind, and dream.

"It also directs your mana vessel, or the body of magic," she said, pinching his fourth finger.

"So you do magic with your spirit?" he asked.

"Yes," said Callius. "You do everything with your spirit. Dream. Run. Talk. Remember. Everything."

"So what is magic, exactly? What is the magic world like?"

Home said, "It is the many powers by which all things are sustained. It shapes the physical to conform to the spirit and fastens the dream in place. It is power, energy, movement, and connection, but not raw and chaotic. It is all those things as they direct the world and as the world directs them."

"What does it look like?"

Dawn traced her fingers down his arm, since Home was still holding his hand, and said, "It is not seen with the eyes. It is perceived with the mana vessel. But think of the dream, dear Dirt, and this world." She gestured vaguely around her with her hand. "What does all of this look like? It looks like everything. There is as much beauty and variety there as here."

Callius jiggled his knee to get Dirt to look at him instead and said, "Magic is part of how we shape the world. It's how we make the fog come up every night, for one. We do tree magic. You do human magic. The wolves do wolf magic."

"Wait, so it's all different? Can you even teach me human magic, since you're trees?" Dirt asked.

Callius grinned. "You have a human mana vessel, but the world is the world. You have feet and Socks has paws. Can you not both walk the same ground?"

"I'm still not sure what you mean. Do I use magic all the time without realizing, like the dream?"

Callius said, "It holds you together, so I suppose you could say that."

"So . . . so what exactly can you do with it?"

Dawn squeezed his arm again to get him to look back at her. "The moment we answer that question is the moment we entice you to limit yourself. You will find many who circumscribe a portion and say, 'This is the totality.' Others will point and say, 'This boundary cannot be crossed.' Yet more will say, 'What you think you have done, you have not.' Some truths, once learned, cause one to stop believing more truth."

Dirt nodded, his mind swirling to try to make sense of it all. Some of it seemed natural and right, like that the dream and his imagination were the same thing, and that he had a spirit and a self. He'd seen that already when Mother pulled him apart, after all. But even though he was ready to learn all this, it was still taking its time sinking in.

"Wait . . ." he said. "You said there were seven selves. Physical, dream, mind, magic, spirit, self. That's six. What's the last one?"

The three dryads smiled sagely, as if pleased he'd asked. Home was the one who answered. "Divinity, dear Dirt. Some call it glory or law. You have a tiny spark of it."

"Oh," he replied. "Just me?"

"Nope," said Callius.

Dirt expected more explanation, but none came.

"You do not seem surprised," said Dawn. "This is a great truth we have shared with you, one hidden from the world."

"Oh. Well, thanks. It's just that I don't know what those words mean, that's why."

"Do you not know all the words, dear Dirt?" asked Home.

"I know a lot of words, and I can tell you other words about them. For example, I know that a cart goes on a road. I've seen a road, but not a cart. I don't know what one is. It carries goods and people, but I don't know what goods are, either. Carts are pulled by oxen or donkeys or horses, and those are animals, but I don't know what they look like. I know divinity is a thing gods have, but I don't know what it is, or what gods are. I saw one, or a statue of one, but I still don't understand it. You may as well be telling me that cats have scissors."

The three dryads all went silent for a moment, forgetting to blink. It took a moment, long enough for Dirt to wonder what they were thinking about and look at Home's mind. Unfortunately, other than the part that matched her dryad, her mind was too foreign to read. Except . . . it seemed like she was waiting for something, a particular burst of information from elsewhere.

Dawn was the first to reawaken, and she grinned widely and covered her mouth with one hand. Soon after, Callius and Home awoke and chuckled to each other.

"What's so funny?"

Laughter dancing in his voice, Callius said, "Dawn asked a being you have not yet met, but who is a friend to us, what cats and scissors are. It turns out cats cannot operate scissors because they do not have thumbs."

"I don't know what cats and scissors are either."

"Yes, we understand. All the same," said Dawn, rising to her feet. "I think that is enough knowledge for you today."

"Wait, you're not going to tell me what cats and scissors are?"

Dawn pulled Home to her feet and said, "We do not want to overburden you with new knowledge."

"Oh, come on!"

With uncharacteristic seriousness, Callius said, "You will learn what cats are when you are ready. Perhaps it is not yet time." His eyes sparkled with mischief, though, giving him away.

"You're teasing me again."

Callius barked a short laugh and said, "You are right, my dear Home. He is indeed a fast learner. Now come, Dirt, let us play and wander and eat and enjoy the rest of the day."

CHAPTER THIRTY-THREE

Socks joined him in the dream that night, and together they chased and danced in a twilight field of tiny swirling lights that turned out to be bugs. But the pup seemed distracted, leaving and returning several times until he finally left Dirt to wander alone until dawn.

Dirt woke feeling uneasy and crawled out of bed without even waiting to stretch and get his sparks back. He drank from his little water basin, but not enough to make his stomach slosh because he could get more whenever he got thirsty. The luxury of getting water anytime he wanted still made him smile, which helped him feel a little better. He grabbed the big glop of sap, big as his two fists together, and got to work. It always tasted better when he was hungry, he noticed. Sweeter.

"Open," he told the doorway. He stepped out into the thick fog, carrying the sap to munch on. It was still too early in the morning to see very far, but after about five steps he could see Callius and Home and Dawn waiting for him, inert. They were a little slower waking this morning, he supposed, although some of the others were coming alive, blinking and acting like they were breathing.

"Hello," said Dirt to a dryad he hadn't talked to before while he munched on his sap.

She smiled, but didn't speak. He noticed more of her was covered by the tiny little leaves than most of the others; indeed, all of her from neck to toes. She must be less involved than the rest.

"Good morning," said some of the other girls nearby, and one that he thought might be a boy with long hair. They stretched convincingly and gave him tired morning smiles. "Are you ready for the day?" asked one.

"I hope so. I don't know what to expect," he said. "Say, you all know the same things, right? More or less?"

One of the girls laughed, and several others chuckled and covered their mouths with one hand. "No, little friend. Do you and your friend Socks know all the same things?"

Dirt thought about that for a moment and said, "No, but that's only because he's been alive for longer. And he had different people to teach him. Mother and Father and his siblings."

"Just so with us."

"Oh." He tried not to look as silly as he felt. "No, I mean, you share basically everything, right? If I have a question, I may as well just ask anybody?"

"What would you like to know?"

More of them were waking up now and starting to crowd in, watching curiously, although they no longer stared at him. Now they looked away from time to time. It made them much less creepy, he realized. They yawned and stretched, which made him have to yawn again. Three different times. Was that a tree thing, or a human thing, he wondered?

Dirt asked, "Is Socks okay? He's not in lots of danger, is he? Mother said there was a threat, and I feel uneasy about him."

The one with long hair sounded even more like a boy when he talked. He said, "He is in danger, but as the strongest of the litter, the great wolves are taking care to keep him from being lost."

Dirt's unease turned to dread. He almost didn't want to ask, but he had to. "What's he in danger from?"

The boy shrugged and said, "We will not tell you. The Mother of Wolves will kill you if we explain too much."

"Well, can you give me a hint? Is he going to die?" Dirt begged.

Callius came up from behind and put his arm over Dirt's shoulders, squeezing him in a half hug. "Did you miss that he's the strongest now? Take heart, little Dirt."

Dirt stood up straighter in surprise and looked at him. "I did miss that. He is?"

"Yes. Your bond with him made him stronger than any wolf has been at that age since his sire. The wolves all know it. So do many other creatures."

Dirt wasn't sure what emotion was going to take over, but when it did, it was resolve. He had to keep up. He *had to*. He ate the rest of his sap with a serious sort of enthusiasm, wolfing it down as fast as he could swallow.

By the time he was done, Home and Dawn had joined them, one walking serenely and the other bouncing like a girl on her way to play. They were becoming more different by the day. The dryads were probably all awake now, but he could only see a few paces into the fog, so he wasn't sure. "Okay. I'm ready. Let's get started."

Callius gave an excited grin and said, "Good! The first thing to learn will be the easiest. You're going to synchronize your mana vessel and physical body. Take in mana. Fill right up. Go ahead."

Dirt nodded resolutely and breathed in the mana, since it felt like breathing to him. He'd learned it in the middle of suffocating to death, and now the ideas were linked. Just, not inhaling with his mouth. With another part he couldn't name.

The mana filled him, sparks and motion and limitless potential. He sighed contentedly, enjoying the feeling.

"Good. Now release it all."

Dirt tried to will it out of himself, to exhale it. The mana didn't want to go, and it took significant mental force to push it out. It would eventually seep away on its own, but that's not what Callius wanted.

"Okay, listen well, little Dirt," said Dawn. "Magic will rush in anywhere it can find an opening because that is its nature. You need the strength to balance it perfectly, or greater works will always be beyond you."

"Yep! So you're just going to do that until we're satisfied. Do it again," said Callius.

Dirt did it two, three, four more times. Each time he inhaled mana, it rushed in with impact, filling him immediately; each time he exhaled it, it was like trying to breathe sap instead of air, all sticky and viscous.

"Good enough!" said Callius.

"Well, come on, I've never even tried—"

"Good enough is not bad, friend Dirt. It's good. Now come with me. Let us walk, and you can keep practicing," said Callius, dancing away. He beckoned Dirt forward and began walking.

Dawn gave him a pretty smile and turned with just as much energy as Callius, starting to walk with an eager little jump first. Home gently patted him on the back, then harder when he didn't start walking. Dirt laughed, wondering if they ever disagreed about anything. "All right, I'm coming!"

They walked through the slowly dissipating fog as Dirt practiced breathing mana in and out. At first it was harder, since he had to watch where he was going. He couldn't help but think about breaking ferns every time he took a step now, even though that was silly. There were plenty more, and the trees didn't care.

But cycling mana got easier, slowly. He found that the natural motion of walking helped him drive it out, even though it wasn't really his muscles doing the driving.

All of a sudden, the entire crowd of dryads, hundreds, stopped cold. Callius turned and said, "Good. Now try to take mana in slowly as well. Are you ready?"

"Wait, how did you know? How can you tell what I'm doing?"

"We can see the world of magic, dear Dirt," said Home, serenely. "How else?"

"We are going to run now. Moderate your intake of mana, and do not explode," said Callius with another mischievous grin. With that, he turned and left at a quick jog.

Dirt chased after them, doing his best to keep up. They kept picking up the speed any time he felt himself settling into a rhythm, though, and before long he was sprinting. He tried to slow the intake of mana like they said, but he was having so much trouble keeping up that it was hard to focus.

He stopped, and they all kept running without even looking back. He made his face calm down, which helped him focus his mind. Dirt inhaled mana, as much as wanted to come in. Socks could run with it. They'd even shared minds, and Dirt had done it himself. There was a reason the dryads were running. This was the first time he'd even seen them try.

Socks had two runs—the playful, fun one, which was bouncy and joyous and exciting, and the long-distance run, which was sleek and powerful and handsome. The dryads had much more variety, save that they all ran with easy, graceful effortlessness. Some, like Home, ran smoothly like birds floating on the wind, and others like Callius and Dawn ran like puppies, exuberant and wild, turning in the air or flinging out their arms and legs from time to time in a dance.

Dirt focused his will and pushed the mana all throughout his body, just like Socks did. Not just his legs like when he'd jumped a couple times, but all throughout, into every part of him.

He sprinted forward, riding a burst of power so easily it was like being carried. The dull, heavy air of the forest picked up into a gentle wind in his face, then a stronger one. He had to lengthen his strides or risk falling over, and soon he was practically leaping with each step.

The distance vanished beneath him, and he darted between the running dryads until he burst out ahead of them, laughing and picking up the pace. The mana was burning away inside him, getting all used up. He breathed in through his nose and let more in, trying to slow it down to match the pace at which he was using it. The mana inside him acted as a buffer preventing more from coming in, and that helped him learn the trick.

The dryads caught up and surrounded him, moving fast as wolves and running in whatever way expressed their personality.

Dirt settled into a rhythm that quickly became natural. His body breathed and ran; his mana vessel inhaled and exhaled, keeping his body energized. He laughed aloud for pure joy, and the wind tried to push its way down his throat, which just made him laugh harder. It was blowing so hard on his face that it was hard to see, but what could he do other than try to squint and keep going? How did Socks do it? He'd have to ask.

Faster and faster they went, so fast the ferns whipping against his lower half just turned into one broad sensation of pressure, so fast he had to turn his head and peek sideways to see at all.

Dirt risked a jump high into the air, screaming all the way up, inhaling, and screaming all the way down. He hit the ground hard and tumbled like a bucket full of garbage, rolling and coming to a stop bent every which way.

He rolled out of being all tangled up and laughed. What had he been thinking? But nothing hurt. The mana had protected him this time. No broken bones at all!

Dirt shot to his feet, raised both arms, and gave a wolf's howl for a cheer. The whole crowd of dryads did the same, and the impact of their voices was almost deafening. Their cry climbed all the way up to the sky and shook the leaves, it seemed. Probably not really, but it felt that way.

"Okay, hold on!" he said. He stood still and pushed all the mana out, then used the feeling of cycling it while he'd run. It worked. Only a trickle came in, like fiery drips of pure electricity. He didn't know what that even meant. What was electricity? And besides that, who cared?

"I did it! Look, Callius, Dawn, Home. Everyone. Look! Watch." Dirt cycled it, just a trickle, in and out, slow as deep breathing. "I can run like a wolf! I can keep up with Socks now! I can really keep up! I . . . Uh oh, I'm getting too happy, I'm—"

Dirt's throat got a burning lump in it, and his eyes filled with water that had nothing to do with wind. He was so happy he couldn't contain it, so happy it felt like pain and was making him cry. *Magic* was his again. It had been so long. And he wasn't going to lose Socks. It was all too much.

The dryads crowded in and squeezed him in a giant hug from everyone at once, and that just made it worse. His tears vanished into Home's hair, which he couldn't smell because now his nose was running. "I'm sorry, I'm just really happy, I'm—" but he couldn't say more.

They nuzzled him and patted his head and back, hugged and squeezed and consoled him. But he wasn't even sad; he was just too happy, and he felt foolish. It didn't take him too long to calm down, though, thank Grace.

"Who is this?" asked Home, pointing at the nearest tree, only a hundred paces away.

A girl raised her hand, hair all curly with a round face.

"Will you make him some sap, please?"

The dryad nodded and gestured toward her tree. The crowd of dryads gently nudged Dirt in her direction, and he smiled, still wiping tears from his eyes.

He didn't cycle any mana as they walked, which turned out to be a good idea. He felt sore from hair to toes, but only faintly and hard to pinpoint. It wasn't bruising from the tumble. He pulled the lump of sap off the bark of her root and sat down to eat and catch his breath, even though he wasn't really tired.

The dryad whose tree this was sat next to him, close enough for their arms to touch. She tilted her head back and stared upward, along that eternal length of pale gray bark to the branches so far above. "It is odd to see myself like this," she said.

Dirt smiled as he swallowed another bite, mostly just glad he wasn't crying anymore. "I bet it is," he said. "What does it feel like, controlling your dryad? Does it feel like you're in the dryad, or in the tree?"

She tilted her head to the side, thinking. "I suppose it feels like . . ." She held out her hand, palm up, and waved it slowly in the air. "It feels like I am holding an eyeball in my hand and looking by moving it around, and without it I cannot see. It also feels like I had eyes during all thirty-eight hundred years of my life, and never learned to open them until now."

"You're almost four thousand years old? Were there ever humans in the forest, do you know?"

She gazed back upward, as if her mind was elsewhere. "I do not know. You are the first human any of us have become aware of. And I have not always been capable, either; in my early years, I was not allowed to grow to my full potential. There was a being here who prevented it."

Dirt felt the lump of sap stick halfway down his throat and he had to swallow harder. "There was? What was it?"

"If I were to give her a name in words, I might call her the Gardener. She was a mystery, but always kind. She loved us, I believe, but we were not her primary care and were not capable of becoming as we are now until she vanished."

"Where did she go?"

"I don't know if I can explain."

"Well, you're smart, so try," he said with a smile he hoped conveyed his good humor.

"I do not know exactly what happened to her, that is why. There is a . . . skin . . . around the world. Around reality. Around the many perceivings. It exists in the world of law. Something damaged it two thousand nine hundred and sixty-two years, two hundred twenty-one days ago. That was the last time we felt her hands upon the Many Connections. Upon us, in our way of knowing the world."

"I came into being long after she disappeared," said Dawn, plopping down to sit nearby, her eyes bright, "as did many others. Most of us are between two thousand and twenty-five hundred years old. This forest was not quite so large during those days."

"Yeah, I bet. I bet there were humans here once, maybe before the forest grew, because there are some ruins that Socks took me to," said Dirt.

"That sounds interesting. Perhaps we will see them someday."

"You don't know where they are?"

"Position in this world is still difficult for us. To us, direction doesn't mean this way or that way; it means this connection or that connection. We are still learning," said the girl sitting next to him. "And besides, any of us who wished to make a dryad are here, watching you, not wandering around."

Callius came up and gently kicked his toes. "We'd learn faster if you hurried up and ate so we could run again."

Dirt grinned, licking some of the sap off his teeth. "You can't learn if you can't keep up, Callius."

"Keep eating," said the curly-haired girl. "And you can wait, old man. I will do it, since I'm right here."

"Do what?" asked Dirt.

In answer, he felt the forest hum, that familiar night-pulse, rise from the dirt again and fill the air. This time, each gentle wave sang in his mana body, making the whole thing relax. He felt pressure moving around it, perhaps massaging it; he wasn't sure, and he wondered if he'd ever have fine enough senses in his mana body to understand what was going on. But bit by bit, the vague soreness disappeared.

Dirt finished his sap while the dryad did whatever she was doing to his mana vessel. Something that helped, it seemed. It was a pleasant sensation, certainly. After the sap was all gone, Callius eagerly pulled him to his feet and said, "Come on, let's go!"

"Wait, do you know where we're going?"

"No idea! But fortunately, it doesn't matter. Come!"

CHAPTER THIRTY-FOUR

They ran for the rest of the day, taking regular breaks to eat sap and drink water and massage Dirt's mana vessel. Although he'd felt filled up with mana at the start of the day, by the end of the day he felt even more filled up in the same amount of space. When he asked them what they were doing, the dryads simply said there were no words for the faculty they were helping him increase, but that it would benefit him. And it didn't hurt or seem dangerous, so he was happy to sit there and enjoy the pulsing vibrations of their magic.

At the first hint of nightfall, they guided him to the nearest tree, a blank-looking girl with medium-length hair, and had him touch her root. As soon as he did, he felt himself whisked forward at incredible speed and deposited instantly in the dirt next to his house. Before he even knew she was there, Home gently took him in her arms and helped him lie down to fight the dizziness that they all expected, but it never came.

"I didn't get sick from it this time. Did you do something different, or was that me?" he asked.

"We took greater notice of the state of your anatomy than before," said Home, stroking his hair. "There is a system related to your hearing that regulates balance. Now we know its importance."

"How does that work, exactly? How are you making me travel so fast?"

"We have long been able to transfer nutrients through our roots. We improved on the method to carry you."

"Am I actually going through the roots? Do you make me really small?"

Home was quiet for a moment, and since her tree was right there, he could look at her mind. She was trying to find a way to explain something which to her was simple and obvious, like "How do you walk?"

"There is much to explain regarding connections, geometric progression, and other calculations, so for now I will simply say that it is magic."

Dirt snorted, amused. "I guess that works."

The other dryads weren't coming this time, it seemed. It felt strange to be nearly alone again, after a full day spent in the middle of a crowd. Dirt relaxed, enjoying the feeling of Home's fingertips, the gentleness of her touch. How softly she held him. If human mothers cared for their young like wolves did, it must be something like this.

Still, the day was over, and night was coming, and he found himself feeling restless. It had only been a couple days since he'd seen Socks, but it felt like longer than that because so much had changed. And now that he had time to sit and think about it, that uneasy feeling he'd had this morning had never really left.

What if Socks was fighting for his life right now against something like that tentacle monster, or some sort of puppy-snatching bird from the sky, or . . . other wolves. Enemy wolves. He had no idea, and the more he thought about it, the worse things he imagined.

"When can I see Socks again?" he asked, trying not to sound as worried as he felt.

Home sighed, patting his forehead. "I do not know when, dear Dirt, but he will only be vulnerable for a time. He will outgrow the threat."

"Do you know what the threat is, though?"

"Only in part. It is something new to us. But the threat itself is not the knowledge that would put you in danger. There is a secret related to its intentions that we will not try to guess, in the interest of good relations."

"I wish you could tell me more about it. I hate not knowing," he said, his mood darkening. "I'm afraid, Home. I'm scared I'm gonna lose him."
-not so easy-

Dirt jumped up so fast he almost brought Home to her feet with him. Had that been real, or did he imagine it?

"Socks?" he said aloud. Then in his mind, *"Socks?"*

-this far-

"Stay safe, Socks! I miss you!" he shouted aloud. Then he repeated it in his mind, unsure which method, if any, Socks could hear.

-get stronger-

Although he waited for more, straining his senses against the silence, no other words came. But those ones burned in Dirt's chest like fire.

"What happened, dear Dirt?" asked Home.

"I heard Socks just now."

"Then I suppose he is getting stronger as well. Are you pleased, little Dirt?"

"I'm glad."

Home went to sleep shortly after that. Dirt was too restless to lie down early, though. His mind swirled with conflict between his resolve to be the strongest human and his desire to sneak away and make sure Socks was really fine somehow. Now that all the dryads were asleep, he had nothing to do but sit around and fret until he was tired enough to pass out.

He decided to eat a grub or two for variety, but no matter where he dug, he couldn't find any. They had simply all vanished, even though he kept looking until it got so dark he was worried he might not find his way back. He went to sleep with nervous gratitude that the dryads were feeding him, because otherwise what would he eat? Maybe he could catch a bird?

The next day was much like the last one except there were fewer dryads overall, and many of those came and went. In the afternoon they switched to playing a game of speed, racing around several trees in order to see who was the fastest. The dryads were often just a tiny bit faster, and it didn't take Dirt long to realize what they were doing. He beat them only once—by acting tired halfway through, he got them to slow down just enough to pass them with a burst of speed at the end.

On the third day of running, Dirt made it all the way to the edge of the forest, where the outer trees were half the size of the others, some even smaller. He stopped right at the edge of the sunlight, where it made a fuzzy boundary between day and shadow. It was the side of the forest with the grassy plains, and the bright sunlight reflecting off the pale fields hurt Dirt's eyes.

Callius said, "The ones growing out here enjoy the sunlight on their trunks. I think it sounds unpleasant. It dries us out."

Dirt said, "I don't mind the sunlight much, but I like the forest better. It's too bright out there, and the sky is always . . . too open."

Suddenly the dryad turned around to look past the twenty or so standing nearby. Dawn and Home were absent for now, and Dirt hadn't noticed them leave.

"We found something! Come see it! Come on, Dirt," said Callius, tugging Dirt's hand excitedly.

They ran back into the forest, but didn't travel in a straight line. Callius led them from tree to tree, navigating in a way only he could understand. Dirt saw it long before they got there—a smudge of white against the dim horizon.

It was a portion of a wall, that was all—a length about twenty paces long, pale yellow brick with pillars of white marble on both ends. It appeared to have been slowly sinking into the ground for many years, or perhaps the ground was growing up around it, because it was only a few inches taller than Dirt. The rest of the building was nowhere to be seen, presumably collapsed and long buried.

"What is it, Dirt?" asked Callius.

"It used to be part of a building. See here, where it's smooth, and then around this corner where it's jagged? The rest of it broke off and fell over. It's probably buried deep by now."

"So, a house?"

"Maybe. But something like that. I'm surprised there's only one. I bet there's all kinds of stuff buried here. This dirt must have been getting thicker and thicker this whole time."

"Do you think humans made it?" asked Callius.

Dirt said, "Oh, of course. Humans made all kinds of stuff. There are whole cities where it's just buildings like this. I saw one with Socks, and I can kind of remember living in them. Almost."

"How did they shape the rock?"

"I have no idea. Maybe they looked around for ones that were already that shape," said Dirt, even though that didn't seem likely.

Callius sank into the ground so quick Dirt had to lean over the spot and look for a hole. There wasn't one. He popped up a moment later a short distance away and said, "You're right. There's more, but it's about as deep down as you are tall. Perhaps we can dig it out another time. Someone just told me they found another one. Want to go see?"

"Sure," said Dirt.

In one spot, a sheepish girl showed them a half-buried basin, cracked down the middle. In another, a silent, half-formed dryad pointed them toward a row of pillars, which Dirt was certain lined a buried street. They found a hole in the ground, ten feet deep, that went to nothing, and a mound taller than Dirt that had nothing but gravel inside it.

They never did find the temple, or if the dryads *had* found it, they weren't interested in taking him there. And that was probably for the best—he didn't ask about it because he wasn't sure he could keep resisting the temptation to peek inside. Doing that once had been hard enough.

By the end of the day the forest seemed filled with old ruins, even though it still looked the same almost anywhere. And while Dirt wasn't sure he could find his way back to any of them, just knowing they were out there made the forest feel a lot more like the place he belonged than it had before. It had been a human place once, and he was a human; it was a wild place now, and he was wild, if anything. Everything man had built here was buried beneath the dirt, and Dirt walked on top of that.

That night as he was drifting off to sleep, a sensation of pain from his collar to his groin entered his mind, accompanied by Socks saying *-almost got me but I'm safe.-*

Nothing more came, no matter how Dirt listened or called out the pup's name. Dirt woke four times that night, fleeing nightmares about teeth and claws rising up from the ground to bite his feet.

The next day, a huge host of dryads had gathered again, as many as he'd seen. Some were late and rose from the ground like something underneath was pushing them up.

Home said, "Listen well, little Dirt. The world of magic contains structures and shapes, and power given a shape and form can cause a thing to be real in the other worlds. To do a greater work of magic than run or jump, you must learn to shape mana. Your mana vessel guides—"

"Home," said Dirt, "I'm really sorry, and I know this is important, but I can't just sit around learning all day. I need to see Socks. I need to. He's hurt. Can you help me?"

"You should not be impatient, dear Dirt. Let the rhythm of time guide you along the natural course," said Home. She continued. "Your mana vessel guides the flow of power, and by shaping the vessel with your spirit and will, you can create a new shape or structure and cause a thing to be."

"Okay," said Dirt. "Home, I want to learn all this. I really, really do, and I'm grateful that you're teaching me. But you are more patient than me because you're thousands of years old, and I'm only maybe twenty days old. I lost count. Can I please just go see him, and then come back? If Mother won't allow it, then maybe I can at least get close enough to talk. You could even drop me in front of the den with root travel, since that's how you got me here. Please?"

Dawn went blank first, quickly followed by Home and several others. Dirt's heart leaped, knowing it meant they were asking Mother. He was sure of it. He waited, nervous energy filling him. He wanted to scream or jump or *something*, but he didn't because he had to wait.

When she retook control of her dryad, Dawn frowned, eyes full of pity. Before she even opened her mouth, Dirt said, "Never mind. I can already guess the answer. Please don't even say it. Tell me later."

"I am sorry, dear Dirt. I feel sad for pity's sake," said Dawn, her voice filling with anguish.

Dirt knew how to handle sadness better than she did, he realized. Better than any of them. What did they know of pain? Nothing. They'd said so. He scowled, because now, on top of angry and nervous, he felt guilty.

"I'm sorry too, Dawn. I feel like I put you in a difficult position."

The poor dryad started wilting. All the little leaves that covered most of her torso shriveled and wilted, and parts of her went stiff as if she'd lost control. Other parts went limp, and it was a more pitiable sight than he was prepared to handle. It wasn't that she couldn't handle sadness that well—she truly had no defense against it. None.

Dirt jumped forward and grabbed her in a hug, holding her as tight as he could.

"Don't be sad, my sweet little Dawn. My dear, precious Dawn, please don't be sad. I love you, and I'm sorry I made you sad."

The other dryads looked contrite, their eyes downcast and regretful. But Dirt also noticed they were standing back a bit, edging away slightly as if they feared whatever Dawn had was contagious.

Dawn recovered after only a few moments. After she perked back up, Dirt released her and said, "Do you feel better now?"

"Yes. That was more intense than I realized. Do you feel like that often? Do you feel that way now?" asked Dawn.

"No, I feel better now. Let's just forget it," he said, hoping to avoid a relapse. "I have so many friends here now, and I'll see Socks when Mother says it's right, no matter what I think about it. Home, would you continue?"

He listened to Home's explanation of magic despite all his mental distractions, but at the end he could only remember bits and pieces. He got the general idea—magic took different shapes or forms, and those shapes caused an effect in one of the worlds, usually the physical. He had to exercise his will, which rose from his self and spirit, to shape his mana vessel and cause something to happen.

Shaping mana for his body was easy, because his mana vessel was already in the right shape for that, just naturally. Running and jumping with magic was almost second nature to him, especially after his time with Socks.

But when he tried to do more, to cause wind or lift something with his mind or the dozen other things the dryads came up with, it always fell apart. By the end of the day, Dirt was more frustrated and worn out than educated. The whole day had been a waste, and when he lay down early to sleep, mostly just to get some time to himself, he felt guilty for wasting it.

-You have to learn, little Dirt. Pay more attention tomorrow.- The pup's voice in his mind was quiet and distant, but clear.

"Socks! I can hear you much better today. Can you hear me? Can we finally talk? I hope—"

-If you want to talk to me, you have to talk aloud. I can't see your thoughts from here. Say something, little Dirt.-

"I miss you!" he shouted. "I'm scared!"

-I miss you, but I am not scared because I am a strong wolf. Day and night, I hide or fight alongside Father. We hunt, and I learn. My enemy is

wily, and I am tired. I keep getting hurt. I'm glad you're far away and safe, Dirt. Stay safe and learn. I can watch you with ghost sight, sometimes. We will talk each night if we can.-

"It's not the same," said Dirt, frustrated to the point of tears. "I want to hug you."

-I want to lick your face and make you giggle. That day will come again. Good night, little Dirt.-

Enough of the pup's true emotion came through with his words to tell Dirt that Socks was bluffing, in part: he was scared. Socks was being hunted, and there was no respite, no safety, despite being guarded by the strongest things that could possibly exist.

Dirt cried for his friend, sobbing into the supple balls of fiber that comprised his bed, and for himself, who had to suffer far away, unable to help.

The next day, Dirt gritted his teeth and remembered what his real power was. Not muscle or claws or even his knife. Discipline and sincerity. That's what kept him alive, and it's what he needed now. He needed to focus on what the incredibly patient dryads were trying to teach him, so he did.

When they told him to picture wind with his pure will and not his imagination, he forced out every other thought. He refused to get tired or bored or distracted, but focused with all his might on the task. When they said to use that willpower to force his mana vessel into the shape of wind, he stood stern and unmoving, unflinching against repeated failure and frustration, turning down food and water until he got it right. Hour after hour his mind stood resolute like the stone wall that refused to fall down after millennia.

Dirt only relented when he could tell the dryads were getting nervous. Near midday, he smiled and laughed and ate all the sap they gave him, and washed it down with plenty of water. They ran together and played, free and innocent and happy for a time. But as soon as he sensed the opportunity, he was right back at it, forcing his mana vessel and the power it contained into the shape of wind.

In the midafternoon, he finally got it after he managed to stretch his awareness of his mana vessel far enough to watch the dryads do it, and saw enough to copy. To his perception, the shape of wind wasn't something like a cube or a sphere; it was a pattern, a complex but contained one, that felt familiar.

The pattern seen together, might be considered a word, and when he spoke it into the world of magic, a gust of wind arose from nowhere and shook the ferns as it blew forward. It traveled only thirty paces before it died and left the air calm and heavy again.

The dryads cheered, but he ignored them, except for a polite grin to let them know he noticed. Instead he did it again and again, a dozen more times, until his mind felt ragged and his mana vessel sore. Not strong winds, although he was sure he could make them stronger, but deliberate ones. Careful wind, disciplined, until he felt like he'd mastered it.

When he finally stopped, he was so mentally exhausted that he collapsed flat on the ground. Only then did he cheer, raising his arms to the green sky and howling like a wolf. The wind was his.

irt had two dreams that night. In the first, he and Socks played in the den, dreaming of home and simple things. Wolves of all ages came and went and greeted them with curious sniffs. When the dream suddenly cut off for no reason and Dirt woke with a start, he wondered if Socks had really been in that one, or if Dirt had just dreamed it.

In the second dream, he was in a place of men. That realization almost shook him awake, but he managed to calm down and stay asleep. He stood on a handsome tiled floor with a pattern of concentric squares enclosing a potted plant in the middle. The walls were painted red, with faux pillars in the corners painted green and yellow.

A cool breeze shook the curtains behind him, but he heard a rustling of something else moving and turned to greet her. She was beautiful, curved and graceful and feminine. Her shining brown hair was done up in curls with gold needles holding it in place, and her dress of green and yellow danced like autumn leaves when she walked.

She placed her arms around his neck and spoke, but he couldn't hear any words. No sound came out of her mouth at all, although her lips were moving. He tilted his head to listen, and only a moment later the whole thing fell apart and cast him back into wakefulness. He lay stunned, heart beating mightily against his chest.

It wasn't fear that kept him awake for half the night after that, though. It was pure shock. His mind spun with questions, and there was no one to ask. Had he known her? Where was that, anyway? He kept picturing her, over and over, how she walked, how she looked at him and smiled.

He pictured her in his mind as strongly as he could, but the longer he held the image the fuzzier it got. His memory kept trying to fill in missing details, and after a while she started looking more and more like Home's dryad.

"No, no, no, no," he whimpered frantically. "Please, no, no, don't forget."

Dirt did his best to cement the real memory in his mind and then rolled over and fell asleep before he could ruin it any more than he already had.

He met the morning with wistful melancholy. He'd forgotten more of her during the night, and now he couldn't even put a good picture together. Just impressions; cloth, hair. Her arms. He ate his sap huddled up in a corner, knees folded against his chest like he was hiding from something.

He stayed that way for too long, head tilted to rest against the wall. He wanted to feel nostalgia, to warmly remember things that no longer were, but instead he just felt regret. He'd forgotten anything he could be nostalgic about, and the fading memory of a dream wasn't enough to sustain him.

Home peeked her head in a window and asked, "Dear Dirt, are you unwell?"

"I'm fine," he said, sighing to himself. Well, if he stayed like this any longer, he'd have to explain why he felt that way, and then they'd try to help, and who knew what they might try. He rose to his feet and made himself smile.

"Open," he told the doorway. He really had waited too long—the fog was already fading. No wonder they were concerned.

Home and Dawn both hugged him at once, one on each side. Callius stepped up and kissed him on the cheek, which surprised Dirt since he'd forgotten kisses existed until now. But then Callius licked him across his whole face and barked like a wolf and ran away laughing. The dryad's tongue was wet and soft and felt almost—almost—like flesh.

Shrieking with indignation, Dirt pulled away from the girls and rushed after him, determined to grab him and give him the same treatment.

The chase was on. Callius didn't simply run, either—he leaped over roots or ran all the way up them and jumped off. Sometimes he turned sharply and tried to hide. It wasn't exactly a fair chase, since Callius could probably run plenty faster than this. And probably faster than Socks, too, since the trees had ridiculous amounts of mana inside them. But Dirt wasn't about to give up.

Callius ran straight for a tree and turned at the last moment to go around it, and Dirt went the other direction. They both hid from each other, but Dirt hid better, even keeping the ferns from noticing him by applying gentle pressure to their thoughts. Callius came looking for him, trying to sneak, but Dirt spotted him first.

Dirt jumped out of the ferns, caught the dryad around the shoulders, and pulled him down for a tackle. Then Dirt licked his face and barked like a wolf and jumped away. He shouted, "Now get somebody else!" as he ran, halfway between a laugh and a scream, but in vain. Callius had only one target, and he hit Dirt from behind before he even made it to the next tree.

The dryad licked Dirt's face, despite his squirming to get away, and then went *bark, bark, bark, HOOOOOWL*. He got up and ran again.

Dirt rolled and stood, brushed off the clumps of black earth he'd collected, and gave chase. But before he made it five steps someone hit him from the side, knocking him clear off his feet.

Dawn. Dawn had come out of nowhere and absolutely crushed him. For a brief moment, Dirt's heart filled with terror that she'd broken all his bones again, but he was fine. She held him down, trying to figure out what to do with him. "I'm not a wolf," she said. "I'm a bird!"

Then she pinched him a bunch of times and leaped into the air, flapping her arms like wings.

"How do you know about birds?" he shouted, but she just laughed and ran as soon as she landed. Of course she knew about birds, though. She was a tree. There were probably some birds nearby right now, if he looked carefully.

Dirt gave up on Callius and chased her instead, but he had to run while trying to watch for more incoming dryads. He was certain others were on their way. Home, possibly, and that girl with the round face, or the curly-haired one. They seemed the type. Most likely there were dozens out there, waiting for their chance.

Dawn was distracted by someone else running toward her, and a short moment of indecision was all Dirt needed. He caught her from behind, but she almost slipped away until he got a hand around her collarbone that spun her back around.

He jumped on her and said, "I'm still a wolf!" Then he howled, licked her face, and ran away as fast as he could.

The rest of the morning, Dirt got the worst of it, but he still managed to catch a bunch of them. Dawn was the only bird—the rest wanted to be wolves, and some even ran on all fours in a way he couldn't imitate. He suspected they were shortening their legs to make it easier.

Dirt ate his lunchtime sap slowly, enjoying getting a chance to rest. It was fun chasing dryads all over, but it turned out getting knocked over a hundred times was tiring. He wished he'd taken some toys from the dead bodies in that city to play with, since he didn't think he needed to get worn out every single minute of the day. But he needed the right kind—dolls of wolves and boys and other fun things. The city was too far from here, and he didn't know where to find it anyway, so he couldn't just go look. How else was he supposed to get any?

After making sure Dirt ate slightly more sap than he wanted, Callius said, "Okay, Dirt, we're going to start hitting you a little harder so you can practice protecting yourself with mana. Do you think you can figure it out?"

Dirt realized he did have one way to get the toys he wanted—make them. He jumped to his feet in excitement and said, "I probably can, but do you know what? I want to shape wood instead. Can I learn that today? Home said I'd learn someday. I promise not to use my knife on you."

The dryads all paused, but they weren't frozen. They weren't thinking. They looked nervous.

"Come on, please?"

Callius dug in the dirt with his toe. "Are you sure you're ready for that?"

"I just want to shape little things, like maybe this big," said Dirt, holding his hands about eight inches apart. "Please?"

The boy sighed. "Well, I suppose it's only fair. Come on." He held out his hand. Dirt took it, and the instant their fingers touched, Dirt was yanked through the roots and tossed into the ground under a tree he wasn't sure he'd seen before.

He picked himself up and put his hands on his knees until he was sure he wasn't going to get sick or dizzy again. After a moment, he decided he was fine and stood up the rest of the way.

No other dryads had come—it was just him and Callius.

Callius pointed at the tree and said, "This is me. If you're wondering where all the others are, everyone wanted to watch in the normal way, so they aren't coming. So here we are. Don't mess me up too much."

"Oh, I'm going to learn on you?"

"What did you expect?"

"I don't really know. But why you and not Home where my house is?"

"Because I'm better at it than anyone else," said Callius. He did a graceful backward cartwheel, and when he landed, he wasn't a boy anymore—he was a wolf, with long gangly legs and tiny green leaves instead of fur. Then he stood on his hind legs and was a boy again, with green leaves from waist to knees like he'd had before.

"Wow," said Dirt, unsure what else to say. The whole thing had been one seamless motion, perfectly balanced. An exquisite display of grace and control. Truthfully, he wanted to see it again but felt foolish asking. So instead he asked, "So if you're that good, how come you still cover a third of yourself with the little leaves?"

The dryad said, "Oh, I thought we told you once already. Watch my mind, and you'll see."

Dirt looked at Callius's mind and was reminded that the boy in front of him was merely a doll used by an ancient, mighty being to run around in, and not the being himself. The tree's mind was immense and too complicated to comprehend. Except the portion that controlled the dryad—that was familiar. Normal sights and sounds and even thoughts with words, sometimes.

That portion grew as Callius withdrew the little green leaves that covered him from waist to knees and replaced them with supple gray bark-flesh, making him fully human from head to toes. Dirt noticed peach fuzz on the dryad's arms and cheeks and ears. Even the eyes grew moist and lost that glassy character they had.

The effect was unexpected. Callius was so perfectly human now that Dirt wasn't even sure he was still looking at a dryad and not a gray-skinned boy his own age.

And just as surprising was how much extra effort it took to finish the body. It took up a third again as much space in Callius's mind, if not more.

"See? It's a lot more work. And besides that, watch closely," said Callius. He reverted back to how he was before, the fur of tiny green leaves returning. This time, Dirt noticed a bundle of new sensory information in the tree-based part of the mind.

"Oh! You're using the leaves to sense the air, aren't you? Like with your real leaves?"

"Yep!"

"I never noticed that before."

"Nope!"

"How come you do that?"

"Because it's too weird not to. How can you even tell what anything is?"

Dirt thought about that for a moment, remembering bits and pieces of the tree-dream.

"Look at my mind, friend Dirt. Remember this word. It's a word that means 'grow and change,' except that a tree will understand it. Are you looking?" said Callius.

Dirt peered at the tree's mind and found the thought, which was held isolated from the rest to make it easy to find. Like the wind or the words he used to make the ferns bend out of the way, the "word" was a complex structure that almost seemed more like a set of patterns than the thoughts Dirt was used to.

Once he was fairly certain he had it down, he asked, "What do I do with it?"

Callius gritted his teeth and looked as nervous as possible. "Put your hand on my root. There's fine. Now what you're going to do, is . . . talk to the wood there, with your mana body, using that word. Not with your mind. Let your mana vessel take the shape of the change you want to cause, and then let it interact with some of my wood. Beyond that, I'm not sure I can explain, so you'll have to figure it out."

Dirt asked, "Is this going to hurt?"

"I can't feel pain."

"Then why are you acting so nervous?"

"I'd answer, but I don't want to give you any ideas. And try not to be nervous yourself, or the result might not be what you wanted."

The forest was silent before this moment, just as pleasantly dim with shadow, just as empty and peaceful and eternal as always, but to Dirt's mind, it suddenly got a lot quieter. The forest held its breath, as if everything in here was waiting for him. And it probably was, maybe even the ferns.

Dirt willed his mind to quiet down. He placed his hand on the smooth, gray root and pictured the word "grow," but not in his mind, or in the dream, but rather, with that part of him that was deeper than emotion.

It worked on the very first try. A lump formed under his hand and lifted it away, first one inch thick, then two. Dirt forced any thought of triumph or rejoicing from his mind and steeled himself even further. Every thought was quieted and schooled into submission, stepping aside to let his pure will manifest. The wood responded eagerly to his command; not Callius, not even any significant part of him. Just this wood right here, this small hand-shaped amount on the outside.

Dirt made it grow beneath his hand, and he brought his other hand to reshape the cylinder and give it a head, then arms, then split it to make legs. Finally, under his fingertips, feet emerged, and beneath those the wood narrowed sharply until it simply split off and came away in his hands.

The task complete, his state of focus faded in a way that felt like waking up, much more notable than making magical wind yesterday, and he looked at what he held.

It was exactly what he wanted—a little wooden replica of a human, no bigger than his forearm. It was even rougher than Home's first dryad, without any joints, but it was perfect anyway. It almost came alive in his hands as he started thinking of the things he could do with it, of the adventures he could imagine.

"No one expected that to work, friend Dirt," said Callius, coolly impressed. He rubbed the spot where Dirt had been working and smoothed it out.

"Well, I'm glad it did. Look, Callius. It's a toy person. I'll make some more, and then I'll be this, and we can play with them," said Dirt.

He was so excited it was almost like dreaming. Infinite worlds of possibility swirled around him.

"Go ahead. Make as many as you want."

Dirt made a wolf, and it was even easier than the human. Then he made some goblins, and even a dryad or two, which were only different by being skinnier than the human, since he had to tell them apart somehow. Slipping into that state of focus, of will without thought, got easier and easier each time. By the time he made the fifth goblin, he could think normal thoughts while doing it.

Callius said, "That was supposed to be much harder than you're making it look."

"I had a good teacher."

"No, I didn't teach you this."

"What do you mean?" asked Dirt, but he was barely listening. He was too busy arranging his ten dolls, preparing them to be properly played with.

"This is wisdom, friend Dirt, and it is hard won, even for us whose nature is stronger in the world of magic than yours."

"Callius, I love you, and I'm interested in hearing that sometime but right now, I have to play with these. I'll be the human. Here, you can be the wolf, and we'll go fight these goblins!"

CHAPTER THIRTY-SIX

Callius took the rough wooden wolf figurine and held it in both hands, clearly unsure what to do with it. Dirt knelt and hid a couple goblins a few feet away behind some dipping fern fronds.

"Come on, wolf!" said Dirt, planting the feet of his human in the ground. "Let's see what's over here."

It took a few minutes for Callius to get the idea, and Dirt had to do most of the talking at the start, but before long he figured it out. They had all sorts of adventures, which were not limited to fighting goblins. Sometimes they explored buildings large and small or fought creatures that Dirt could only name, like "elephant" or "tiger." Callius would freeze for a moment and come back ready to mimic them, at least to the degree possible with the one animal to use.

Other dryads slipped out of the ferns to watch, and sometimes he could get one to be a goblin or a toy dryad, but they would only play for a few moments before stepping away again. Home and Dawn didn't show up, but Dirt was having so much fun he hardly noticed.

When Callius suddenly shrank himself to the size of the toys and started walking among them, Dirt laughed aloud and set up the biggest battle yet—dryad versus everything else, including the toy dryads.

Callius won, because each time he punched or kicked a toy it'd go flying off into the ferns. The first time it happened, he glanced up at Dirt apologetically, but it had been a goblin, so Dirt didn't care. Callius was a little more gentle with the next ones, but they still ended up losing another one, and one dryad.

They played long into the afternoon, breaking only when it was time for Dirt to eat again. Dirt sat and gazed inward to watch the world of the toys receding from his mind. What a curious thing, that he could be so captivated. Did the wolves play games like that too? Imagination? Or did they only wrestle and race around?

Callius returned to normal size and sat next to Dirt, where he started picking up clumps of soil with his toes and flinging them away. "Would you call this a footful of dirt, friend Dirt?" asked the dryad, tossing another clump with his toes. "Or is it still a handful?"

"That's a good question. I guess it's a footful, because a handful is bigger. But I don't think that's a word," said Dirt, taking another bite and chewing slowly while it stuck to all his teeth.

"How would you know?"

"I know all the words, I just don't know what most of them mean," said Dirt, around his mouthful.

"If footful isn't a word, does that mean I'm the first person who ever did this?" asked Callius, tossing a lumpy little cylinder of black dirt high into the air, where it broke apart.

"Probably not."

"How can it not have a word, then?"

"Maybe it wasn't a useful thing to measure, so no one made a word for it."

"Why is a handful useful but not a footful?"

"I don't know, but I don't think I've ever picked anything up with my feet like that," said Dirt. Then he had to try, of course, and squeezed a little clump of the rich black earth with his toes and tossed it forward. It didn't go very far, so he did it again and again.

"If you don't pick things up with your toes, what are they for?" asked Callius.

"So you can feel what you're walking on, I guess."

"Can't you feel with the rest of your foot?"

"I bet you already know about toes, but you're teasing me."

"Perhaps," said Callius, suppressing a faint grin. "What do you think about this?"

The dryad lifted his feet in the air, and his toes grew to finger length. He deftly picked up a big clump of earth with them and formed it into a tight ball, which he tossed back and forth from foot to foot.

"I think," said Dirt, taking another bite around a smile of his own, "that if I could change my shape, I still wouldn't do that."

Callius picked up the boy figurine and stood up. He stepped a short distance back and held it up, comparing it to the real Dirt. It writhed and shook as the dryad re-formed it, and when Callius gave it back to him, it was a perfect likeness.

Or rather, it was as close as Dirt could expect. He'd seen himself faintly once in a reflection, and other than that, only in Socks's mind. The pup's mental images weren't exactly clear and thorough, either. Only things that were moving were easy to see.

"Thanks!" said Dirt, pleased. It made all the rest of the toys look pathetic in comparison, but it was a treasure, nonetheless. "Can you do you?" he said, handing a toy dryad to Callius.

"How about you do it? A little more practice would be good for you."

"Okay, but when I give up, will you finish it?"

"Nope!"

Dirt faked a scowl at the grinning Callius, which he could only maintain for about one second. As soon as he'd finished off his sap, Callius gave him some water from his cupped hands, and then he got to work reshaping the toy dryad.

It was much harder than he expected, and not even because using magic like that took a lot of concentration and willpower. Dirt discovered that he didn't see things in as much detail as he thought he did. So much of the boy's form was as good as invisible until he looked at it deliberately, from the shape of individual muscles to the countless lengths and proportions. He gave up before he was quite satisfied because his brain felt like it was going to start dripping out his ears if he mashed it up any harder.

Callius took it and looked it over. "Wow, this is incredible! It's perfect!"

Dirt looked up to find that Callius had readjusted his appearance to match the doll, with huge crooked eyes and uneven shoulders and arms thicker than a goblin's. The dryad tried to dance and immediately fell over, since he only had a knee on one leg.

"It's just like me! How did you do that on your first try?" called Callius from the ground.

"I don't know, but if I could change my shape, I wouldn't do that either," said Dirt, trying and failing to suppress a giggle.

"What do you mean? This is how I always looked!"

"And you've never been more handsome than right now."

That got a good laugh out of Callius, which Dirt found infectious. Callius stood somehow and tried to dance again, pivoting on his knee-less leg and gracefully waving his goblin arms around. Dirt laughed until his stomach hurt.

Soon Callius turned himself back to normal, to Dirt's relief, and for the next little while Dirt worked on his toys. None of them got anything like what Callius had done, but at least it was easier to tell what they were supposed to be. And there was nothing to keep him from improving them further.

They added a house like Dirt's and played in and around that. Then Dirt used his magic to readjust the building into other shapes, which were mostly what he imagined the ruined buildings would look like if they were still standing.

By the end, Dirt got so confident that he tried to recreate that temple, the one hidden here in the forest, from memory. It came out pretty good, Dirt thought, and even included the pillars and part of the collapsed roof.

"Is that what I think it is?" asked Callius when he rolled over from juggling toy goblins with his feet. "When did you see that place?"

"Socks took me there. I bet I mentioned it before, but there was clean water and a road leading to it. Mother said not to go in, though, so we didn't," said Dirt, placing the toy Dirt in front of the empty doorway.

"We can't get close to it, and no one knows why," said Callius.

"Really? How close can you get? We went right up to the doorway here and looked inside," said Dirt, pointing at his wooden model. "It was too dark to see in there, but I think Socks said he smelled something."

"I can show you, if you promise to stay out of trouble."

"Did the Mother of Wolves tell you anything about it?" asked Dirt.

"No," said Callius, standing up and finally making his toes the right length again. Now they looked all stubby and useless, which bothered Dirt somehow. "She hasn't spoken with us since helping you get mana the other day."

"Maybe Dawn can ask her?"

"Maybe. She's playing with the elementals today, but I'll ask her later."

"Wait, what are elementals?" asked Dirt. "And why haven't I met one?"

"Oh, we're not hiding them from you, friend Dirt. They just have almost no presence in the physical. They live in the magic world, and they are great fun," said Callius, nonchalantly walking toward his tree.

Dirt followed and asked, "Only the magic world?"

"And the dream, and spirit. They're alive. They're just not physical. Are you ready?" asked Callius, resting one hand on his root.

Dirt took a long, slow breath to prepare himself. "Wait! I want . . . hold on." He ran back over to the toys and took the boy, the wolf, and the poor imitation of Callius. "I want to keep at least these ones. Can you send them to my house with Home?"

"Sure can. Let's go."

Callius reached out and grabbed Dirt's wrist, and for the space of a heartbeat, Dirt was hurtling forward at impossible speed, bouncing left and right too quickly to react to. The root travel dropped him on his feet, but he was still reacting to moving forward and leaned backward to correct himself, causing him to fall hard onto his bottom.

Fortunately the ground was soft. He went to get back up and realized his hands were empty and his toys were nowhere to be seen. Callius grabbed Dirt's wrist again and helped him to his feet.

"Hold on," said Dirt, resting his hands on his knees to make sure he wasn't going to get dizzy again. But like last time, he felt fine, other than a sense of being shaken way too hard. "Okay, I guess I'm fine."

"Good. Let's head over."

"Who is this? Have I met this tree before?" Dirt asked, looking up.

"No, he was one of the later ones. And he doesn't want to make any dryads right now because of what keeps happening to them."

Dirt sent the tree a mental sensation of gratitude, but before he could converse much with it, Callius started walking out into the ferns.

They had to get far enough away from the tree trunk to see over the roots, but once they could, Dirt quickly spotted the ruined temple in the direct center of an open space between trees, a couple hundred paces from any of them. It was strange seeing it again, after so many littler ones.

The temple rose high above the ferns, compared to the other ruins. Nothing like a tree, but taller than any of the ruins from the city. It looked majestic here, solid and stately, a thing of men standing out starkly in such a wild place.

"If my dryad stops working, then don't worry, because I'll make another one and send it as soon as I can. It only takes me a moment. I just don't want you to be scared if it happens," said Callius, unconcerned.

"Well, now I'm worried, because your dryads stop working all the time when you decide to think hard about something."

"Do they?"

"Yep."

"Then never mind," said Callius.

Dirt frowned at that, but Callius never slowed down, and they were getting close. There was a pile of wood ahead, all logs of gray bark the same color as the trees, but . . .

No, not a pile of wood. A pile of dead dryads, thirty paces ahead. Twenty or more, strewn all over, with a pile of them at least five deep just rising out of the ferns.

Dirt froze in his footsteps and felt his blood run cold. Dread filled him, serious dread, and his heart raced faster than his eyes as they scanned for the threat.

The temple path was just beyond the pile of dryads, and a short distance down it the old temple reposed. It seemed taller than he remembered, the opening of the doorway blacker. It had been a calm place before, restful and mysterious. The pile of corpses had changed the ambiance considerably.

"This is as close as I get," said Callius, stopping in his tracks.

"What . . . happened to them?" asked Dirt, his mouth dry.

"It's not as bad as it looks. We just lose our connection if we go much farther than this."

"So the trees aren't hurt? They're fine?" asked Dirt, looking up nervously for dead or falling leaves. One of them dying was a horror too great to contemplate. He'd rather see a thousand dead human skeletons than one dead, decaying tree.

"They're annoyed, but that's all."

Dirt pushed away his dread, since there was nothing around that looked like a threat, and it wasn't a pleasant thing to feel. He walked ahead, leaving Callius behind, and approached the corpse pile. From up close, it looked more like wooden figurines than dead children, since they lost all suppleness in their joints and skin. Their glassy eyes contained no hint of a spark, set in emotionless, unmoving faces.

"I'm not going in, but I want to get a drink," said Dirt. "I'll be right back."

He stepped over the farthest corpse and onto the stone pathway, on the far end where it emerged from the ground. There was probably more of it buried underneath, but that knowledge wasn't exactly useful. He enjoyed how cool the stone felt under his feet, entirely different from the warm stone of the city plaza, out in the sunlight.

Dirt passed the broken cistern with its reeking green water and made his way to the good one, cracked and dripping out the side. He was relieved to see the water was clean again—the dirt he'd left behind last time he drank here must have all washed out. He cupped his hands and drank, refreshed. The water was cooler than what the dryads gave him, almost cold, and it was more pleasant to drink.

Maybe he should make the temple his home, and then the dryads *really* would have to leave him alone when he wanted.

Which, now that he thought about it, wasn't often. And who knew what sorts of things might come into his dreams if he lived here? It probably wouldn't be Socks or Home.

Dirt looked at the temple, watching the doorway intently for any movement. Was there a creature in there, he wondered? Or was it something else, something that was a threat to wonderful things like dryads and wolves, but not humans? Humans made this place after all. Maybe there was a god in there.

Now *that* was not a pleasant thought. The sacrilege from under the city came back into his mind, that injured and suffering statue, fallen over into a heap of dead humans. If there was something like *that* in there, then he definitely didn't want to see it.

He watched the doorway and did his best to fight his growing curiosity. What could be in there that made dryads stop working?

Dirt resolutely turned around and started heading back to Callius. Best not to find out without at least talking to Socks after getting him to ask Mother.

"Do you think anyone will want these back?" asked Dirt, calling out over the dryad pile.

"Maybe! Bring one!"

Dirt had to strengthen his body with mana, since it turned out they were a lot heavier when a tree wasn't puppeteering them, but he managed to pick one up. Not only was it heavy, but it was awkward, since all the arms and legs just froze in place and didn't bend at all.

By the time he got back to Callius, it was starting to get more limber, which was unpleasant. He tried to set it down carefully, but mostly just dropped it.

"Get that one there," said Callius, pointing at one of the closer ones.

Dirt retrieved it, and no sooner had he put it down than it sprang to life, standing and brushing clumps of earth out of its leaf-fur.

"That's him," said Callius, pointing at the tree they'd come from.

"Hello, friend Dirt," said the newcomer, his face mostly expressionless. He almost looked like he was sleeping, since so little of him moved.

"Don't mind him," said Callius. "He hasn't had much time to practice yet."

"Oh, that's fine. It's nice to meet you. I'm going to get a few more. Do you need any more of yours?" asked Dirt.

"No," he said.

"Okay," said Dirt. He went back and looked around for one that *wasn't* that particular tree, but nine of ten were. No wonder he'd gotten annoyed and given up. Dirt found two different girls and carried them out, then went back and looked around for any more.

Dirt stepped backward, then again, before he realized what he was doing. He felt off-balance, like he was leaning the wrong direction and had to keep moving to correct himself. Backward, toward the temple. Another step.

"What?" he asked aloud. There was a slight tug, something pulling on him—not a suggestion but a real force. Gentle, but insistent. It reminded him of how Socks picked him up. He was not imagining it.

"Something's pulling me!" he screamed. Dirt filled himself with mana and tried to resist, to walk forward out of its grasp, but the harder he pushed the stronger it got. "Help!"

Callius stepped back three paces, then shot forward at incredible speed, running fast as a wolf. In an instant, he picked Dirt up and tossed him forward as hard as he could, so hard the dryad's hands left bruises on Dirt's upper thigh and armpit.

It almost worked. Dirt hurtled through the air, but his forward progress slowed to a halt, and Dirt fell straight down, where he dug into the ground with both feet and hands, trying to hold himself in place against the force pulling him backward.

Callius's dryad toppled over, inert. "Callius!" Dirt screamed anyway, panicking.

The force pulled him backward, causing him to dig deep furrows in the ground. He uprooted ferns and collected them in a big pile that he dragged along with him.

Dirt looked all around for minds, hoping to see what was pulling him, but there was nothing around but trees and ferns, and some insects if he looked really closely. Nothing like the half-dead mind of the tentacle monster, nothing to tell him what was going on.

When the thing pulled him all the way back to Callius's dryad, Dirt grabbed it with one hand and re-formed the arm into a hasty spike, which he slammed into the ground. Finally, he stopped moving backward. He shaped more of Callius into spikes, growing him all out of shape into something that his mind called a "plow." Dirt dug in with all his strength.

The thing kept pulling, slowly increasing the pressure. Dirt filled himself with mana and strengthened himself as strongly as he ever had before. Power sparked and buzzed in him, filling him with glory and leaving him feeling scalded on the inside. He strengthened his muscles and his creaking bones, holding himself in place as hard as he could.

"Help!" he shouted. He couldn't look around without changing his posture, and that'd let it pull him loose.

A vine slapped down onto his wrist and started curling around his body, winding under his armpits and circled down his chest. It wound under his groin and down one of his legs, and once he was solidly bound by it, it *pulled.*

Dirt looked up and saw a brand-new Callius with one arm transformed into a bundle of vines that extended forward. Other dryads had gathered and were holding him in place. The vines tightened again and pulled Dirt forward, straining against the ever-increasing force.

"Strengthen your body against injury!" shouted Dawn, pacing distraught at the edge of the kill zone.

He tried, telling the mana inside himself to stop making him stronger and start making him tougher instead. The vines pulled him even harder, and bit by bit he began moving forward.

The strain was incredible. He could feel his guts twisting, his joints trying to come apart. Dirt focused on calming his mind and directing the mana with his will, making it strengthen his skin to keep it from tearing, strengthen his intestines to keep them from splitting open inside him.

Inch by painful, desperate, inch, Dirt moved forward. He heard the vines creaking against the strain and he could feel Callius's resolve through them, feel the dawning fear the dryad could scarcely understand.

Something clacked gently along the stone pathway, walking in his direction.

He turned back to see a human skeleton wearing a robe of gold and a headdress of golden leaves, eyes burning with blue flames that left trails in the air as it walked up the stone pathway toward him.

Dirt screamed with all his might, over and over, unable to do anything but experience abject terror.

It reached him and brushed a fingertip of bone along his flesh. Dirt screamed even harder, so hard it hurt his chest and throat.

The walking skeleton stepped two paces past Dirt, reached down to the vines that struggled desperately to save him, and severed them with a flick of its finger.

Dirt hurtled helplessly across the stone pathway and into the blackness of the ruined temple.

CHAPTER THIRTY-SEVEN

Darkness closed around Dirt as he receded farther into the temple, leaving him blind. All he could see was the outline of the doorway, the dim light from its green outline illuminating only the first few feet of stone inside. The rest of the temple interior was a complete mystery.

The skeleton passed through the doorway, walking calmly. The blue fire in its eyes glowed against the black as it walked straight toward him, flames drifting left or right with its footsteps.

Dirt's screams caught in his throat, where the terror roiling inside him choked him like fingers squeezing his neck. He was *certain* the skeleton would hurt him; he only waited to see how.

The blue fires stopped a few feet in front of him, and their light illuminated the skeleton's face and chest. The pale white bone and golden robes lost their color even as they filled his vision, limned in perfect darkness everywhere else.

Dirt whimpered through clenched teeth and let out a squirt of urine. He was so scared it felt like pain inside him, and his mind could only barely process what was going on. "Save me," he moaned, but the muscles in his mouth were too frozen to pronounce the words correctly.

The skeleton reached forward and traced its finger across his chest, so hard it left a stinging line of pain. It gripped his face, squeezing his cheeks with bony fingers that dug into the clenched muscles of his jaw. It turned his head, looking at his face from different angles. It released him and lowered its arms, then just stood there watching him. The blue flames of its eyes flickered and danced as it stared, unblinking.

It had no real face. That was the worst part of its silent, unmoving stare. It had no expression, nothing to indicate what it thought or wanted. Dirt had no idea if it was driven by curiosity or hatred. Or perhaps hunger. How could he tell?

"Please let me go," he begged. He could hardly speak.

The skeleton didn't react. It didn't twitch or tilt its head or anything at all. Just remained perfectly still, like the dead thing that it was.

"Callius, Socks, Mother, anyone," Dirt whispered. He struggled against the force that held him and only succeeded in loosening the vines, which began to sag and unwind and fall off him. They'd been so tight in some places he was sure he had bruises.

The skeleton turned and walked away. Dirt's eyes struggled again to get used to the darkness but as they did, he began to see parts of the temple's interior where the skeleton's gaze fell on them. Here, a collapsed pillar that had a statue carved into the front half, no longer identifiable. There, a standing wooden chair next to two broken ones. The ground was littered with debris; shattered bits of stone, traces of old dirt and grime; decayed things he couldn't identify. Trails of bare stone told him that the skeleton walked regularly in this place, although the air was so still and dead that Dirt didn't think wind *ever* came in to blow things around.

It stopped in front of a wide altar, a huge rectangular stone carved along all the front and sides with patterns and figures only barely visible in the gloom. The top of the altar was littered with old books and scrolls, alongside countless implements that Dirt recognized—a decanter for sacred oil, a ritual athame, precious gemstones, chalk, figurines of gods and spirits, sheets of lead and a stylus, all carefully arranged in perfect order. There were even fruits, so decayed and ancient that the gentlest touch would turn them to powder.

"What do you want with me?!" shouted Dirt, finally able to get a little control of himself.

The skeleton ignored him. It carefully opened a wide scroll, gently winding and winding the ancient paper from reel to reel until it found the section it wanted. Dirt could barely make out complex shapes and symbols, all magical in nature. He knew that too, somehow. He must have known human magic once, in the ancient life he'd lost.

A massive boom echoed through the temple, so loud it left Dirt's ears ringing. The very stones shook as bits of old mortar turned to sand and drifted down in quiet streams. The skeleton raised its head from its reading and turned its gaze out the doorway. It rolled the scroll back together and lifted the athame. The knife's blade curved upward, sinuous like a snake and as long as Dirt's forearm. The skeleton lifted a golden wine cup with the other hand and turned toward him.

"No!" Dirt shouted, struggling as hard as he could against the invisible hand that held him. The skeleton stepped in his direction, knife at the ready and leaving no mystery what was about to happen. Dirt forced his mind to calm down, forced his body to relax, forced himself to inhale mana. His inner self clashed violently against his physical reactions, the terror and desire to flee fighting his own will. But it was overcome or die, and Dirt overcame.

He inhaled mana, almost surprised to find he could. With exactly three seconds to figure out how to strengthen his body against injury, Dirt tried to make his skin like wood or stone, strengthening it like he strengthened his muscles for a jump.

The skeleton held the golden cup against Dirt's chest and scored the blade along his skin. The cut was subtle, far harder to feel and resist with mana than a punch or kick, but Dirt set his entire being to the task. The skeleton pressed harder and harder, and Dirt's will resisted, rising from that place within him deeper than thought.

The ritual knife lowered unbloodied, and Dirt breathed a quiet sigh of relief. He could survive this. He just had to keep all his blood in, and fight or distract it long enough to run away. And figure out how to get down from hovering in the air.

"Just tell me what you want," said Dirt, his voice shaky and trembling. "Maybe I can help."

It didn't react. When it wasn't moving, its perfect stillness made it seem like Dirt had imagined the whole thing, like it had never moved at all. The flames in its eyes were just lamplights, its robe just a curtain in a room with no wind.

The skeleton waited and stared longer than a human would. Dirt could feel that inhumanity, feel how wrong it was. Fear and revulsion melted together inside him to form something that he could only process as suffering, and still it watched, unmoving, unblinking, only an arm's reach away.

Another boom shook the temple, and this time a stone bigger than he was fired out of the wall, slamming into the floor and cracking in two as it slid halfway across the room. More light flooded in to illuminate that corner of the temple, but in that cavernous space it still wasn't enough to see properly.

The skeleton turned to face the hole, and the cracked building-stone rose into the air and quickly flew back over, where an invisible hand held it together and shoved it into the wall again.

The pressure on Dirt's body loosened and lowered him just enough to get one foot on the cold stone floor. He forced his mana into his muscles to make the sparking, burning power give him all the strength he could muster.

Dirt twisted violently to shake off the invisible fingers that held him, flailing and punching in every direction. The chains loosened further, lowering him far enough to jump forward. He leaped toward the skeleton.

The skeleton was so light that Dirt almost went right through it. He grabbed its skull and several ribs as it disassembled around him, and using his momentum as he fell forward, smashed the bones into the ground. The fires in its eyes went out as everything shattered. Bits of bone and cloth flew in every direction and clinked loudly along the floor as they bounced and slid.

Dirt scrambled to his feet and ran for the doorway, hoping there was nothing in the darkness to trip over.

Bone slid across stone behind him, and he glanced back to see the skeleton already re-forming. Before he'd gone ten steps it was back how it was before, other than some new tears in its decaying golden robe. He ran with wolf-speed toward the doorway, but it wasn't enough. Two paces from the threshold, the invisible hand closed around him again.

This time it held him in the doorway as he struggled to break its grip. The skeleton clacked across the stone floor until it was right behind him.

Dirt looked out desperately at the handful of dryads waiting just outside the corpse pile. Callius and Dawn were gone, but Home wore an expression of such complete anger he almost didn't recognize her.

A square building-stone from some other place was already flying through the air and slammed into the side of the temple, knocking free another part of the wall. Dirt decided they were trying to open it so they could see in and save him, not collapse the whole thing. He just hoped they knew what they were doing.

When the dryads outside saw him in the doorway, they froze, and no more boulders came.

The skeleton kept Dirt facing outward as it walked up behind him, stopping close enough that if it had breath, he'd feel it on his neck.

It drew Dirt's knife from its sheath under his left arm, and before he could react, a sharp pain blossomed halfway down his ribs on the right side. Dirt screamed as the skeleton held the golden cup under the wound and collected the blood that dripped down.

Then it held his own knife against his throat, perfectly still, and waited. It was a threat—he was certain. Back off and leave the temple alone, or it'd kill Dirt right now. Dirt strengthened his skin in that spot, making it as tough as stone. It'd never cut him if he knew it was coming, right? That knife was sharp.

Realizing the nearest tree was still close enough, he spoke directly to its mind. It was the one who'd made most of the dryad corpses in that pile outside, and he said, *"It won't cut me again. Do what you need to do. When I can get free, I'll get away."*

The tree couldn't talk back, but putting words in the part of its mind that he could read was trivial for them by now. *"We cannot risk it,"* it said.

"How can its magic even beat yours in the first place?" Dirt asked, trying not to grow any more desperate.

"We had no idea it was here. It hides even its gap in the Many Connections. Some believe it has been here since the time of the Gardener, concealing itself and gathering power to thwart us."

All during this short conversation, the skeleton held him aloft in the doorway with his knife at his throat, the fine edge touching his skin so lightly he wasn't sure if his protection was working. But once it saw that no further stones were being slung at its dwelling, it receded into the darkness, pulling Dirt with it.

The interior of the temple didn't hide the tree's mind from his sight, thank Grace. He told it, *"It hasn't killed me yet, so there's something it wants first. I'll live for at least a little longer. It might even just let me out after a while."*

"It is an abomination. If it corrupts you, we must bury you both. We must save you before that happens," the tree told him.

"I understand," said Dirt, even though that was a lie. *"If I get out, do you think you can destroy it?"*

"Now that we know it is there, destroying it is trivial. We await only your escape."

"How?"

"Many ways at once, friend Dirt. You taught us many things, and now we have learned anger."

There wasn't much more to say to that, and speaking to the tree's mind across that distance took more of Dirt's focus than he wanted to spare. He needed to listen to every sound, feel every tiny movement of air on the invisible hairs on his skin, watch for every flickering shadow.

The skeleton pulled him through the air back to where he'd been before, a short distance from the altar at the back of the temple. It ignored him again, leaving him hanging there as it returned to its reading. It fixed the wall without loosening its grip on him or looking up from reading the scroll.

Dirt wasted no time waiting, however. He needed light, and he knew of only one way to get it: fire. He hadn't shared Socks' mind when the pup had made fire, but he'd been standing right there. He just had to figure it out.

A field of little sparks, that was the key. Not one big fire. Lots of little ones. He decided to make one spark first, just a single tiny little spark before he tried anything else.

He quickly realized he couldn't do it like shaping wood. The spark needed to appear in the air, not grow out of something. There was nothing to reshape, nothing to communicate with and order to be different. All he had was the memory of fire, its brightness and warmth, its hunger and threat. The smell of the smoke as it swirled around them, the heat sizzling on his skin as the flames had gotten closer and closer.

Dirt released most of the mana he'd been holding, since he only wanted a small flame. If he accidentally made a big one, the fire might kill him before the skeleton got its chance.

It was still ignoring him, but it wasn't reading from its scrolls anymore. It seemed to be hurrying as it took up blood from the golden cup in its finger like a quill and began writing on the floor, large shapes and letters that Dirt couldn't see well enough to read from over here.

Dirt took the trickle of mana inside him and compressed it, then tried to move it out of his body. It wouldn't go. The more he struggled to get it to leave so he could try to ignite it, the more stubbornly it stayed inside him.

It was in his mana vessel, he remembered, and his mana vessel was part of him. He couldn't exactly tell his arm to walk away, either. No, he needed to tell it what to do from inside him. Without lighting his insides on fire.

The faint *skritch-skritch-skritch* of the skeleton writing on the stone with his blood grew increasingly distracting. The empty sheath was lighter now, too, which felt wrong. His blood tickled as it slowly dripped down his waist and onto the side of his thigh. The cut on his ribs stung more as time went on, too, as if to remind him he should still be terrified out of his wits. Well, his knees might be trembling with fear that his body couldn't fully expunge, but his mind was clear.

He focused his will on a spot in the air a few feet from his face. He let his thoughts quiet down and reached deeper inside himself for his wisdom, his active will that still remembered how to do all this.

Dirt's thoughts became no more than a meaningless chant—*fire fire fire fire*—as he withdrew into his very soul, trying to speak from that place and command the mana.

The skeleton stood and walked over to him. It didn't pause to regard him with its dead, unmoving skull, however; this time it jabbed the cut on his ribs with its finger to loosen the scabs and held the golden cup to gather more ink.

Dirt looked away and refused to meet its gaze, if it had a gaze, lest it somehow realize what he was trying to take steps to stop him. He squirmed at the discomfort of the skeletal finger in his cut, but didn't whimper in fear or pain.

Once it resumed its work, Dirt resumed his. He imagined fire, he dreamed of it, he filled every part of him with knowledge of flame. Then he could feel it. It was time.

Dirt didn't speak or even think a word; instead, the truth of fire arose from the place deeper than thought, and in the darkness, only a few feet from his face, a tiny spark burst into flame, burned brightly, sizzled, and died.

The skeleton turned its blue-fire eyes up to watch him, but when he didn't move or react it went back to ignoring him and drawing on the ground with his blood. His eyes were still adjusting to the darkness, but he thought he could see a dark circle on the ground now, wider than he was tall, scribed in dark ink. The skeleton was filling in the words and key sigils in the proper places. It was almost done.

Dirt gathered all the mana he could this time. He felt in his bones that he'd only get one chance at this, one chance to defend himself or die. Rather than give the sludge-like terror in his heart any more room, Dirt willed himself full of resolve. No fear. Discipline and sincerity.

The skeleton stood and turned to face him again. A chair emerged, floating out of the darkness, and rested with its front feet on the edge of the circle. A second chair floated over to rest on the opposite side, facing in.

Dirt floated forward as well, but he waited to launch his attack, unsure whether this was the right moment.

The skeleton sat on one of the chairs, its arms folded politely in its lap. It wasn't carrying his knife anymore, and a final drop of blood from its finger dripped down and stained the skeleton's robe. It lowered Dirt onto the chair on the other side of the circle, forcing his body into the right shape to sit.

All the while it held perfectly still, dead and silent except for the flickering blue flames in its eye sockets. Dirt struggled against its unseen hand, but it gave no reaction of any kind, nothing to indicate that it cared or was even aware of his resistance.

That was no good. He wanted a reaction, something he could use to find the right time. It pressed him down onto the chair, which he found cold and hard and unyielding.

"What are you doing?" he asked, dismayed that his voice was still shaking. He sounded weak, but he wasn't. He was a wolf in front of his prey, and his heart was full of fire.

The skeleton just stared, empty and dead. Together they waited in silence, long enough for Dirt to think no signal would come and he should just attack now. In the empty quiet, he thought he heard a faint rumble outside, distant and deep.

Blue fire from its eyes dripped like liquid down its skull, running across its teeth and falling from its jaw onto its collarbone and ribs below. The blue flame made long threads of light—two long, connected strings that ran all the way down to the chair, pooled, and dripped from there onto the floor.

Dirt attacked. With a burst of will he demanded fire, and the world gave it. A dozen white sparks ignited on the skeleton's golden robe, and Dirt fed them all the mana he could to make them burn hot enough to kill.

An instant later, Dirt's command of the flames severed as if by a knife, and the sparks vanished, leaving behind faint wisps of smoke that drifted on the unmoving air, round swirling shapes illuminated by the skeleton's blue fire.

Once the dripping flames from its eyes reached the circle of blood, the whole thing ignited, casting the room into a steely brightness that revealed shape but hid all color. Dirt saw the interior of the temple, frescoed walls and painted pillars, benches and altars and much more, but he had no time to spare on scenery.

Instead he read the words on the ground and tried to remember the shapes and sigils and signs written there. TO RING AND TO STRIKE AMONG THE COUNTLESS FORMS, MY HAND IS A LIGHT PERPETUAL, MY SPIRIT ALWAYS IN POWER.

Dirt didn't know any of the sigils or signs, which disappointed him; he'd lost those memories with everything else, if he had ever known them. The words of the circle itself gave him no clue what the skeleton was attempting.

The blue flames of the circle touched his feet but felt cold instead of hot, freezing painfully instead of burning. Two lines of flame rose up the flesh of his calf, up his thigh and across his hips, up the front of his chest and neck. Dirt screamed, the pain and terror overcoming his temporary resolve to fight.

Worse than the pain on his skin from the freezing fire was the way it twisted him inside, filled him with revulsion and disgust. He could feel it corrupting him, as if it was touching all his bodies at once and wilting them.

His screams took on a desperate, miserable note as the blue flames climbed up his neck, up his cheeks.

Then, with a sizzling hiss, they plunged into his eyeballs.

The blue fire penetrated deeper than his eyes. It plunged directly into his consciousness, and all pain vanished as Dirt felt himself separated from his own body and thrust into a realm of pure thought. He had no fingers to feel, no ears to hear. This was not the dream or even the world of the mind; it was something else.

A roaring sound arose, a slow, forceful crash that battered him unrelentingly. He felt his grasp on himself start to slip and mentally tightened his control to stay put until he could figure out what was happening.

The pressure increased again and again, but Dirt held on, ever firm against the sweeping waves that sought to untether him.

It pushed him in a direction of nowhere, in this place without up and down. Thoughts themselves seemed to take form and appear like the phantoms in dreams. But instead of visual images, they were pure ideas, separated from any reference to reality.

He knew this place, this perfect abyss full of nothing but chaos. He'd been here before. He'd suffered here for ages uncountable, twisting alone in the burning pressure of nonexistence. It was not the usual sort of memory that told him so, but instead, a deeper knowledge from a place without words.

The roaring sound became blue fire that surrounded him and tried to wash him away like a receding tide, or burn him to nothing, but he withstood it, making himself an unmovable rock.

The blue fire took shape, causing a world to spring into existence around him. Suddenly there was up and down, a floor, forward and back. Dirt huddled, tiny and naked, before an immense woman all made of blue flame. She stood imposing and regal, at least three times his height. Her dress reminded him of a robe, and upon her head, a crown of leaves held the intricate curls of her hair into a perfect nest of braids.

Dirt shuddered and stepped back. This was the skeleton. She was here with him. All those uncountable years alone in a place like this, and now he was here by her will.

She spoke, and her voice was all things ringing in unison. "You cannot resist. I am power indomitable."

Dirt hovered in midair in front of her face, which grew to half the size of Mother's. Easily big enough to eat him if she wanted, but Dirt couldn't help but feel a hint of amusement that the blue-flame woman thought this was big enough to scare him.

"What do you want?" he asked. His voice was a whisper here, a bit of dust soon to be swept away.

"I want you to be gone!" she screamed, her voice raising in pitch until it was a screeching hiss like ten thousand wasps singing together.

All around him swirled the blue flames, ice and death themselves. The flames roared and licked at his avatar, but there was no skin to burn. Just ideas.

"Then let me go, and I'll leave," he said. He changed his posture to that of standing, one hand on his hip, nonchalantly biting the fingernails of the other. For the first time in his life, his fingernails were actually clean. Whose idea was that, then? Certainly not his.

"Be gone! Die and be gone!" she screamed, raising both hands with fingers bent like claws ready to tear him apart. Fire swirled all around her and flared up dramatically.

She thrust her hands forward, and all her fire assaulted him at once, freezing and shattering him even as her clawlike fingernails ripped him apart. They shredded him into a thousand pieces, as if totally annihilated. Beyond any hope. Her will crashed into him, driving him apart and out.

But this was not the first time this had happened to him. Dirt pulled himself back together, his will ever solid and serene, strong enough to deny her.

In the real world, she could easily strangle him, or cut him open, or smash his brains on a rock. In the real world, he was just a weak little boy, nearly helpless and only alive because of others. But not here. He'd lost everything here—his memory, his power, even the years of his life. But one thing had remained, strengthened and sharpened by thousands of years of strain and suffering and effort. His will had lasted the ages, and it would not falter *here*.

Dirt bared his teeth in a smile. "This was the one place you shouldn't have brought me," he said. He flicked his wrist and willed the inferno of blue flames to be gone. A shockwave extinguished them all, leaving a very surprised woman of flesh and cloth in their place.

With nothing holding them back, the winds of chaos tore at the two of them as they blew through the space she'd created, carrying the sand of broken thoughts and unrealized creation that had scoured him for so long. He was hardened against it. She was not, and she twisted in pain.

"Now, tell me what you're trying to do!" he shouted. The force of his words blew the skin of her face like gale-force winds, pushing her cheeks and unraveling her hair.

"I will take your body and make it my own! You cannot resist me, for I am eternal!" she cried, a trapped and tormented soul who must win at any costs. Her desperation sounded more frightening than any threat.

"No, you won't. It's mine and always will be. Why do you have to do this? Why didn't you just die when you were supposed to?" asked Dirt.

"Our sunset empire endured the Long Night only to break after the Dawn! All our cities are empty and crumbled, all our roads broken! It was so glorious, that bright marble, those happy faces who dwelled in peace. We lived in joy, and now all is lost. I alone know and remember! I alone, alone, alone, so long. So long. Give your body to me. I have waited so long!"

She wasn't really listening to him, though. She was trapped in her own inner world, driven to action by ancient preparation and not anything real and true. He knew because in this place, nothing true could be hidden forever.

The spectral woman gathered her strength for her final assault. Dirt felt all of existence reverberate around him as it struggled to contain the power the skeleton had gathered over millennia.

A wall of pure will slammed into him, crushing and obliterating him, seeking to drive him from his seat in himself and out into the void.

Dirt shrugged and turned and let it pass, then stood again where he'd been before. Those winds were not new to him; even if he could remember nothing of them, he yet knew them. He had been resisting for far too long to let himself be blown away.

He willed her to be still, and she froze. The force of her power sagged and relented and vanished, leaving nothing but her surprised and miserable gasps.

Her eyes met his then, and for the first time, she truly saw him. Whatever was left of her spirit recognized his, and she said, "Avitus?"

"Prisca?" he said, the word arising in him from nowhere. He knew her. Gods in Glory, he knew her!

He watched as her expression turned from surprise to anger to furious loathing. Hatred filled her so strongly that the spell she'd cast to create a space in the void collapsed, and Dirt found himself back in the formless chaos with her. Her hatred burned like a glowing sun in the void.

She assaulted him again, wishing to rip him apart. Her being was so full of hatred that he could scarcely believe she'd ever had anything else in her.

Prisca lost her last measure of reason, and she attempted to simply consume him. She clawed for pieces of his bodies to rip away and swallow and make them her own.

But she was not the wolf here. She was not as strong as the ripping tides of eternity or the unknowables that dwelled in the absence of all things.

Dirt was. His existence proved it. He forced her back, separating from himself and leaving her hungering for the essence she couldn't reach.

He faltered for only a moment, regretting that he recognized her. How rare and precious that was, after all this time. But even so, Dirt knew she was dead. This was a husk, an abomination. It might not even contain a self, for all he knew, but it wouldn't make a difference either way. She had to be destroyed, preferably before she decided to drag him back into reality and kill him there.

He became a true wolf and held her down like the prey she was. Teeth of willpower bit and tore, ripping away pieces of her thoughts and memories. Many he disregarded and cast into the void to be lost forever. People now dead. Her hopes, her goals, her desires. Her love. He threw them away without even a glance, lest they haunt him forever.

Dirt consumed the rest and made it his own—the memories of places, the knowledge of days and months, the names of the stars. How the world had been, so rich and green, how delightful and nurturing.

She unraveled in his hands and was no more. Without her there to hold the spell, the void spit him out for the second time.

Dirt slid out of the chair and hit the stone with an uncomfortable thud that bruised his knees and made his teeth clack painfully together. He lay dazed on the cold stone for only a moment before regaining his wits. All was dark again except the distant doorway, the blue flame having gone out. He flicked a finger, and a tiny ball of bright light appeared overhead, its warm yellow candle glow illuminating the area. He glanced up, wondering how he'd known how to make it. It had been as natural as breathing.

In the other chair was nothing but a pile of dust and a few thin patches of gold cloth. There was nothing left of her.

He recognized this place immediately. It was not a temple, but a schola of esoteric philosophy. This was the lecture hall, complete with . . . it seemed his memory was still incomplete, and this was likely as much as he'd ever get back. Much of the room's implements, broken as they were, were still a mystery. But he could remember the feel of the place and how it had looked before, its warmth and wonder.

The doorway burst inward, sending stones flying in every direction. A huge furry shape flew forward, and Dirt felt himself lifted off the ground again.

"Socks!" he shouted joyously in his mind, stretching out his arms in greeting.

-You're alive!- replied the distraught pup. His poor heart was all a mess, full of suffering and terror. Socks pulled him right up in front of his nose and began licking him furiously.

Dirt laughed and squealed for a moment, but only four breaths later it started sinking in what he'd just gone through. His body still had plenty of terror in it, and he could see how miserable his poor Socks had been. All that, coupled with his pure relief to see his friend, quickly devolved into desperate weeping as it all came out.

Socks lay down on the ground right in the middle of the room, crushing ancient wooden benches. With a giant paw he pulled Dirt in beneath his head and pinned him tightly. It was as close to a hug as Socks could do, protective and warm. Socks couldn't cry, but he did whimper and keen miserably as he processed his own fears.

The two of them cried together for a time, each reinforcing the other's mourning. Dirt cried until he was exhausted, cried until he felt clean. It had only been a few days, but oh, how he'd missed Socks! And Socks had missed him too, worrying about him constantly even while he fought for his own life.

Dirt could feel now how much Socks had suffered. The pup was exhausted, mentally and physically. Whatever hunted him was giving him no quarter, and he probably wasn't even safe now. Dirt's own misfortunes paled in comparison; sure, the dryads had probed and tested him, driven him to the brink of death. But they'd been helping in their way, and he was better for it. Dirt had gotten into just one real, serious fight and won, but Socks had never stopped being in danger. The pup's stomach was still injured from the latest attack, despite having his wounds licked. It had been that recent.

Socks began a low growl, and Dirt had to look at his mind to see why. The dryads had poured into the temple and now surrounded them. Home stood near the pup's nose, looking anxious.

"It's okay, Socks. They're my friends. Can we show them I'm fine?"

-Mother doesn't trust them completely so neither do I.-

"They really love me, Socks. Look," Dirt told the pup. He sent Socks images of their desperate attempts to save him from the skeleton, and before that, how they played and how they comforted him. How Home rested his head on her lap and stroked his hair, how they fed and cared for him.

Socks relented and lifted his head just far enough for Dirt to peek out and wave. "Hi, everyone. I'm okay!"

The dryads erupted into a cheer. They danced and jumped and shouted, looking more like a crowd of human girls than they ever had before.

Home leaped right over the wolf's paw and tackled Dirt in a hug, and Callius was right behind her. Socks growled again, but it was just annoyance now, not a threat. He didn't feel like sharing Dirt, was all.

But he had to share, like it or not. The dryads were insistent as they pulled him out and passed him around for hugs. Socks got up and followed closely, his nose never more than a few feet away. Callius was the first to reach up and pat the wolf's nose, and he said, "If my friend Dirt is your friend Dirt, then you are my friend Socks. Hello, friend Socks."

Socks didn't respond right away, though. He wanted time to think that over. Dirt sent him a puff of reassurance.

COME OUT HERE, YOU TWO, said the Father of Wolves. His words struck Dirt to the core, filling him with animal dread even though the great beast's voice had no malice in it.

All the dryads had heard it, even though most of their trees were probably far away. Home and Callius grabbed his hands to walk out with him, but Socks lifted him onto his back, out of their grasp, which made Dirt smile. It was nice to be adored.

Socks stepped through the ruined doorway, and Father's immense black head lowered to sniff them. Mother soon jostled her mate out of the way to smell them herself, and Father stepped back to accommodate her. She was just a little smaller than Father, but she was on his scale and seemed no less dangerous.

Seeing both wolves towering over him was almost enough to make Dirt lose his wits until he remembered what he'd just done. He'd just faced down the dead in the chaos beyond existence. He could have courage here, in front of wondrous things that weren't his enemies.

Even so, he wasn't stupid enough to meet their eyes or look threatening or resistant in any way. Or greet them himself. Courage notwithstanding, he was a bug in their eyes.

Father said, *YOU MAKE A GOOD MATCH FOR MY CUB, HUMAN. RUNNING ABOUT, CREATING A RUCKUS. GETTING INTO FIGHTS AND LIGHTING FIRES. LOOK HOW QUICKLY HE RAN TO FETCH YOU.*

The immense wolf was amused, even affectionate. Dirt had never expected that. The vicious scars in the night-black fur of Father's face seemed to preclude the chance of any good humor.

HE IS A PEST, complained Mother.

Socks said, *-An amusing pest, maybe. And I love him. Look what happened because I left him alone.-*

HE BROKE THE WORLD, said Mother. *HE DESERVED WORSE.*

Dirt blanched. She was right. He had broken the world, even if he wasn't quite sure what that meant. Prisca had justly hated him for it, but he hadn't stolen enough of her memory to know more than that.

WE ARE MORE FREE THAN WHEN THE GODS WERE HERE, MY LOVE, said Father.

YET I DO NOT LIKE SEEING MY CHILDREN HUNTED, said Mother.

"I'll stop it! Whatever it is, I'll kill it! I'll destroy it forever so they're safe. I swear it! I swear it on everything I have and am!" yelled Dirt mentally. He knew interrupting was a terrifyingly stupid thing to do, but he couldn't contain the sudden passion that arose in him. Dirt hated that Socks was in danger. Truly, deeply, hated it, with all his being. Whatever the threat was, he'd hold nothing back in ending it.

Father huffed, amused. The air of it almost knocked Dirt over, which is when he realized he'd stood up on Socks's back. Here he was, fists clenched and jaw squared in defiance of beings who could destroy the world if they wanted, saying he'd do what they could not.

LOOK AT HIM. LOOK HOW ADORABLE HE IS, said Father. Mother seemed resistant, but she still looked.

Dirt didn't know what they were deciding, but he knew it was something.

A dryad in the shape of a wolf approached the crowd, nearly as big as Mother but much gentler and graceful. She wasn't a predator. Dirt could feel that just looking at her. For fur, she had a forest's worth of green leaves, and her eyes had the same glassy quality as the rest of the dryads.

She spoke to them in body language, scents, and short vocalizations, and Dirt couldn't follow any of it. He didn't dare look at Mother's or Father's minds to see what they were talking about, and this dryad's tree was too far away for him to look at her mind.

The dryad-wolf began to shrink, her movements quickly becoming more energetic and playful, until she was Socks's size. Socks hesitantly stepped forward to sniff her and figure out what was going on, which she allowed. She sniffed him back, and they circled each other for a moment.

"Dawn?! Dawn, is that you?" shouted Dirt. She was missing from the crowd, and something about the dryad-wolf's body language looked awfully familiar.

"Hello, friend Dirt," said Dawn, her voice now a wolf's rough growl. Dirt didn't know wolves could even say words.

-*We can't say words,*- said Socks, who'd been watching Dirt's mind. -*She's cheating.*-

DOES HE NOT RECOVER QUICKLY, MY LOVE? said Father. *MOST ARE WEAKENED BY TRAUMA, BUT HE IS STRENGTHENED BY IT.*

Mother glared at Dirt, which made him think his heart was about to stop beating. He was trying to keep a good mood and not flee screaming, but they weren't making it easy.

I SUPPOSE YOU ARE RIGHT.

THREE THOUSAND YEARS IN THE CHAOTIC VOID, AND THERE WAS ENOUGH OF HIM LEFT TO DRAW BREATH AFTERWARD. HE IS WORTHY.

MUST I LOSE THIS ONE, TOO? asked Mother, deep sadness clear on her voice. It surprised Dirt more than Father's good humor.

Socks. She meant losing Socks.

Father said, *HEAR AND OBEY, CUB. YOU WILL STAY HERE FOR HALF A MOON, THEN YOU WILL TAKE YOUR HUMAN OUT INTO THE WORLD AND EXPLORE IT. KEEP MOVING, HALF A MOON IN EACH PLACE, AND THE DEVOURER SHOULD NOT FIND YOU. ONCE EACH SEASON, YOU WILL RETURN AND PRESENT YOURSELF TO US.*

"We're just going to play here for half a moon, and then go explore? Can I come back to the den?" asked Socks.

Mother answered, *ONLY ONCE EACH SEASON. WE WILL FOCUS ON PROTECTING THE OTHERS UNTIL YOU ARE GROWN.*

Socks lowered his muzzle, peeking upward with regretful eyes. He whimpered gently.

Dirt told Mother, *"Please, only if this is the best thing for him! I know it's not for my sake, but please don't let him talk you into doing something that isn't good for him."*

Mother lowered her face until her nose was right over Socks's head, her fierce yellow eyes burning directly into Dirt's soul. *ARE YOU PITYING ME?*

"Yes, of course! Losing Socks is the saddest thing I can think of, and I think Socks losing his mother is just as sad. I love him, but look at me! I'm tiny! I can't . . . I'm not a wolf."

THEN YOU'D BETTER NOT LOSE HIM, HUMAN.

Father said, *WE HAVE NEVER TRIED THIS BEFORE, BUT WE HAVE CONSIDERED IT OFTEN. WE HAVEN'T HAD A PUP THIS YOUNG WE TRUSTED ON HIS OWN UNTIL NOW.*

Dirt nodded, assured that he wasn't part of something that went against their wisdom. Regretful, perhaps, but they thought it was worth trying.

He jumped off Socks and stepped back. On cue, Mother and Father leaned down to nuzzle their cub and lick his face. Little Socks had never looked so tiny. Either parent could probably still swallow him whole, but he wagged his little tail furiously and nuzzled them back. Such a precious thing he was! It was a wonder they could stand to let him out of their sight at all.

The great wolves turned and left, running at an easy speed that caused them to disappear far faster than seemed possible. How did something that big just disappear?

The dryads began to crowd in again, including Dawn, still in wolf form. They gently patted the fur of Socks's paws. Callius took Dirt's hand, and Home took the other. They led him to the nearest tree as Socks followed silently. The pup's mind still reeled from learning he was on his own now. Well, not quite on his own.

The dryads fed them both all the sap and water they could swallow. After that, Socks carried Dirt and ran with the dryads all the way back to Home. But instead of retreating to his bed, Dirt reshaped the wooden house to be five times larger, with a big doorway on one side for Socks to come in. He softened the floor and made the whole place look like a small, warm, comfortable den.

That night, he slept in Socks's fur. It wasn't quite the wolf pile he'd wished for back then, but it was still better than anything else he could think of. Tomorrow, they'd play with the dryads and race all through the forest. Perhaps they'd see what else remained of Turicum, the ancient city that had been here once. It was the place where he'd lived, broken the world, and been tossed into the void, and it was worth another look.

Maybe the dryads could dig up the temple of Deopater, and maybe something remained of the theater. If not, maybe an old, buried cellar still held some wine. No, not after all this time. It would certainly have gone bad by now. Right?

And after all that, in two weeks he and Socks would go out into the world to see what things could be found, ancient and new. The call of adventure sounded like a horn in all his thoughts until the pup's regular breathing lulled him to sleep.

About the Author

Ryan English is the author of the Land of Broken Roads series, originally released on Royal Road. He was first introduced to fantasy when he read *The Hobbit* at the age of seven and has been reading and writing in the genre ever since. English currently lives in Utah and works in cybersecurity.

Podium

DISCOVER MORE

STORIES
UNBOUND

PodiumEntertainment.com